Josie

"With her qu... [Viets] combines the perfect list of ingredients to whip up a cozy treat.... Without a doubt, *Death on a Platter* serves up her most hilarious mixture of mystery, love, and adventure to date." —Fresh Fiction

"Each of Viets's titles is top-notch." —AnnArbor.com

"Engaging." —*Publishers Weekly*

An Uplifting Murder

"Entertaining.... As always, Viets creates a heroine replete with wit, intelligence, and a sense of humor and entwines her in complicated plot strands."
—*Mystery Scene*

"Viets designs a flashy murder with just the right amounts of sparkle and shine." —Fresh Fiction

"Fans will laugh at the predicaments this mystery shopper finds herself in on the job and sleuthing."
—The Mystery Gazette

The Fashion Hound Murders

"I've read most of Ms. Viets's work. All of it is good, most of it excellent. This one is superb, maybe the best she's written so far." —Gumshoe

"Elaine Viets does it again! ... *The Fashion Hound Murders* is a hilarious story ... [and] a fun-filled adventure.... Pick this book up if you are looking for a lighthearted read with great shopping tips!"
—The Romance Readers Connection

continued ...

Murder with All the Trimmings

"Viets milks much holiday humor in her novel, pulling out all the wonderfully garish stops."
— *Pittsburgh Tribune-Review*

"Elaine Viets writes exciting amateur sleuth mysteries filled with believable characters; the recurring cast, starting with Josie, adds a sense of friendship that in turn embellishes the feeling of realism."
— *Midwest Book Review*

Accessory to Murder

"Elaine Viets knows how to orchestrate a flawless mystery with just the right blend of humor, intrigue, and hot romance. If you are looking to complete your wardrobe for the fall, you just found the most essential piece."
— *Fresh Fiction*

"The writing and plot are superb . . . no wasted words, scenes, or characters. Everything advances the plot, builds the characters, or keeps things moving. It's what her many fans have learned to expect." — *Cozy Library*

High Heels Are Murder

"A laugh-out-loud comedic murder mystery guaranteed to keep you entertained for any number of hours—the perfect read for a rainy day. . . . Shopping, St. Louis culinary treats, and mayhem abound, providing for a satisfying read." — *Front Street Reviews*

"*High Heels Are Murder* takes Josie into the wicked world of murder, mayhem, and toe cleavage. . . . Viets spans the female psyche with panache and wit."
— *South Florida Sun-Sentinel*

"Viets has written one of the funniest amateur sleuth mysteries to come along in ages. Her protagonist is a thoroughly likable person, a great mother, daughter, and friend. . . . The strength and the freshness of the tale lies in the characters." — *Midwest Book Review*

Dying in Style

"Finally, a protagonist we can relate to."
—*Riverfront Times* (St. Louis, MO)

"Laugh-out-loud humor adds to the brisk action."
—*South Florida Sun-Sentinel*

"A fine, unique espionage murder-in-the-mall thriller."
—The Best Reviews

Praise for the Dead-End Job Mystery Series

"One way for a fugitive to hide in plain sight is to work at low-wage jobs, which is what Helen Hawthorne has been doing in Elaine Viets's quick-witted mysteries."
—Marilyn Stasio, *The New York Times*

"Wickedly funny."   —*The Miami Herald*

"A stubborn and intelligent heroine, a wonderful South Florida setting, and a cast of more-or-less lethal bimbos....
I loved this book."
—*New York Times* bestselling author Charlaine Harris

"Hair-raising.... Viets keeps the action popping until the cliff-hanger ending."   —*Publishers Weekly*

"Hilarious."   —*Kirkus Reviews*

"A fast-paced story and nonstop wisecracks.... Elaine Viets knows how to turn minimum wage into maximum hilarity."
—Nancy Martin, author of *No Way to Kill a Lady*

"Elaine Viets reaches the right equilibrium with well-placed humor and lively plotting."
—*South Florida Sun-Sentinel*

"A quick summer read for fans of humorous mysteries with clever premises."   —*Library Journal*

"Helen Hawthorne is one of my all-time favorite mystery characters—smart and funny with a huge heart."
—Cozy Library

"Laugh-out-loud comedy, with enough twists and turns to make it to the top of the mystery bestseller charts."
—*Florida Today*

Also by Elaine Viets

Josie Marcus, Mystery Shopper Series

Dead-End Job Mystery Series

MURDER IS A PIECE OF CAKE

JOSIE MARCUS, MYSTERY SHOPPER

Elaine Viets

AN OBSIDIAN MYSTERY

OBSIDIAN
Published by New American Library, a division of
Penguin Group (USA) Inc., 375 Hudson Street,
New York, New York 10014, USA
Penguin Group (Canada), 90 Eglinton Avenue East, Suite 700, Toronto,
Ontario M4P 2Y3, Canada (a division of Pearson Penguin Canada Inc.)
Penguin Books Ltd., 80 Strand, London WC2R 0RL, England
Penguin Ireland, 25 St. Stephen's Green, Dublin 2,
Ireland (a division of Penguin Books Ltd.)
Penguin Group (Australia), 250 Camberwell Road, Camberwell, Victoria 3124,
Australia (a division of Pearson Australia Group Pty. Ltd.)
Penguin Books India Pvt. Ltd., 11 Community Centre, Panchsheel Park,
New Delhi - 110 017, India
Penguin Group (NZ), 67 Apollo Drive, Rosedale, Auckland 0632,
New Zealand (a division of Pearson New Zealand Ltd.)
Penguin Books (South Africa) (Pty.) Ltd., 24 Sturdee Avenue,
Rosebank, Johannesburg 2196, South Africa

Penguin Books Ltd., Registered Offices:
80 Strand, London WC2R 0RL, England

First published by Obsidian, an imprint of New American Library,
a division of Penguin Group (USA) Inc.

First Printing, November 2012
10 9 8 7 6 5 4 3 2 1

PUBLISHER'S NOTE
This is a work of fiction. Names, characters, places, and incidents either are the
product of the author's imagination or are used fictitiously, and any resemblance
to actual persons, living or dead, business establishments, events, or locales is
entirely coincidental.
    The publisher does not have any control over and does not assume any respon-
sibility for author or third-party Web sites or their content.

ALWAYS LEARNING   PEARSON

For Mary Alice Gorman,
who was there at Josie's birth.
Enjoy her wedding.

Acknowledgments

Publishing a novel is a team effort, and I'm lucky to have Sandra Harding, my editor at NAL. Thank you for a thorough critique. I appreciate the efforts of assistant Elizabeth Bistrow, hardworking publicist Kayleigh Clark, the NAL copy editor, and the production staff.

Jinny Gender is my bridge adviser and Maplewood expert. My friend and Femmes Fatales blog sister Hank Phillippi Ryan helped with the television section. Thanks to Liz Aton, Valerie Cannata, Kay Gordy, Alan Portman, Molly Portman, Jack Klobnak, Bob Levine, Sue Schlueter, Janet Smith, Jennifer Snethen, and Anne Watts.

Thanks to teacher MarySue Carl's fifth-period biology class at Arroyo High School, El Monte, California, for their help with Amelia's language. Go, Blue Pride!

The Rev. Kalen McAllister's good works include helping the homeless, visiting prisoners—and giving me information about life in the county jail.

The Jewel Box is not open for weddings the day after Thanksgiving, except for Josie. It is, however, a beautiful place to get married.

Thank you, Linda Dattilo, for explaining Molly's trek through the court system and how she could wear a bridal gown instead of a jail jumpsuit in front of a judge.

Doris Ann Norris is not a Maplewood police officer, but a retired librarian and a friend to writers. Big Dave the pizza deliveryman is Dave Kellogg, a pizza driver, reservist, and disabled Iraq-era war veteran who is now a contractor in Afghanistan.

Special thanks to Detective R. C. White, Fort Lauderdale Police Department (retired), and to the law enforcement men and women who answered my questions on police procedure. Some police and medical sources have to remain nameless, but I'm grateful for their help. Any mistakes are mine.

Cath Hoffner is a real person and a true pet lover. She still feels guilty that her cat Audrey swallowed that balloon ribbon, though Dr. Ted said it wasn't her fault and many pet owners wouldn't have paid for the surgery to save a cat's life. Cath's little girl, Kristyn, is now grown up.

Thanks to Rachelle L'Ecuyer, Community Development Director for the City of Maplewood.

Are you a fan of writer John Lescroart? Me, too. He bid one thousand dollars at a Left Coast Crime auction for a character name in this novel. John asked that the character be named after a buddy and former manager at Borders Fair Oaks, Tom Hedtke. John's money will go to the Sacramento Library Adult Literacy Program. Thank you, John, for helping writers and readers.

Many booksellers help keep this series alive. I wish I could thank them all.

Thank you to the librarians at the Broward County Library, the St. Louis Public Library, and St. Louis County Library. Librarians are the original search engines.

For my husband, Don Crinklaw, a heartfelt thank-you for listening to Josie's wedding plans. Thanks also to my agent, David Hendin.

Amelia's cat is based on my striped writing partner, Harry, who snores by my monitor while I write. Stuart Little is a real shih tzu. His owner, Bill Lichtenberger of Palm City, Florida, made a generous donation to the Humane Society of the Treasure Coast to see Stuart's name in my novels.

Thank you, blog sisters. I rely on the advice and encouragement of the wise women in the Femmes Fatales (www.femmesfatales.typepad.com). Stop by our blog.

Harry and Stuart's photos are on my Web site at elaineviets.com. Please e-mail me at eviets@aol.com.

Prologue

"Joshcy." The man's voice was followed by a crunch like a roof caving in. "Hwcjsh wejing ghocinng?"

Josie Marcus was pretty sure she wasn't getting an obscene phone call at nine in the morning. Then the man added a wet slurp, followed by another massive crunch. What was he doing with that phone?

"Excuse me?" Josie asked. "Who is this?"

The gulps sounded like a boa constrictor swallowing a whole pig, followed by juicy smacking. "That was good," he said.

Now Josie recognized the caller—Harry the Horrible, her boss at Suttin Services. Josie mystery-shopped for the company's St. Louis office.

Harry repeated his question. "I asked how's the wedding going? You and Dr. Ted ready to tie the knot?"

"Almost. It's five weeks away," Josie said. "What are you eating?"

"A deep-fried cheeseburger." Satisfaction oozed from Harry's voice. Even Josie's phone seemed greasy. She wanted to wipe it down. She wanted to wipe out the picture of Harry forming in her mind. Her boss had a thick brown pelt all over his body—at least the parts Josie had had the misfortune to see. Harry had hair on his flabby arms, fish-belly ankles, and stubby hands. Hair peeked through his straining shirt buttons, but so far Josie had been spared the full view of his chest.

Only Harry's dome was follicle free. Mother Nature had compensated by giving him a luxuriant unibrow.

"Thanks for your wedding invitation," Harry said. "I can't come, but I got you a present. Wait till you hear what it is."

"You're going to tell me before I unwrap it?" Josie asked.

"You don't have to unwrap this gift," Harry said. "It's your latest mystery-shopping assignment. I want you to shop wedding flowers and wedding cakes for a St. Louis wedding Web site. You can go as yourself—a bride shopping for her wedding."

He paused dramatically, like a game show host announcing a gigantic prize.

Harry's serious, Josie thought. He really is giving me a good assignment as a present. Well, it is a gift. Working for Harry has been awkward since I reported that surly sales assistant. I didn't realize Saber was his niece. She deserved to get fired.

Since then, Harry had given Josie nothing but bad assignments. She even had to mystery-shop pig ear sandwiches—and eat one.

Niece or no niece, Josie lived by her code. Her mission was to protect Mrs. Minivan, her name for the backbone of America's shoppers. Mrs. Minivan was overlooked, ignored, and disrespected. Josie fought to right those wrongs against the average shopper.

"You want me to mystery-shop wedding flowers," Josie said. "Do you mean all the flowers—the bouquets and boutonnieres, church flowers, and reception centerpieces?"

"Naw, just the whatchamacallits for the reception," he said. "The centerpieces. That's why this assignment is a gift. It's easy."

It would be easy, Josie thought. She'd spent hours deciding whether her bridesmaids should carry bouquets or wear wrist corsages. International trade treaties were signed after less debate.

She'd take this gift—and hope Harry's anger had finally cooled.

"I'll do it," Josie said.

"Good," Harry said. "I'll fax you the details. I need you to start today with a flower shop called Denise's Dreams. They sell other stuff, but our client only cares about the flowers."

"That's near my house," Josie said.

"See? I told you it was a present," Harry said.

Josie heard a rustling noise and guessed Harry was stuffing his take-out box into his office trash.

"Did you really eat a deep-fried cheeseburger for breakfast?" she asked.

"You need protein for the first meal of the day," Harry said. "I need man food. The Carnival Diner makes deep-fried cheeseburgers. The chef used to work at the state fair. You should try his chicken-fried bacon."

"Does he deep-fry the patties?" Josie asked. "How does he keep the cheese from melting away?"

"The chef takes the whole cheeseburger," Harry said. "Meat, cheese, pickles, bun and all—batters and deep-fries it. The cheese turns into a warm pocket of melted goodness. His french fries are sensational."

"They're battered, too?" Josie asked.

"Of course not," Harry said. "That would be stupid. You gonna go to work? That shop opens at nine thirty. You're supposed to be a bride on a budget at Denise's Dreams. At the other two, you have to say money is no problem."

"I've had plenty of experience with wedding budgets," Josie said. She and her veterinarian fiancé, Ted Scottsmeyer, had agreed to follow a budget. But their plan kept encountering unexpected expenses. Josie knew their wedding cake would cost about seven hundred dollars, but she hadn't factored in the fifty-dollar delivery fee. This job would help pay for the cake and the delivery.

She dressed quickly, pulled the still-warm mystery-shopping paperwork out of her fax machine, read it, and tucked the pages into her purse.

On the way to Denise's Dreams, she passed Ted's veterinary clinic and checked the parking lot. It was crowded with cars, but the big blue St. Louis Mobo-Pet van was gone. Ted was making house calls today while his partner, Christine, handled the clinic patients.

She turned the corner and saw Denise's Dreams. The shop looked like a midcentury bride's dream: a one-story white rambler with ruffled tie-back curtains and a picket fence.

Inside, the front room was devoted to flowers. The hothouse flower smell was sweetly overpowering. A big cooler along one wall was crammed with cold, colorful blossoms. Pink roses and blue hydrangeas were massed around the counter. On closer inspection, Josie saw those flowers were silk.

A young blonde in a ruffled dress with blue ribbons in her hair was behind the counter, arranging pink gladioli in a glass vase.

Behind her, Josie could see a room with snowdrifts of bridal veils. In a third room, labeled HAIR JEWELRY, Josie glimpsed a blue velvet Victorian sofa and a showcase sparkling with tiaras and jeweled combs.

The beribboned and ruffled blonde smiled and said, "May I help you? My name is Molly."

At first Josie thought the slender saleswoman was a girl. But the harsh morning light showed tiny lines around her eyes and mouth. Molly was at least thirty, but she dressed like a little girl going to a birthday party.

"I'd like some information about flowers for my wedding reception," Josie said. "I'm getting married in five weeks. I've chosen everything but the reception flowers."

"Are you on a budget?" Molly asked.

"Definitely," Josie said. Two points in Molly's favor, she thought. She greeted me promptly and asked if I was interested in budget offerings.

"May I suggest silk flowers for your reception?" Molly said. "These look real, and after the wedding, you'll have a lasting memento."

"I like live plants," Josie said.

"We have a fine selection of tropical plants you can rent," Molly said. "You can also rent the vases for your centerpieces. That will save money, too. Let me show you."

She plunked a heavy binder with sample photos on the counter and they paged through it. Josie was impressed with Molly's sales pitch. She didn't pressure, but she gave several useful options. Josie selected one and Molly prepared a contract.

"I can't sign it until I show it to my fiancé," Josie said.

"That's fine. Denise, the owner, or Rita, the other sales associate, will be happy to help you when you come back," Molly said. "I'm getting married next week. This is my last day at work. I'm going to be a full-time homemaker, the career I've always wanted."

"Who's your fiancé?" Josie asked.

"Ted," Molly said, her eyes turning dreamy soft. "He's so kind and handsome. He loves animals."

"I'm engaged to a Ted, too," Josie said. "He's a veterinarian. Next week Channel Seven is coming to his clinic to tape a pilot for his new show, *Dr. Ted's Pet Vet Tips*. Each week, Ted will talk about how to care for pets. His first show is how to clip a cat's toenails."

"I don't like Channel Seven—or cats," Molly said, and made a face. "I'm sure my Ted would have nothing to do with that awful TV station. And cats are sneaky."

Josie didn't like this double insult, but she was on the job. She searched for a polite answer. "Channel Seven does sensationalize the news," she said. "But Ted's show will be part of their community service programming. Once his show gets going he can move to a better station. I wasn't a big fan of cats, either, until we got our cat, Harry. Now my daughter and I love him. He's funny."

"I'll take your word for it," Molly said. "I'm a dog

lover. I have a little white Maltese, Bella. When is your Ted's TV show taping?"

"Next Tuesday at eleven," Josie said.

"That's my wedding day," Molly said.

Josie could see she was lost again in bridal dreams.

"Congratulations," she said. "I think you were such a big help because we have so much in common."

Next Tuesday, Josie would find out exactly how much they had in common.

Chapter 1

Tuesday, October 23

"Josie dear, it's Lenore. I wanted to touch base with you about our luncheon today."

The patrician accent of Lenore Scottsmeyer Hall triggered an instant physical reaction in Josie Marcus. Her hand shook so much, her phone seemed to be struggling to escape.

Josie wished she could run away. She was terrified of her future mother-in-law, a fearsome woman who looked like she'd stepped out of the society pages. A stylish sixty-two, Lenore would rather walk naked through Walmart than admit her true age.

"I couldn't forget you," Josie said, willing her voice not to wobble. "I'm leaving now for Ted's taping at the clinic. I'll meet you there and then the three of us can head out to lunch afterward."

"My son the doctor is a natural for television," Lenore said. She never mentioned that her son's patients were animals. "After the taping, we'll discuss your wedding plans over luncheon."

"Discuss" means Lenore wants to hijack our wedding, Josie thought. She was marrying Dr. Ted Scottsmeyer exactly one month from today—the day after Thanksgiving.

Lenore clearly didn't intend to follow the advice for the modern mother of the groom: Show up, shut up, and

wear beige. Josie had already signed the important contracts and paid the deposits. It was too late for Lenore to
make changes, wasn't it? But Lenore was rich enough to
get her way—except in the choice of her down-market
daughter-in-law.

"Looking forward to it," Josie lied. "Gotta run. We don't
want to miss the first episode of *Dr. Ted's Pet Vet Tips*."

"Wait!" Lenore said. "You are dressed nicely, aren't
you? Our reservations are at the Ritz."

"Don't worry," Josie said. "I always wear shoes in res-
taurants."

Lenore gasped.

Josie hung up, feeling slightly ashamed. She'd done it
again. She knew Ted's mother had no sense of humor. Her
plastic surgeon husband had probably removed it to prevent smile wrinkles. But Josie couldn't resist teasing her.

She took time for a final mirror check. I'm way over-
dressed, Josie decided, but I want to please Lenore and
look good for Ted. Josie had snagged her curve-hugging
designer pantsuit at a steep discount. Her black heels
were polished and her brown hair had bounce. Her hat
brim did a glamorous dip over one brown eye.

Josie grabbed the wedding plan notebook that had
become an extension of her right arm, and stepped into
a golden fall day. She hoped her wedding weather would
be this glorious. She gleefully crunched fallen leaves all
the way to her battered gray Honda.

Josie couldn't wait to marry Ted. She'd never expected
to marry, and certainly not a man as good as Ted. Not
with her past. But Ted had fallen in love with Josie, a
single mom with a lively eleven-year-old daughter and a
nowhere job as a mystery shopper.

The veterinary clinic lot was nearly filled. Josie spotted the TV truck, the blue minivan that belonged to
Ted's partner, Christine, and his tangerine '68 Mustang.

There was barely room for the white Bentley that
pulled in front of the clinic door. The car looked like an
elegant iceberg.

A Bentley? Ted's clients didn't drive two-hundred-thousand-dollar cars. Who did that belong to?

Oh no, Josie thought. Even Lenore wouldn't rent a Bentley. Well, she was staying at the Ritz-Carlton. She'd been reassured to find that outpost of civilization in St. Louis when she'd had to leave her Boca Raton mansion to set her son's wedding to rights.

Josie stashed her beat-up Honda next to Ted's vintage car and watched a gray-uniformed chauffeur open the Bentley's door. A white satin-sheathed arm handed the chauffeur a ribbon-trimmed basket with a tiny white Maltese. A rhinestone collar sparkled at the dog's neck.

Lenore wouldn't wear white satin to lunch, Josie decided. And she didn't have a dog. The vet's mother didn't like animals.

Josie forgot about the dog when a blonde in a wedding dress like a summer cloud stepped out of the Bentley. She caught her filmy veil as the breeze whipped it across her face, nearly dropping her trailing bouquet of white orchids. Josie noticed the bride's shapely white satin heels. She'd been looking for shoes just like that. Wonder where she got them . . .

Josie snapped out of her wedding daze. She knew that woman. Where had she seen her? The bride turned her head and Josie recognized her. That was Molly Deaver, the sales associate at Denise's Dreams. Molly had said she was marrying Ted today.

Her Ted, not mine. What was Molly doing at Ted's clinic on her wedding day? She watched the bride reclaim her dog and adjust her bouquet. Then she sailed into the clinic. Josie followed like a sleepwalker.

They were greeted by a chorus of woofs, yelps, and meows. A white-haired man held a gray-muzzled beagle on his lap. A woman in a lumpy red coat sat next to a beige plastic carrier. Josie heard the cat inside hissing at the old beagle.

Lenore was in a sleek black Chanel suit, pressed against the waiting room wall as if surrounded by savages. She regarded the hairy animals with distaste and ignored the black Labrador who trotted past her. That was Ted's Lab, Festus.

The Lab went straight to the bride and licked the little Maltese.

"Festus!" Molly said. "You're so sweet to welcome your new sister, Bella."

Sister? Since when did Ted's dog have a sister? Josie wondered.

Kathy, the clinic receptionist, was unflappable. She stepped up to the counter and said, "You look so pretty, Molly. Is something wrong with Bella? You don't have an appointment."

"Of course I have an appointment," Molly said. "Ted and I are getting married in an hour. I came to pick him up."

Josie felt the floor cave in underneath her. She leaned against the clinic counter for support and tried to figure out what was happening.

Kathy remained unfazed. "Married?" she said. "Oh, no. Dr. Ted isn't getting married today."

"Of course he is," Molly said. "I know it's bad luck for the groom to see the bride before the wedding, but I don't go by those old superstitions. I'll just go back there now." She powered past the clinic counter.

"No! Wait!" Kathy called. "You can't!" She struggled to raise the countertop to stop Molly, but the bride ignored her.

Molly pushed open the door to the surgery. Josie saw a balding man with a TV camera trained on Ted. Her fiancé looked so professional in his blue shirt and white coat. They set off his muscular shoulders. Josie admired his glossy brown hair.

Marmalade, Ted's easygoing orange cat, sat on an exam table next to him. Ted held the cat's paw and said, "There's no need to declaw your cat if you clip its claws regularly. Old Marmalade here likes it. I give her lots of treats, which helps. It's best if you start getting your cats used to nail trimming when they're kittens, but I got Marmalade when she was grown-up.

"Before you start trimming, get your cat used to the process by gently stroking her paws."

Ted touched Marmalade's orange paw and the cat gently patted his hand. He chuckled and ruffled her fur.

"Don't try to trim your cat's claws if she's upset. Wait till she's relaxed or sleepy. Marmalade is one cool cat right now. See how I'm holding the paw and pressing the toe pad gently?"

The camera lens moved in to focus on Marmalade's paw.

"That makes the cat extend her claw. Then I—"

Ted's talk was interrupted by a low growl from the bride's Maltese. The orange-striped cat outweighed the tiny dog by several pounds, but the good-natured Marmalade ignored the dog.

Ted did not. He looked up, puzzled by the vision of a full-rigged bride in his surgery. "Molly Deaver?" he asked. "Do you have an appointment?"

"I certainly do," she said. "So do you. We're getting married in an hour."

"I am getting married," Ted said. "But not today and not to you."

"No, you're marrying me," Molly said. "We talked about it in my kitchen. You said you wanted a small wedding."

"Yes, I did," Ted said. "But Josie is my bride. You're my patient. I mean, Bella is."

"Ted, you can't leave me at the altar," Molly said, her voice climbing to a screech. "Today is more than our wedding day. It's our anniversary. Exactly six months ago Bella had her surgery. She brought us together. I'm not only Bella's mother. I'm your fiancée. You've visited my house at least twenty times."

"To see your dog," Ted said. "My partner, Christine, and I take turns working in the mobile pet van."

"Chris has never been to my home," Molly said. "Just you." Josie heard her desperation. "I only want you."

"Miss Deaver, you've been following me everywhere these past few weeks," Ted said. "I've run into you at the store, the supermarket, and the dry cleaner. I see you sitting in the clinic parking lot. You've called this office more than two hundred times in three weeks. You leave gifts I don't want."

"You love my homemade blueberry muffins," Molly said. "You said so."

"I liked the first one," Ted said, "but you've made me four dozen so far this week and it's only Tuesday."

"I love you and I want to be with you," Molly said, softly. "That's why we're getting married. Hurry, sweetie. The minister is on his way to the church. Time to change into your tux." Now she was a mother coaxing a reluctant little boy to get ready for church.

Ted seemed too stunned to argue. Josie stayed rooted to the waiting room floor. Only Ted's mother took action. She stepped into the surgery and said, "Young woman, you're demented. My son has no intention of marrying you. He's marrying Miss Marcus. We're lunching at the Ritz to discuss their wedding plans."

Molly unleashed an agonized "Nooooooo!"

"Call 911!" Lenore shouted.

The bride screamed again, and Bella jumped out of her white basket and bit Marmalade. The cat swatted the little dog. Molly rushed forward to rescue her pet, then slapped Ted. That's when Marmalade attacked, scratching Molly's hand.

"You got blood on my wedding dress," Molly cried. She whacked Ted with her bouquet.

Josie threw open the surgery door and ran to Ted. "He's my fiancé. Here's my engagement ring."

"Mine's bigger," Molly shouted, and held out her hand. Her rock was a solitaire, three times the size of Josie's twin diamonds.

"Ted belongs to me," Josie said, taking his hand.

"He's mine!" Molly grabbed a scalpel from a tray of

instruments and held it to Ted's throat. "Drop his hand or I'll cut his throat."

Josie saw a tiny drop of blood on Ted's throat, near a pulsing vein.

"Drop the knife," Lenore said. "Drop it now or I'll shoot."

Josie saw her future mother-in-law in gunslinger black with a pearl-handled pistol.

Molly still held the knife to Ted's throat. Josie stared at a single drop of blood as it trickled down his neck.

Ted's mother calmly took the scalpel out of the bride's hand, while she kept the gun trained on Molly.

The bride wailed along with the approaching police sirens.

Josie heard the cop cars roar into the lot. "The police are here," she said.

That was when she saw that the TV camera had been taping everything.

Chapter 2

Josie's day broke into a kaleidoscope of crazy scenes. She focused on these fragments:

One perfect drop of blood on the bride's white dress.

The elegant Lenore serenely stowing the pearl-handled pistol in her Chanel bag.

A trail of glistening red running down Ted's neck. He'd been slashed by Molly the bloodstained bride.

Ted's injury tore Josie out of her trance. "You're hurt!" she said. "Where do you keep the bandages?"

Ted gently took her hand to stop her. "Josie, the cut doesn't even deserve a Band-Aid," he said. "Marmalade's given me deeper scratches."

At the mention of her name, the big orange cat slid soundlessly under the exam table.

Josie heard harsh, hopeless sobs and saw Molly crying by the exam table. Her extravagant orchid bouquet had been tossed on the floor next to the overturned dog basket. The bride held her fluffy dog in a desperate grip, as if Bella could save her sanity.

The full skirt on Molly's wondrous white dress was deflated, and her wilted veil hid her tear-streaked face.

What was that filmy material called? Josie wondered. She had a sample somewhere in her wedding plan notebook. Silk illusion. That was it. Perfect for this surreal occasion.

Josie felt a twinge of pity for the bedraggled bride. Then she remembered Molly wanted to hijack Ted and marry him — and she'd stabbed him in the neck.

Lenore stood between Molly and Ted, still holding the bloody scalpel in her manicured hand. She was poised to attack the bride if Molly moved toward her son.

The door burst open and two blue uniformed police officers ran into the room, holsters unsnapped. A buzz-cut Rock Road Village officer shouted, "Drop the knife, ma'am, and stand back." His brass nameplate said EDEL-SON. He looked to be in his late twenties, but he had the voice of command.

Lenore placed the scalpel on a counter out of Molly's reach.

"I took the weapon away from that woman," Lenore said, and shot the shivering, sobbing bride a venomous glare. "She broke into this room and said she was marrying my son this morning. Of course, there is no such wedding."

"Yes, there is!" Molly said. "I have the ring, the church, and the minister."

"But not the groom," Lenore said, her voice hard. "When my son refused to go with this creature, she attacked him with that scalpel."

"It's just a scratch," Ted said.

"I was attacked, too," Molly said. "She knifed me." She pointed at Lenore, whose carefully made-up face was rouged with red fury.

"I did not," Lenore said. "The cat scratched her when she stabbed my son."

"Look at the blood on my dress," Molly said. "That witch tried to shoot me. There's a gun in her purse."

"Quiet!" Officer Edelson cried. "I'm putting you all in separate rooms so I can sort this out. We're using the exam rooms."

Edelson turned to the soft-bellied bald man with the TV camera. "Cameraman, did you film this?"

"I'm a photographer for Channel Seven," he corrected. "Bill Madfis. Our station uses tape, not film."

"Then I want that tape," Officer Edelson said.

"Can't give it to you," Madfis said. "You have to check with my boss at the station first."

"Then I'll just take it," Officer Edelson said.

"Go ahead. You'll have the station lawyers all over your ass," Madfis said. "You have no way to play it, anyway. It's a DCV-Pro tape. For TV professionals. Doesn't work in a regular tape machine."

A coffee-skinned officer whose name tag said PHILLIPS herded a chunky woman in cargo pants and a khaki shirt toward an exam room.

Where did she come from? Josie wondered.

"You can't do this! Do you know who I am? I'm Rona Richley, Channel Seven producer." Rona had a honking New York accent. "I won't talk to the police without our station lawyer. I'm calling him right now." She held up a black iPhone.

"That's your right, ma'am," the officer said. "But you don't need a lawyer. You're not being taken into custody."

The TV producer was speed-dialing as Officer Phillips shut the exam room door on her.

The officer then came back for Lenore, trying to steer her by the elbow toward another empty exam room. Ted's mother shook off his hand and walked coolly into the room, shoulders back and head high, as if this was precisely what she wanted.

The bride was not corralled as easily. She backed against the wall like a cornered animal. "I'm the victim," Molly said, her voice heavy with tears. "Why are you locking me up?"

"We aren't locking you up. We want to hear your side in private," Officer Phillips said.

"Can I take Bella?" the bride asked. "My little girl?"

"You got a kid here, too?" the cop asked.

"Bella is my Maltese," Molly said, petting the white fluff ball in her arms. Bella licked the bride's hand with a pink tongue.

"Can't see where a girlie dog would be a problem," the officer said. "Does she bite?"

"Of course not," Molly said.

Does, too, Josie thought, making a mental note to tell the police that Bella bit Marmalade and started the chain reaction that ended with Molly's bloody bridal gown.

The cop's question triggered a fresh outbreak of weeping. Officer Phillips handed Molly a tissue from the counter and she blotted her tear-swollen eyes.

"My mascara is running," Molly said, sniffling. "I paid two hundred dollars for bridal makeup. The makeup artist promised it was waterproof and now it's smeared."

"Yes, ma'am," the officer said, his voice neutral.

She really believes she's going to marry Ted, Josie thought. That can't be.

Then a thought slammed Josie so hard, she staggered backward. What if Ted really was marrying Molly? Josie had read about bigamists on the Internet. Some men had two or three families stashed in different cities and their other wives never suspected.

Josie knew Ted was too perfect to be real. She couldn't believe her good luck when he'd proposed. She still expected their wedding plans to fall apart before the minister pronounced them man and wife.

No, I'm the crazy one, Josie decided. Ted is no bigamist. Why would he schedule a TV interview the morning he was marrying Molly—and ask me to be here? Bigamists don't invite a TV station and their other fiancée as witnesses.

This is just bridal jitters, Josie decided. No wonder, after this nerve-racking morning. Molly really seemed to believe she was Ted's fiancée. Where did she get that idea? Did Ted accidentally encourage her? She watched Molly maneuver her full skirt across the crowded surgery. A flounce trailed on the floor, sweeping dog hair along with it.

"Watch that table," Officer Phillips said. "Can you get your dress through the exam room door? There. You're fine. The officer will be in to see you shortly."

Josie could hear Officer Edelson still arguing with the cameraman—no, the photographer. That was what Bill Madfis called himself. "Look, dude. I can't give you the tape unless the station agrees," he said. "You can put me in jail, but before I hand it over, I gotta get clearance from the station. From the way my producer is carrying on in that room, I think you'll be hearing from them shortly."

Josie saw the producer standing at the window of her exam room door, shouting into an iPhone and waving her other hand wildly. Rona Richley's dark frizzy hair had escaped its clip and tumbled down her back.

"Ma'am, we'd like you in the next room," Officer Phillips told Josie. He escorted her into a blue-tiled exam room that smelled of disinfectant and dog hair.

Josie dropped her purse and hat on the exam table next to a plastic model of a dog pelvis and plopped down in the blue client chair. She leaned her head wearily against the wall and heard a low-pitched whine coming from next door. Was Molly's dog hurt?

No, wait. That was Molly crying. The walls were so thin, Josie could hear her in the next room. Molly's door opened, and Officer Edelson greeted the bride. Josie caught bits of their muffled conversation. Molly's higher voice carried better than the police officer's deep rumble.

"My name is Molly Ann Deaver," she said. "My dog is Bella Deaver. Her full name is Bella's Snow Fantasia. She's a purebred Maltese. I don't know why my fiancé is behaving like this. You have to believe me."

"Why would he say he was marrying another woman, ma'am?" Edelson asked. At least, that was what Josie thought the officer said. She pressed her ear harder against the wall.

"I don't know. I saw that other woman when she came to Denise's Dreams, the shop where I work. She said she was marrying a vet named Ted, but there are other local veterinarians with that name. I never dreamed she was talking about my Ted. There's something wrong with that poor woman."

What? Josie was shaking with anger. Molly thinks there's something wrong with me?

"Ted loves me," Molly said. "He wants to marry me."

Another low sound, like distant thunder, from the officer.

"No, I've never met his mother. How do I even know she is his mother? She pulled a gun on me. What kind of mother-in-law does that?" Molly's voice grew shriller.

"I—I did put that knife thingie to Ted's throat, but I was upset when he said we weren't getting married today. We're definitely engaged. See, here's my engagement ring. It's a two-carat round-cut rose-gold ring. I bought it at Forever Diamonds in the Galleria."

A short mumbled question.

"Yes, I bought it myself." Molly said. "And paid for it, too. He's a struggling doctor and I have money. I wanted the right engagement ring. My wedding day is the most important day of my life."

Another bass rumble from the officer.

"Of course I can wait here a little longer," Molly said. "This is just a misunderstanding. I'll wait here as long as you want. After all, Ted and I will be married forever."

Chapter 3

"My son is *not* marrying that demented woman, Officer," Lenore said. "She's not fit to be a doctor's wife."

Josie didn't need to press her ear to the wall to hear Ted's mother. Lenore's imperious voice sliced through the thin exam room walls.

"I don't know that . . . that . . ." Words failed the well-bred Lenore — polite words, anyway. "That creature wearing that ridiculous dress. I thought she was dressed for Halloween. I've never seen her before. Ted's never mentioned her. He's marrying Josie Marcus, the girl in the hat."

Josie couldn't hear Officer Edelson's next question, but she didn't have to. Lenore's answer was enough.

"No, he didn't discuss his engagement to Miss Marcus with me," she said. "I had no say so in the matter. I introduced him to a number of suitable young women, but he's ignored my efforts."

Ouch, Josie thought. I don't think I'll be calling Lenore "Mom."

"But Miss Marcus is a thousand times better than that escapee from a lunatic asylum," Lenore said. "Even if she does have a child out of wedlock."

Did she call Amelia "a child out of wedlock"? Hot anger blasted through Josie. Nobody disparaged her daughter. Nobody. Josie gripped the door handle, prepared to march on Lenore, when she saw Officer Phillips was planted in her path. No way she'd get past that wall of mahogany muscle.

Josie sat back down. She'd discuss Lenore's attitude toward Amelia later, in private. Ted didn't need two crazy brides in one day.

Officer Edelson must have asked Lenore another question. Josie caught the phrase "brandished a weapon" in his deep rumble.

"I do carry a pistol," Lenore said. "It's a small thirty-eight. I'm licensed for concealed carry and I practice at the gun range every week."

Another rumble. Josie strained her ears so hard, they practically flapped, but she couldn't hear the officer's question.

But Lenore's outrage was loud and clear. "What! You believe there's an incompatibility with the Florida and Missouri concealed carry laws? I am in a building owned by my son and I was protecting both of us from a knife attack. That's why I carry a gun—for protection. It's my constitutional right."

The rumble was deeper and darker this time, a subterranean earthquake.

"Of course I didn't carry it on the plane in my purse," Lenore said. "I don't fly commercial. I came on my husband's plane, and brought my weapon with me. Good thing I had it, too. If I'd waited for you to respond, that lunatic would have cut Ted's throat. And I didn't threaten that so-called bride. I saved her from a murder charge. I hope you're locking her up for assault."

A soft rumble was cut short by Lenore's clipped response. "What? Only if my son presses charges? Of course he will. And if he doesn't, I will."

The rumble sounded more tentative now.

"No, I wasn't hurt," Lenore said. "But I could have been. Really! If Ted doesn't press charges, you can Baker Act her. You do know what that is, don't you?"

Another short rumble.

"Missouri doesn't have a Baker Act?" Lenore said. "Even this backwater must have a law so people who are a danger to themselves and others can be committed, whatever you call it. And that young woman qualifies as both! How long are you going to detain us? We'll miss our luncheon reservation."

The next rumble sounded apologetic. Josie heard the exam room door close softly. When Officer Edelson knocked on Josie's door, she felt absurdly relieved, like a patient waiting for a doctor.

Edelson looked like a schoolboy who'd escaped expulsion with a stern lecture. Even his buzz cut seemed wilted. Josie was tempted to commiserate but decided he wouldn't want to be reminded he'd been tongue-lashed by a sixty-two-year-old woman.

Josie offered him her chair. "I prefer to stand, ma'am," Edelson said. "State your name and address."

She told him, then added, "I'm engaged to Dr. Ted Scottsmeyer. Really engaged. He proposed to me in Tower Grove Park."

For a moment, she remembered the sunlit splendor of that fall day and her sheer happiness. Then she was back in the clinic exam room, staring at a plastic dog pelvis and wondering if Molly's bizarre intrusion would wreck her future with Ted.

"Do you work here at the clinic?" Edelson asked.

"No, I'm a mystery shopper for Suttin Services, but I wasn't working today. That's how I met Molly Deaver. I mystery-shopped the store where she works. I gave her a good rating, too. She's a good salesperson. She told me she was marrying a man named Ted. I had no idea she meant my fiancé. She must have something wrong with her."

Two can play that game, Josie thought.

"I came here to watch Ted's TV taping," she said. "Then Ted and I planned to have lunch with my future mother-in-law."

An hour ago, Josie had dreaded that lunch. Now she longed to be sitting at the table with Lenore.

"I got here just as that bride arrived in a Bentley," Josie said. "It was surreal. She marched right inside with a huge bouquet and her dog in a basket. Kathy, the receptionist, tried to keep Molly out of the back room where Channel Seven was taping, but she forced her way in and made a scene.

"And her dog bites, too," Josie said. "She bit Ted's cat, Marmalade."

"Does the cat need medical attention, ma'am?" Officer Edelson asked.

"I don't know," Josie said. "Marmalade jumped off the exam table when you arrived."

She glanced through the exam room window. "That's Marmalade, the orange cat under the table, curled up with the black Lab, Festus. The dog is also Ted's. The cat is licking the Lab's ear. That's so cute."

"Ma'am," the officer said. He was losing patience.

"The cat seems fine," Josie said. "But Ted is definitely wounded. His so-called bride cut him, and his neck is bleeding. She said, 'Drop his hand or I'll cut his throat.' Before I could do anything, she sliced him. She's seriously disturbed."

"Did Ted ever mention Molly Ann Deaver to you?"

"No. Never," Josie said, then wondered why Ted hadn't.

"Look, Officer. There's no way Ted's going to marry that woman, today or any other day," Josie said. "I can prove Ted is marrying me. I have a wedding plan notebook with all our information."

"So does the other bride," Officer Edelson said, and was gone before she could answer.

Josie heard the door open in the exam room where Ted waited. At first, Josie could hear every word her fiancé said. Then she wished she didn't.

"No, don't call the paramedics," Ted said. "I know Josie and my mother are upset, but women make a big deal out of a little scratch. I've had worse cuts shaving."

The two men gave a "we guys" chuckle and Josie silently seethed. They were laughing at her expense.

"How long has Miss Deaver been your patient?" Edelson asked.

"Her Maltese, Bella, has been my patient for six months," Ted said. "I met Miss Deaver when I spayed Bella here at the clinic. I made two follow-up visits in the clinic van to her home and the dog was fine.

"But Miss Deaver kept asking me to treat her dog for minor ailments at her home. She said Bella had a limp. I checked the dog and there was no problem. Miss Deaver insisted, so I referred her to a veterinary orthopedic specialist."

"They have those for dogs?" the officer asked in a surprised tone.

"And cats. Veterinary medicine is very advanced," Ted said. "They have ultrasound, reconstructive surgery, CT scans, even neurosurgery."

"Yes, well. About this dog of hers," Edelson prompted.

"Bella," Ted said. "The ortho doc said Bella was healthy and Miss Deaver complained to me about the specialist's bills. She'd spent more than two thousand dollars on Bella's nonexistent limp."

The police officer whistled.

"Good veterinary care isn't cheap," Ted said. "Bella was home from the referral clinic two days when Miss Deaver said her Maltese had an upset stomach. I went to her home in the clinic van, but the dog seemed fine. She claimed her dog was vomiting, but said she'd cleaned it up.

"Next, Miss Deaver said Bella was scratching her ear and it was infected. I found no evidence of irritation or soreness on either ear. I took blood for tests, and the results were normal."

Josie noticed he called her Miss Deaver, not Molly. Was he trying to show the police officer she meant nothing to him?

"Miss Deaver called the clinic more than thirty times in four months with imaginary illnesses for a healthy pet. When I was at her house, she would have the kitchen table set for a snack or a meal. I often don't have time for lunch, so I'd grab a bite and we'd talk."

Humpf, Josie thought. Ted fell right into her trap.

"She liked to discuss her wedding. I thought it was harmless. I told her I was marrying Josie and she wanted the details, so I told her our plans. She talked about hers. She mentioned everything but the groom."

"And you didn't find that suspicious?" Edelson asked.

"Well, lots of brides lose sight of the groom when they plan their weddings. Josie isn't like that, but there aren't many women like Josie."

Josie could hear the warmth in his voice, even through the wall. She smiled.

"I guess you could say I was dense, but even I started getting suspicious," Ted said. "Bella was sick only on the days when I drove the van. If Miss Deaver found out my partner, Chris, had van duty, she'd say Bella felt better and would cancel the appointment. Chris and I discussed it. She said she would handle Bella and Miss Deaver would have to bring her into the clinic. There would be no more house calls.

"That's when Miss Deaver started following me. I'd leave the clinic and find her sitting in her car in the lot here. She'd leave gifts for me with Kathy, our receptionist. She baked cakes and muffins. Dozens of muffins. One day, after she took Bella to Chris for a checkup, she ambushed me in the hall here and gave me a Rolex watch. I told her to take it back. She said she couldn't. She'd had it engraved with what she called 'our anniversary date'— the day I'd spayed Bella."

"She thought that was your anniversary?" Officer Edelson asked.

"Sad, isn't it?" Ted said. "I did everything to help her see reality. I showed her photos of Josie. I talked about the afternoon I'd asked Josie to marry me. I told her how much I loved Josie. It didn't do any good.

"I kept thinking if I ignored her, she'd get discouraged and go away. But she didn't. The more I refused to see

Miss Deaver, the more she was convinced I wanted to marry her. She wouldn't stop following me."

"She wasn't following you, Doctor," Edelson said. "She was stalking you. That's a crime in all fifty states. You should have reported it to the police."

"I thought only women have stalkers," Ted said.

"Men who stalk women are more common," the officer said. "Male stalkers tend to be more dangerous. But two percent of the men in this country have been stalked by women."

"You know a lot about stalkers," Ted said.

"It's a serious problem," Edelson said. "Our department got a grant to send me to a seminar. Stalking is often tied in with domestic abuse. Miss Deaver has assaulted you with a deadly weapon, so she's already demonstrated she is dangerous."

"What can I do now?" Ted asked.

"Press charges for assault," the officer said.

"I can't," Ted said. "She needs a psychiatrist."

"We can lock her up for seventy-two hours in a mental health facility," Edelson said.

"That will get her the help she needs," Ted said. "But I feel sorry for her."

"That's dangerous," Edelson said. "What if she harms your fiancée? In her mind, she may believe getting rid of Miss Marcus will set you free to marry her."

"No!" Ted said. "That's crazy. Josie has an eleven-year-old daughter. What can I do to protect them? Miss Deaver is already barred from the clinic."

"You saw how well that worked this morning," Officer Edelson said. "You need to file charges for assault, Doctor. She needs a dose of reality. Does she have family here?"

"I don't know," Ted said. "I know very little about her."

"Well, her family needs to take steps to get her the care she needs. Meanwhile, you should develop a paper trail documenting evidence of stalking so we can prosecute her. We'll need your phone records, her dog's charts and bills, and the logs of your phone calls."

"I'll get you my cell phone records," Ted said. "Our receptionist, Kathy, will get you the clinic records. Christine and Kathy will both testify that she's been a nuisance."

"Do you have photos or security tapes of Miss Deaver waiting in your clinic lot?" Edelson asked.

"No," Ted said.

"You definitely gave her back the watch?"

"Yes," Ted said. "But I remember the jeweler's name on the box."

"That's a start," Edelson said. "You can also take out a restraining order, though in my experience that won't make the stalker go away."

"What does?" Ted asked. Josie could hear the fear in his voice.

"Most stalkers don't respond to treatment," he said. "They simply move their fixation from one love object to another. Many experts recommend that you move to another state."

Josie wondered if they could hear her gasp through the wall. She could practically see Ted running his fingers through his unruly brown hair. She heard him pacing the small room.

"What! I have to give up my life and my veterinary practice because of a crazy woman?" Ted said.

"You'll have to give it up anyway, Doctor. If she's seriously delusional, only death will stop her."

Chapter 4

Molly Deaver's screams were torn from her heart. "No! You can't arrest me. I'm the victim. What did I do to deserve this?"

She's not acting, Josie thought. She really believes Ted loves her. She wrapped her arms possessively around her fiancé, as if Molly could take him away.

The deluded bride shrieked again, and Josie felt Ted flinch. Josie patted his hand and whispered, "I know this is painful for you, but the arrest is the best way to get her the help she needs."

"She's insane," Lenore said, not bothering to lower her voice. "Ted has no reason to feel guilty."

The large open surgery seemed crowded. Molly's dress, suitable for a Victorian ball, took up most of the floor. Lenore, Ted, and Josie leaned against a cabinet, as far away from Molly as they could get. Crouched beside a counter, Bill Madfis was taping the scene, while Rona, the producer, muttered instructions. Officer Edelson didn't seem to notice the Channel Seven photographer. He was trying to reason with Molly.

"You stabbed Dr. Scottsmeyer with a scalpel, Miss Deaver," Officer Edelson said. "That's a felony assault. Dr. Scottsmeyer is pressing charges."

"He doesn't mean it," Molly said. "Tell him, Ted." Her

denim blue eyes, brimming with tears, pleaded for his help.

The police officer didn't give Ted a chance to answer. "I'm afraid that's for the court to decide," Edelson said.

"But what will happen to Bella, my little dog?" She cuddled her pet like a baby.

"Yap!" said the Maltese.

"We can call animal control," the officer said.

"No!" Molly wept.

Ted started to say, "I could—," but Josie guessed he was offering to take care of Bella. "Don't offer," she said. "You'll only enforce her delusion."

"Don't you dare," his mother said. She gripped Ted's arm.

He nodded. "You're right," he said.

Officer Edelson said, "Do you have a family member we can contact, Miss Deaver?"

"Yes, my sister," Molly said, sniffling. "Emily Deaver Destin. I don't have my cell phone with me, but she's waiting at the church. She must be frantic by now."

"Officer Phillips will make the call," Edelson said.

Molly recited her sister's cell phone number in a shaky voice. Phillips punched it in and retreated to an exam room to make the call.

"Ted, won't you change your mind?" Molly asked. "For the sake of our love? Look Bella in the eye when you answer."

Lenore gripped Ted's arm so hard, Josie was afraid she'd leave bruises, but Ted didn't seem to notice. Josie gave his hand a comforting squeeze. "Be strong," she whispered. "It's the only way to help her."

"Molly, I don't love you," Ted said in a soft voice. "I can't marry you. I'm marrying Josie."

Tears rained down Molly's face, washing away her expensive makeup. She kissed her dog and said, "You're an orphan now, Bella. Daddy doesn't want us anymore."

"Don't answer her," Lenore said through gritted teeth. "You can't win an argument with a crazy woman."

Ted stayed silent, to Josie's relief.

The exam room door opened and Officer Phillips said, "Your sister is on her way to take custody of your dog. I told her we'd leave it here in a cage." He reached for the fluffy white dog.

"She's going to be locked up, just like her mommy," Molly said, kissing Bella on her head. More tears threatened.

Lenore gave an unladylike snort.

"It's time to go, Miss Deaver," Officer Edelson said gently.

"May I freshen up, please?" Molly asked. "The ladies' room is right across the hall."

"Officer Phillips will wait outside the door," Edelson said.

Ten minutes later, Molly emerged, looking like she'd stepped off the cover of a bride's magazine. Somehow, she'd combed her blond hair and repaired her makeup. She gave Officer Edelson a heartbroken smile and squared her shoulders.

"I'm ready," she said.

"If you go quietly, I won't cuff you," he said.

She upped her smile to radiant. He put his hand on her elbow and escorted her out of the clinic surgery. Madfis followed with his camera trained on the couple, a grotesque parody of a wedding photographer.

He was back five minutes later, grinning. "I got the money shot—the bride getting into the cop car, with the Bentley in the background."

"Good work, Bill," said producer Rona Richley. "Now, Mrs. Scottsmeyer Hall, we'd like to talk to you about that pearl-handled pistol."

Lenore looked absurdly pleased. She checked her makeup in her compact mirror, fluffed her already perfect hair, and pulled out her pistol.

"I always carry my weapon in my purse for self-protection," she said. She held her pearl-handled pistol as if it were a piece of fine jewelry.

Madfis, the Channel Seven photographer, pointed his lens at the shining silver gun.

"Pretty, isn't it?" she asked. "Pretty deadly. I don't carry this for looks. It's a weapon—a snub-nose thirty-eight."

Lenore was a natural for television. The bridal invasion at the clinic had been dramatic and potentially deadly, but Lenore seemed unruffled. She faced the camera, relaxed and comfortable, looked it right in the eye, and smiled at it like a lover.

The camera loved her back. Josie could see Lenore on producer Rona Richley's monitor. Television gave Ted's mother an actressy glamor and newfound youth. She barely looked forty on the small screen. It was a tribute to her style and her second husband's plastic surgery skills.

Lenore pointed to the pistol's inlaid-pearl grip with a manicured nail. "These are my initials in silver. *LSH*—Lenore Scottsmeyer Hall. My son, Dr. Ted Scottsmeyer, says I use too many monograms, but I want everyone to know this is my weapon."

Ted, standing next to a cabinet, winced at the mention of his name. Josie patted his hand and he smiled at her. She thought he was too pale. The blood spot on his shirt collar had dried and his thick hair stuck up. Josie smoothed it back into place.

"Don't underestimate this little beauty," Lenore was saying. "It's small but deadly. This thirty-eight is a self-defense handgun for close quarters, designed to be easily concealed. It fits right in here."

Lenore held up her black Chanel purse with the signature double *C*s. "If necessary, I can fire right through this," she said. "But I'd hate to ruin a good purse."

She laughed, dismissing her deadly skill as a charming eccentricity. Rona smiled at her. The Channel Seven producer was crouched behind Bill, the photographer, nodding encouragement to Lenore. Rona had explained that she'd ask Lenore questions, but they would be edited out of the actual TV interview. She didn't need to ask many. Lenore almost interviewed herself.

Josie thought Lenore gave her gun lesson with professional polish, except she ignored the most basic safety rule: Never point a gun at anyone. Lenore aimed her thirty-eight straight at Bill. The photographer didn't flinch.

"A short-barreled revolver like this is useful for its speed," Lenore said. "I can draw, sight, and fire by the time an attacker with a long-barreled gun is still trying to get me in his sights."

She stuffed the snub-nose back into her purse. "I'm licensed to carry concealed and I practice religiously. I can empty my weapon into a pie plate at seven yards in five seconds—including the time it takes to draw it from this purse. I practice, practice, practice. I have to. That's the mistake most people make. They buy a gun and then don't practice. That laziness will cost you your life.

"I practice point shooting, too. If I'm threatened and have to fire at close range, I may not have time to align the sights. I can pull out this gun, look over the top of it, hopefully get the front sight on the target and shoot."

Lenore whipped the gun out of her purse and once again pointed it at the camera. Josie winced and backed away. The photographer moved in closer. Bill was either fearless or foolish.

"I prefer the sighted fire method," Lenore said, "but I'm prepared to defend myself when I don't have that luxury. I believe self-protection is an important women's issue."

The chunky Rona nodded and her dark hair danced. Bill kept the tape rolling as he focused on the .38.

"I carry my pistol in a purse instead of a holster, but it's just as deadly as any man's long barrel," Lenore said. "Maybe deadlier, because I can open my purse quicker than he can unsnap his holster. Besides, I'm an expert shot."

Josie didn't think Lenore was bragging, not from the confident way she handled that pistol. Ted stifled a groan. Rona nodded like a dashboard dog. Josie wondered if the frizzy-haired TV producer was as enthusiastic about concealed weapons away from Lenore's spell.

"Why do you carry a gun?" Rona asked her.

"Because I live in South Florida," Lenore said, as if that were an explanation. "Protection is important everywhere, not just Florida. Today's problem with that, uh, unfortunate person is a prime example. We were in a clinic in a quiet neighborhood, surrounded by decent people. There was even a large dog, but he was no use."

She glared at Festus, who'd come out from under the table to watch. Ted's Lab wagged his tail.

"None of that made any difference when that deluded woman burst in here," Lenore said. "No one stopped her. She would have killed Dr. Scottsmeyer if I hadn't had this weapon."

Lenore brandished the pistol and gave a dazzling smile. The producer applauded. "Perfect!" she said. "Now could you twirl your pistol and blow on the barrel as if you've just fired it?"

Lenore did more stylish moves while Bill, the photographer, taped the glamorous gunslinger. He even climbed on a chair to shoot her from another angle.

"Do you have enough tape for your interview?" Lenore asked.

"More than enough," Rona said. Josie noticed the producer's ecstatic smile and felt uneasy.

"Good," Lenore said. "What's going to happen to my son's show? Are you going to finish taping it?"

"Uh, we're meeting about that later at the station," Rona said. She avoided looking directly at Lenore.

Josie's heart sank. The producer is dodging the question, Josie thought. Molly not only wounded Ted; she'd killed his TV show.

"I hope you won't abandon a useful program like *Dr. Ted's Pet Vet Tips*," Lenore said. Josie thought she was trying to frown, but the Botox injections had left her smooth forehead immobile.

The producer gulped. "Right now we'd like to interview Dr. Ted about today's incident."

Ted shook his head. "I'd rather not," he said. "I'm hoping Miss Deaver can be cured of her . . . problem. She is a former patient. No, I mean, Bella's my patient. That's her dog. Well, not my patient. Dr. Chris took over her case. But Miss Deaver is a client. I want to give her a chance to recover."

"Ted, you should talk to the TV station," Lenore said. "Any TV time is good."

"At least give us a statement about today," Rona said. "We need something for the record. Stand over there by the table, where you were with the cat."

Ted obediently got into place. Josie tried unsuccessfully to straighten his white coat and the rumpled blue shirt underneath.

"You stand over here," Rona said, and pulled Josie over near Lenore.

"We're rolling in one, two, three," Rona said.

"Were you engaged to Molly Ann Deaver?" she asked Ted.

"No! Never," Ted said. "I went to her home to check up on her dog, Bella. I'd spayed her Maltese. Miss Deaver misunderstood my visits. She thought I was calling on her. She began to make excuses so I'd see her—I mean, her dog—more often.

"There was nothing wrong with Bella. I even sent her to a specialist who confirmed my diagnosis. It seemed wrong to take Miss Deaver's money and subject Bella to blood tests, X-rays, and other procedures when the dog wasn't sick. I discussed the situation with my partner, Dr. Chris, and we decided that she would handle any future appointments for Bella and we'd treat the dog only if Miss Deaver brought her to the clinic. After she ambushed me in the hall and gave me an expensive watch, we declined to treat her dog at all."

Ted was sweating. Big drops ran down his forehead and splashed on his bloodstained shirt. He kept running his fingers through his hair and it was standing up again. Josie longed to give him a fresh shirt.

"So you never planned to marry Molly Deaver today?" Rona asked.

"Not today or any other day," Ted said. "I've never dated her. I've never met her family. I am engaged to Josie Marcus and we're getting married in a month, the day after Thanksgiving. Josie—not Molly. She's my bride, my real bride."

Ted had seemed so sure of himself when he talked about how to trim a cat's nails. Now he was tongue-tied. It was painful to watch him stumble over his words. Festus seemed to notice his distress. The black Lab bumped his big head against Ted's leg, and the vet absently scratched the dog's ear.

A worried Festus jumped up on the table next to Ted and licked his neck. The vet tried to calm his dog with reassuring pats. Festus was not fooled. He leaned protectively against Ted.

"Dr. Ted," Rona said, "you didn't answer my question. Where did Miss Deaver get the idea that you wanted to marry her?"

"I don't know," Ted said, his voice sad. He scratched his head.

Festus threw back his head and howled.

Josie wanted to join him.

Chapter 5

"I'm so sorry your mother couldn't make our little luncheon," Lenore said.

Josie knew she wasn't. Lenore and Jane had met once and disliked each other instantly.

"I am, too," Josie said. "Unfortunately, Mother had a previous engagement. But she's looking forward to seeing you at the Blue Rose Tearoom tomorrow."

Jane had a church committee meeting today—and no idea she'd been invited to this lunch at the Ritz-Carlton. Josie didn't dare bring her fierce little mother. She knew when Lenore started hinting that her son could have found a better bride, Jane would leave blood on the white tablecloth.

When the polite lies were out of the way, the server took their orders and delivered their drinks—white wine for the women and a beer for Ted.

"Well," Lenore said, "this morning was interesting, wasn't it? I'm glad that woman is locked up."

Ted's mother was fresh and prettily flushed after her television triumph. She glowed in the sunlit softness of the restaurant.

Ted still looked bedraggled, even after he'd stopped at home to change into a fresh shirt. He refused to wear his white doctor's coat, even after Lenore begged him.

"She'll be out on bond soon, Mom," Ted said.

"And then the judge will put her away," Lenore said. "That nice policeman said her attack on you is a second-degree felony assault. She's looking at five to fifteen years in prison."

"I don't think so," Ted said. "Pretty blue-eyed blondes don't get maximum sentences."

"It doesn't matter," Lenore said. "She's out of the way." She dismissed mad Molly with a wave of her hand.

"Josie, you already received my wedding guest list weeks ago," Lenore said. "We're expecting some fifty friends and family members to attend Ted's wedding. He's my son and I want to make this an occasion."

Josie felt a jab of fear when Lenore said "Ted's wedding" and "make this an occasion." Josie and Ted wanted their wedding to be a celebration, not a circus.

"Our guests have received their invitations," Lenore said. She produced one from her bag and tapped the heavy cream-colored paper with her fingernail.

"These aren't engraved," she said. The frost in her voice could have chilled their wine.

"No," Josie said. "But we chose the best paper, one-hundred-ten-pound cotton stock. They look engraved."

"But everyone knows this isn't real engraving," Lenore said. "If only you'd let me, I could have helped you. The invitation says the ceremony is at the Jewel Box. What's that?"

"Wait till you see it, Mom," Ted said. "It's an art deco greenhouse in Forest Park—that's the big city park—with these incredible palm trees and tropical plants. The Jewel Box was built in the 1930s. It's on the National Register of Historic Places. The out-of-town guests will see something really cool."

Ted brightened as he described the Jewel Box, his enthusiasm overcoming his lost look.

"We were lucky to get it," Josie said. She managed a lopsided smile and fortified herself with a sip of wine. "Our timing is perfect. Our wedding is at the start of the winter poinsettia show and hundreds of them will be on display, ranging from white to deep ruby. It's dazzling. I have a photo of the Jewel Box in my wedding plan notebook." She leafed through it and found the page.

"Here," she said. "Not only is the building gorgeous, but there's lots of free parking."

"Very nice," Lenore said. A historic building seemed to meet her exacting standards. "What about music?"

"We've picked some lovely CDs," Josie said. "We chose music that meant something to both of us."

A shadow crossed Lenore's face. Was that an attempted frown on her Botoxed forehead? Josie wondered.

"I was thinking of a string quartet for the ceremony," Lenore said.

"Mom, that's not in our budget," Ted said.

"I'll give it to you as a gift," Lenore said.

"That's very generous," Josie said, and meant it. "I'll get the names of some local quartets and you can choose one."

"Oh, you hire one," Lenore said. "Just send me the bill."

Well, that was easy, Josie thought. Maybe I've misjudged her.

"Will you have the reception at the Jewel Box, too?" Lenore asked.

"No, we've only rented it for two hours," Josie said. "There's another wedding after ours. But we have the reception at a nice banquet hall, the Royal Saint Louis."

Lenore frowned at the photo of the hall.

"Is that a public banquet hall?" she asked. Her tone implied it was a public toilet.

"A good one," Josie said. "The food is delicious. See. Four stars."

"In St. Louis," Lenore said. Her collagened lip curled. "I was hoping we could have the reception here at the Ritz."

"That's—," Ted said.

Josie cut him off before he could say "out of our price range." "Taken," she said. "That date has been booked already."

Josie had no idea if that was true, but she'd already signed the contract for the Royal Saint Louis.

"Of course," Lenore said. "I should have known. For your wedding reception, I was thinking of booking Peter Duchin."

"Peter Duchin?" Josie said. Wasn't that old people's dance music?

"Surely you've heard of his orchestra," Lenore said. "He plays at the White House, premier charity galas, and society weddings. I doubt if we'll be able to get Peter himself at this late date, but any of the bands booked by his organization are top notch."

"We already have a band," Josie said. "A good one. We've got the Smash Band. It has ten members."

"Smash is playing all the wedding reception favorites," Ted said. "'Proud Mary,' 'Raise Your Glass.'"

"We even paid an extra hundred dollars for the twist contest," Josie said.

"A twist contest!" Lenore looked like she'd bitten into a lemon.

"It's fun," Josie said. "We have a cool trophy for the winner."

"I was hoping my son's wedding would be small but tasteful," Lenore said.

"That's what we want, too," Josie said. "That's why we decided not to have a dollar dance."

"I've never heard of that," Lenore said. More frost.

"It's a bridal tradition," Josie said. "The bride and groom dance with guests who pay for the privilege. The money usually goes to the honeymoon fund."

"I should think not!" Lenore said. She clutched her wineglass and took a stiff drink. "At least I've heard of that song, 'Proud Mary.' But what is 'Raise Your Glass'?"

"A song by Pink," Ted said. "It's a wedding favorite for . . . uh, my generation."

"This Pink," Lenore said. "That isn't Pink Floyd, is it? I heard one of their songs, something about a brick. It's loud and depressing."

"I agree," Josie said. "'Another Brick in the Wall' isn't wedding music. Pink is a rock star. She won a Grammy."

"I don't know her," Lenore said, as if that were a failing on Pink's part.

Josie was relieved. That meant Lenore hadn't heard of another Pink hit—"Fuckin' Perfect."

"And I'm quite sure none of our guests have heard of this Smash," Lenore said. "But they definitely know Peter Duchin. He plays all the time in Boca Raton."

Lenore drawled Boca Raton as if it meant something more impressive than "mouth of the rat."

"If they haven't heard of Smash, they should have," Josie said. "He was an MTV DJ, and he's been on national television and radio stations all around the country. Since he moved here, he's become a St. Louis institution."

Lenore sniffed. "Half of our out-of-town guests haven't heard of St. Louis," she said.

Josie pressed her lips together, forcing herself not to answer back. She looked around wildly, hoping the server would appear with their lunch, but saw no sign of approaching rescue. She wished Ted would defend their choice, but he was scanning the horizon for signs of food.

"We've already signed a contract," Josie said.

"I'll buy it out," Lenore said quickly. "With a thousand-dollar bonus for this Smash person."

Josie tried counting to ten to keep her temper. She quit at four. "No, thank you," she said "We want Smash. Amelia asked for him."

"You're letting a ten-year-old dictate your wedding choices?" Lenore didn't hide her disbelief.

"Amelia is eleven," Josie said. "She's happy that Ted and I are marrying, but our marriage will be a big disruption in her life. She asked for Smash, and Ted and I were happy to go along with that. Smash is our choice, too."

She looked at Ted, waiting for him to support her.

"Yum," he said. "My Reuben sandwich with duck fat fries is on its way."

"What are duck fat fries?" Lenore asked.

"Potatoes fried in duck fat," Ted said.

Lenore shuddered delicately. She'd already banned the bread basket and wanted her salad served with the dressing on the side.

There was a lull in the conversation while the server set down their meals.

Josie inhaled the fragrant steam from her soup. "Mm. This tomato bisque smells delicious," she said, hoping to keep the topic safely on food. "How's your lunch, Lenore?"

Ted's mother brushed aside Josie's question like an annoying fly and said, "Will Amelia's father be at your wedding?"

"No," Josie said. "Nate is dead." He was murdered, but Josie wasn't giving Lenore that detail. "But her grandfather, Jack Weekler, will be flying in from Toronto."

Duck fat must have had amazing powers of revival. After three fries, Ted perked up and said, "The rehearsal dinner is the groom's responsibility. Maybe we could have that at the Ritz."

Josie gave her fiancé a relieved smile.

"What a splendid idea," Lenore said. "I'll make the reservations right after lunch."

Ted had rescued the difficult meal. They chatted happily about safe subjects after that: Josie's colors—red, white, and pink—to go with the Jewel Box flower display. The dinner table decorations would be big pots of poinsettias. "My best friend, Alyce, will be my matron of honor and Amelia is my junior bridesmaid."

"Very sensible," Lenore said. She glanced at her watch. "Well, if you two don't mind, I'll get the check and then make the arrangements for the rehearsal dinner. Josie, I'll meet with you and your mother tomorrow."

"I'll take Ted back to his car at the clinic," Josie said.

"I'm glad that Molly Deaver won't be lurking in the parking lot," Ted said.

"Oh, she won't bother you again," Lenore said. "That's all taken care of."

Josie hoped her future mother-in-law was right.

Chapter 6

"I need to stop by my place right away, Ted," Josie said. "Before I take you back to your car."

Josie was pacing outside the Ritz, waiting for the valet to return with her car. The droopy-brimmed hat made it hard to see Ted. She took it off and held it by the brim.

"Any time," Ted said. "I like your mom. You seem worried. What's wrong?"

"I don't want Jane hearing some twisted version of the scene at the clinic today," Josie said.

"Dr. Chris and Kathy won't talk," Ted said.

"Maybe not, but the waiting room was crowded. You can't believe what the local gossips will do to that juicy story."

"Call her now," Ted said.

"No way I can explain that on the phone," Josie said. "Besides, Mom won't believe you're safe until she personally inspects you for damage."

The tinny notes of "Here Comes the Bride" sounded from Josie's purse.

"You come with your own entrance music now?" Ted asked.

Josie looked embarrassed. "Amelia reprogrammed my cell phone to play the 'Wedding March.'" She fished her phone out of her purse and said, "Hi, Mom. What's wrong? Is Amelia hurt? Why are you crying?"

Ted hovered close by, looking concerned. Josie tried to give him both sides of their conversation.

"Good. She's safe," Josie said. "Thanks for picking her up at school. No, Mom, Ted didn't have his throat slashed by a crazy lady."

Ted's eyes widened.

"He's fine. Well, she did cut him, but it was tiny. Really. He wasn't hurt at all. We've just finished lunch. He couldn't eat if his throat was cut. We're on our way to see you now. You can check him out yourself.

"Is our wedding off? Of course not," Josie said. She tried to laugh, but it sounded high-pitched and fake.

"Who told you that? It was Mrs. Mueller, wasn't it?" Josie sighed. "That interfering old bat never gets anything right. No, Mom, Ted is *not* engaged to another woman. He's never been engaged to anyone, not since he graduated from vet school."

Ted nodded his agreement.

"Yes, that part is true. A bride in a Bentley pushed her way into his clinic this morning. She was wearing a wedding dress, carrying a bouquet and a dog. She interrupted Ted's TV taping. Her name is Molly and she announced that she was marrying Ted, but she isn't. Ted didn't know anything about that wedding. Their romance existed only in her head."

Josie took another deep breath.

"Yes, Mom, that's right. The poor woman is unbalanced. She does need your prayers. The police took her away. No, they didn't take her to a psychiatric hospital. She was arrested for second-degree assault. Who'd she assault? Ted. But it's just a scratch. He's okay, Mom. Really."

The conversation was back where it started. Josie saw the valet driving her rattling Honda. Her old car trailed a sleek black Porsche and a shining navy Cadillac. Ted paid the valet while Josie said, "We're on our way, Mom. We'll be home in ten minutes."

The valet opened the dented door to Josie's beater as if it were a luxury car. She tossed her wide-brimmed hat in the back and sank gratefully into the driver's seat.

"I gather there's trouble," Ted said as Josie drove toward her home on Phelan Street.

"Mrs. Mueller got to Mom first with a wild tale that your throat was slashed by your other fiancée."

Ted groaned. "Maybe Festus and I should hide under my desk at the clinic," he said.

"Don't underestimate Mom," Josie said. "She'll have that rumor straightened out in no time—once she confirms you're well. We're almost home."

Maplewood was more than a hundred years old, an inner-ring suburb of St. Louis with generous two- and three-story homes, shady yards made for children to play in, and front porches where people could rock and relax. The late-fall sun was kind to the old homes. It gave the timeworn brick on the two-story Marcus flat a rosy glow.

Jane was outside in the front yard, her face pink with exertion.

"Look at your mom trying to drag those huge pots onto her porch," Ted said. "What's she going to plant in them—oak trees?"

"Mums," Josie said. "She and Mrs. Mueller outdo themselves with their fall-flower displays."

"Those pots are as big as beer kegs," Ted said. "Hurry up, Josie, before she hurts herself."

He didn't wait for Josie to parallel park. As soon as she stopped the car to back it into place, Ted leaped out and ran up the walkway.

Josie didn't have to hear his conversation with Jane. She could see it. Her fiancé gave Jane a quick hug, then pried the first pot out of her hands and carried it up the porch steps as if it were foam rubber. Jane tried to carry the other end. Ted shooed her away, then picked up the second pot.

Josie's car seemed safely parked, but she got out to make sure the back bumper didn't cross the boundary of

Mrs. Mueller's yard. Their troublesome neighbor believed she owned the street in front of her home and yelled at anyone who dared park in "her" area.

Mrs. M was planted on her porch, arms on her hips, glaring at Josie. From the way her head was tilted, Josie thought Mrs. M was also trying to eavesdrop on Jane and Ted. She locked her car door and heard her mother say, "Well, there is a bag of potting soil, Ted."

"Your car's in the garage, right?" he said. "I'll go get it."

"You don't have to do that," Jane protested, but not too much. Josie thought her mother looked pleased.

Amelia came around from the garage, balancing a cardboard box of bronze mums. Josie's daughter was tall for her age. Her flat little-girl's body was rounding into womanly curves. Her personality was changing, too, and not always for the better. Josie was glad Amelia still wanted to help her grandmother.

"Those mums will look good on Grandma's porch," Josie said.

Amelia shrugged. "Whatever," she said. "Are you still going to marry Ted after he got engaged to that other woman?"

Mrs. Mueller, digging in her own freshly potted yellow mums, froze like a forest deer, then swiveled her iron gray helmet head toward Josie to listen better.

Josie blasted back her answer. "Ted *isn't* engaged to anyone but me," she said. "He's not going to marry that demented woman, AND I WISH PEOPLE WOULD QUIT SPREADING FALSE RUMORS!"

Mrs. M backed away from her mums, squeezed through her front door, and slammed it. Josie heard the lock click.

"Okay, okay, you don't have to beast me," Amelia said. Her lip trembled.

Beast? Josie wondered. Oh, right. She had been screaming.

"I'm sorry, sweetheart. I wasn't yelling at you," Josie

said. "That was for Mrs. M's benefit. She's the one spreading that rumor and she upset Grandma."

"Her," Amelia said. "Nosy b—" She saw her mother's frown and said, "Uh, person."

"Good catch," Josie said.

Ted hurried past them lugging a forty-pound bag of topsoil as if it weighed half that. "Hi, Amelia," he called as he ran up the porch steps.

"Put that bag next to the pots, Ted," Jane said. "And that's enough work. You're coming inside so I can look at that cut."

"It's nothing," Ted said. "I've already checked it."

"You're an animal doctor," Jane said. "You need an expert. That's me. Upstairs to my flat, and if you're good, you can have chocolate chip cookies."

"Never turn those down," Ted said, and raced up the stairs two at a time. Amelia ran behind him. Josie moved a little slower. Her feet hurt in those high heels.

Jane's pale green living room was so clean, it made Josie feel guilty. She could see the vacuum cleaner tracks in the wall-to-wall carpet and smell the lemon polish. The magazines were lined up precisely next to the TV clicker on the dust-free coffee table. Jane's shih tzu, Stuart Little, barked a greeting.

Ted started to scratch the dog's ears, when Jane commanded, "In the kitchen and unbutton your shirt."

"But—," Ted said.

Josie hurried into her mother's kitchen. Ted was seated in a chair with Jane hovering over him. Amelia was crunching cookies at the table. The air was perfumed with fresh coffee.

"No cookies until I look at that cut," Jane said. She had an open first-aid kit on the counter. "Just as I thought. This wound wasn't cleaned properly." She tore open an alcohol wipe and gently dabbed at Ted's neck.

"Ow!" he said.

"Don't be such a baby," she said. "Big strong man like you. You carried those heavy pots, so you can put up with this." She squeezed a drop of medicated ointment on a Q-tip, applied it to the cut, then covered the wound with a Band-Aid.

Despite his protests, Ted seemed pleased by Jane's fussing. Josie realized his own mother had never even looked at the cut. Lenore had been too busy swanning in front of the TV cameras.

"There," Jane said. "Much better. Now tell me about this terrible business."

Josie did while Ted sipped coffee and munched cookies. When she finished, Jane said, "Goodness." Jane never used four-letter words, so this was extreme disapproval for her. "Amazing," Amelia said, finishing yet another cookie. Josie had lost count at six.

"At least that Molly won't be bothering you anymore," Jane said. "What are the latest plans for the wedding, Josie? I need to know, since I'm meeting with you and Ted's mother tomorrow."

"Can I turn on the TV?" Amelia interrupted.

Amelia was bored by the constantly changing details. So was Josie, but she didn't dare admit it. She told Jane about Lenore's offer to hire a string quartet for the wedding and left out her attempted takeover of the reception music. No point giving Jane ammunition.

"Mom!" Amelia shouted from the living room. "Ted's mother is going to be on TV."

"What?" Ted, Josie, and Jane stood up and sprinted for the living room. They arrived to see Molly Ann Deaver weeping before the camera.

"That's your crazy bride?" Jane said. "She looks normal to me."

"She isn't," Josie said. "She—"

Josie stopped, shocked speechless when the announcer said, "Channel Seven has a special report at five p.m. about the double-brided doctor and his pistol-packing mama."

Then Lenore Scottsmeyer Hall smiled and pointed her pearl-handled pistol straight at the screen.

Chapter 7

"Yes, Your Honor, he left me at the altar." Molly Deaver, a snowstorm of white satin and silk illusion, wept scenically for the TV camera—and Judge Fletcher Hornsby.

The judge was a dried-up seventy with a fluff of white hair like a rooster comb. Only his black robes gave him majesty. He peered over the top of the high oak bench like a hungry chicken looking over a fence at feeding time. His small eyes glittered while he surveyed the bride.

Josie, Ted, and Jane stood silent in front of the television in Jane's living room, Stuart Little next to them. They knew they were watching a disaster.

"That's your bridezilla?" Jane said. "She seems sweet."

"She's not," Josie said. "But she's delivering an Academy Award–winning performance as an abandoned bride."

"How did she get on TV already?" Ted asked. "And why isn't she wearing a jumpsuit to enter a plea?"

"There's your answer sitting at the table. Renzo Fischer," Josie said. "She must have called the best lawyer in St. Louis. Renzo has a real talent for getting around the rules."

"Fresh wedding dress," Amelia said from the couch. "You should get one like it, Mom."

"Be quiet, Amelia," Josie said, then instantly felt bad. "I'm sorry, honey. But this crazy woman is trying to wreck our lives."

Josie tried to hug her daughter, but Amelia shook her off. "Whatever," she said. "If you ask me, you're the crazy one."

"I agree with Amelia, dear," Jane said. She moved behind a green armchair, as if it were a shield. "Not about the dress," she added, quickly. "Ruffles are not your style. But that Molly bride seems surprisingly sane."

"I know she does, Mom," Josie said. "That's the problem. I hope the TV station will show the crazy stuff she did at the clinic."

"What about Ted?" Jane said. "That station should have interviewed you."

"They did," Ted said. "I sounded like an idiot. This will be a massacre."

Josie's heart went *ka-chunk*. Ted was right, she thought. Even if Rona showed Molly with the scalpel at Ted's neck, the viewers had already seen her looking sweet as a six-tiered wedding cake.

The horror show continued to unfold in the courtroom with mournful Molly. "And—and he said I was crazy, too," she said, soft and wounded.

Judge Hornsby straightened his scrawny shoulders and said, "He did? A pretty little thing like you!"

"Oh, thank you, Your Honor." Molly batted her eyes at the dried-up judge and squeezed out more tears.

"You've made me feel like a woman again," Molly said. "It helps that an important gentleman such as yourself thinks I'm attractive."

Her lawyer was beaming like a proud parent at a school play.

Ted groaned.

"Any man who doesn't think you're beautiful is insane," the judge said. "You are charged with a second-degree felony assault."

"No!" Molly said. Her eyes widened dramatically.

"I'm sorry, my dear," Judge Hornsby said. "I cannot reduce the charges. Only the prosecutor can do that. You did cut a man with a scalpel." He chuckled, as if a knife attack were adorable.

Josie yelled at the TV screen. "She drew blood!"

"Not that much," Ted said.

"Any blood is too much," Jane said.

"Hey, everybody, I can't hear with you talking," Amelia said.

Molly was still explaining her attack on Ted to the judge. "I did cut him, Your Honor. I was so upset. It was only a little cut."

"How do you plead, Miss Deaver?" the judge asked.

She looked at Renzo. The little lawyer nodded.

"Not guilty," she said, her voice sweet and firm.

"Your Honor, may I say something else?" Molly asked.

The judge nodded gently.

"Ted's mother went crazy and pulled a gun out of her purse—an actual gun—and threatened to shoot me. I would never hurt Ted. You understand, don't you?"

"I certainly do," the judge said, eyes twinkling.

"Gag me," Josie said to the TV.

"Mom!" Amelia said. "How can I find out what happened if you keep talking?"

"This isn't what happened," Josie said.

"Josie, please," her mother said. "We have to hear what she's saying. That way we'll know how to answer her lies."

Brave Molly had switched to another mode—righteous indignation. "Do you know what happened next, Your Honor? After Ted left me on our wedding day and my mother-in-law tried to shoot me? They both went to lunch at the Ritz with the Other Woman."

Josie shrieked so loud that Stuart Little yelped. "The Other Woman! How did I get to be the Other Woman?"

"Sh!" Jane said. "I want to hear this."

"You're lucky you didn't marry him, Miss Deaver," the judge said. "I have to send the case to trial, since this Dr. Ted Scottsmeyer has pressed charges." His lip curled at Ted's name. "But I'm releasing you on your own recognizance."

"Oh, thank you, Your Honor. You've saved me and my baby."

"She's got a baby?" Amelia asked.

"A dog," Josie said.

"Miss Deaver, there's one more thing you must do," the judge said.

"Anything, Your Honor."

"Find a man worthy of you!" The judge banged his gavel.

The camera left Molly smiling bravely through her tears, and moved outside the courtroom to a TV reporter with a red suit and a blond bubble of hair. "This is Wendy Lee Chase, Channel Seven news, reporting live at the courthouse," she said. "We just heard Judge Fletcher Hornsby. The judge believes that Miss Molly Ann Deaver was left at the altar by Rock Road Village veterinarian Dr. Ted Scottsmeyer. Dr. Scottsmeyer claims he was attacked by Molly."

Claims? Josie's heart dropped like a rock out of a skyscraper window. The TV station had turned on Ted.

"I have an exclusive interview with Molly, the abandoned bride," Wendy Lee said.

A commercial for a floor mop flashed on the screen, but Josie, Ted, and Jane didn't see the woman dancing with delight while cleaning her floors. Ted plopped down next to Amelia.

"This couldn't get any worse," he said.

Josie tried to rub the tension knots out of his shoulders. "It's a smear," she said.

Jane gave him a reassuring hug. Stuart Little licked his hand, and Ted scratched the dog's chin.

"It's not so bad," Amelia said. "It makes Ted look studly."

The show returned to Molly, seated on a pale peach couch, wearing a soft blue dress with a lace collar. Wendy Lee Chase sat across from her, oozing sympathy. "We're here with Molly Ann Deaver in her home," Wendy Lee said. "She was left at the altar this morning by Rock Road Village veterinarian Dr. Ted Scottsmeyer. Molly expected to be Mrs. Scottsmeyer by this time today. Instead, she's facing felony assault charges. Can you tell us what happened, Molly?"

Molly managed a mournful smile. "About six months ago, I took Bella, my Maltese, to Ted's Rock Road Village clinic to be spayed," she said.

The camera focused on the little white dog asleep on Molly's lap.

"I spayed her because I am a responsible mommy," Molly said. "After Bella's operation, I called the clinic and asked Ted to come to my home in the St. Louis Mobo-Pet van for her checkup. I didn't want to stress Bella by taking her out so soon. Ted works such long hours, he didn't have time to eat. I fixed us a little lunch. He was grateful. The Other Woman doesn't cook."

Josie stifled another shriek.

"Ted told me so," Molly said, her eyes wide. "He also said he wanted to get married."

"To you, Josie," Ted said.

"I know," she said. "I can tell she's twisting your words."

"I wanted to get married, Wendy Lee," Molly said. "I'm an old-fashioned girl who believes marriage is the most important career a woman can have. I'm working at Denise's Dreams, a bridal shop, helping other women plan their big days. But I longed for my own wedding. And Ted is the perfect man. He loves me, and we have so much in common."

"Like what?" Wendy Lee asked.

"We both love animals," Molly said. "And he loved my cooking. He was starved for good, home-cooked food—and for love. Soon we were planning our wedding.

He'd come over and we'd talk about the perfect way to start our new life together. You could say Bella brought us together." She petted the little dog in her lap.

Ted stared at the screen, speechless.

Wendy Lee switched to a confiding "we girls" mode. "May I ask you a personal question, Molly? When did you and Ted consummate your love?"

Molly blushed prettily. "Do you mean, did we have sex?" She lowered her eyes. "Like I said, I'm old-fashioned. I wanted to be pure for my wedding night. Ted agreed to respect my wishes. He said he didn't want to make love to me."

Ted said, "That's the only true thing she's said so far. Except she left out the word 'ever.' I said I didn't *ever* want to."

"I know," Josie whispered.

Wendy Lee forged ahead. "So, tell us how your happiest day turned into your worst nightmare."

"This morning, I came to the clinic to pick up Ted in a white Bentley. I know renting a luxury car is extravagant, but I'd always wanted to ride in one. I thought Ted would enjoy it, too. They say it's bad luck to see your groom before the wedding, but I didn't believe that old wives' tale. Maybe I should have." She gave a sad smile.

"Everything went wrong from the moment I walked into the clinic. Kathy, the receptionist, has always been so kind. This morning, she tried to stop me from seeing Ted. I went right past her into the surgery, where your channel was taping Ted. He looked so handsome, but he wasn't dressed for our wedding. I reminded the silly boy he was going to be late. He gets so wrapped up in his work, he forgets, you know."

She smiled fondly at Ted's foible, before her face turned sad.

"Except he said he wasn't marrying me," Molly said. "Ted said he was marrying the Other Woman a month from now. I had no idea. She came to the store where I work, but I thought she was just another bride. She said she had an engagement ring, but I had one of my own, and let me tell you, my diamond is a lot bigger than her little chips."

Josie looked at her ring finger. "They're not chips, Ted. I love my ring."

"Sh!" Jane and Amelia said.

Molly's voice wobbled on the edge of more tears. "The Other Woman told me to leave Ted alone. She said he was hers. I wouldn't listen to her crazy talk. Not on my wedding day. Our conversation got a little out of hand, and the next thing I knew, I was holding a scalpel and a woman who said she was Ted's mother pulled a gun and threatened to shoot me. I couldn't believe she was Ted's mother. He's naturally handsome and she looks like she's had more facelifts than Joan Rivers."

"Poor Mom," Ted said. "She doesn't deserve that."

"Did Dr. Scottsmeyer's mother fire the gun?" Wendy Lee asked the would-be bride.

"No," Molly said. "The police came busting through the door and she hid the gun in her purse. The police arrested me and I called Mr. Renzo Fischer, the best trial lawyer in St. Louis. Mr. Fischer asked that nice Judge Hornsby if I could make my plea in my wedding dress instead of an awful jail jumpsuit. Judge Hornsby said it was okay for your station to be in the courtroom, Wendy Lee. Otherwise, I would have been all alone."

"Molly told me she didn't like Channel Seven," Josie said. "She sure changed her mind fast."

This time Josie got a triple "Shhh!"

"And how did you plea?" Wendy Lee asked.

"Not guilty, of course," she said. "But my wedding — and my life — is over."

Molly sobbed again, but her mascara held fast. "Ted loves me. I know he does."

Wendy Lee turned to the camera. "And what does the groom have to say for himself?" she asked. "Not much. We asked Dr. Ted Scottsmeyer twice why Molly thought he wanted to marry her. Finally, Channel Seven got this answer from the doctor in his clinic surgery."

Josie winced when she saw this interview. Poor Ted looked like he'd been left out in the rain.

"I don't know," he said, and scratched his head.

"As you can see, the two-timing groom has no explanation," Wendy Lee said. "But his pistol-packing mama has plenty to say."

Lenore looked beautifully cruel on the small screen, twirling her pistol like a gun moll. She held up her weapon and bragged, "Don't underestimate this little beauty. It's small but deadly. This thirty-eight is a self-defense handgun for close quarters, designed to be easily concealed. It fits right in here."

Then she showed her black Chanel purse. "If necessary, I can fire right through this," she said. "But I'd hate to ruin a good purse."

Lenore was still laughing when the show ended.

Chapter 8

Lenore was still cackling on Jane's TV screen when three cell phones erupted. Ted's phone barked, Jane's rang like an old-school phone, and Josie's played "Here Comes the Bride." All three phone owners retreated into separate corners to answer.

Josie recognized her caller's number: Alyce, her best friend and matron of honor.

"I saw that horrible television show," Alyce said. "It's wrong. I know it's wrong. Ted would never do that."

Josie could practically see Alyce, her creamy skin flushed with indignation and her pale hair floating about her face.

"Every word is a lie," Josie said.

"I knew it," Alyce said. Josie's friend was as generous as her build, and a good listener.

"Molly Ann Deaver is insane," Josie said, "but Channel Seven loved her abandoned-bride act."

"Fletch the Lech sure bought it," Alyce said. "But I expected that."

"You know Judge Fletcher Hornsby?" Josie asked.

"My husband does," Alyce said. "So does the rest of the legal community. That old publicity hound. No, he's a real hound. They call him Fletch the Lech because he drools over every pretty face in his courtroom. Women lawyers dress like nuns to avoid that nasty old man. So far, he's managed to dodge any serious complaints, but the bar association is watching him."

"He was definitely watching Molly," Josie said. "She's been stalking Ted."

"Poor Ted," Alyce said. "I figured it had to be something like that. I don't trust that station. I got sucked in while I was channel surfing. First I saw Fletch, then the bride. I know her sister, Emily."

"Of course you do," Josie said. St. Louis was the kind of big small town where everyone was connected.

"She lives in my subdivision," Alyce said.

No wonder the fake bride wore a big rock and rode in a rented Bentley, Josie thought. If her sister lived in the Estates at Wood Winds, there was money in that family. Alyce's subdivision was a pricey gated ghetto in West County.

"Is Emily as crazy as her sister?" Josie asked.

"No, she's super sane," Alyce said. "She snagged a primo Wood Winds committee—the Thanksgiving food bank fundraiser. She and my friend Connie will be selling crafts at the Blue Rose Tearoom tomorrow."

"I'm going there for brunch with Mom and Lenore," Josie said. "We're discussing the wedding. At least, I hope it's a discussion. Mom and Lenore didn't hit it off the first time they talked."

"I saw your pistol-packing mother-in-law on TV," Alyce said. "Is that what she's like?"

"She's forceful," Josie said, "but better-looking in person." She mentally patted herself on the back for her diplomacy. If Ted hadn't been in the same room, she would have been blunter.

But Josie couldn't fool her best friend. "Ted nearby, Josie?" Alyce asked.

"Yes."

"Thought so," Alyce said. "At least your mother-in-law will live twelve hundred miles away in Florida."

"That's right," Josie said carefully.

"You can't talk, can you?" Alyce said.

"You know me too well," Josie said. "I'll be sure to buy something tomorrow." She clicked off her phone, relieved someone saw the real situation.

"How bad was your call?" Ted asked her.

"It was good," Josie said. "That was Alyce and she didn't believe Channel Seven's report. Who'd you talk to?"

"My partner, Chris," Ted said. "After the judge cut her loose, Molly headed straight for the clinic again. She flounced in, still wearing her wedding dress, and demanded Bella. Didn't even say thank you. She picked up her dog and left. Our clients stared and a Rottweiler growled at her."

"I wish he'd bitten her," Josie said. "What's Chris hearing from your clients?"

"Reaction is mixed so far," Ted said. "Two women canceled their appointments. They said they didn't want to deal with a hound like me. Six women requested me — and only me — to examine their pets at their homes. Chris said I wasn't making house calls this week."

"Amelia was right," Josie said. "The controversy has made you more attractive."

"Notorious," Ted said. "That's not the same. I don't like it. I'm an animal doctor, not a dog."

Amelia giggled.

"Alyce says the judge is known as Fletch the Lech," Josie said. "He's the real hound."

"Well, that explains something," Ted said. "That judge —"

The rest of his sentence was drowned out by Jane's shouting. "Ted's a good man and I'm proud to have him as my son-in-law. That's right, proud! That crazy Molly Deaver lied through her teeth. We're lucky to have him, AND IF YOU DON'T BELIEVE THAT, YOU CAN LOSE MY NUMBER, ESTELLE!"

Jane punched her phone off extra hard. "The nerve of that woman!" she said. "And she irons the altar cloths, too!"

She hugged Ted again. "This will blow over," Jane said. "Too many people know you're a good man and a good doctor. I hope you'll stay for dinner."

"I should have Josie take me to my car," Ted said.

"You should eat," Jane said. "I've got homemade beef stew in the freezer. Dinner will be ready as soon as I make a salad. Amelia, set the table for four, please."

"Mom's right," Josie said. "You need a good meal."

"Please stay, Ted," Amelia said.

"Well, I can't refuse three ladies," he said, and grinned at Amelia.

At dinner, Jane heaped Ted's plate with her savory stew, thick with beef, carrots, and potatoes. Ted speared a beef chunk and pushed it around his plate. Josie waited for him to eat it, but he abandoned it and stuck his fork in a potato hunk.

Conversations started up suddenly, then quickly died.

"I got those mums on sale at the garden center," Jane said. "I'll plant them after dinner."

"Need help?" Ted asked.

"No, you've done enough," Jane said. "I'm so upset, after that show, I'll feel better digging around in the dirt."

That killed the conversation for a long minute.

"While we're talking dirt," Josie said, "Alyce's husband is a lawyer, Ted. He can recommend a good attorney if you want to sue Channel Seven."

"What's the use, Josie?" Ted said. "Molly Deaver has been painted as a victim. If I sue her, I'll be the monster who attacked her in court after I abandoned her at the altar. I'll just hope the story dies away soon."

Josie didn't think it would, but if she said so, Ted would feel worse. More silence descended while Ted took a carrot on a tour around his plate.

Amelia tried the next conversation. "Zoe wore the freshest outfit today," she said.

Josie braced herself. Zoe was eleven going on forty. She was the first in her class to wear makeup, drink beer with older boys, even sext a picture of her budding breasts to a boyfriend.

"She had this leopard blazer over a floral dress."

"Flowers and a leopard print?" Jane said. "I don't think those would go together."

"You wouldn't expect it to work, Grandma, but on Zoe it totally did. I loved her kicks. She wore Converse low tops. And she had this awesome Alexander Wang tote. You could find me something like that, couldn't you, Mom? You're an amazing shopper. It's your job."

"Wow, that's a lot of butter, Amelia," Josie said. "You've slathered it all over. I might be able to find one of those for your birthday, the dress or the blazer. Or I could score the Converse shoes. But the tote is out."

"Maybe I could buy the tote for Amelia's birthday," Ted said.

"I don't think so, Ted," Josie said. "It's more than six hundred dollars. That's too expensive. I can get a good knockoff cheap."

"It's not the same," Amelia said, and stuffed a big bite of beef into her mouth.

Ted resumed pushing chunks of stew around his plate until Jane said, "Does your food taste bad?"

"No, no," Ted said. "I ate too many cookies before dinner. Now I'm not hungry."

"I'm finished, too," Josie said. "You've had a long day, Ted. I'll drive you to the clinic to pick up your car."

"After we do the dishes," he said.

"Don't bother about the dishes," Jane said. "Amelia and I will do them. You two run along."

They both thanked Jane and ducked out. Josie was grateful the awkward dinner was over. Mrs. M, arms crossed over her chest, was on her porch, staring at Ted and Josie as they walked to her car. Josie stuck out her tongue.

"That was mature," Ted said, and grinned.

"It was. I could have flipped her the bird," Josie said. "I don't like the way she stared at you."

"I'd better get used to it," Ted said.

Josie unlocked her car and Ted sat down heavily. Josie kissed him and said, "I'm so sorry you have to go through this." She felt content with her head on his shoulder.

"I'm sorry I didn't recognize Molly was a stalker and

report her," Ted said. "Now I've dragged you into my mess."

"You didn't drag me anywhere," Josie said. "I love you. We'll face this together." She wanted to stay in her car, safe and isolated from the world, but her mother came outside in her gardening outfit. Time to leave.

Josie steered her car into the street and asked, "Did you call Lenore about the show?"

"I don't have the nerve," Ted said. "I'm hoping she never sees it."

A block from the clinic, Josie slowed down behind a line of cars. "What's going on?" she asked. "Is there an accident ahead?"

"There's a parade," Ted said. "They're all slowing down at the clinic." He craned his neck. "I see at least five TV news vans. Don't go into the lot. Just cruise on past so I can see what's going on."

Josie inched toward the clinic.

"I see Channel Five's truck," Ted said. "And Channel Two, Four, Eleven, and Seven. That's Molly's blue Bug, parked next to my car."

"She's back at the clinic?" Josie said.

"Yep. Talking to Channel Four."

Josie didn't recognize the reporter, a telegenic type in a shirt the same blue as Molly's dress. The abandoned bride was carrying her fluffy white dog like a baby. Bella's rhinestone collar sparkled.

"Quick, Josie. Keep driving before she sees me!" Ted said, and ducked down.

Josie stepped on the gas and swung around the line of gawkers.

"What do you want to do about your car?" she asked.

"Can you take me home?" he asked. "Kathy and I open the clinic at nine tomorrow. I'll ask her to swing by and pick me up. I wish that woman would go away for good."

"Maybe if we wish together, we can make it happen," Josie said.

Chapter 9

"Josie! It's Ted. She was here again." Ted didn't take time to wish her good morning. His words were quick, clipped, and angry.

Josie knew exactly who he meant. "What's Molly done to you?" she asked.

She had her hairbrush in one hand and her cell phone in the other.

"Molly was at the clinic, waiting by my car. At eight thirty this morning. Wearing some frilly dress like it was 1950," Ted said. "Kathy was driving me to work. When she saw Molly, she blasted the horn and called 911. Molly dumped a package on my car hood and took off in her blue Beetle."

"A package! Was it a bomb?" Josie asked.

"That's what I thought," Ted said. "I wanted to call the bomb squad, but Kathy calmly walked over and ripped open the package. Molly made me more blueberry muffins."

"You didn't eat them, did you?" Josie asked.

"Of course not," Ted said. "Kathy showed them to the police when they arrived."

"What did they do?" Josie asked.

"Nothing," Ted said. "These weren't the same two officers who were here yesterday. They treated the whole thing like a joke. One said he wished he had cute blondes chasing him with pastries. Kathy said that wasn't funny— Molly was dangerous. He finally asked if she'd damaged my car or the property."

"Did she?" Josie asked.

"No. The cop said, 'We'll file a report, Stud Muffin,' and they both drove off, laughing."

"It isn't funny," Josie said. "Are you able to work today?"

"I'm fine," Ted said, and switched the subject. "When is the moms' wedding summit?"

"I'm getting ready now," Josie said. "Jane's already dressed. She went outside to see if her flowers needed watering."

Josie heard a shriek. So did Ted. "Uh-oh. That's Mom," she said. "Hope bridezilla hasn't done something. I'll call you back."

Josie dashed to the front porch, wearing her black pantsuit and no shoes. Jane was standing over the two massive pots Ted had carried there yesterday. The morning sun gilded the gaping holes in the soil where the flowers had been.

"Somebody stole my mums!" Jane said. "Those . . . buzzards!" That was the worst B-word Jane used, a sure sign she was furious.

Josie looked up and saw their neighbor, Mrs. M, rolling up their walk like a tank in a flowered housedress.

"Jane! Someone stole your flowers," Mrs. M said. "They took mine, too. I saw who did it."

"Then why didn't you stop them?" Jane asked, exasperated.

"I saw the thieves, but I didn't actually see them stealing," Mrs. M said. "Last night, a carload of young men from the city drove down Phelan Street about nine o'clock, playing loud rap. They were gangbusters for sure. I should have called the police because they stole my Mammoth Football mums."

"Young men from the city"—Josie translated that as

"African-Americans." "You mean 'gangbangers,' Mrs. Mueller," she said. "And I don't think they drive around stealing flowers."

"You can laugh, Josie Marcus, but those people start by stealing and then their crimes escalate. Soon they'll be attacking us in our beds. I'm doing what I should have done last night—report this to the police. What about you, Jane?"

"I don't have time," Jane said. "Josie and I are leaving to meet with Ted's mother. To discuss the wedding."

"That's still on?" Mrs. M asked. She raised one eyebrow. "You're letting your daughter marry that Bluebeard?"

"That TV story was one big lie," Jane said. "Anybody with half a brain could see that."

Ooh. A year ago, Jane wouldn't have zinged Mrs. Mueller. Back then she'd been Jane's best friend. She was still a neighborhood power, in charge of the choice committees. But when Mrs. M insulted Josie and Amelia, Jane lashed back. The two women eventually mended their broken friendship, but it was no longer strong.

"Ted is a good man and I'm proud to have him in my family," Jane said. "Let's go, Josie. I'll wait in my car."

She stomped back toward the garage, leaving Mrs. M on their porch, chins trembling with outrage. "You have a civic duty to report this," she shouted at Jane's back.

Josie ran inside and slipped on her stylish new red heels, grabbed her purse, and dashed out the back door.

Jane was still fuming when Josie sat down in the passenger seat. "I've half a mind to rescind that woman's wedding invitation," she said, starting her car. "She doesn't deserve to be part of your special day."

"Don't, Mom," Josie said. "I want to see what awful gift she gives me and Ted. Ted! I forgot to call him."

She speed-dialed Ted's cell phone. When he answered, she heard the clinic background sounds: arfs, woofs, and an occasional cat screech.

"Ted? Mom's fine. She was upset because someone

stole her mums last night. Pulled them right out of the pots. Took Mrs. Mueller's plants, too. Mrs. M says it's 'gangbusters' from the city. No, we're fine. Mom's not worried and neither am I.

"How are you after this morning's surprise? Busy. Good. I'm glad that stupid TV show didn't hurt your business. I've gotta go, too. The wedding summit is starting soon. Mom's parking at the Blue Rose Tearoom. Twenty-nine days and we're together forever. Take care. I love you."

"What was that all about?" Jane asked.

Josie told her about the stalker bride's morning visit. "I was talking to Ted when you discovered your flowers were stolen," Josie said. "He was worried."

"How he got to be such a good man with that witch of a mother is beyond me," Jane said.

"I gather Ted takes after his late father," Josie said.

The Blue Rose Tearoom was a two-story Victorian from the days when St. Louis County was mostly farmland. Now it was surrounded by acres of asphalt. The old white house had gingerbread trim and freshly painted blue shutters. Hooked rugs, flowered china, and softly grayed turn-of-the-century photos made the inside cozy. Even on a Wednesday morning, the parking lot was packed.

"There's a good crowd here," Josie said. "That will help the fund-raiser. Alyce's subdivision is selling crafts for the Thanksgiving food bank."

"We'll have to buy something," Jane said.

"And watch what we say at the craft table," Josie said. "Emily will be here selling, and she's Molly Deaver's sister. Alyce says she's nothing like her crazy sister."

"I don't trust anyone in that family," Jane said. "I won't mention our connection to Ted."

"We won't have to," Josie said. "His pistol-packing mama will be at our table."

"Lenore." Jane made a face. "I'm trying for your sake, but I don't like her."

"Me, either," Josie said. "That's her navy Chevy rental

car, next to the dented red pickup. Who drives a pickup with a gun rack to a tearoom?"

"At least the gun rack is empty," Jane said. "Do I look okay?" She patted her sprayed gray hair and checked her pink plastic earrings. Jane had been through some hard times, but she had a pleasantly worn look, as if the struggle had improved her.

"You look pretty, Mom," Josie said. "That's my favorite pantsuit."

"Lenore is so chic," Jane said. "I don't want to embarrass you."

"Can't happen," Josie said, and hugged her mother.

Inside, Lenore waved at them from a corner table. Josie recognized her blue suit as a stylish St. John Knit. Her gold earrings were Tiffany diamond starfish. Josie waved back and they sat at a roomy table for four with a fat Blue Willow teapot.

"Josie, your future mother-in-law is a local celebrity," Lenore said. She had a glow that wasn't makeup. "Everyone recognizes me. They've been coming by the table here to look at me—even the men brave enough to come into this place. They want to know if I have my gun. I showed it to them."

"You saw the TV show last night?" Josie asked carefully.

"No, but the nice young waiter at the Ritz did," Lenore said. "He said I was 'awesome'—that was his word. The rest of the staff congratulated me. Even the housekeeper knew who I was. What did you think of me?"

"You were amazing," Josie said. She thought that safely covered the subject. She noticed Lenore never mentioned her son. Josie could feel the curious eyes aimed at them. A parade of women passed by, taking the long way to the restroom to look at Lenore.

A server in a blue gingham dress appeared with a basket of warm cranberry bread and honey butter. "Remove that bread," Lenore said, waving it away. "It's fattening."

"I'll take it," Josie said.

"Josie, dear, remember your wedding pictures," Lenore said.

"I am," Josie said. "A happy bride makes a beautiful picture." She chose the thickest slice and slathered it with honey butter, then passed the basket to her mother.

"Are you ready to order?" the server asked. Josie felt sorry for the stout older woman, forced to wear a girlish dress with puffed sleeves.

"I'll have the eggs Benedict," Lenore said, "with no sauce, no Canadian bacon, and fruit instead of fried potatoes."

"That's just a poached egg on an English muffin," the server said.

"That's right," Lenore said.

"I'll have the bacon-cheese scramble," Josie said as she deliberately buttered her second piece of cranberry bread.

"And fresh fruit instead of fried potatoes?" the server asked.

"No," Josie said. "I want the potatoes."

"I'll have the same," Jane said.

After the server left, Jane said, "Lenore, what color dress will you be wearing? I'd like pink."

"Fine with me. I'm wearing black," Lenore said.

"To a wedding?" Jane asked.

"I don't buy the old-fashioned idea that mothers have to wear pastels with pearls. That's so dowdy."

Jane's face fell.

Josie knew she was planning to wear her wedding pearls with a pink long-sleeved dress. She longed to stab Lenore, but she only had a butter knife. Change the subject, she told herself. "My matron of honor, Alyce, is wearing red velvet," she said. "It will look good with your black."

"Do I know Alyce?" Lenore asked.

"You'll meet her at the rehearsal," Josie said. She thumbed through the photos on her cell phone. "That's her there. The pretty blonde."

"Rather large, isn't she?" Lenore said.

"Largehearted," Josie said.

"Here comes our food," Jane said.

The three women ate in uneasy silence until Lenore said, "I was able to book the rehearsal dinner at the Ritz."

"Congratulations," Josie said. "I know you wanted to hold it there." They talked about the rehearsal plans and other harmless matters while a stream of diners passed their table, some sneaking glances at Lenore, others outright staring.

"I have things to do," Lenore said. "Shall we get the check?" She signaled the waitress.

Finally, Josie thought. She pulled out fifty dollars. "Here's my share and Mom's," she said. "Mom and I would like to look at the craft sale. It's a charity fund-raiser."

"Oh, I could take a look," Lenore said, a queen bestowing her presence on the peasants.

Josie, Jane, and Lenore examined the handmade scarves, jewelry, and other artfully displayed items. A pleasantly rounded woman with golden-brown eyes smiled at them.

"I'm a friend of Alyce Bohannon's," Josie said. "Are you Emily?"

"No, I'm Connie," she said. "Emily's taking a brief break. How may I help you?"

"I want these two wool scarves," Josie said. "And the pink necklace for my daughter."

"I'll take this green pet quilt," Jane said. "My dog watches the soaps with me. This will keep the dog hair off the couch cushions."

"What about you, ma'am?" Connie asked.

"I don't like homemade things," Lenore said. "I'll settle the check at the table."

Josie was mortified. "I'm sorry," she said, slipping Connie an extra ten dollars.

"You don't have to do that," Connie said, "but thank you."

"My purse!" Lenore said.

Josie heard her cry of distress across the room.

"I can't pay without my purse," Lenore said.

Once again, their table was the center of attention. Jane and Josie rushed over and helped Lenore and the server search for the missing Chanel bag. Other customers began looking for it.

"It's not on the floor," Josie said.

"It's not hanging on your chair back," Jane said.

"Here it is!" the server said. "It was sitting on the fourth chair. The tablecloth hid it." She handed Lenore her Chanel bag with the double *C*s.

"That isn't where I put it," Lenore said. She checked inside. "There's my wallet." She opened it. "My cash and credit cards are untouched. Thank heavens, everything is here. Let's go."

Lenore didn't even thank the waitress. Josie pressed a five-dollar bill into her hand and followed her mother outside.

"How many days before she goes back to Boca?" Jane asked as they waved good-bye to Lenore.

"The day after tomorrow," Josie said. "I wish someone would lock her up until the wedding."

Josie was about to get her wish.

Chapter 10

Back at home, Josie slipped off her red heels, wiggled her newly freed toes, and poured herself a cup of coffee. Then she sat down in her office, a corner of her bedroom with a computer and a fax machine on a garage sale table. Josie went online to find string quartets for her wedding.

The search was easier than she expected. Most of the online groups had sample videos or recordings. Several were photographed playing in the Jewel Box. She narrowed down the groups to four, e-mailing each their music selections and asking if they had the date open.

Josie e-mailed her fourth choice, carried her empty coffee cup into the kitchen, and saw it was two o'clock—time to pick up Amelia at the Barrington School for Boys and Girls. The school was financial light-years away from the Marcus family, but Amelia went there on a full scholarship. A full scholarship didn't mean a free ride. Josie had to pay a thousand dollars a year, plus books and fees. It was a struggle to keep Amelia in the school, but she wanted the best education for her daughter.

But she was beginning to dread these short trips to school. Her tween daughter had started speaking another language. "Don't beast me," Amelia would complain.

Sometimes Josie wasn't sure what her daughter said.

But she understood one thing: Amelia was distancing herself from her mother.

That was a healthy part of growing up—or so Josie read on the parenting blogs. She still felt sad she was losing her little girl. They used to make "guerilla gorilla raids"—quick, impulsive trips to the St. Louis Zoo after school.

Last week, Josie had said, "Let's go see the penguins. It will be cool."

Amelia had rolled her eyes and said, "Mom, nobody talks that way."

Josie hoped there would be no sarcasm this afternoon. She pulled into the school's half-circle driveway. The austere redbrick buildings with white trim shouted money in well-bred tones.

The Barrington students didn't shout, either. Nor did they leave the school in noisy herds. These were the children of old money, power couples, or the doctors and researchers who staffed the powerful St. Louis medical centers. They were precious to their parents, and potential kidnapping targets. The children were not released until their parents or designated drivers were parked at the school.

Josie smiled at the other Barrington mothers waiting for their offspring. Many could afford to be stay-at-home moms. They gave her cool nods, letting Josie know she was not one of them.

"Amelia Marcus!" the loudspeaker announced. Josie's heart sank. Amelia did not come running across the Barrington lawn. Shoulders hunched, backpack dragging, she moved as if she had anvils strapped to her shoes.

It's going to be one of those days, Josie thought.

Amelia tossed her backpack into the backseat and flopped down. Josie could smell her strawberry shampoo. A frown marred her smooth forehead and she'd covered the sprinkling of freckles on her nose with Josie's makeup again. She decided to let it go for now.

Josie tried to kiss her, but Amelia shied away.

"What's wrong?" Josie asked. She carefully steered past a green Land Rover.

"Nothing," Amelia said, her voice flat as a doormat.

"That means something," Josie said. "Are you feeling down?"

"Chill, Mom."

"I'm not chilling. You're my daughter and I want to know."

They were barely out of the school and Josie was already raising her voice.

Amelia responded with surly silence. Josie said nothing.

After a mile, Amelia said, "Oakley, that know-it-all, said Ted was some kind of player because he was engaged to you and that weird stalker. I said she was scandalous and Oakley was dumber than Miley Cyrus, and only an idiot would believe anything as lame as Channel Seven."

This was the ultimate insult. Amelia hated Miley Cyrus.

"Oakley? Is that a first name or a last?" Josie asked.

Tween names at Barrington could be difficult. Josie knew that "old" names like Kathy, Susan, and Linda were never used. Barrington parents preferred unisex names: Dakota, Peyton, Jordan, Sierra, Cassidy and now, apparently, Oakley.

"She's new," Amelia said. "Her parents are doctors from Boston. Oakley is her first name. I call her Annie and she hates it."

"Wonder why you don't get along," Josie said.

"We didn't even before she saw that video. And she said my grandmother was a weirdo with a gun."

"Jane?" Josie said.

"No, Ted's mother. She's my grandmother, isn't she?"

"Well, technically, she'll be your stepgrandmother, but I doubt Lenore will be happy if you call her that."

"Fine with me," Amelia said. "I don't like her anyway. Her skin's all stretched funny. She doesn't look nice like my real grandma."

"Lenore's had a facelift or two," Josie said. "She's proud that she doesn't have any wrinkles."

"She did that to herself on purpose?" Amelia asked.

"Ted's stepfather did it. He's a plastic surgeon."

"I don't get it," Amelia said. The surly tone was vanishing.

"Me, either," Josie said. "And I wouldn't worry about what Oakley says. That TV show will soon be forgotten."

"Mom, it's gone viral," Amelia said. "Somebody posted it on YouTube. Oakley showed it to me on her iPad while I was waiting for you. Ted's mom is grinning and twirling her gun. She's called 'the pistol-packing mama.'"

"How viral?" Josie asked, and ran a stop sign. A burgundy Buick gave her a horn blast.

"Mom!" Amelia said. "You rolled right through that stop."

"Sorry," Josie said. "How many hits did that video get?"

"Thirty thousand," Amelia said.

Chapter 11

Josie breathed in the rich, steamy scent coming from her kitchen. "Chicken and dumplings," she said. "My favorite perfume."

"Not quite chicken and dumplings," Amelia said. "I'm making them now."

Changeable as a spring day, Amelia was currently in a sunny mood. On the ride home from school, she and Josie had bonded over their dislike of Ted's mom.

"I know what I want to be for Halloween," Amelia said. "A witch."

"It's only a week away. Are you making a costume?"

"Emma said I could borrow her teen witch costume. It's a black pointy hat and black cape with pink satin lining. She's going as a vampire this year."

"Sounds good," Josie said. She knew Emma wouldn't have a teen porn star costume with bustier and thigh-high boots.

"You get to wear costumes on campus," Josie said. "But you won't have the afternoon party now that you're in middle school."

"Parties are for babies," Amelia said. This was her first year at that lofty level.

When they got home, Amelia had finished her homework, chased her cat, Harry, and texted her friend Emma (not necessarily in that order), then announced she was making chicken and dumplings for dinner.

Josie was amazed that her daughter seemed to enjoy cooking. Amelia was at the kitchen counter, expertly cutting the shortening into the flour with two knives, an old-fashioned method Jane had taught her.

Josie pulled two plates out of the cabinet and Amelia asked, "Isn't Ted coming over for dinner?"

"Can't make it tonight," Josie said. "He called and said he had a sudden emergency at the clinic."

Amelia looked disappointed. "He loves my chicken and dumplings."

"Once we're married, you two can cook together every night," Josie said. "I'll do the eating, for better or worse." She smiled, but Amelia didn't notice. She was slowly adding the milk to the dumpling mixture with the concentration of a chemist.

"There," Amelia said. "Perfect. Not too lumpy or too watery. Ted's gonna be sorry he missed these."

She dropped spoonfuls of dumpling dough on top of the chicken and vegetables, then covered the pot tightly. "Now, it has to stay that way for fifteen minutes," she said. "No snooping, Mom. That's why your dumplings are tough and soggy."

"No, it's not," Josie said. "I didn't inherit Grandma's cooking gene."

"You sound proud of that," Amelia said.

"I'm not," Josie said. "I'm proud of you." Amelia had an adorable flour smudge on her nose, but Josie didn't dare say anything in case it triggered another sulk. Hoping for a taste, Amelia's striped cat sat at her feet, ears up, tail curled in a question mark.

Josie reached down and scratched his ears. "No people food, big guy," she said. "Ted says it's not good for you."

"What kind of emergency did Ted have, Mom? Another dog hit by a car?"

"Not this time," Josie said. "A cat ate the ribbon on a balloon. Ted has to remove it."

"Stupid owner letting ribbons near her cat," Amelia said.

"Ted says it wasn't Cath Hoffner's fault," Josie said.

"Cath? The lady who lives down the street?" Amelia asked. "With the cute little girl Kristyn?"

Josie took the butter dish out of the fridge and set it on the table next to the bread and milk. "That's her," she said. "Cath also has an orange tabby named Audrey.

"Her daughter brought home a party balloon on a curly ribbon. Cath thought she'd tied the balloon high on the banister, but the cat got it anyway. She heard Audrey throwing up and saw the ribbon hanging out of her mouth. Cath rushed her to the clinic. Ted x-rayed the cat and said Audrey ate several feet of ribbon. She needs surgery to remove it. Ted told his partner, Chris, he'd handle it.

"Cath said she'd pay for it. She feels bad her cat ate the ribbon. Ted says you'd be shocked how many people abandon their sick pets because they don't pay the vet bills. That's how he got Festus and Marmalade."

"That's how Grandma got her dog," Amelia said.

"Stuart Little really did have a stupid owner," Josie said. "He told Ted to put him down—a perfectly healthy dog—because he didn't want to pay the vet bill. Ted refused and Grandma took him. He's been a good dog."

"I'm glad Harry doesn't eat things he's not supposed to," Amelia said.

Harry jumped up on the table and began licking the butter. Amelia giggled.

"Hey!" Josie said. "You know better, cat!"

Harry stared at her with saucer-sized green eyes, then slid snakelike off the table. Josie caught him. "Time-out, Amelia," she said, and handed Harry to her.

"Aw, Mom, he didn't mean it."

"He didn't mean to get caught," Josie said. "A little time in your bathroom will help him remember his manners. We only have one stick of butter left."

"Couldn't you just cut off the chunk he licked?" Amelia asked.

"He licked the whole top of the stick. He cleans himself with that tongue and I don't care for his brand of toilet paper."

"Ew, Mom, you're gross," Amelia said.

"Not as gross as your cat," Josie said.

Josie expected that remark to trigger another sulk. Instead, Amelia shrugged and carried Harry off to his temporary prison in her purple bathroom. Then the two sat down to Amelia's dinner.

"Your chicken and dumplings tastes even better than it smells," Josie said. "There's a reason why they call it comfort food." She was ladling herself a second helping when her cell rang. She checked the display and said, "It's Ted. Maybe he can still join us for dinner."

She opened her phone. By the way Ted said her name, Josie knew he wasn't calling with good news. "What's wrong? Did Audrey die?"

"She came through her surgery just fine," he said. "I hope I also removed her taste for ribbons. I was getting ready to lock up and leave when I saw Molly's Beetle in our parking lot again. I'm here by myself."

"Did you call the police?" Josie asked.

"After the way they laughed at me this morning?" Ted said. "What good would that do?"

"Can she get in the clinic?"

"No, I locked the doors after Kathy left an hour ago. I can see Molly's VW parked next to my Mustang. It's right under the security light."

"Is she getting out of her car?" Josie asked.

"No, she's sitting in the front seat, watching the door."

"Stay right there," Josie said. "I'll come get you and walk you to your car. Then you can follow me to my house. Amelia's made chicken and dumplings."

"I can't wait," Ted said. "Her dumplings are the best."

"I agree," Josie said. "Amelia's dumplings are the best."

Amelia grinned.

"And I can't wait to get to the clinic and give bridezilla a piece of my mind."

"What if Molly attacks you?" Ted said. "She's crazy."

"I'm armed," Josie said.

"You don't have a gun, do you?" Ted asked.

"No, I've got that pepper spray you gave me for protection," she said. "Stops rabid dogs and berserk brides. I'm on my way."

She punched her phone shut. "Did you hear that, Amelia? The stalker bride is lurking in Ted's lot. I'm picking up Ted and telling that nut bar to leave my man alone."

"By yourself?" Amelia asked. "Shouldn't you take Grandma? Or me?"

"I can handle her," Josie said. "I'll have Ted with me. Just keep the chicken and dumplings warm, and we'll be right back."

Josie combed her thick brown hair, slashed on fresh lipstick, and dragged on a clean white blouse, wondering why she was dressing up to confront a stalker. Because I'm meeting Ted, she decided. And I want Molly to see he's mine.

She ran out into the warm October night and wished the weather would be as good on their wedding day. Too bad St. Louis weather was as unpredictable as Amelia's moods.

The clinic was only three minutes away, a practical cube embedded in a parking lot. The lot was deserted except for Ted's '68 Mustang and Molly's Beetle, bronzed by the security lights.

She saw Ted's tall, muscular frame outlined in the clinic doorway. Josie parked on the other side of Ted's tangerine car. She glanced at Molly sitting upright in her Bug, eyes aimed at the clinic door. Ted was outside, already locking the door and setting the alarm.

Josie ran straight to him and gave him a fierce kiss, making sure Molly could see them. They walked hand in hand to Ted's Mustang.

"I'll follow you back to my flat as soon as I talk to her," Josie said.

"It's useless, Josie," Ted said. "She won't listen."

"I can at least try," Josie said.

"Then I won't leave until you're back in your car."

Josie kissed Ted's cheek, then turned toward Molly. The stalker ignored her. Molly kept staring straight ahead. Josie was prepared to pound on Molly's window, but it was rolled down. No surprise on a warm October night.

"Molly Ann Deaver," Josie said. "You can fool that horny old judge, but you can't fool me. You aren't engaged to Ted and you know it. He's marrying me."

Silence. Molly didn't move.

"I said, do you understand Ted's marrying me? Are you going to leave him alone?"

More silence. Josie could hear her car's engine pinging as it cooled.

"ANSWER ME!" Josie shouted.

The silence grew louder. Now even Josie's car was quiet.

A furious Josie bent down to get a better look inside the car. Molly still ignored Josie. Her eyes were fixed straight ahead. In the dim light, Josie saw Molly wore her seat belt and a dress splashed with pink roses. She had a dark flower behind her ear.

"Molly?" Josie said.

Her car smelled funny—like iron and something worse.

"Molly!" Josie screamed, and shook her. Molly slumped forward. That wasn't a red flower in her hair. She had a bloody wound blooming by her ear.

Molly Deaver had a bullet in her head.

Chapter 12

Molly Ann Deaver was murdered.

The bullet wound was a deadly bloom of dark red that spattered down her pink dress.

Josie made a thin mewing sound that morphed into a straight-out scream. Ted leaped out of his car and said, "Josie, what did she do to you?"

"Nothing," Josie said, her voice flat. She felt as if she were watching herself from a long distance. The bronze glow of the mercury-vapor lights added to the effect, as if Josie were looking at a sepia-tinted photo taken long ago. "She's dead. Someone shot her in the head."

Ted gathered Josie into his arms. Something shattered inside when she leaned her head on his shoulder. She caught his work smell—coffee, disinfectant, and dog hair—and cried. "I wanted her gone for good and now she is, but not this way."

"Me, either," Ted said.

"What's going to happen to you?" Josie wept. "First that terrible TV show. Then that stupid judge. They're going to blame you."

"Sh!" Ted said, holding her. "I'll be fine. I didn't kill her. I was inside when it happened. Are you sure she's dead? Maybe I should check."

"She's definitely dead," Josie said. "Don't touch her! You don't need to get your fingerprints on her car."

"Her eyelids look bruised," Ted said. "I wonder if she was beaten first? She must have been shot at fairly close range. I can see the black gunpowder marks on her skin. The blood has clogged and the top stuff is dry, but the thicker stuff is still wet."

"Stop!" Josie said. "It's horrible standing out here discussing her dead body. We need to call the police."

With fear-numbed fingers, Josie punched in 911 and blurted that she'd found a dead woman in the clinic lot. The 911 operator tried to keep her on the line, but Josie hung up and called her mother.

"Mom, I only have a few moments before the police get here," she said. "I'm with Ted. Molly Deaver's been shot in her car and the police are on their way. Will you make sure Amelia gets to bed on time? Yes, Ted and I are fine. No, we weren't hurt. The only—"

Josie's sentence was interrupted by the sirens. "The police are here," she said. "I've gotta go, Mom. Love you."

Josie thought she was frightened when she found the body.

But her fear grew when two Rock Road Village police arrived on the scene. She and Ted didn't recognize the officers.

She thought the officer who interviewed her was somewhere in his forties, but later she couldn't recall his name or his face. All she remembered were his hands: strong, calloused, with a gold wedding band and a deep scratch on his right thumb. He used those hands to pat down Josie for a weapon. She didn't like a strange man touching her, but he was quick and professional. He searched her for trace blood, examining her clothes and making her take off her shoes. He also swabbed the front and back of her hands with little test-tubelike collection doodads with sticky tops.

"I'm testing for GSR, ma'am," he said.

Gunshot residue, she figured out later.

They didn't find any on Josie or Ted. Josie's officer told her to sit in the back of his car.

"Can I call my mother?" Josie asked.

"Not until the homicide detective gives permission, ma'am," he said. "He's on his way." He locked the door to his car.

A bald, baggy-faced officer took charge of Ted. He was a stickler for procedure. "Empty your pockets, sir," he said, his voice neutral.

"Where should I put my things?" Ted asked.

"On the hood of your car, sir."

Ted set his cell phone, keys, wallet and pocket change on the Mustang's hood. The officer gave Ted a cautious but thorough pat-down.

Ted's phone barked. "Can I answer my phone?" he asked.

"No."

"What if it's a patient?"

"Don't you have a partner?"

"Yes, but—"

"Let your partner take the call."

After Ted's clothes and shoes were checked for blood spatter, the officer told him, "You can sit in that car and wait until the homicide detective arrives."

All that was bad. But when a Dodge Charger pulled into the lot and the homicide detective stepped out, Josie felt something claw her heart. It was Detective Richard Gray, the man who thought she'd murdered Amelia's father, Nate. The same man who'd once thought Ted was a killer, too.

He was wrong both times. Now Josie and Ted were together, and there was another murder.

Detective Gray dressed like his name: gray suit, darker gray tie, silver gray hair, eyes like chips of dirty ice and just as cold. His last name was so perfect for him, Josie thought he must have felt complete when his hair finally grayed.

"Miss Marcus," he said. "We have to stop meeting like this." His voice was mocking.

"But wait, you're not alone. You have a partner in crime now. It's my old friend, Ted. As I recall, you were a person of interest in one of my cases, *Dr.* Ted." He made Ted's title into a sneer.

"Why am I not surprised that you and Miss Marcus have joined forces and the result is another victim? A famous one, too. The little blonde you left at the altar, Dr. Ted. Shot in the head. Miss Molly Deaver is—or should I say was—a nice-looking woman. That TV show made her into a jilted bride, but I didn't believe it. If Channel Seven says the sun is shining, I look out my window to confirm it."

A wave of relief washed over Josie when she heard that.

"I talked to Officer Edelson and he said Miss Deaver was a stalker. He told me stalkers don't get better with treatment. Your only escape is to move away and hope they'll fixate on someone else.

"But this clinic says you've got a major investment in the area. Looks like you took the sure-fire route to freedom: I'm going to read you and Miss Marcus your rights." He began the familiar chant.

"Am I being taken into custody?" Ted asked. Josie was too afraid to speak.

"Not yet," Gray said. "But I want to make sure I have the bases covered. Are you going to call your lawyer?"

"No. I didn't kill her and I can prove it," Ted said. "Kathy, our receptionist, was the last person to leave the building at five thirty today. I locked the door after her and used my code to turn on our security system. None of the clinic doors was opened again. I noticed Molly in our lot at six thirty, sitting in her car. I thought she was watching the door, and so I called Josie. She got here about ten minutes later. That's when I opened the clinic door. Check our security system. It will prove I'm right."

"You got a camera on the lot here?" the detective asked.

"We do, but it wasn't working last night. Kathy called it in today. The company will be out tomorrow to fix it."

"Very convenient."

"You can check that with the security company, too," Ted said.

"Why didn't you call the police when you saw Miss Deaver?" Gray asked.

"Did that this morning," Ted said. "The patrol officers treated my complaint like a joke."

"New hires," Detective Gray said, and shrugged.

"Since I knew the Rock Road Village police wouldn't help, I called Josie."

"How do I know you didn't shoot the victim while you were waiting for Miss Marcus to ride to your rescue?" Gray asked.

"Check Molly for livor mortis," Ted said. "You should find the blood is starting to pool in her lower extremities. That doesn't start until twenty minutes to three hours after death. Also, I bet you'll find her car engine is cold. Josie's car is still warm."

"You got it all figured out, Sherlock," the detective said.

Extra lights had been erected in the parking lot, and a cloth shield was put up to hide Molly's car from curious eyes. The doors were opened, and white-suited techs were examining the Volkswagen. Police photographers and other crime investigators crawled around the scene like ants on an overturned hill. Uniformed officers knocked on neighbors' doors. The baggy-faced first responder was searching the bushes around the clinic.

"Detective, we found this inside the victim's car. It's been fired, sir." The uniform was so young, he looked like he was out past curfew.

Josie could see the weapon in the police car's side mirror—a pearl-handled .38 with *LSH* in silver. Lenore's pistol.

"Are you holding that firearm by a pencil in the barrel?" Detective Gray asked.

"Y-yes, sir," the officer stuttered.

"Didn't they teach you anything at the academy? Not only is that unsafe," he said, "it could damage potential evidence. You pick up a gun by the textured surface on the grips."

"These are pearl-handled grips, sir. There's no texturing. There are initials. They look like *LSH*."

"So they do. Package that firearm in an envelope so the lab can process it for prints."

"Yes, sir."

"But first, take out the ammunition and put each bullet in a cardboard pillbox."

This time, the uniform nodded.

"I've seen that weapon before," Gray said. "*LSH*. That's Lenore Scottsmeyer Hall."

He turned to Ted. "Aren't you the son of the pistol-packing mama?"

"Lenore Scottsmeyer Hall is my mother," Ted said. "That's what they called her on Channel Seven."

"She still in town?" Gray said.

"She's flying home Friday morning," Ted said.

Josie fought to banish the image of her future mother-in-law riding a broom.

"Where's she staying?" Gray asked.

"At the Ritz in Clayton. But there's no way she'd shoot Molly Deaver."

"That's not what I saw on TV," the detective said. "Your mother whipped out that thirty-eight snub-nose mighty quick to defend her darling boy. Used a gun that looks just like this one. Aren't those her initials?"

"Looks like them, yes," Ted said. "But I've never seen her gun up close."

Detective Gray motioned to two more uniforms combing the parking lot. "Go to the Ritz and pick up Mrs. Lenore Scottsmeyer Hall," he said. "Bring her in for questioning. She's a person of interest."

Josie could see Ted's face had gone pinched and pale.

She longed to comfort him, or at least hold his hand, but she could do nothing.

The Ritz was ten minutes from Ted's clinic, but Josie thought the wait took hours. Her thoughts ran wild. Would Lenore really shoot Molly? Ridiculous. But Lenore was ridiculous. And her interview while she twirled that stupid gun had gone viral.

Josie tried to think about what she'd seen and block out the vision of Molly staring glassy-eyed into eternity. She erected a kind of mental screen, a version of what the crime scene workers had put up.

Why would Lenore leave her beloved pistol behind in the car? Wouldn't she take it with her? If Lenore didn't kill the bride, how did someone else get her gun?

Detective Gray's cell phone rang. Josie could hear him talking. "What do you mean she's checked out? Did the front desk say where she was going?

"The airport!

"That woman is fleeing. Stop her."

Chapter 13

Lenore was a stylish standout in the airport security line. Most of the straggling travelers stood slump-shouldered in saggy jeans or dreary sweats. Ted's mother wore a sleek tan Chanel suit draped with gold necklaces that would have sent TSA's metal detectors into a tizzy— except she never made it through security.

She was pulled out of the line by a TSA agent and two Rock Road Village uniforms. And—wouldn't you know it?—a Channel Seven crew happened to be in the airport. They taped the fugitive's "takedown" as reporter Wendy Lee Chase called it. She was breathless with excitement. Lenore had gone from pistol-packing mama to Florida felon in half a day.

Ted and Josie watched Lenore's arrest on television. They couldn't be with her at the airport when it actually happened. They were still being interrogated by an angry Detective Gray.

They missed the ten o'clock news that night. But Ted stopped by Josie's for breakfast the next morning after she'd dropped Amelia at school. They sat on her living room sofa watching the morning news, their plates of eggs abandoned on the coffee table.

Channel Seven newscaster Wendy Lee, eyes wide with artificial excitement, said, "Lenore Scottsmeyer Hall, the pistol-packing mama, was arrested last night at Lambert International Airport. A police spokesperson says Mrs. Scottsmeyer Hall was allegedly fleeing St. Louis after murdering abandoned bride Molly Ann Deaver."

A photo of an artistically tearful Molly flashed on the screen.

Ted and Josie groaned together as Wendy Lee recapped her version of Molly's suffering and death.

"Miss Deaver was found shot to death in her car in the parking lot of the St. Louis Mobo-Pet Clinic Wednesday evening," she said as a helicopter videoed the clinic lot. Molly's Beetle, Josie's battered Honda, Ted's Mustang and a horde of crime scene workers were bronzed by the mercury-vapor lights.

"Police searched the area and found a snub-nose thirty-eight revolver believed to belong to Mrs. Scottsmeyer Hall. Rock Road Village police were dispatched to the Ritz-Carlton to question Mrs. Scottsmeyer Hall and discovered she had fled the luxury hotel. She was arrested trying to board a flight back to her home in Florida."

"Wonder how Channel Seven knew to go to the airport?" Ted said.

"I don't think Detective Gray called them," Josie said. "He hates that station."

"Maybe it was the young officer who found Mom's gun," Ted said.

They watched the camera pan the long line of travelers dragging rolling suitcases, then stop at Lenore. Her designer suit glowed in the dreary airport lighting. The two uniforms and the TSA agent surrounded her and they blocked her progress.

"What is the meaning of this?" Lenore asked. Her voice was haughty, exactly the wrong tone to take. "I need to leave immediately or I'll miss my flight."

Ted winced. "Oh, Mom," he said to the TV screen. "This is no time for your Boca Diva act."

On camera, Lenore glared at the gawky pink-faced Rock Road Village cop.

"Sorry, ma'am, but we need to question you." He gulped and glanced uneasily at his older partner, a muscular officer with a military haircut.

"About what?" Lenore demanded.

"Miss Molly Ann Deaver," Officer Muscle said. He spoke with smooth reassurance.

"That demented bride?" Lenore said. "Why should I care about her?"

Ted warned the TV, "Mom, you're walking into a trap." Josie patted his hand, but he didn't notice. He was watching his mother's downfall.

"When did you last see her?" Officer Muscle asked. His scrawny partner shifted uneasily from foot to foot.

"Tuesday afternoon, when she invaded my son's clinic," Lenore said. "You people showed some sense and hauled her away." She gave the officers a frosty smile. "But that judge is crazier than she is. He turned her loose after she attacked Dr. Ted Scottsmeyer with a knife."

"Mom!" Ted said to the TV set. "Did you have to use my name?"

"And you haven't seen her since?" Officer Muscle said. Josie thought she detected a hint of sarcasm.

"No? Why would I want to? Is something wrong?"

"Please, Mom," Ted begged. "Please watch what you're saying."

"You could say that, ma'am," the officer said. "She's been murdered."

"Why is that my concern?" Lenore looked down her nose at him.

He looked right back. "We believe you are fleeing the scene of the crime."

"That's absurd," Lenore said. "I'm going home to my husband, Dr. Whitney Hudson Hall. He's a board-certified plastic surgeon in Boca. I'm so worried about him, I didn't wait for our plane. I'm flying commercial. Now, if you'll step aside."

She tried to push her way past the men, but TSA had

removed the barricade rope and smoothly guided her outside the line.

"No, ma'am. You have the right to remain silent . . ." By the time he finished reading Lenore her rights, the foursome was near the terminal exit.

"I want my lawyer," Lenore said. "I won't say a word until attorney Shelford Clark arrives from Boca Raton. I won't have a St. Louis hick representing me. I want a real lawyer."

Ted was still talking to the screen. "Oh, Mom," he said. "They're going to lock you up and throw away the key. Please don't say anything else."

After insulting the local legal community, along with the citizens of St. Louis, Lenore Scottsmeyer Hall was finally, blessedly silent.

That was when the TV report cut to Lenore's old pistol-packing mama interview. Wendy Lee said, "Mrs. Scottsmeyer Hall gave Channel Seven this exclusive interview before the murder of Molly Ann Deaver."

Now Lenore was in dead black, grinning at the camera. "I carry my pistol in a purse instead of a holster," she said, "but it's just as deadly as any man's long barrel. Maybe deadlier, because I can open my purse quicker than he can unsnap his holster. Besides, I'm an expert shot."

The camera focused on Lenore twirling her pistol as Wendy Lee said, "Police sources say Mrs. Scottsmeyer Hall's fingerprints were found on both the murder weapon and the bullets, and she cannot account for her whereabouts at the time of the shooting. Mrs. Scottsmeyer Hall declined to comment.

"Channel Seven is the only station with this interview of the victim's sister, Emily Deaver Destin, at her home in the exclusive Estates at Wood Winds in West County."

The camera panned the subdivision's entrance and a view of the lush lawns and eclectic architecture, from Victorian mansions to Tuscan villas.

"That's where Alyce lives, right?" Ted said.

"She has the Tudor mansion with the half-timbered garage," Josie said.

"Is her subdivision exclusive?"

"It's expensive," Josie said. "I'm not sure that's the same thing."

Emily's home jutted out of the ground like a cantilevered crystal. Josie thought it looked interesting but cold, like Emily.

"Emily doesn't seem anything like her sister," Ted said.

She was a big-boned woman of about thirty. Her brown hair had been chopped short. Everything about her seemed designed to save time, from her brown turtleneck to her flat shoes.

"I don't know why anyone would hurt my sister," she said. "Molly couldn't wait to marry Ted Scottsmeyer. Her wedding was all she talked about. She never hurt a soul. Molly liked ruffles and flowers and antiques and loved her fiancé. I'm glad the police caught her killer."

"So you believe that Lenore Scottsmeyer Hall murdered your sister?" Wendy Lee asked.

"I have no doubt the police arrested the right person," Emily said. "I know she's a killer." She stared right into the lens.

"Mom's been tried and convicted on TV," Ted said. "What are we going to do?"

"I don't know," Josie said. "Channel Seven has set up Lenore to look guilty as hell." And she helped them, she thought. But she couldn't say that to Ted.

"Mom didn't kill Molly," Ted said. "I wonder who'd want Molly dead? And how did the killer get Mom's pearl-handled pistol?"

"I think I can answer that," Josie said. "She misplaced her purse at the Blue Rose Tearoom the other day. The server, Jane, and I searched for it. Half the restaurant helped look for her lost purse. The server found it on the empty chair at our table. Your mother insisted she didn't put her purse there."

"Did she notice her gun was missing?" Ted asked.

"She opened it and said her wallet, money, and credit cards were there. I don't remember her mentioning the gun."

"Was the restaurant crowded?" Ted asked.

"Packed," Josie said. "People were coming by the table to see your mom. She was quite the celebrity. Anyone could have swiped her purse, taken the gun, and returned her bag during the search."

"No cop will believe her story," Ted said. "There are too many coincidences, Josie. The clinic security camera broke, so there's no video of the parking lot. Somebody stole the gun out of Mom's purse at the tearoom and she didn't notice. And Mom wasn't fleeing the city; she was going home to be with my stepfather. It doesn't help that she tried to fly commercial instead of waiting for their plane."

"Or that my stepfather, Whit, just happened to break his ankle at the wrong time."

"Have you talked with him?" Josie asked.

"Three times so far," Ted said. "Whit loves Mom and he says he'll spend every dollar he has to save her. He's already hired Shelford Clark and he's flying him here. The lawyer will be in St. Louis in about an hour."

"Then we should pick him up at the airport," Josie said.

"That's sweet, Josie, but a lawyer like Clark expects to be treated like a king. He has a limo meeting him. Whit makes major bucks sculpting Boca babes. Lucky for Mom, he's also a good guy."

"Is this Clark a good lawyer?" Josie asked.

"Remember the Boca Babe Case?" Ted asked.

"Was she the twenty-something wife of the rich old furniture store heir?" Josie asked. "Wasn't she accused of murdering her husband?"

"She was," Ted said. "Most people thought she did. Shel Clark got her acquitted. She not only inherited the old man's millions, but Shel helped sell her life story for another two million.

"He's the best in South Florida," Ted said. "How well he'll play in St. Louis is another question."

"I wish your mom had been more tactful," Josie said.

"Mom has a lot of fine qualities, but tact isn't one of them," Ted said. "Whit says he likes smart, forthright women."

"Is your stepfather coming here?"

"Can't. He really did break his ankle on the golf course," Ted said. "His ortho doctor says he has to stay off it for four weeks. He won't even let him do surgery."

"Who'll take care of Whit now that your mom can't come home?" Josie asked.

"Mrs. Garcia, their live-in housekeeper," Ted said. "Their chauffeur will drive him. If he's lucky, Whit will get to come here for our wedding."

Our wedding. Less than a month away. Josie knew even the best lawyer couldn't get Lenore acquitted on a murder charge in that time, and Lenore couldn't get bail for murder.

Ted and Josie couldn't walk down the aisle with Lenore in jail.

Josie had one more thing to do before their wedding—solve Molly's murder.

Chapter 14

Jane had her garden supplies spread out on the front porch. Ted and Josie saw the flat of rubbery bronze mums turned toward the morning sun. Lined up on newspaper were a slightly rusty trowel, a three-pronged cultivator, and six mousetraps.

Mousetraps?

"Mom, do we have mice out here?" Josie asked.

Ted picked up a trap. "These are the old-school snapping traps," he said. "That long metal spike is dangerous. There are better ways to catch mice."

"I don't want to catch a mouse," Jane said. "I'm after the rat who stole my mums. If he comes back, he'll get a nasty surprise when those traps snap his fingers."

"You'll get a nasty surprise, too," Ted said. "The plant thief can sue you if he's injured."

"Even if he's sticking his hands where they don't belong?" Jane said. "That's ridiculous." She stuck out her jaw. Josie tried not to snicker at her small, furious mother.

"I agree," Ted said, "but it's the law."

"But I have to stop them," Jane said. "Mrs. Mueller planted poison ivy with her mums. It looks pretty. See?" She pointed her trowel toward their neighbor's porch. The trailing red leaves of poison ivy made a handsome frame for her mums. "But I'm not going out into the woods to dig it up."

"Mrs. M better hope her mail carrier isn't allergic to poison ivy," Ted said, "or she'll be picking up her mail at the post office."

"Mom, how much were those mousetraps?" Josie asked.

"Four dollars each," Jane said. "I'm using three traps per pot."

"So you've spent twenty-four dollars to save twenty-five dollars' worth of mums," Josie said.

"Thirty dollars and seventeen cents," Jane said. "It's not the money—it's the principle."

Ted checked his watch. "I have to be at work in an hour, but I think I can help you," he said. "Do you have any canned food?"

"Dog food, tuna, and corn," Jane said. "I use the little cans of tuna. Take your pick."

"I'll need six cans. Tuna would be best," Ted said. "I'll help you wash them."

Josie followed Ted and Jane upstairs. Jane emptied the three-ounce cans of tuna into a plastic container. Then Ted peeled off the labels and washed them while Josie dried. Next, Ted used an ice pick to poke holes in the bottoms of the cans and threaded three each on a piece of string. The cans clanged against one another.

"They're noisy," Jane said.

"That's the idea," Ted said. "Let's go bury these in your plants' roots. Anyone who tries to pull up your mums will make enough noise to wake you or Stuart."

"In that case, I've got some old jingle bells in the junk drawer," Jane said, rooting through it. "Here. Use these, too."

"Only if you promise to call 911 if you hear the trespasser," Ted said.

"Deal," Jane said. "I'm so lucky to have you as my son."

"You already treat me like one," Ted said.

Better than his own mother, Josie thought, then felt her heart contract. What if the wedding couldn't go off because Lenore was in jail? She couldn't bring herself to discuss that possibility with Ted.

Instead, she asked another question she never thought she'd say. "We're seeing Lenore at the county jail tonight, right? Seven o'clock?"

"I'll pick you up at six thirty," Ted said. "And now I really do have to go." His voice was soft with love and reluctance.

"I think I hear my cell phone," Jane said, and disappeared inside.

Ted gave her such a deep kiss, she wanted to say, Forget the big wedding and let's elope today. But she knew Amelia wanted her to have a real wedding with real photos.

Jane rattled her front door, and Ted and Josie parted. She watched wistfully as he drove off in his tangerine Mustang.

"More wedding errands today?" Jane asked.

"Always," Josie said. "And I still have Harry the Horrible's gift, those wedding-related mystery-shopping assignments. I'd better get going."

Josie never left home now without her wedding plan notebook. She kept it next to her bed. She collected it, along with the mystery-shopping material Harry had faxed her. She almost made it out the door when her cell phone played the tune that was starting to grate on her nerves.

It was Alyce. "Josie, I saw the story about Lenore's arrest. How awful. What really happened?"

"She's in the county jail," Josie said. "Whit, Ted's stepfather, flew in the best lawyer in Boca."

"The best lawyer in St. Louis would have worked better," Alyce said.

"I know that, but Lenore thinks this city is the frontier. I'm worried she'll be in jail on our wedding day. I can't marry her son if she isn't at the wedding."

"Oh, sweetie, what are you going to do?"

"Try to figure out who killed Molly."

"The police won't like that," Alyce said.

"Then they should have arrested the real killer," Josie said.

"I told you Molly's sister lives in Wood Winds," Alyce said. "Molly's body has been released. The visitation is tonight and the funeral is tomorrow. We can go to the funeral together."

"Do you think Emily will recognize me from TV?"

"That big-brimmed hat hid your face," Alyce said. "If anyone asks, you're my best friend, Joanie."

"I'll do it," Josie said. "The visitation could be risky, but there will be a bigger crowd at the funeral. We can sit in the back. Where is it?"

"St. Clifton's Church on Ballas Road. I'll meet you there at nine thirty Friday morning."

Josie studied Harry's notes for her mystery-shopping assignment at Flowers by Namorita. She was supposed to order flowers for the tables at a mythical reception and get a contract.

"Don't sign contract," the notes said, "and get all quotes in writing." There was one cryptic note for Flowers by Namorita. "Unusual designs. Rumors of possible scam." Trust Harry not to give her any extra clues.

Flowers by Namorita was on Manchester Road, but a far different section than Josie's segment in Maplewood. Manchester Road ran more than one hundred twenty miles through the state of Missouri. Flowers by Namorita was in Wildwood. That part of St. Louis County had lived up to its name when Josie was a girl. Now it was turning into a tame suburb.

Josie liked the shop and its spare Japanese décor, but not the cloying scent of hothouse flowers. A thin woman in black greeted Josie.

"I'm Namorita. How may I help you?"

Josie guessed Namorita was an elegant fifty and thought her sophisticated style needed a cigarette holder.

"I want to order flowers for my wedding reception," Josie said. "I didn't like the choices the florist who's doing my wedding offered. They were too old-fashioned. I heard that you do creative designs."

"What's your price range?" Namorita asked. Her

shrewd eyes seemed to size up Josie and weigh her wallet. A fashionable woman like Namorita would know Josie was wearing last season's shirt. Her black pants were good quality, but not an up-to-the minute style. Her flats were the best—French Sole, spotted at a garage sale in the rich neighborhood of Ladue.

"I'm so lucky," Josie said. "My future mother-in-law is paying for the reception flowers and she says money is no object."

Did a flash of greed flicker in Namorita's eyes? Josie couldn't tell. She felt so carefree saying, "Money is no object"--and getting paid to do it.

"The problem is my wedding is less than a month away," Josie said. "It's the day after Thanksgiving."

"That's not a problem," Namorita said. "It's an opportunity. Let's look at some of our sample books. What are your colors?"

"Red, white, and pink," Josie said.

"Good," Namorita said. "Start with our red arrangements here."

Josie paged through dizzying displays of roses, lilies, chrysanthemums, carnations, and tulips, until they blurred into crimson blobs. "Wait!" she said. "I like that arrangement—red tulips surrounded by a cuff of white orchids in the tall glass vase. It's exactly what I'm looking for—simple, dramatic, unusual."

"Excellent choice," Namorita said. "Now, how many arrangements do you need?"

"Twenty tables with one vase each," Josie said. "And four vases for the head table, so twenty-four. It's hard to tell in the picture, but how many flowers are in that arrangement?"

"Six Radiantly Red tulips and five white *Phalaenopsis.* Those are moth orchids," Namorita said. She punched the keys on a black calculator and showed Josie a figure. Josie hoped her eyeballs didn't pop and her eyebrows leap up.

"That should do," Josie said.

"Good," Namorita said. "I'll prepare the contract."

She returned with a contract that said Josie wanted twenty-four arrangements of Radiantly Red tulips and white *Phalaenopsis* (moth orchids) along with the price she'd quoted Josie.

"Now you fill in your information and the hall where you'd like the arrangements delivered," Namorita said, "as well as your payment information."

"I need to show this to my mother-in-law," Josie said. "She's paying. I'll fax it back to you." When those *Phalaenopsis* turn into real moths, she thought.

All the way to the next florist, Josie's encounter with Namorita nagged at her. Something was wrong with that contract, but she couldn't figure out what.

Gretchen's Flowers and Gifts was in Rock Hill, a community much closer to Josie's home. This flower shop was in a brick cottage. Once again, the bell jangled. This time a motherly woman with a comfortable bosom and softly graying hair met Josie at the door.

"I'm Gretchen," she said. "How can I help you, dear?"

Josie repeated her "money is no object" pitch, but Gretchen didn't get the slightly feral look that Namorita had.

"It's lovely that your mother-in-law is so generous, but you mustn't take advantage of her," Gretchen said. "That's no way to start your marriage. Let me give you this list of wedding flowers in season this time of year. And don't turn up your nose at chrysanthemums and marigolds. I can do clever things with them. Zinnias are interesting, and so are asters and dahlias, and I'm very creative with dried leaf accents and candles."

Gretchen might appear motherly, but her designs were edgy. Josie paged through her sample book and finally settled on an arrangement of red dahlias and white zinnias with white tea lights.

"I like that," she said.

"Good choice," Gretchen said. "It's striking, but the arrangement is not so big it will overwhelm your tables. Your guests will be able to chat with one another."

She showed Josie a price that was one-quarter of the amount quoted by Namorita. "Now let me prepare your contract. My computer's in the back room."

"I can't sign the contract," Josie said. "I'll have to show it to my mother-in-law first."

"Of course you do," Gretchen said.

Josie felt guilty making Gretchen do all that work for nothing. She'd been so protective and sweet. Josie liked her arrangement and wished she really could have it for her wedding reception, but even at Gretchen's reasonable prices, it was too expensive.

I'll make it up to you, Gretchen, she thought. I'll give you a glowing report and the new wedding Web site will bring you bigger and better customers than me.

"Here's your contract," Gretchen said.

It called for arrangement number 548, with five red dahlias, stems twenty-four to twenty-eight inches long, heads three to four and a half inches in diameter, four White Wedding zinnias, stems twelve to fourteen inches long, with four-to-five-inch-wide double blooms, and six white tea lights on a silver metal S-stand.

"White Wedding is the name of the zinnia?" Josie asked.

"It's perfect, isn't it?" Gretchen said. "The right look and the right name."

"You've listed the number of blooms," Josie said, "along with the stem length and bloom width."

"Of course, dear. Shortchanging the flowers in a centerpiece is one of the oldest scams in the business. It makes me ashamed of my profession. A bride meets with a florist, who shows her a photo of the decorations and offers a price. She signs a contract, and then at the reception finds out the florist put a lot more flowers into the photo sample. She's been shorted. It's a sneaky trick and I won't stand for it. I spell everything out."

"I can't thank you enough," Josie said. "Now I have to go see my mother-in-law."

She didn't add "in jail."

Chapter 15

How do you dress when you have a date with your fiancé to see his mother in jail? Josie wondered. Maybe I should get a tattoo and a tube top. Instead, she chose Ted's favorite outfit — black pencil skirt, cobalt blue blouse, and high heels.

He whistled when she answered her door.

"You're the best-looking thing I've seen all day," he said, and wrapped his arms around her. Josie felt that lovely flutter she always had with Ted.

"You see cats and dogs," she said, sinking into his chest. "But I'll take that as a compliment."

He returned her kiss, hot and sexy.

"Mm. You have nice lips," she said.

"You, too," he said. This kiss lasted longer and he unbuttoned her top button.

She rubbed her spike heel along his leg. "You smell like coffee and wood smoke."

Another button undone. "I wish we could stay here all evening," he whispered.

She licked his earlobe. "Soon," Josie said. Unless your mother derails our wedding, she thought.

"Mom! I forgot. We're going to miss the seven o'clock visiting hour unless we leave now," Ted said.

Lenore's name worked better than a cold shower.

Josie buttoned her blouse, straightened her skirt, and picked up her purse.

"Where's Amelia?" Ted asked.

Did I unbutton Ted's shirt? Josie wondered, slightly dazed.

"Upstairs with Mom," she said. "They're eating tuna casserole. She'll save some for you. What's the latest on your mother?" That question killed her last lingering bit of passion.

"Nothing good," Ted said. "I talked with Whit. Mom's being arraigned tomorrow at ten. The charges are first-degree murder."

Josie winced. Missouri was a death-penalty state, but Ted didn't need that reminder. "I'm sorry. I'll be in court with you then," she said.

"No, you won't," Ted said.

"I want to."

"And I appreciate the offer. But Mom wouldn't want you to see her like that. She's a proud woman. Please, Josie. Don't be there. I mean it."

Josie could tell he did. "Have you talked to her lawyer?"

"My stepfather did. Shelford Clark says there's no chance of bail because Mom's charged with murder and the prosecutor says she was fleeing the state. The murder weapon was definitely Lenore's."

"But her purse was missing," Josie said.

"Misplaced, according to the prosecutor. The waitress found it and Mom announced to the entire Blue Rose Tearoom that nothing was missing. The waitress says she'll testify."

"Lenore should have given her a reward," Josie said.

"Wouldn't make any difference," Ted said. "The police have twenty other names. Mom must have made quite an impression there. The police found her fingerprints on the bullets and her partial print on the murder weapon."

"Where did the police get her prints?" Josie asked.

"From her damned concealed carry permit," Ted said.

She'd never heard him criticize his mother before. "She had to brag about that gun on TV."

"Her lawyer could explain the prints," Josie said.

"What about the security video?" Ted said.

"I thought the clinic's camera wasn't working," Josie said.

"A house two doors down has one. Its outdoor camera caught a dark Chevy Impala approaching the clinic at 6:12, then go flying by in the other direction at 6:21. Lenore rented a navy blue Chevy Impala."

"Is she the Impala's driver?" Josie asked.

"No," Ted said. "You can't really identify who the driver is. You can see a shape behind the wheel, but it could be a woman or a man. Can't see the license plate, either. But the car fits with the time of death and Lenore can't account for two hours after she left the hotel. She says she got lost going to the airport. The police say she made a detour to Rock Road Village and killed Molly, then became a fugitive. Mom says she needed to fly home two days early because Whit broke his ankle."

"Did Lenore leave you a message that she was rushing home?" Josie asked.

"No," Ted said. "Mom says she was going to call me from the airport but never got a chance. The police think that's another sign of her guilt. So is flying commercial for the first time since she married Whit. It doesn't help that she threatened Molly with a gun and it was on TV."

Running endlessly, Josie thought. And it had gone viral on YouTube. No point in saying that, either. Ted was miserable enough. She stared at the lights of downtown Clayton, a concrete canyon in St. Louis County. The county jail looked like another office tower—except its criminals had been caught.

"I didn't tell you the best part," Ted said as he pulled into a parking garage near the jail. "Lenore had a rolling suitcase when she was taken into custody in the TSA line. The police got a warrant and opened it. Guess what they found?"

"Clothes?" Josie said hopefully.

"The suit she wore at the clinic," Ted said. "Still in the dry cleaner's bag with a note that the cleaners couldn't get the stain out."

"What stain?" Josie said, her heart sinking.

"Blood. Molly's blood. Remember when she attacked me with the scalpel?"

"Not likely to forget that," Josie said.

The bizarre chain reaction replayed in her mind: Bridezilla trying to drag Ted off to the minister. Bella jumping out of her basket and biting Marmalade. Ted's cat swatting Bella, and Molly swooping in to save her dog and slapping Ted. That was when Marmalade scratched Molly and she started bleeding.

She wished she could wipe away the image of herself, frozen in place.

"Your mother stepped in and took the scalpel out of Molly's hand," Josie said. "That's when she got the blood on her suit."

"That's what Mom told them," Ted said. "The police didn't have enough for DNA testing, but they can show it's Molly's blood type."

"But they can see what happened at the clinic," Josie said. "Channel Seven has it on tape."

"The prosecuting attorney issued a subpoena for it. Channel Seven says it's station policy to erase all tape except what's used in the actual shows. They claim they don't have room to store all that tape."

"Do you think that's true?" Josie asked.

"The judge believed them," Ted said. He eased the Mustang into a parking spot. They joined the line for the jail's metal detectors. Some visitors were tired workers finishing a long day. Others were swaggering young men, flirty young women, and a scattering of children.

To Josie, the air was charged with rage and weariness. She and Ted stowed their cell phones and Josie's purse in a locker.

Lenore sat in a booth behind a plastic glass screen. Josie tried to hide her shock. Her mother-in-law's complexion was drained by the dull beige scrubs. Her face looked different, too. Josie realized Lenore wasn't wearing makeup—but her hair looked perfect.

Josie forced herself to smile and said, "Lenore, how are you?"

"Stuck in this hellhole," Lenore hissed. "Surrounded by hicks."

"Mom, please. Your voice carries," Ted said. "You don't want to upset people."

"Oh, I'm not talking about the inmates, Ted. I get along fine with the girls. They know all about me. Call me the Pistol-Packing Mama. Isn't that a hoot? We have so much in common."

"You do?" Josie said.

"Tabitha—she's the one at the end talking to the older gentleman—has been charged with shooting her boyfriend. But the police arrested the wrong woman. Just like me. And Lizzie—I call her Liz, because she's a distinguished-looking young person—didn't mean to shoot her man. He came in drunk at three a.m. and she mistook him for a burglar."

"Right," Ted said.

"She's trying to make something of herself," Lenore said. "She's been to beauty college and she worked wonders with my hair. I would have paid two hundred dollars for this in Boca." She patted her hair.

"Aren't you worried about the murder charge?" Josie asked.

"No, I'm innocent and I have a good lawyer," she said, and made a brushing motion with her hand as if she could flick away a first-degree murder charge. "Well, enough about me. Let's get down to business. Josie, did you bring your wedding plan notebook?"

"I'm not allowed to bring it inside here," Josie said. "Jail rules."

"Then fax a copy to my attorney," Lenore said. "He

can bring in the paper. I'll convey my instructions through him."

"It's not necessary," Josie said. "Ted and I have everything planned."

"Not everything," Lenore said, and narrowed her eyes at Ted. "I want to know why you didn't invite your brother, Richard, to be in your wedding."

Josie braced herself. She knew this fight was coming and Ted had promised to handle it.

"Because I can't trust Dick, Mom," Ted said.

"His name is Richard, not Dick," Lenore said. "He was named for your grandfather."

"Grandfather would have been ashamed of his namesake's stupid practical jokes. Dick started doing this"— Ted stopped and searched for a word—"nonsense at age eight when he short-sheeted my bed."

"Ted, you're such a grouch, darling," Lenore said. "Even when you were a little boy."

"You thought he was cute, Mom. Every night was a misery—ice cubes in my pillows. Pies in the sheets. He never stopped. On his last visit here, he superglued a tennis ball to my dog's paw. That was the last straw."

"And you value a dog over your own brother?" Lenore asked.

"My dog is smarter—and kinder," Ted said. "I haven't spoken to my idiot brother since."

"It was a prank gone wrong," Lenore said.

"You make excuses for him, Mom," Ted said. "Dick—"

"Richard," Lenore corrected.

"Has been fired from ten jobs for his so-called pranks," Ted said. "And Whit got him most of those. Last time, Dick—"

"Richard," Lenore said.

"Put the manager's stapler and pen set in Jell-O."

"He saw that on *The Office*. Everyone thought it was hilarious. His employer had no sense of humor."

"How funny was it when he Saran Wrapped Whit's car and he was nearly late for surgery?"

"We spoke to him about that, dear."

"He nearly cost you your country club membership after he put itching powder on the men's locker room toilet seats."

"Whit made a generous donation to the expansion fund and it was forgotten," Lenore said.

"He's thirty, Mom, and acts like he's fifteen," Ted said. "One of these days he's going to hurt someone."

Lenore fixed her son with a look.

Uh-oh, Josie thought. He's going to cave.

"Ted, I don't ask for much, but I'm begging you to include your brother in your wedding. Please."

"What if he pulls one of his stupid tricks?" Ted asked.

"I'll speak to him," Lenore said. "I'll cut off his allowance if he misbehaves."

"It's up to Josie," Ted said.

Wait a minute, Josie thought wildly. How'd I get in the middle? She looked for an escape, then realized she was trapped—in a jail.

"Uh—" Josie stalled for time.

"Then it's all settled," Lenore said. "Richard will make an excellent best man."

"What! No freakin' way," Ted said. "I already have someone. My clinic partner, Christine, will stand up for me."

"But she can't be your best man," Lenore said. "She's a woman."

"Dick doesn't act like a man," Ted said. "And I can't uninvite her."

"Male attendants for the groom are so old-school," Josie added.

That did it. Lenore had to be cutting-edge. "Then Richard can escort Whatchamacallit. Josie's—"

Josie glared at Lenore. If she says "illegitimate," I'll tear out that plastic glass and strangle her with my bare hands, Josie thought.

Even the clueless Lenore must have caught the look in Josie's eyes. "Lovely daughter," she finished.

"Her name is Amelia," Josie said, fighting down her anger.

"Sorry," Ted said. "Christine's son, Todd, is escorting Amelia. They'll make a cute couple. And he's Amelia's age."

"What about the matron of honor?" Lenore asked.

"Alyce's husband can escort her. He owns a tux," Josie said.

"But you haven't asked him yet," said the crafty Lenore. "Please say yes, Josie."

Can I do that to my best friend? Josie wondered. Alyce was a strong woman. She was married to a demanding lawyer and she had a toddler. Dick didn't act much older. She could control him for one day.

"I—," Josie said.

"Josie, don't say yes until Mom agrees to the conditions," Ted said. "Dick will be properly dressed in a tux, black socks, bow tie and black dress shoes."

"*Richard* will wear his *dinner jacket* with the appropriate accessories," Lenore said.

"And he will keep his clothes on for the wedding and the reception," Ted said. "I don't want him mooning anyone. Plus there will be no jokes—or what passes for a joke around Dick."

"I guarantee that Richard's behavior will be impeccable or he will lose his allowance for three months."

"Twelve months," Ted said.

"One full year," Lenore said.

Oh, Alyce, Josie thought, what am I doing to you?

"Josie, please say yes," Lenore said. "I so want to see Ted married and then I want to fly home."

"And I'll do everything in my power to make sure you board that plane to Boca," Josie said—and meant every word.

Chapter 16

St. Clifton's Church was crammed with Molly's mourners. Josie didn't know if people were there to gawk or grieve, but the crowd—and the suburban Gothic chapel's gloomy recesses—helped her slip into the funeral unnoticed.

Josie and Alyce squeezed into a back pew behind a stone pillar. Josie sat next to a pair of gossips. Both women were somewhere south of fifty. One had fluffy brown hair and an orange flowered dress like a slipcover. Her thin, angular friend was encased in black as if mourning her lost youth. Josie thought the woman's dark hair streaked with steel was striking. She mentally named them Mrs. Flower and Mrs. Steel.

"I never thought Molly would get herself murdered," Mrs. Steel said. There was disapproval in her voice.

"She didn't 'get herself murdered,'" Mrs. Flower said. "She was killed by that doctor's witchy mother."

"I might prefer death to *that* mother-in-law," Mrs. Steel drawled.

No, you wouldn't, Josie thought. Not if you knew Ted.

Mrs. Flower simpered and said, "Stop! You're terrible."

Josie figured fluffy Mrs. Flower considered herself a "nice" person but reveled in Mrs. Steel's snarky comments. "Molly was a good sales assistant," Mrs. Flower said piously. "So helpful when my Gracie married."

The angelic-looking blonde on their left glared at the pair, then slipped her BlackBerry out of her purse and began texting. Josie stared straight ahead and pretended to study the stained glass.

"Wasn't she going to marry someone else before that vet?" Mrs. Steel asked.

"Yes, what was his name? George," Mrs. Flower said. "George somebody. Had a beard. He sold carpets."

"Until he took off out west somewhere," Mrs. Steel said. "For months it was 'George this' and 'George that,' and then suddenly she was marrying that vet."

"The vet was better looking," Mrs. Flower said. "Molly was pretty, too."

"I guess, if you like ruffles," Mrs. Steel said. "Did you go to her visitation last night?"

"Yes. So sad," Mrs. Flower said.

"I wouldn't be caught dead in that dress she's buried in."

Mrs. Flower snickered.

"Here comes the sister, Emily," Mrs. Steel said. "She had to work to find a black suit that ugly. Her husband, Brad, is an accountant and looks it. A no account-ant, if you ask me. I heard he invested her inheritance and lost every penny."

"That can't be true," Mrs. Flower said. "They have that big house in Wood Winds and they both drive expensive cars."

"Big dreams, big house, big debts," Mrs. Steel said. "Just because they have expensive things doesn't mean they can afford them."

"You're awful," Mrs. Flower said. She giggled, then smoothed her face into a solemn expression. "Emily is sitting next to that older woman with the cane. That's Aunt Martha, the girls' only close relative after their parents died. She must be eighty. Hasn't stopped crying since she sat down. You'd never guess Emily and Molly were sisters. Molly loved antiques and pretty things. Emily likes everything new, plain, and practical. Almost like a man."

"Look how short her hair is," Mrs. Steel said. "Do you think Emily is gay?"

"She's married," Mrs. Flower said.

They watched the pallbearers roll Molly's white casket up the aisle.

"So? Could be a cover if her husband's gay," Mrs. Steel said. "I've heard in some old St. Louis families the rich father showers money on a gay man to marry his lesbian daughter. Then the couple live as they please as long as they don't cause a scandal."

"I don't think being gay is a scandal anymore," Mrs. Flower said. "And their family money isn't old."

At that, a woman in a navy suit swiveled around and hissed, "Shut up, both of you! Have the decency not to run down that poor girl at her own funeral."

Mrs. Steel paled. Mrs. Flower's cheeks turned red as roses. Both were silent for the rest of the ceremony. That was more respectful, but not as informative, Josie decided.

She learned nothing from the eulogies except that Molly had been a good friend, a sweet person, and a dedicated employee of Denise's Dreams. A young woman with a shiny cap of brown hair said, "Molly helped me realize my dream wedding, but she never got to have hers." She left the podium, weeping.

Her sister Emily said simply, "I loved my sister. Her life was short and ended tragically, but she brought happiness to others. Rest in peace, dear Molly."

The choir sang "O God, Our Help in Ages Past" as Molly's coffin was rolled to the hearse. The funeral service was over.

Josie was surprised to see a receiving line after the ceremony. A frail old woman sat on a folding chair, her cane beside her. Her liver-spotted hands shook and her wrinkled face was wet with tears. Aunt Martha. Emily and her husband stood side by side. Brad the accountant had a pleasant face and a comfortable paunch. Emily was nearly a head taller than her husband.

"Thank you for coming, Alyce," Emily said. "And for dropping by that chicken and artichoke casserole yesterday. That was so kind."

"That's what neighbors do," Alyce said. "I'm so sorry about Molly. Would you like to come to my home tomorrow for lunch at noon? A change of scene might help. It will just be me and my friend Joanie." Alyce presented Josie by a name close enough to her own that she'd answer to it.

"Joanie was a customer at your sister's shop," Alyce said.

"It would be nice to get out of the house," Emily said.

"There's a long line behind us. I don't want to monopolize you. We'll see you tomorrow." Josie and Alyce patted Aunt Martha's hand and quick-marched out the church door.

"Nice work," Josie said on the way to their cars. "I was hoping to get a chance to talk to Molly's sister. I want to ask Emily about something I heard those two awful women next to me say."

"Was there anything useful in that toxic spew?" Alyce asked.

"One mentioned that Molly had a fiancé before Ted named George. I didn't get a last name, but George had a beard and he moved west. I wondered if he was a real fiancé, or if Molly was stalking him, too. He might be the killer."

"He'd have to be in town to shoot Molly," Alyce said.

"Maybe she stalked other men and one of them wanted rid of her. Emily might know. I have less than a month to find out who killed Molly," Josie said. "I wanted to talk to her coworkers at Denise's Dreams."

"We saw the owner at the funeral," Alyce said. "Better check if the store is open today."

Josie put her cell on speakerphone and called the

shop. They heard this recording: "We are closed today due to a death in the family. We'll open tomorrow at ten o'clock for all your bridal needs."

"That was sweet to say Molly was a member of the family," Josie said, "but it delays me another day. Do you have to get home, or do you want to mystery-shop wedding cakes with me? Harry wants me to shop two branches of the Cakes by Cookie chain."

"If we get to eat samples, I'm in," Alyce said. "But you can't get a cake-tasting appointment at the last minute."

"I have to ask," Josie said. "It's part of the customer service evaluation. Let's try the store on Big Bend, near me."

Josie put her phone on speaker again. "Cakes by Cookie," said a cheery voice. "This is Shirley. How may I help you?"

"I'd like an appointment for a wedding cake tasting," Josie said.

"Congratulations," Shirley said. "When do you want to come in?"

"This afternoon," Josie said.

"You're joking, right?" All the sweetness vanished from Shirley's voice. "You're supposed to make tasting appointments two to three weeks in advance."

Josie could feel the frosting on her phone, and it wasn't butter cream. "I'm sorry," she said.

"You're lucky we happen to have a cancellation," Shirley said. "Get here in half an hour and you can have a tasting. How many in your party?"

"Two," Josie said. "Me and my matron of honor. How many other couples will be at this tasting?"

"None. I was going to throw away the cake samples when that bride cancelled. But you can try them if you get here. I don't have all day to gab on the phone." Shirley hung up.

"Well, that sounds appetizing," Alyce said. "We get to eat the cakes she was going to throw away."

"I think Shirley flunked the 'dealing with unexpected

requests' test," Josie said. "I have my mystery-shopping paperwork in my car. You want to go with me?"

"As Shirley would say, let's not stand around gabbing," Alyce said. "I have a nanny until two."

Traffic was light on the way to the cake tasting. It was a good time to talk. "Are you working until your wedding?" Alyce asked.

"This is my last assignment," Josie said. "Ted still has six months on his lease. Amelia and I will live at his house until we find our new home. I'm starting to move a few things into Ted's place and getting my flat ready so Mom can rent it. Now I'm wondering if I should hold off moving my things until I know if Ted and I are getting married."

"Of course you are, Josie," Alyce said. "You'll find Molly's killer, and you and Ted will live happily ever after."

"That hasn't been the story of my life so far," Josie said.

"It will work out," Alyce said firmly. "What else needs to be done for your wedding?"

"Not much," Josie said. "The invitations were mailed, the flowers are ordered, the reception and the ceremony are planned down to the last detail, and the contracts are signed. Ted went with me for our wedding cake tasting."

"What kind did you get?" Alyce asked.

"Three tiers with three flavors: vanilla, chocolate, and lemon, iced with white butter cream. We're using my mother's wedding cake topper. Amelia says it's vintage."

"Maybe she can use it for her wedding," Alyce said.

"We still have to shop for Amelia's dress and I need high heels. You've chosen a gorgeous red dress. My gown is ready except for the final fitting."

The polka-dot CAKES BY COOKIE sign appeared over the next hill. The Big Bend location was sandwiched between a bridal boutique and a jewelry shop.

"Good location," Alyce said. "What a cute junior bridesmaid's dress."

"Maybe I can bring Amelia here to look at it," Josie

said. "Mm. No doubt there's a bakery here. The air smells like sugar."

"Let's see how sweet Shirley is in person," Alyce said.

Shirley turned out to be surprisingly helpful after her rude comments on the phone. She reminded Josie of a small bird. Shirley bobbed her dark head and seemed to hop as she herded them to a white table with plates, silver forks, and samples of cakes on a white china platter. The table was covered with a snowy cloth and a glass bowl of orange and red gerbera daisies. A white leather album held numbered photos of wedding cakes.

"Number 128 is a traditional three-tiered wedding cake," Shirley said. It was decorated with swags of white icing and roses. Shirley served Josie and Alyce slices of iced vanilla cake the size of business cards.

"That butter cream icing tastes rich," Alyce said.

"It is," Shirley said. "That cake is iced with six pounds of sugar, six pounds of sweet cream butter, vanilla, and a little shortening to cut the richness."

"Delicious," Josie said.

"But we can take a traditional cake and build on it," Shirley said. "This cake has three bridges to three other cakes."

"Interesting," Josie said. She thought the ornate cake looked like a model for a Victorian bandstand.

"Number 129 has a fountain in the middle," Shirley said.

"Won't that get the icing wet?" Josie asked.

"Of course not. It's peaceful."

Peaceful? It was a cake, not a park.

"Number 130 is our most exciting wedding cake," Shirley said. "It's a six-bridge fountain cake."

Josie counted fourteen different cakes joined by bridges, overpasses, ramps, plastic pillars and Corinthian columns with a fountain in the center.

"Looks like Caesars Palace in Las Vegas," she said.

Alyce kicked her under the table.

"In a good way," Josie added.

Shirley cocked her head like a puzzled sparrow, then said, "That cake serves five hundred people. We can use almost any fruit or custard filling in our wedding cakes. This is a sample of our apricot filling. And here's a slice with chocolate pudding."

Josie scarfed up both. "I like the chocolate," she said.

"It's very popular," Shirley said. "We can also personalize your cake. Isn't this adorable?"

She showed Josie a wedding cake topped with two troll dolls.

"Was that for a computer programmer's wedding?" Josie asked.

"How did you guess?" Shirley said.

"Perhaps you'd like a more elegant cake. Number 131 is a European style white mousse frosted with white chocolate."

"What are those icing decorations that look like big sculpted flower petals?" Josie asked.

"Fans," Shirley said. "You can get them in dark chocolate, too. We also have the yin and yang cake, frosted in dark and white chocolate."

"Very New Age," Josie said.

All the samples had disappeared. Shirley recited the rest of the required information about delivery charges, down payments, and last-minute changes.

"Well," she said, "what do you think?"

"I'm a little overwhelmed," Josie said.

Shirley handed her enough paperwork to buy a house. "You can go over this with your sweetie and then call me. I've helped hundreds of brides. The month before your wedding can be murder, but you'll forget that on your special day."

"Promise?" Josie said.

Chapter 17

Molly Deaver, Ted's stalker bride, sold wisps of silk illusion to starry-eyed women at Denise's Dreams. Now Josie had to return to the shop to find out who really killed her.

Exhausted after a day of eating cake samples, she crawled into bed at nine thirty. Worries attacked like swarms of mosquitoes. These weren't bridal jitters—Josie wasn't even sure she'd have a wedding. She and Ted couldn't start their new life when Lenore's was ending.

What is the proper wedding etiquette when your fiancé's mother faces murder one? Josie wondered. Should we wait to marry until after her trial?

Josie had heard about the "*CSI* effect": Juries demanded forensic evidence to convict. Lenore's case had a truckload, from the murder weapon to the victim's blood on her Chanel suit. Her actions could be twisted into guilt. The police said she was a fleeing felon. Lenore said she was running home to her injured husband. The jury pool was polluted by the tape of Lenore cackling over her pearl-handled pistol. She'd insulted the whole city and demanded a "real" lawyer from Boca.

Josie thought Lenore could wind up behind bars.

Then what? Will Ted and I marry later? Josie had a horrible vision of herself in her wedding gown and Ted in his tux, waiting in line for the prison metal detectors. Each year, we could alternate holidays, she thought: Christmas at my mother's house, Thanksgiving at the pen with Ted's mom.

If this wedding is canceled, who'll pick up the bills? I signed the contracts for the hall, the wedding cake, the caterer, the band, even the Jewel Box.

What if Ted doesn't want to marry until he finds Molly's real killer? He'll blame himself because he didn't recognize his fluffy client was a predator.

He might not marry me at all, she thought. I'm a thirty-one-year-old single mom with a sulky tween daughter. His mother thinks Ted is too good for me. I think he's too good to be true.

By 2:10, she was tired of trying to sleep. She got dressed and made a pot of coffee.

Josie forced herself to remember the details when she'd discovered Molly's body: She saw the dark red wound in Molly's temple. The blood was clogged around it and the thicker stuff was still wet and yucky. Her mind veered away, and now Josie remembered something important:

Molly's window was down.

It had been a warm fall night. But if Molly was frightened, she would have rolled up her window and tried to drive away. And the gun-toting Lenore scared Molly. She would have run if she'd seen her.

That meant Molly was killed by someone she knew.

Someone else wanted rid of the relentless stalker bride, Josie decided. I have to find him. I will solve this murder and marry Ted. We'll honeymoon on St. John. Then Amelia and I will move into his house until we buy our own home.

She felt better making those resolutions. She checked the kitchen clock: 2:35. Josie poured herself more black coffee. She was going ahead with her life. She'd clean out her closet, starting at the top.

She pulled out Amelia's baby album, sat on her rumpled bed, and thumbed through the photos.

There was a red-faced newborn Amelia in a pink knit cap. Amelia had been born with silky dark hair like her father's. Josie had been wildly in love with Nate. She'd been engaged to another college student, a man she could barely picture now. Josie tossed her secure life when she threw away her engagement ring and started dating the high-flying pilot.

Their daughter had had a beautiful beginning. Josie didn't need photos to remember that night: She'd lit a zillion candles. They'd talked and drank champagne until Nate carried her to bed. The next morning, Josie found empty bottles, burned-out candles—and the unopened condom box.

Nearly four months later, Josie was pregnant, frightened, and delighted. She and Nate would marry. He made good money as a pilot—Nate always had cash. They'd buy a house and she'd finish college.

She never got a chance to tell him she was pregnant. He was arrested in Canada with a planeload of drugs. Now his spendthrift ways made sense: Nate was dealing drugs.

Josie wanted nothing to do with him. Nate went to a Canadian prison for a decade and Josie sentenced herself to life without romance.

Jane was furious. She wanted Josie to give up the baby for adoption. Josie refused and dropped out of college to become a mystery shopper.

Josie brought Amelia to meet her grandmother. She'd been terrified when she rang Jane's bell. Jane fell in love with her new granddaughter.

Josie turned the album page. Jane had snapped the next photo of Josie cradling a three-week-old Amelia. Josie still had her baby-belly fat and dark circles under her eyes. Her daughter's color had gone from red to pink and Josie admired her tiny starfish fingers.

Jane insisted that Josie and Amelia move into the downstairs flat. Josie's mystery-shopping barely covered the bills, even with Jane's artificially low rent and free babysitting. But she had one luxury: more time with her daughter. Josie smiled at the photo of a laughing seven-month-old Amelia crawling toward the camera. She'd had to get down on the floor for that photo.

The photos comforted Josie. She knew she'd been tired and worried when Amelia was a baby, but now she remembered that time as happy. She'd survived. She would get through this crisis. Josie packed the album, then sorted her clothes into piles: things she'd wear now, clothes she'd donate, clothes she'd store in the basement until she and Ted found their home.

She carried a box down to the basement, threw in a load of laundry, and went back upstairs for more.

By seven o'clock, Josie had stashed the last box in the basement and finished three loads of laundry. She carried the donated clothes out to her car, then stretched in the sun. Amazingly, she didn't feel tired.

She checked on Amelia. Her daughter was cocooned in her purple spread with her cat, Harry. Amelia would sleep till at least nine on a Saturday morning. Josie could drop off the clothes at the church donation box and be back in fifteen minutes. She pinned a note to Amelia's bathroom door in case she woke up.

Josie dropped the clothes off and was slammed by a sudden wave of weariness after being up most of the night. She went home, set her alarm, and napped. She heard Amelia fixing herself breakfast and checked her bedside clock: 9:04. Amelia was spending the day at her friend Emma's house. She could trust Emma's mother to watch the girls but not smother them.

Amelia sat in sullen silence on the drive to Emma's.

"Don't forget, we shop for your bridesmaid's dress this afternoon," Josie said.

"Grmpf," Amelia said. She slammed the car door, then smiled and waved at Emma.

Josie drove to Denise's Dreams in Rock Road Village, passing Ted's clinic on the way. Josie was relieved that the lot was almost filled with cars—and there were no TV trucks.

Good, she thought. But something niggled at her brain. Something that might help Lenore. Something about . . . She turned onto the shop's street and the helpful thought vanished.

Josie hoped Denise's Dreams could end her wedding nightmare. The picket fence and ruffles looked solid and comforting. She was greeted at the door by a blonde who looked so much like Molly, they could have been sisters. The hothouse flower smell hit her in the face. It reminded Josie of funerals, not weddings.

"Hi, I'm Rita," the blonde said. "May I help you?"

"I'm getting married," Josie said, "and I need a tiara." She braced herself for the bridal gush.

"Well, you've come to the right place!" Rita said. "All our tiaras are one of a kind, handcrafted by Denise herself. What's your price range?"

"No limit," Josie said. "My mom's buying and she says I can pick any style I want."

"Super," Rita said. Her pale skin flushed with excitement—or maybe greed. "Have a seat. Would you like coffee?"

"Yes," Josie said, hoping it would jump-start a conversation. "Black, please."

Rita steered Josie to the room furnished like a Victorian parlor and Josie settled onto a tufted blue velvet armchair. Rita set two flowered cups of coffee and a plate of sugar cookies on the marble-topped table in front of Josie. Then she carried a stack of velvet boxes from a back room and sat gracefully in the chair next to Josie.

"So many celebrities are wearing tiaras at their weddings now," Rita said, opening a red velvet box. "Carrie Underwood had an amazing tiara with real diamonds—forty carats. This one is similar. Those aren't real diamonds, but they have a wonderful sparkle."

Josie tried not to wince. "Nice," she said, "but I'd like something simpler."

Rita reached for a gray velvet box. "This tiara is like

the one Jennifer Lopez wore when she married Marc Anthony."

"Didn't they split?" Josie asked.

"Well, yes." That box disappeared. "We have so many types of tiaras: silver, gold, rhinestones, Swarovski crystal, and pearls."

"Pearls," Josie said.

"A warm look," Rita said. She showed Josie a blue velvet tray with two pearl tiaras.

"I like that one with the three pink pearl roses," Josie said.

Rita smiled her approval. "Pink and cranberry pearls with green baroque pearl leaves," she said. "The tiara is twelve hundred dollars and sure to become a family heirloom."

Josie examined the second tiara, an elegant band of pink pearls.

"Pretty and affordable," Rita said.

"It's difficult to choose," Josie said.

"Don't wait too long," Rita said. "These are one of a kind."

"Denise would make a fortune selling these online," Josie said.

Rita laughed. "That's what I tell her, but Denise can barely manage e-mail. She believes her designs should be sold personally. I don't want to pressure you, but your favorites won't last long."

"Maybe I need to come back with my friend Alyce," Josie said.

"That's how I made my major choices," Rita said. "With my best friend, Molly."

Josie noted that "made"—past tense. "Molly," she said. "Wasn't she the poor bride who was tricked by that awful doctor?" Forgive me, Ted, she thought.

"He's not a real doctor," Rita said, her eyes narrowing. "He's a vet. He treats animals because he's not fit for people. His horrible mother shot poor Molly. I saw her, you know."

"Molly?" Josie asked.

"The killer," Rita said. "It was before—" She stopped. "Before it happened. I was at the Blue Rose Tearoom with a bridal shower, and she was flaunting her gun, bold as brass. And then she—"

Crystal tears started in Rita's eyes.

Josie pulled a tissue from her purse. "It must be hard to lose a good friend," she said, her voice soft with sympathy. "I don't know what I'd do without Alyce."

Rita wept openly, the tiaras abandoned on the table. "You understand," she said. "Some people thought Molly and I were unlikely friends. Molly inherited money and didn't have to work. But I do."

"Just like Alyce," Josie said. "She's a rich lawyer's wife. I have an office job, but she's a full-time homemaker."

"That was Molly's dream," Rita said. "She planned to quit work after she married. She stayed at the shop because she loved helping other brides.

"I was thrilled when Molly said she was marrying Ted Scottsmeyer." She spat out Ted's name.

"It seemed perfect," Rita said. "I was engaged to Ben. He was a sales associate for a department store. Molly and I adored planning our weddings. Then Ben dumped me. Molly was there for me. She understood my pain because she'd suffered, too. She'd been jilted by someone else."

Josie hesitated, then decided to chance the question. "There was another man before that vet?" she asked.

"George," Rita said. "She was madly in love."

Success, Josie thought, holding back a sigh of relief. "Did you know George?"

"I met him once," Rita said. "He was okay. Sold Molly the blue broadloom for her home. That's how they met. George was kind of ordinary cute—turned-up nose, brown hair, and a beard. I didn't like the beard, but Molly thought it was manly. She'd bought her wedding dress when George ran off to Billings, Montana."

"How cruel," Josie said.

"It was," Rita said. "Molly saw George at the supermarket. Naturally, she went to talk to her fiancé. He said he was leaving for Montana the next day. They were in the produce department. Molly held her head up until she got to her car, but her heart was broken.

"She was sick, physically sick. She sat in my living room and cried her heart out. I took her to lunch; we went to movies and the art museum—anything to help her get over George. Then she met *that vet*. Molly didn't deserve what those men did to her."

"Did you ever meet the vet?" Josie said.

"Once," Rita said. "I was at Molly's house when he came to check on Bella. He was definitely a hottie. Soon Molly was planning her wedding to Ted. She was happy again.

"We had such a wonderful time planning that wedding. I was more like her sister than Emily. She's Molly's half sister. They have the same father but different mothers. And totally different personalities.

"Emily is just plain greedy. Molly was generous. Too generous for her own good. You'd never guess Molly and Emily were related." Rita took a sip of coffee and blotted her eyes.

"Molly and Emily didn't look anything alike. Emily doesn't care how she dresses and Molly was so feminine. She liked animals and Emily doesn't. Molly and I love antiques and Emily's house is modern. I think modern furniture looks sterile, don't you?"

"I have nothing but old furniture," Josie said truthfully.

"I was at Emily's once. I felt like I was sitting in a doctor's waiting room."

Josie peeked at her wristwatch. She had to get to Alyce's for their lunch with Emily.

"Doctor!" Josie said. "You just reminded me. I have an appointment at noon. I'll be back. You've been a big help."

More than you realize, Josie thought to herself.

Chapter 18

Finally, Josie thought. Information I can use to find Molly's killer.

Rita gave me a name, city, and job. No last name, but how many carpet dealers can there be in Billings, Montana?

Do cowboys even use carpet?

Josie's car skimmed along the highway to Alyce's house, but she put the brakes on that last thought. She hated when Easterners treated St. Louisans like barefoot hicks. Lenore's digs at her city made Josie grit her teeth.

I'm no better, assuming everyone in Montana is a cowboy. I don't know a thing about that state. I'll need to do some research.

She waved to the guard at the gate to the Estates at Wood Winds. The hilltop entrance gave the best view of the subdivision's richly bizarre architecture: a Norman castle, Victorian mansion, and a Tuscan villa.

Josie parked in the driveway of Alyce's Tudor mansion and knocked on the side door.

"I'm in the kitchen," Alyce called.

Alyce's kitchen was more than the heart of her house—it was the showcase for her creativity. She was a skilled, imaginative cook.

Josie always took a moment to marvel at the kitchen's

golden linenfold oak paneling. No boxy fridge or pantry intruded on the view. They were hidden behind the warm wood.

Alyce, with her Renaissance curves, milk white skin, and corn silk hair, was filling soup bowls from a stockpot on her six-burner stove.

Josie inhaled the delicious steamy perfume. "Yum," she said. "French onion soup?"

"With sherry and a touch of thyme," Alyce said. "The bread slices are toasting in the broiler. As soon as Emily arrives, I'll float the toast in these bowls, add the cheese, and pop them under the broiler until the tops are brown and bubbly."

"What can I do?" Josie asked.

"Serve the salad on those plates and carry them to the table." Three plates, painted with an ornate design of leaves and flowers, were stacked next to a wooden salad bowl on the kitchen island.

"Pretty china," Josie said. "Looks antique."

"The plates belonged to my grandmother," Alyce said. "It's a Rosenthal pattern called Bavarian Autumn."

She filled the first plate using the salad tongs, and started on the next. "Are those cranberries in the salad?" Josie asked.

"Pomegranate," Alyce said, "along with avocado and mache. And before you ask, mache is a sweet-tasting green also known as lamb's lettuce. You'll like it."

"I like all your food," Josie said, filling the last plate.

"That apple crumb pie there is for dessert," Alyce said. "I thought Emily would appreciate comfort food, so I made my mother's recipe."

Josie carefully carried the plates to the table in the breakfast room. "I've made some progress in the search for Molly's killer," she said. "I talked with her coworker at the bridal shop. Molly had a fiancé before Ted. He ran off to Billings, Montana. I'm getting hints that Molly may have stalked him, too. Do you think her sister knew that Molly had a stalking problem?"

"You can ask her yourself," Alyce said. "I hear a car in the drive. Must be Emily's."

"Didn't she walk?" Josie asked. "It's a nice day."

"Walk!" Alyce said in mock horror. "No one walks in Wood Winds. Not without a baby stroller, a dog, or exercise weights. Walking upsets the natural order of subdivision life. We must burn fossil fuel to the gods of suburbia."

Josie opened the side door for Emily. She didn't look like a typical Wood Winds wife. She wore jeans, a black flannel shirt, and no makeup.

Lumberjack mourning, Josie thought, then regretted her unkind thought.

Alyce gathered Emily into a hug and asked, "How are you?"

"Okay," Emily said with a shrug that said she wasn't. "People have been very kind."

Alyce handed her a glass of wine, then said, "Have a seat in the breakfast room and start your salads. I'll bring in your soup shortly."

Josie noticed that Alyce didn't introduce her again. She hoped she could get through this lunch without Emily discovering she was engaged to Dr. Ted.

"How's your aunt Martha?" Alyce asked as she carried in two soup bowls.

"Molly's murder was a terrible shock," Emily said. "Poor Aunt Martha had to be sedated after the burial. I can't believe that horrible woman would shoot my poor little sister."

"Do you think she did it?" Josie asked.

"Not a doubt in my mind," Emily said firmly. "She's a nutcase. Did you see her on TV with that gun? I hope they lock her up and throw away the key."

"Did you ever meet the groom's family?" Alyce asked.

"He was supposed to meet our family at an engagement dinner at my house," Emily said. "I'd planned it for weeks. Twelve people, including Aunt Martha and Molly's friend Rita from work. Had a lovely crown roast of beef because Molly said he was a meat eater. An hour before dinner, Molly said he called her and canceled. Said he had emergency surgery on some dog. We ate dinner without him."

"Molly must have been upset," Alyce said.

"I was more upset than she was," Emily said. "She said that's what it was like being a doctor's wife. Aunt Martha said it was a sign he was ambitious. She approved.

"He's a vet, and I don't think he's all that successful. He didn't contribute a penny to the wedding. Molly paid for everything. She wouldn't use anything she'd bought for her other engagement, not even the wedding dress."

"What other engagement?" Alyce said.

Josie forked another bit of salad, alert for the crucial answer.

"Molly was engaged to another man before the vet," Emily said. "A carpet salesman. Aunt Martha thought she could have done better, but Molly said she was in love. My sister was obsessed with weddings ever since she was a little girl. Our cousin got married at Disney World in Orlando, and Molly was the flower girl. She never got over that. When she played with her dolls, it was always a wedding. Then she started being a bridesmaid for her friends, but she really wanted to be a bride. I think she accepted George because he asked her."

"George is the carpet salesman?" Alyce asked.

Come on, Josie thought. Give us his last name.

"Right," Emily said.

Josie decided to risk jumping into the conversation. "That isn't George"—she searched her mind for a last name and saw her empty salad plate—"Rosenthal at Bavarian Carpets, is it?"

"No, George Winstid with Brenhoff Carpet and Flooring," Emily said. "It's a national chain."

Thank you, Josie thought.

"Molly spent a fortune on that wedding and then George backed out. Said he was moving to Montana.

Molly was devastated. Then she met this Dr. Ted and they got engaged in a hurry and she was planning a whole different wedding. I thought she could use the dress she'd bought for George, but Molly insisted on a fresh start.

"This wedding was even more extravagant. It's a good thing she inherited money from our parents. Brad is just starting his business and we couldn't contribute money, but I gave her my time. I said she could have her wedding presents delivered to our house since Molly worked and wasn't home to get deliveries.

"She got some gorgeous presents. I think people felt sorry for her after George dumped her."

Josie shifted uncomfortably in her chair. She hoped it was grief that made Emily talk that way about her sister.

"Molly always did have all the luck," Emily said.

Luck? She's dead, Josie thought.

"Now I'm stuck with her dog, Bella. Yappy little thing pees everywhere. I have to keep her in the basement or she'll ruin my carpet."

"Maybe one of Molly's friends will take Bella," Josie said.

"Oh, I'm not giving her away," Emily said. "Bella is a purebred with papers and has all her shots. I put her on Craigslist and sold her for five hundred dollars. The new owner is picking her up tomorrow. I'm sorry, but I didn't catch your name."

My name, Josie thought. What name did Alyce give me?

"My fault," Alyce said. "This is my friend *Joanie.*"

"And it's time for me to pick up my daughter at her friend's house," Josie said. "It was a pleasure meeting you. Thank you for another amazing lunch, Alyce."

Josie escaped to her car and tore off to Emma's house. This afternoon, the Amelia who jumped into her mother's car was totally different from the grumpy morning child. Now she was all sunshine and smiles.

"So, where are we shopping for my dress, Mom?" Amelia asked.

"Thought we'd start with a bridal boutique near our house called Cassie's."

"Can I get a long or a short one?" Amelia asked.

"Whatever you want," Josie said, "as long as it's under a hundred dollars."

"Can I have a black dress?"

"No," Josie said. "My colors are white, pink, and red." The dreaded pout appeared, but before Amelia could say anything else, Josie turned the car into a strip mall. "That's Cassie's shop," Josie said.

Cassie herself waited on them. Her manner was firm but helpful, as if she was used to dealing with dithering bridal parties. Everything about Cassie was straightforward, from her dyed black hair to her deep red lipstick.

"Amelia is my daughter and my bridesmaid," Josie said. "We'd like a dress that's either pink or red. Amelia is a size seven junior."

Cassie sent them to a spacious dressing room with a triple mirror, a carpeted platform, and a satin love seat. "You sit down, Mom," Cassie said. "Amelia, you're onstage. You can wear this robe while I bring some selections."

Amelia had worn her Ed Hardy skulls and roses bra and matching panties. She put on the pink satin robe and vamped in the mirror. Josie thought her daughter looked more dyspeptic than sexy, but knew better than to say anything. Motherhood at this stage required lots of silence.

"I brought your new dress flats," Josie said, "so you don't have to wear the sample shoes in the corner."

"Good. They're gross," Amelia said.

"Here we are!" Cassie carried in an armload of dresses. Amelia rejected a watermelon bubble skirt as lame. The long hot pink chiffon was voted "okay" by Josie and earned a lackluster "whatever" from Amelia.

A fuchsia satin ball gown with ruching at the side seam was next. "That's cute," Josie said.

"Makes my butt look fat," Amelia said.

"You don't have any fat," Cassie said.

"Oh, honey, don't talk that way," Josie said. "I hate how women torment themselves over their bodies."

Nice speech, Ms. Steinem, she told herself. You should practice what you preach. How often did Alyce hear you say the same thing when you were shopping for a wedding dress?

"This is a tea-length formal," Cassie said. "Petal pink satin with a lace overlay."

Josie's eyes teared when Cassie zipped the dress and Amelia turned around. The medium pink flattered Amelia's complexion and brought out the natural red highlights in her hair.

"You look beautiful," Cassie said.

Beyond beautiful, Josie thought. What was that phrase the kids used? "That dress is the bomb," Josie said.

"Oh, Mom," Amelia said, rolling her eyes. "Only cheerleaders say 'the bomb.'"

Cassie took control. "What do you think, Amelia?"

"This dress is flawless," Amelia said.

"Sold!" Josie said.

Chapter 19

Billings, Montana, was bigger than Josie thought—more than a hundred thousand people. The old railroad town was near Yellowstone National Park. "Near" meant somewhere between 127 and 178 miles, depending on the route visitors took to the park.

The West has a different definition of "near," Josie decided.

She pictured Ted, Amelia, and herself on a scenic drive through the mountains to Yellowstone. A real family vacation with horseback rides, hiking, kayaking—and lots of photos for Amelia to show off at school.

Another dream that wouldn't come true unless she found Molly's killer.

Josie called up the nationwide Brenhoff Carpet and Flooring Web site and clicked her way to the Montana store. The page showed six staff photos, framed by lariats.

ROPIN' IN GOOD DEALS! the headline said.

George Winstid was "ordinary cute," as Rita called him. Maybe better than ordinary. George looked about Ted's age—thirty-five—and had the alert, eager-to-please expression of a good salesman. Josie liked his tip-tilted nose and didn't mind the face fur. George kept his beard neatly trimmed.

"Congratulations, Mr. President!" it said under his

photo. "George Winstid, September's Red Carpet Seller, has been elected president of the National Carpeting and Floor Covering Association, 1,700 members strong. He'll be inducted at the NCFCA Expo in St. Louis, Missouri, Oct. 22–27. We're proud our top seller is nationally known."

George was in St. Louis this week, Josie thought. Before Molly was murdered. He'd run to the wilds of Montana to get away from Molly Deaver—if she really did stalk him.

Josie had to know. But how was she going to find George at a huge convention?

She kept clicking through more sites. The NCFCA Expo was at the downtown convention center. More than twelve hundred industry people were registered. George was featured in NCFCA's "Our New Officers" section. "It's especially fitting that St. Louis native George Winstid be installed at the expo in his hometown," the online press release said.

Josie looked up the NCFCA schedule. The expo had a cocktail party and banquet tonight at seven o'clock at the convention center. It was almost five now. Even with his photo, she'd have a hard time finding George in a thousand-plus partygoers. If her hunch was right and George really had been stalked by Molly, he'd be wary of lone women.

Josie reread the site and had an inspiration. She knew how to get around that obstacle.

She started calling the convention hotels. Josie found George at the fifth one, the Drury Plaza Hotel at the Arch. Here goes, she thought, as she asked for his room.

His phone rang. Once. Twice. Three times. Four times. Next it would be routed to the message center. Should she leave one?

Wait! He answered, "George Winstid."

"Mr. Winstid," she said, "I'm a reporter with the *St. Louis City Gazette* business section. My editor received a press release about your election as president of the

National Carpeting and Floor Covering Association, and we'd like to interview you about your post. It's news when a hometown boy makes good. Would you have time for a short interview?"

"That's nice of you," George said. "My mom lives in Ballwin. She can show the paper to all her friends. We have a big do at the convention center at seven tonight. I could get you a press pass."

"Actually, I have another assignment this evening," Josie said. "The *Gazette* offices are fifteen minutes away. Could we meet at the bar at your hotel? I'll buy you a drink on my expense account."

George hesitated.

"Please?" Josie said. "I promise you'll be free by six o'clock. Plenty of time to make your party."

"Meet me in the lobby for happy hour," George said.

Josie pushed her old car to the limit, slowing down only in the known speed traps. She parked in the hotel garage with minutes to spare.

Josie loved the Drury Plaza Hotel at the Arch. The dark wood, Waterford crystal chandeliers, and Italian marble were part of the building's elegant past. The hotel also had a seriously loony bronze sculpture of Native American Sacajawea guiding explorers Lewis and Clark through the lobby.

Business travelers easily found their way to the happy hour buffet. The suits were filling their plates with free chips and salsa, hot dogs, and nachos. All the men were clean-shaven except for one in a dark suit, nursing a beer.

"Mr. Winstid?" Josie asked.

Now Josie saw his convention name tag. "You're the reporter, right? Take a pew," George said.

"Thank you for meeting me here," Josie said. "Before I sit, may I buy you a fresh drink?"

"The hotel gives us some free drink tickets," he said. "Let me get you one."

"White wine," Josie said.

"Help yourself to the buffet and I'll be right back," George said.

Josie piled a few chips on a plate, but she was too nervous to eat. George set a cold wine in front of her and said, "Now, what do you want to ask me?"

Here goes, Josie thought. "Mr. Winstid, I'm not a reporter."

His face darkened.

"I need your help," Josie said. "I want to marry Ted Scottsmeyer next month. He's a veterinarian, and Molly Ann Deaver—"

George made a growling noise, but Josie forged ahead. "Molly Deaver showed up at Ted's clinic in a wedding dress and said they were getting married that morning. The whole marriage was invented in her twisted brain."

"That bitch!" George slammed his beer bottle on the table. Two women at the next table stared at him. George lowered his voice and said, "I moved to the other end of the country to get away from her. I thought I was safe. I come back here to be president of a national organization and take my mom to lunch and Molly's da—" He stopped short and amended the word. "—dang sister was at the restaurant peddling homemade junk."

"You were at the Blue Rose Tearoom?" Josie asked.

George looked embarrassed. "I did it for Mom. I'm no tea drinker, but she likes the place. She can't afford lunch there, so I took her as a treat."

"You're a good son," Josie said.

"Look, I'm sorry for your trouble, but I can't waste any more time talking to you. I have to get to that cocktail party."

"I think the police would be interested in knowing Molly's ex-fiancé was in town this week," Josie said.

"We were never engaged," George said. "I opened up the *Gazette* one day and saw the announcement of our engagement. I took a lot of ragging about that. I tried to get the paper to print a retraction, but they said it was a paid announcement, not a news story. I had to get a lawyer before they'd even say it was a 'misprint.' Wouldn't even retract it.

"That woman is a complete head case. We never even dated. She stalked me because I sold her some carpet. That sale cost me my St. Louis career. Why would the police care where I am this week, anyway?"

"Because she was murdered," Josie said.

"You don't say." George seemed stunned by the news. "When?" He could hardly say the word.

"Wednesday night," Josie said, "between six and six thirty."

George sipped his beer, maybe buying time to recover. His tone went from shocked to belligerent. "Go ahead and tell the police. I've got an alibi. I was at the conference meet-and-greet from six to eight that night. A thousand people saw me there.

"Besides, that move to Montana was a blessing in disguise. That's where I met my Renee. Sweetest little girl I ever met. We're engaged for real." His face softened into a smile.

"Congratulations," Josie said.

"I'm sorry Molly got her hooks in some other man, but she's not my problem anymore."

"But you must understand mine," Josie said. "We need to find Molly's real killer, or Ted and I will have to cancel our wedding. Did you take out a restraining order against her?"

"I don't see the point in those things," George said. "A piece of paper wouldn't stop Molly. Besides, I didn't want something like that in the public record. Not good for my career. My boss told me there was an opening at the Billings store and that town was growing, so I transferred there."

"Do you know of any other men Molly might have stalked?"

"I know very little about her," George said. "I knew she had a sister—Emma, Amy."

"Emily," Josie said.

"She seemed decent enough, but she refused to believe her sister has mental problems. She blamed me for 'leading Molly on.' I was happy to get away from the whole crazy bunch. I wish I could tell you more, but I don't know anything else. Now I have to go to that cocktail party."

"You've been a big help," Josie said.

On the walk back to the parking garage, she realized George had been more of a help than she thought.

He said he was in town the day Molly was murdered. But George never asked how she was killed.

Chapter 20

Saturday, October 27

George Winstid said he had a thousand witnesses to prove he didn't kill Molly Deaver.

Josie wondered if he had any.

She felt a slight flicker of hope: George had given her some useful bits of information, but she didn't see how they could free Lenore.

She slammed on her brakes at a red light. While she waited, Josie tried to analyze what he'd told her.

George had a thousand witnesses only if he'd been onstage at the convention center.

But he wasn't. He'd been at a cocktail party. The convention center was bigger than an airplane terminal. George could have flitted around and said hello to a dozen people, slipped out, shot Molly, and returned before he was missed.

No one was watching him the whole time.

The traffic light changed and Josie's car crawled another block. St. Louis didn't have Saturday traffic jams unless there was a game downtown. What was the holdup? She had to be at Ted's in an hour.

She was making the big move tonight—carrying her first things to his place. This was also a romantic evening, maybe their last chance to be together. Next week, they'd be swept into the wedding whirlwind.

Jane had warned her daughter. "You need to spend time with Ted before he forgets why he asked you to marry him," she'd said. "Don't worry about Amelia. I'll watch her. We'll start packing her things and then we'll have a cooking lesson."

Josie was touched. "Thanks, Mom," she said. "You're thoughtful."

"I'm not too old to forget what it's like to be in love," Jane said.

Poor Mom, Josie thought. Amelia calls you the princess bride because your wedding picture is so beautiful. Too bad your prince turned into a toad.

What my father did wasn't right or fair. He promised to love and honor you. You promised to be a full-time homemaker. Then he ran off and started a new family in Chicago, and you had to take a dreary bank job and raise a daughter on your own.

"You deserve your happiness, Josie," Jane had said. "I'll feel a lot better when I walk you down that aisle and give you away."

"You and me both," Josie had said. "Mom, what if we can't get married because of Lenore's arrest?"

Josie's small mother wrapped her in a protective hug and said, "You *will* get married. Don't even think about the alternative."

But Josie did. Constantly. Lenore's arrest could ruin her chance for happiness unless Josie got the Rock Road Village police to reopen Molly's murder and find the real killer.

Josie's Honda crept forward. She still couldn't see what caused the slowdown. Wait! The road suddenly opened up. If she moved quickly, she'd make it through the intersection.

Then the light turned yellow and Josie saw the warnings for the red-light cameras. So did the blue BMW in front of her. The Beemer slammed on its brakes. Josie did, too, nearly rear-ending it. Her seat belt yanked her back.

So much for safety, she thought. Red-light cameras

were spies on stilts, causing more problems than they prevented. Now she saw the holdup in the intersection — a fender bender blocked traffic.

While Josie waited for the light to change, those cameras nagged at her. Who had been talking about cameras? The police! They'd been angry that the security cameras in Ted's clinic lot were out of order. They didn't capture Molly's killer on tape.

Now Josie remembered: There were cameras *inside* the clinic.

They would have recorded the bizarre, bloody chain reaction that started with bridezilla cutting Ted with a scalpel and ended with the cat scratching Molly and the bride's blood dripping on Lenore's suit.

Those tapes would tell the true story, unbiased and unedited. The police would have to reopen Molly's murder investigation.

The traffic light changed again, but the cars still didn't move. Josie's fingers felt on fire when she punched the SPEED-DIAL button for Ted's phone.

"Please don't cancel on me tonight," he said before she even said hello.

"Wouldn't dream of it," Josie said. Just the sound of his voice made her feel tingly.

"I'll come over and help you move," Ted said. "You shouldn't carry those boxes."

"Amelia can help me," Josie said. "I have other plans for you."

"That's a sexy giggle," Ted said. "Want to tell me about them?"

Ted sounded so hot, he almost melted her cell phone. Josie remembered the feel of his strong back and broad shoulders and nearly forgot why she'd called.

"I had a brainstorm," she said. "Your clinic has security cameras inside. Were they working when Molly barged into your TV taping?"

"I think so," Ted said.

"How long do you keep your tapes?"

"The security company has them for a week," Ted said.

"Then they caught Molly," Josie said. "Lenore's lawyer doesn't need those Channel Seven tapes. Have your security company e-mail the files to Shelford Clark. The light's green. Gotta go. Love you." She clicked off her phone and sailed through the intersection at last.

At home, she found Amelia in her room texting. How does my girl get her thumbs to move so fast? she wondered.

Josie changed into Ted's favorite white blouse and her black clam diggers, put on fresh lipstick, and slipped her overnight bag into the top box.

Where was her purse?

She checked her room, the bathroom, living room, and finally found it on the kitchen table. She also saw three liters of Diet Coke stacked next to the fridge.

"Amelia!" Josie called. "When did you start drinking Diet Coke?"

"I'm not drinking it," Amelia said. "It's for a science experiment. It will be gone shortly. Can I help carry your boxes to the car?"

Amelia was volunteering to help? The National Weather Service couldn't track Amelia's changing moods. Might as well enjoy this sunny spell.

"They're stacked by my bedroom door," Josie said.

"Grandma's teaching me how to make round steak tonight," Amelia said, balancing two boxes. Josie took two more.

"Good," Josie said. Round steak was maybe her least favorite meal. They went back for the next load.

"Can I paint my new room purple?" Amelia asked as she carefully stacked the last boxes in Josie's car trunk.

"When we buy our new home," Josie said.

"I mean at Ted's place," Amelia said.

"No, he's renting," Josie said. "That room has to stay 'renter white.' But we aren't going to live there long."

"Whatever," Amelia said, and shrugged.

That word had more inflections than Mandarin, but Josie decided this one was neutral.

She kissed her daughter good-bye. "By summer, you'll have your own room in our own house with our own wedding pictures. Now go see your grandmother."

Josie hoped she could keep that promise. She gave Ted such a warm welcome, they didn't get around to ordering pizza for more than two hours.

"What time is it?" Josie finally asked.

"Almost ten o'clock," Ted said. "How about dinner?"

"Mushroom and pepperoni for me," Josie said.

"Same here," Ted said. "I'll order two large." He found his jeans on the floor and put on his shirt.

"I don't know if I can eat a large pizza," Josie said.

"I can," Ted said, sliding into his shoes. "The leftovers make a good breakfast. I'll carry in the boxes. Don't get dressed. I like you the way you are."

Josie unpacked the boxes and put her clothes in the dresser drawers Ted had cleared, then hung her clothes in her half of his closet. Now it was their closet. Almost.

Thirty minutes later, Ted brought in their pizzas, along with the wine and two glasses. They ate pizza in his bed.

"What will we do if your mother is in jail on our wedding day?" Josie asked.

"She won't be," Ted said. "Mom didn't kill Molly."

"Innocent people go to jail," Josie said.

"Most are black, poor, or had bad lawyers. That's definitely not my mother."

"But—," Josie said.

Ted's phone rang and he checked the display. "It's Shelford Clark, Mom's lawyer. I bet he's seen those tapes."

"On a Saturday night?" Josie said.

"Believe me, he's being paid for his time," Ted said. He put the phone on speaker so Josie could hear their conversation.

"My associate e-mailed me those tapes," Clark said.

"Good, huh?" Ted said.

"Bad," the lawyer said. "There's no sound and I can see the cat jumping off the table, but there's no blood except yours. It's very clear that crazy bride is attacking you, Ted. All those tapes will do is show the jury why your mother wanted to kill that woman."

"Oh," Ted said.

Josie felt like someone had let the air out of the room.

"I may have an expert enhance them," Clark said, "and see if the tapes can help establish reasonable doubt. But for God's sake, we can't let them near the prosecution until the last possible moment. Then I'll send a mountain of material and pray they never find those tapes."

"Maybe we could just forget about them," Ted said.

"Can't. I play by the rules," Clark said. "Anyway, you left a paper trail when you called the security company and requested the tapes. Too late to unring that bell."

Ted and Josie sat wrapped in heavy, hopeless silence.

"I'd like to speak to your bride, Ms. Marcus," Clark said.

"I'm here," Josie said.

"Mrs. Scottsmeyer Hall has asked me to convey to you her dismay over your bridal registries."

"My what?" Josie said. Lenore was worried about wedding gifts when she was facing murder one? "Which one? Honeyfund is a good online service. We're also registered at Crate and Barrel, Macy's, and Williams-Sonoma."

"But not Tiffany and Co.," the lawyer said.

"We don't need anything from Tiffany," Josie said.

"No one does, my dear. Except my wife." Clark chuckled at his own joke.

"In Mrs. Scottsmeyer Hall's circle, a proper bride registers at Tiffany." Clark's tone turned avuncular. "Humor her. What harm can it do? All it costs you is a little time. I think you can register online. Pick out a few things."

"But we don't live a Tiffany life," Josie said.

"You want my advice, Josie?" Clark asked.

She didn't, but she knew she'd get it anyway.

"Even if you never use those gifts from Tiffany," Clark said, "you can sell them on eBay. And you'll make Ted's mother happy during a very trying time."

What about me? Josie wanted to say. This is supposed to be my day. But I have to pick my battles. This one isn't worth fighting. "I'll do it," Josie said.

After Shelford Clark hung up, Ted asked, "Is it a problem to register at Tiffany?" He was back finishing his pizza.

"It's not a big deal," Josie said. The problem, she thought, is Lenore is trying to control our life long distance.

She stared at her pizza as if the answer were written in pepperoni.

Long distance. Who else had a long-distance mother?

"That's it!" Josie said. "George's mother is in St. Louis. If your mom can be arrested for murder, so can his. Molly stalked George so persistently, he had to leave the city."

"So wait," Ted said. "You think that Mrs. Winstid was so angry at Molly for driving her son away from St. Louis, she killed her?"

"It's the only way George could come back home," Josie said. "That's why I need to talk to Mrs. Winstid in Ballwin."

"Tonight?" Ted said. "It's nearly midnight." He looked bewildered.

"First thing tomorrow," Josie said. "Should I register at Tiffany before or after I find Molly's killer?"

Chapter 21

Josie felt a warm, wet slurp on her ear.

"Mm," she said. She sighed luxuriously and rolled over to Ted's side of the bed.

She felt lazy and languid after last night's lovemaking, and wanted to linger a little longer on his sexy gray pin-striped sheets. It felt wicked good to sleep in this morning.

Eyes still closed, she reached for Ted and felt a cold wet nose.

Cold wet nose?

Josie opened one eye and stared at Ted's black Lab sprawled on his side of the bed. Festus slurped her again.

"Did Ted let you in?" she asked. "Or did you open the door when he got up?" Ted had banished the scratcha-holic Lab to his basket in Ted's office last night.

Josie scratched Festus's warm velvety ears until he whimpered, then licked her face again.

"You've been in the pepperoni, pizza breath," Josie said. "You ate Ted's breakfast." She checked the floor on her side of the bed and saw greasy paw prints in the open pizza boxes.

"You've blown your diet," she said. "But I don't blame you. Nobody should have that much temptation at his feet."

Now Josie detected the aroma of hot coffee drifting

in from the kitchen. Was it really eight thirty? She put on her pink satin robe and followed the coffee scent to the kitchen, where Ted was pouring batter into a waffle iron. His chocolate brown robe was the same color as his eyes.

"Morning, gorgeous," he said. "Sleep well?"

She wrapped her arms around him, leaned her head on his shoulder, and felt that delicious flutter. "Never better."

"I thought you'd still be asleep," he said. "I'm making you breakfast in bed."

"I hate to snitch," Josie said, pouring herself a cup of coffee, "but Festus ate your leftover pizza."

"Guess we'll have to get by on Belgian waffles. I'll bring your tray into the bedroom."

"Don't you have to work today?" she asked.

"Not till ten," he said. "On your way back to bed, check out the new bookcases in my office."

Ted's home office was the third bedroom in his rented home. Lined with bookshelves, the cozy room was Marmalade's favorite haunt. The cat snoozed on Ted's desk, next to his open laptop.

Josie thought the two new bookcases were an odd choice. They cut the room in half and blocked the window view of Ted's yard. The backs of the bookcases faced Ted's desk and were decorated with posters. One showed a pack of dogs panting outside the National Postal Museum in Washington, DC, waiting for it to open. The other was the classic "Ski Missouri" poster— a skier chewing on a piece of straw in a muddy corn-field.

Now Josie saw why the bookcases were in the middle of the room. Ted had used them to create a second small office with an oak workstation and a cushy office chair. The desk had a two-drawer file cabinet and enough space for a fax machine and computer. Right now, the desktop had a black lacquer pencil cup and matching in and out trays. The eight oak shelves were bare and the wooden floor was covered with a bold red and black rug. She plopped into her new chair and spun around.

Ted watched from the doorway. "What do you think of your new office?" he asked.

"I've never had such a beautiful work space," Josie said. "But you gave me half of your office and all your view."

"Along with all my problems and the rest of my life," he said. "For better or worse. In our new home, you'll have your own office. If you don't like the chair, you can take it back."

"It's perfect," she said. She got up, put her arms around him, and rested her head against his chest. "Thank you."

"I'm glad you like it, but you can admire it later. Your breakfast is getting cold. Off to bed."

Josie's Belgian waffle took up the whole tray. The sweet-smelling confection was crowned with strawberries and lightly dusted with powdered sugar. There was barely room for the pitcher of warm maple syrup.

Festus jumped up on the bed to investigate the waffle, and Ted took him by the collar. "Outside, my friend," he said, and ejected the felonious Festus out the back door. Ted returned with his plate and climbed in beside Josie.

"I'm in a sugar swoon," Josie said.

She was mopping up the last bit of warm syrup when Ted asked, "Want anything else?"

Josie grabbed him by the belt on his robe and pulled him toward her. "Yes," she said. "Something hot."

Last night's love had been quick and urgent. This morning's was slow and sensual.

"You have just the right amount of hair on your chest," Josie said, and sighed. "Some men are hairy all over, even their backs. You have no gorilla growth. Yours is perfect."

"I love your back," Ted said, tracing his finger from the nape of her neck down her spine. "It's so graceful. And you have such a round, pillowy . . ."

"How about some deeper appreciation?" Josie said.

Afterward, Josie fell asleep in Ted's arms. They were awakened by Ted's ringing phone. Ted fumbled for it, and said, "Kathy? Sorry. I overslept. I didn't realize it was after ten. I'll be in the office in fifteen minutes."

Ted leaped out of bed, jumped into the shower, and threw his clothes on in seven minutes flat. He let in Festus and hooked on his leash. They were ready for work.

"I'll wash the dishes and lock up," Josie said.

She smoothed Ted's wet hair into place and gave him a good-bye kiss. Soon she'd do this every morning.

Ted's kitchen was the most impressive part of his home. The owner had upgraded it with sleek dark cabinets, black granite countertops, stainless steel appliances, and a six-burner stove. Josie loaded the dishwasher and tidied Ted's living room. It was done in basic bachelor pad—a brown corduroy couch, two occasional chairs, and a fifty-two-inch television. The room was spare and clean, except for a light dusting of pet hair.

Josie made the bed, and wished her computer were already in her new office. But she could use Ted's phone. She had a plan to talk to George's mother.

First, Josie called the Blue Rose Tearoom. Rachel answered the phone.

"What's your special for this Tuesday?" Josie asked.

"Cranberry scones with clover honey and salmon and cucumber sandwiches," Rachel said.

"Perfect," Josie said. "I'd like a reservation for two at noon on Tuesday."

Now Josie was ready for the crucial step. Mrs. Phoebe Winstid was old-school, and that made her phone and address easy to find in the phone book.

She sat at Ted's desk, punched in Phoebe's phone number, then made her voice squeally-girl high. "Mrs. Winstid?" Josie asked. "Mrs. Phoebe Winstid?"

"Yes?" The woman sounded too young to be George's mother.

Josie heard her hesitation and pressed on in a girlish

gush. "I'm with the Blue Rose Tearoom and you've won a free customer appreciation lunch!"

"I have?" Mrs. Winstid said. All hesitation was gone. "I don't remember entering a contest."

"We got your name from your son," Josie said. "He said you just loved our tearoom! We're trying to build our customer base in certain St. Louis areas. Each month we choose two suburbs. In October, we're concentrating on Ballwin and Maplewood. Isn't that exciting?" Josie thought she must sound like a cheerleader on speed.

"Is there a catch?" Mrs. Winstid asked.

"No catch, no obligation, nothing to pay," Josie trilled. "But this offer won't last forever. Would you like to join us for a free lunch this week, Mrs. Winstid?"

"I'd be delighted," she said. "This is lunch for one, right?"

"Correct. Perhaps you'd like to lunch with our Maplewood winner, Miss Josie Marcus? Miss Marcus adores tea and she seems like a nice young woman."

And a big liar, Josie thought. But a convincing one, I hope. I'm about to make my final move.

"How about lunch Tuesday at noon?" Josie asked. "Wait till you hear our specials." She squeaked down the list.

"Why, yes, I'd like that very much," Mrs. Winstid said.

"Wonderful!" Josie said. "I'll make reservations for both of you. Just come in and ask for Josie Marcus. You're all set."

She hung up, relieved that her scam had succeeded. She was sweating, she'd been so nervous.

Since she was already sitting in front of Ted's computer, Josie registered at Tiffany to please Lenore. She found a porcelain china pattern that was shatteringly expensive: Black Shoulders Limoges. A sugar bowl was eleven hundred dollars. So were a cup and saucer. If guests really wanted to go for broke, they could buy the platter for $2,250.

She requested four sterling silver picture frames for

six hundred fifty dollars, handblown wineglasses at sixty bucks each, and a set of sophisticated Elsa Peretti flatware that was almost five thousand dollars. She added four handsome glass vases at five hundred a pop, and a dozen hand-painted blue Limoges poches at two hundred fifty dollars each. Josie had no idea what a poche was, but it looked pretty.

Josie doubted that any of Lenore's friends would give her gifts so expensive, but if they did, Josie would keep them in a safe-deposit box and sell them to help finance Amelia's schooling.

From the Tiffany wedding registry, her mouse drifted to other bridal sites. She still needed shoes. Josie found exactly the right pair for her wedding dress—in her size. She clicked and ordered them.

From there, she found herself browsing wedding tiaras on several sites, including eBay. Then Josie saw the photo that stopped her search cold.

It was a tiara with three pearl roses. It looked like the tiara she'd seen at Denise's Dreams.

"Pink and cranberry pearls with green baroque pearl leaves," the description read. "Sure to become a family heirloom."

Hm. That was what Rita had told Josie. She also said Denise didn't sell her tiaras online. The price was nine hundred dollars—three hundred fifty dollars less than it had cost at Denise's shop. The eBay information said the seller had a four-star reputation, but gave no name.

Was this the same tiara from the shop where Molly used to work? Was it somehow connected to her death?

Josie had to know.

Chapter 22

Josie shut the door on her own domestic dream and drove to Denise's Dreams. After Ted's comfortable home, the bridal shop's picket-fence perfection seemed fake.

So did Rita's smile.

"I knew you'd come back," she said, blond curls bouncing. "Which tiara do you want?"

"The baroque pearl roses," Josie said, and mentally crossed her fingers. She hoped her hunch was right.

"Oh, I'm sorry," Rita said. "Denise sold it."

Josie didn't think Rita sounded a bit sorry. She didn't look it, either. "Really?" she said. "When?"

"Yesterday afternoon," Rita said. "Another bride saw it, loved it, and bought it on the spot."

Rita's sad smile was as sincere as a deadbeat's promise that the check was in the mail. Josie didn't believe any bride would pay twelve hundred dollars for a tiara, turn around and try to sell it on eBay the next day—for much less.

Josie suspected that Rita stole it and was trying to sell it. But she needed a motive. She had to find out if the saleswoman needed quick cash.

Rita's dress looked new—powder blue with puffed sleeves and a cascade of ruffles down the front. She hovered nearby while Josie tried to stare wistfully at the tiaras on display. They were fairy-tale jewelry for princesses, pageants, and personages, she thought. I guess a bride is all three.

"Would you like to look at the pink pearl tiara again?" Rita said. "It's elegant."

Josie sighed. "My heart was set on those baroque pearl roses. Mom didn't mind the price and it was perfect for my dress. I wanted it to become a family heirloom. Could Denise make another one like it?"

"No," Rita said. "Denise's unique designs are her specialty. She used the highest grade baroque pearls for that tiara. Each pearl was different. They can't be duplicated and neither can the design."

So there isn't another tiara like it, Josie thought. I've connected the tiara on eBay to this shop.

"I'd hoped my daughter would wear it on her wedding day. Now that will never happen," Josie said as if she were mourning the loss for the future generations of Marcus women.

"At least look at the other tiara again," Rita said. "Come sit down. Sunday afternoons are quiet. I have time to help you make the right choice. Have some coffee and chocolate fudge."

"No fudge," Josie said. "My final dress fitting is coming up."

"Black coffee, then," Rita said. She took Josie by the shoulders and practically forced her into the blue chair. "Sit."

Josie sat like a well-trained hound. Rita brought black coffee in a bone china cup, then took the pink pearl tiara out of its velvet box.

Josie studied it, then shook her head. "I thought this looked elegant last time," she said. "Now it just seems plain."

Rita wrapped a blond curl around one finger and absently tugged on her hair. Josie thought her unease was genuine.

"Maybe I can help you choose if I know the kind of

dress you're wearing," Rita said. She handed Josie a heavy ring binder with photos of smiling brides in sample dresses. The styles ranged from sexy strapless numbers suitable for nightclub singers to billowy skirts for long-lost senior proms.

Josie pointed to a ruffled dress much like Molly's. "That's my dress. I went all out with the ruffles and lace. I'm old-fashioned when it comes to weddings."

"Me, too," Rita said. Her ruffles bobbed as she nodded her head. "That's so much like my dress. I can show you lots of good choices for it." She rushed into the back and returned with a teetering pile of velvet boxes, like a shoe salesperson with a selection of wares.

"Now sit back and sip your coffee," Rita said, opening the top velvet box. "This one has an intriguing diamond design."

"Too modern," Josie said.

"Then how about this scroll design?" Rita asked.

Josie pretended to consider it. "Better. But not quite."

"This swirly tiara would look good."

Josie shook her head. She nixed the hearts, butterflies, and bows. Rita offered stars, circles, and crystals. Josie said no. Now they were both exhausted.

"I'm not giving up," Rita said. "But let's take a little break."

She brought a fresh cup of coffee for Josie and one for herself, then settled into the chair for a chat.

"I can't stop thinking about your poor friend," Josie said. "The one whose fiancé ran off to Montana."

"Molly," Rita said.

"I'm surprised she could stand to work here."

"It was hard for her," Rita said. "But keeping busy helped her recover after George abandoned her."

"Did she get stuck with the bills when George ran off?" Josie said. "I'm asking because my mother is nervous. I signed all the contracts and paid the deposits for the hall, the caterer, the flowers. My fiancé travels so much, if I had to wait for him to cosign, we'd never have a wedding. Mom says if he walks away this close to the wedding, I'm stuck paying for everything."

"You don't think he'll do that, do you?" Rita looked alarmed.

"No," Josie said. "I'm sure he won't. But Mom says I'm a fool and it's happened to smarter women than me—like your poor friend Molly. And you, too."

"But that doesn't mean your fiancé will break off your wedding," Rita said. "I've helped hundreds of brides and ninety-nine percent had beautiful weddings."

"Bridal nerves," Josie said. "Heaven forbid, but if the worst happened, I'd survive. I'd be in debt, but I'd go on. I'd be strong like you and Molly. It didn't ruin your life. You didn't go bankrupt."

Rita sipped her coffee, then said, "Molly spent forty-five thousand dollars on her wedding, but she'd have to spend a lot more to go bankrupt. She and her sister both inherited about two hundred fifty thousand dollars."

"Nice," Josie said.

"It got nicer," Rita said. "Molly had a gift for making money. She more than doubled her inheritance through shrewd investing. People underestimated her because she was blond like me. But Molly knew her way around the markets. She was smarter than Emily's husband. Brad was supposed to be this big-deal accountant. Hah! Molly knew more about investing than he did. Molly and Emily didn't really get along, and Brad didn't help. I think Emily was jealous of her sister. Molly was so pretty and feminine. When Molly was engaged to that Dr. Ted"—Rita spat out the name again—"Emily said Molly could have her wedding gifts delivered to her house because Molly worked all day. Personally, I think Emily was trying to get her mitts on some of Molly's gifts. Molly was also going to get a lot of money."

"Was that delivered to Emily's house, too?" Josie asked.

"No, but Molly put her sister's name on the joint wedding account," Rita said.

"Why would she do that?" Josie said. "What if Brad got his hands on her money?"

"Molly made it very clear that neither of their men—Brad or Ted—would spend that money. It was supposed to go toward a house for Ted and Molly. Their aunt Martha gave Molly fifty thousand dollars to help her buy a house, and she suggested the other family members give money to help the couple get started. Molly said it should have been my name on that joint account because I was really her sister, but Aunt Martha didn't like that the sisters had had a falling-out. Molly put her sister's name on the account to show Aunt Martha there were no hard feelings."

"Sounds like Molly didn't hold a grudge," Josie said.

"She was a good person," Rita said, her voice wobbly with tears. "I'm sorry. I shouldn't cry like this at work, but I miss her so much."

"Of course you do," Josie said. "You don't get over a loss like that. What about you? Did you get stuck with the bills for your canceled wedding?"

Rita seemed grateful for the topic change. "Yes, I did," she said, sniffling. "I'm still paying the caterer and the hall. Denise did me a favor. She refunded my deposit for the flowers and took back my tiara and veil, so I didn't owe her. I made an arrangement with my other creditors. I pay them two fifty a month."

"Molly wouldn't lend you money?" Josie asked.

"I didn't ask her. I have my pride," Rita said.

Now she seemed to regret her spurt of plain speaking. "Well," she said, taking a last sip of coffee, "shall we look at more tiaras?"

Rita returned with a daunting pile of velvet boxes. "This is a sweetheart style," she said. The tiny pearl hearts looked like valentine candy.

While Rita talked tiaras, Josie tried to sort through what she'd just learned. If Molly spent forty-five thousand dollars on her aborted wedding to George, Rita had to owe almost that much. "Here's a wave design," Rita said, showing her another tiara. "And this . . ."

After all, Rita and Molly had similar tastes, Josie thought.

"Pear-drop design is popular. So is this saddled tiara."

Rita was saddled with a staggering debt and a sales salary.

"I like this pedestaled tiara," Rita said.

Paying down a debt that big was a monumental task, Josie thought. Even if Rita did negotiate a monthly payment.

"But maybe you'd like these lovely swooning hearts," Rita said.

Rita had nursed Molly through a broken heart, but her good friend wouldn't help her out in her own time of need. Did they have a one-sided friendship?

"I also like these Victorian flowers. Very complex," Rita said.

But what if the answer was simple? Josie thought. What if Rita wasn't really too proud to ask Molly for help? What if Molly had refused to help her best friend? Then Rita turned light-fingered to pay her debts and Molly caught her stealing from the store she loved. A small store couldn't survive big losses.

I'll have to check with Denise.

"I'm sorry," Josie said. "I don't really see anything I like. I have to pick up my daughter at school. Maybe I could come back later this afternoon."

"That's a good idea," Rita said. "Denise will be back this afternoon with more handcrafted selections. The only bad thing is I won't be here."

"You're off work?"

"I'm so excited," Rita said. "I've bought a vintage Coke machine and it's being delivered this afternoon at two. Denise is letting me go home and wait for the delivery people. Could I ask a favor?"

"Sure," Josie said.

"I've enjoyed working with you, but I get a commission. If you come back this afternoon and buy one of the tiaras I showed you, would you let her know?"

"Don't worry," Josie said. "I'll make sure you get credit for all you've done."

Chapter 23

"Stop treating me like a baby, Mom," Amelia said.

Josie was a tired judge listening to her daughter plead her case to be home alone today. The hearing was held in Amelia's room. Harry sat on her bed, a sympathetic jury with wide green eyes.

"I'll only be alone for an hour," Amelia said. She pulled off her crochet-stitch hoodie and hung it in her closet, then dropped her pale pink skinny jeans into her dirty clothes basket.

Exhibit A that I'm an adult now, Mom, Judge Josie thought. Amelia was a good kid, but she had a streak of con artist. Josie decided her daughter needed another reminder of her indiscretions.

"The last time I left you alone—," she began.

"I totally blew it," Amelia said quickly, stopping the familiar lecture. She plopped on her bed and dragged on her old jeans.

"But that was last year when I was a little kid," she said, pulling her PEACE T-shirt over her head. Amelia's head popped out of the neck like a rabbit out of a hole. "I'm eleven now. And you're only going to be, like, what—two miles away?"

"If that," Josie said.

Amelia sensed the verdict turning in her favor. "Grandma's getting her hair done on Manchester," she said. "I could walk there—she's that close. She may get home before you do."

Josie deliberated. Amelia was acting more mature now. A year ago she would have abandoned all her clothes on the floor—clean and dirty—to text her friends and play with Harry.

"Please, Mom?" Amelia said. "I'll work on my science experiment." Her smile was brilliant as the afternoon sun, but Josie's heart felt a twinge of maternal unease. Her head overruled those feelings and said it was time for trust.

"Science is important for girls," Amelia said. "I could maybe get a scholarship if my grades were good enough."

I should be grateful she's experimenting with science and not boys, Judge Josie thought, and delivered her verdict. "All right. I'll leave you alone, but only if you promise to work on your science experiment."

"I will," Amelia said. "I'll even clean my bathroom."

"Don't get carried away," Josie said, but she left home lighthearted and hopeful. Her daughter was growing into a smart, thoughtful young woman. Denise, Molly's former boss, might give Josie some information that would shed light on who killed Molly. Then she and Ted would get married and live happily together with Amelia, two cats, and a dog.

This afternoon, Josie didn't mind the picket fence at Denise's Dreams. The store owner was exactly the kind of woman she'd expect to have a picket fence, waiting for her Mad Man to come home from Manhattan.

Denise was petite, with long, wavy brown hair and soulful brown eyes hidden behind the horn-rimmed glasses sexy spinsters wore in classic movies. Her hot pink heels and full-skirted print dress looked oddly summery. Her voice was a June breeze.

Josie felt like a modern-day intruder in Denise's old-fashioned world. She introduced herself and said, "I've been looking at your tiaras."

Denise smiled. "Rita told me you might be coming

back. I'm so sorry we no longer have the baroque pearl tiara you wanted, but I've finished some new ones. Rita said you like pearls, right?"

"Yes," Josie said.

"Well, sit yourself down and we'll get started." Denise carried a stack of velvet boxes to the coffee table and carefully arranged her pink-and-lavender print skirt to cover her knees. She opened a pink box. She had artist's hands: long fingered and slender.

"This is a pearl floral design I call my Enchanted Garden," she said. Her voice was almost a whisper, as if she were sharing a secret. "See the delicate floral vines curling around the bedded plants?" She pointed to a vine with a pink-painted fingernail.

Bedded? Josie wondered. Are the plants supposed to be bedded—or me?

She thought about Saturday night with Ted and hoped she didn't blush.

"This is a magic garden," Denise said, and gave a summery sigh. "The deeper you go into it, the more you will become lost in its sensuality. Love is the force that enchants in this garden, and you'll carry it in your heart—and on your head on your wedding day."

Josie was thinking of other bedded delights. She bit the inside of her cheek to keep from giggling. There was no way she'd put those profligate pearls on her head.

"I don't think so," Josie said.

Denise opened a deep blue velvet box. "I call this Sleeping Beauty," she said. "It's a true princess tiara. When Prince Charming's warm lips first awakened Sleeping Beauty, she woke up something in him, too."

The beast? Josie thought. Oops, wrong fairy tale.

"They lived happily ever after," Denise said. "I like to think it was love at first sight, accessories with the perfect hair jewelry." She smiled dreamily and Josie saw she was wearing blue eye shadow.

Is Denise telling me a bedtime story? she wondered. There she was, back in bed again. Josie was desperate to end the tiara talk before she started laughing uncontrollably. Her future depended on Denise's help. A picture of her mother-in-law popped into her mind, and her giggling fit vanished.

"That is lovely," Josie said. She tried to match Denise's flowery language. "But I fell in love with that baroque pearl tiara. It won my heart and I'm sure it would seal my fiancé's love forever. I was so sad when I learned it was sold."

"Sold?" Denise said. The rosy dream clouds fled before her dark frown. "That tiara wasn't sold. It was stolen from this shop."

"That explains why I thought I saw it on eBay," Josie said.

"You what?" Now Denise's soft eyes were hard with fury.

"Well, it sure looked like your tiara," Josie said. "Rita said you never sell your work online. It's all unique."

"It is!" Denise grew more agitated. "And I don't!"

"I wanted to buy that tiara Sunday," Josie said. "Rita said you'd sold it Saturday to another bride."

"I did nothing of the kind," Denise said. "I sold two rhinestone tiaras and one crystal design that day, but no pearls."

"Maybe I'm wrong," Josie said. "Would you recognize the tiara if you saw it online?"

"Would a mother know her child?" Denise asked. "I'll call up eBay on the store computer and you'll find it." It was an order.

Denise almost ran to the computer perched behind the counter. Her fingers stumbled over the keys, but she found the site. Josie located the tiara in a few clicks.

"There," she said. "That one. It says, 'Pink and cranberry pearls with green baroque pearl leaves. Sure to become a family heirloom.' The seller isn't asking for bids. It's nine hundred dollars."

"That's my design," Denise said. "I spent sixteen hours working with those pearls and I know those green leaves down to the last twist and turn. That lying bitch."

Her anger could have blasted the pretty flowers on her print skirt into ashes.

"Does your store have a shoplifting problem?" Josie asked.

"Problem? I'll say. If the thief isn't caught soon, I'll have to close. I've lost almost ten thousand dollars in merchandise and I couldn't figure out who was doing it. Now I know—it's Rita."

"You don't know," Josie said. She hadn't realized her ruse would ignite Denise's fiery rage. Now she was afraid the shop owner might hurt Rita. She wanted her caught, not killed.

"Rita's not listed as the seller," Josie said. "It could be someone else. It could be a gang of shoplifters, posing as brides and ripping you off."

"No, it's her," Denise said. "I keep my expensive stock under lock and key in the back room. I came in Saturday afternoon. I know we didn't show or sell any pearl tiaras the rest of the day. You were the last person to see that tiara, and you didn't steal it or you wouldn't be here trying to buy it.

"Rita was the last person to have the tiara. She stole it and now she's trying to sell it. If only Molly hadn't died, I would have stopped these thefts sooner. Molly was going to tell me."

"Was she the poor bride shot by that crazy woman from Boca?" Josie asked.

"That was her," Denise said. "Molly was the sweetest girl. She was crazy about weddings, which made her a super saleswoman. I miss her so much. She had a real knack for dealing with customers. When she and Rita were planning their weddings, I gave them generous discounts on their flowers, veils, and tiaras.

"Then they both had bad luck and had to cancel. I felt so bad for them. I refunded their flower deposits and took back their tiaras and veils. That's against my policy, but the merchandise was in perfect condition. I could still sell them, so I made an exception.

"Molly didn't have to worry about money, but she was grateful. She brought me tulips as a thank-you gift. Rita wrote me a little note. I knew she was in debt and gave her extra hours so she could earn more money. And that's how she repaid my generosity—by stealing."

"When did you first notice the thefts?" Josie asked.

"Now that I look back, they started about the time Rita's fiancé broke off their engagement. At first, small things were missing—a short blusher veil with seed pearls, then a cathedral-length veil in tulle. Next I noticed some bridal jewelry missing: a silver bracelet, a little gold necklace, cultured pearl earrings, all mass-produced and under a hundred dollars.

"Then the losses escalated. My one-of-a-kind designs started disappearing. I had to keep them locked up in the back. I thought we were being targeted by a gang of shoplifters, like you suggested. I was at my wit's end and couldn't afford to hire a private detective.

"I knew—well, I thought—Rita loved my store as much as Molly. I asked them to be on the lookout for the shoplifter. I promised a thousand-dollar bonus to whoever found the thief.

"Molly came to me the night before she was shot, very nervous. She said she knew who was taking my merchandise. I wanted her to tell me right then, but she said I'd have to wait until the next day."

"Was Rita at the shop when Molly told you this?" Josie asked.

"Yes," Denise said. "I knew Molly seemed on edge, but she hadn't been herself since that terrible Dr. Ted. I should have paid more attention to what Molly said. But I was so eager to get the thief's name. She refused to tell me until the next day even though I kept badgering her.

"Rita must have overheard us. We were in the back room, but this is a small shop. She could have listened at the door.

"Josie, did I send poor Molly to her doom?"

Chapter 24

"Did I send poor Molly to her doom?"

Denise's dramatic words belonged in a melodrama. But the shop owner's nightmare question fit with the Victorian velvet and frills of Denise's Dreams.

"It's not your fault," Josie said. "You had no idea she was a killer. We'll call the police now."

"No! We can't!" Denise said. "You'll kill my little store." She was wringing her hands like a maiden pleading with a mustache-twirling villain.

"Rita has to be arrested," Josie said.

"I know she does," Denise said. "But I've already had the murder victim working at my store. If customers find out the killer worked here, too, no bride will buy anything from me. My store can't be connected with a killer. I sell happy ever-afters."

Right, Josie thought. Molly is dead forever, and you're worried about your bottom line. The veils on satin stands looked like accusing ghosts. Dainty ruffles and sugar-sweet flowers covered Denise's steely selfishness.

"At least wait till tomorrow," Denise said. "Rita comes in at noon. I'll fire her the moment she walks in this store. Then when she's arrested and the story hits the media again, I can say she doesn't work here."

"You'll be alone when Rita comes in," Josie said.

"She's already killed once. What if she tries to shoot you?"

"I'll shoot her right in the eye," Denise said.

Josie shifted away from those hard, angry eyes.

"Look." The shop owner modestly brushed back her skirt to show a sheer stocking and a pink lace garter with a lipstick-sized gold tube. "Pepper spray," she said.

Josie's eyebrows nearly jumped into her hairline.

"You're right. I'm here alone sometimes," Denise said. "If I'm attacked, no one will hear me scream. I got this to defend myself. It's nice of you to worry, but I'll be safe. Please wait till after twelve before you go to the police."

"On one condition," Josie said. "Only if you fire Rita the minute she comes in here. I can't wait any longer than noon. An innocent woman is in jail."

"I promise," Denise said. "As a reward for helping me, you can have a five-hundred-dollar credit on any item in this store."

"Uh, thanks." Josie didn't want anything from the shop. She didn't like Denise or her dreams.

But she left filled with hope, floating down the path through the picket fence, happily humming "The Wedding March." Josie would march down the aisle to a different tune, but she'd get married the day after Thanksgiving.

She wanted to call Ted with the good news. But she couldn't touch that SPEED DIAL button. Too much could still go wrong. She didn't want to raise his hopes—or Lenore's. She'd tell Ted the moment the cops took Rita into custody.

That small hesitation didn't stop her joy. She felt a river of happiness coursing through her veins. Josie Marcus, anonymous mystery shopper, had solved the stalker bride's murder and tied it up neatly with a big white bow.

It seemed so obvious now.

Rita, deeply in debt after her aborted wedding, started stealing from the store where she worked and selling the items on eBay. The thefts escalated from small, untraceable jewelry to unique designs. The store was in trouble and Denise had offered a reward to her staff to find the shoplifter.

Molly discovered her best friend was the thief destroying Denise's Dreams. She wanted to tell Denise she'd found the thief, but not when Rita was working. Denise insisted and Rita overheard the conversation. Rita must have suspected that Molly was on to her before that day. Rita had been at the Blue Rose when Ted's mom flashed her gun. It would be easy for an accomplished thief to pocket Lenore's pistol.

Rita hadn't boosted a few items at the shop. She'd boldly helped herself to jewelry worth thousands of dollars. She'd committed felonies. The amount she stole was easily documented through her online sales. Rita was looking at serious jail time. Molly had to be silenced before the store opened the next morning.

Rita had no trouble finding Molly. The stalker bride was still obsessed with Ted. Rita followed her to the clinic parking lot and shot her. Then she framed Lenore.

At least Molly's killer will be brought to justice, Josie thought, as she drove home. She had a bright future again. Josie reveled in the pink glow of the sunset and her rose-tinted dreams. She parked her Honda in front of her home, careful that the back bumper was within her mom's property line.

Even that precaution didn't help. Mrs. M shot out of her front door like she'd been launched.

"Josie Marcus!" she screamed. "Your daughter is setting off bottle rockets in your backyard."

"She can't be," Josie said. "Where would Amelia get fireworks?"

"I don't know, but she did," Mrs. M said with an unpleasant smirk. "See for yourself. Before the police arrive."

"The police?" Josie said. "You called the police on my daughter?"

"Bottle rockets are illegal in St. Louis County," Mrs.

M said. She barged right down Jane's walkway and through the back gate, wearing a flowered top bigger than a botanical garden. A bewildered Josie followed, wondering why so many scary women wore flowers.

Mrs. M pointed to the bottle rockets, her bulky body quivering with indignation. "There," she said. "Right there! That girl is a delinquent, just like her mother!"

A geyser of brown liquid as tall as the two-story house shot out of a two-liter Diet Coke bottle. A second geyser erupted after it. Then a third.

"Amelia Marcus, stop that immediately," Mrs. Mueller commanded.

Amelia ignored her. She was clicking at the soda gushers with Josie's digital camera.

Josie had never seen bottle geysers before, but she recognized the scream of a siren. It was followed by running feet on the walkway. Officer Doris Ann Norris burst into the Marcus backyard, and Josie felt weak with relief. She knew the smart, street-savvy Maplewood police officer.

"Is there a problem?" Officer Norris asked. "The dispatcher received a complaint that someone was setting off fireworks."

"No," Josie said.

"Yes," Mrs. M said. "That young troublemaker is setting off bottle rockets."

"She is?" Officer Norris strolled over to the foaming Diet Coke bottles. "Looks awfully wet for fireworks," she said.

She stuck her finger into a brown puddle and tasted it. "You used Diet Coke, Miss Marcus," she said. "You are Amelia Marcus, aren't you?"

"Yes, ma'am," Amelia said.

Josie was relieved her daughter remembered her manners. Amelia's voice shook with fear, and the blood had drained from her face, but she stood straight and tall.

"I knew your daughter was trouble, Josie Marcus," Mrs. M said. "She's known to the police."

Office Norris turned to Mrs. Mueller. "I do know this young woman. I helped Amelia and her mother when they had a vandalism problem some time ago. I barely recognized Amelia because she's so grown-up now."

A smile flitted across Amelia's chalk white face.

"Some people improve with age," Officer Norris said. Her barb bounced off Mrs. M's gray helmet head.

"Using Diet Coke is very thoughtful," she told Amelia. "Regular soda leaves a sticky mess."

"That's what I heard," Amelia said. "I can just hose this away."

"How many Mentos did you use in your bottles?" Officer Norris asked.

"A whole roll of mints in each one. It's a science experiment."

"You load them with a tube or a roll of paper?" Officer Norris asked.

"Paper tube," Amelia said, sounding more confident. Her color was starting to return.

"An old-school scientist," Officer Norris said, nodding her approval. "You used the more difficult method."

"I got three bottles to erupt one after the other," Amelia said. "It was awesome! I was shooting them when I heard screaming and Mrs. Mueller yelled at me to stop, but you can't stop the experiment once it starts."

"You're not arresting her?" Mrs. M looked like she might explode with disappointment.

"Miss Marcus didn't do anything wrong. It's not illegal to test the fizz factor of Diet Coke," Officer Norris said. "Dropping chewy mints into soda to release the carbonation is a legitimate scientific experiment. Steve Spangler blogged about it on his science Web site. Usually the geyser goes about twenty feet in the air. Miss Marcus was smart to conduct her experiment outside, away from the house."

"Well, I never," Mrs. M said, deflating like a week-old balloon. Not only was Amelia escaping punishment, but the police officer praised her. Josie smiled.

"Your generation used vinegar and baking soda," Officer Norris said.

"We did nothing of the kind," Mrs. M said.

"Sure you did," Officer Norris said. "My pop talked about it. He and his friends used glass bottles. Much more dangerous than plastic."

"Your job is to protect and serve citizens," Mrs. M said. "Not encourage hooligans."

"You are so right, ma'am," Officer Norris said. "And we can't do that when people waste our time. You're a church lady, aren't you? Active at St. Philomena's?"

"I am president of the Ladies' Sodality," Mrs. M said, "past president of the altar decoration committee, first vice president of the music committee, and head of the 2013 Harvest Festival."

"Impressive," Officer Norris said. "You must spend a lot of time at church."

"At least an hour every day, not including Mass and novenas," Mrs. M said.

"You've had plenty of exposure to the Gospels then. Might want to reread that part about loving your neighbor as yourself."

"I'm going home," Mrs. M said, and stomped off.

"Am I in trouble?" Amelia asked.

"Not with me," Officer Norris said. "What your mother decides is out of my jurisdiction."

Chapter 25

Jane held a martini glass the size of a punch bowl.

"I bought this for you," she said. She shoved the glass at Josie and walked into her kitchen with her sidekick, Stuart Little.

The monster martini glass felt surprisingly light. "Thanks, Mom, but I don't need a drink at nine in the morning."

"It's not for you," Jane said. "It's for your wedding. It will look cute on the candy bar we're having for the children at the reception. It's acrylic, so if they knock it over, it can't hurt anyone. I could use a cup of coffee."

Jane poured herself a cup and sat down at the kitchen table. Stuart Little sat at her feet. "Woof!" he said.

"Uh, good morning," Josie said.

She filled a bowl of water for the shih tzu and he wagged his tail. His pal Harry gave him a friendly swat; then both pets slurped their water.

While her guests had their drinks, Josie examined Jane's gift. "I like it," she said. "We can put the Hershey's Kisses in it. I've bought all the candy and hid it."

"From Amelia?" Jane asked.

"From me," Josie said. "I'd eat it all before the wedding. Your hair looks nice."

"Aggie did a good job, didn't she?" Jane said. "I got back from my appointment right after the police left. I couldn't believe that old meddler called the police on my granddaughter. Are you going to punish Amelia? You weren't sure yesterday."

"I needed to sleep on it," Josie said. "I was furious at Mrs. Mueller and didn't want to take it out on my daughter. This morning, I told Amelia I didn't like that she'd lied to me about doing a school science experiment.

"Amelia said she didn't lie. She never said it was a *school* science experiment, just a science experiment."

"She's right," Jane said. "That's exactly what she said when we had our cooking class. You missed a good round steak, by the way."

"I'm sure it was," Josie said. "Amelia could have told me she was going to have soda geysers erupting in the backyard."

"It was harmless," Jane said. "She cleaned up afterward, and even recycled the bottles. Science is important for young women. I had to take home ec. Now girls are encouraged to go into the same professions as boys. She could be a research scientist."

"Not by the way she talked about that science experiment," Josie said. "Amelia told me the truth—but only the truth I needed to know. She's going to be a lawyer."

"Like her grandfather," Jane said.

The man who abandoned us, Josie thought. The conversation wilted. The two women sipped coffee and watched Stuart Little chase Harry around the kitchen. The cat skidded across the floor and knocked over his water.

"Time-out," Josie said, stepping over the puddle. She captured Harry, who went limp as a peaceful protester, and shut him in Amelia's bathroom. Harry howled. Stuart followed his pal into exile and sat outside the closed door, whimpering.

Josie mopped up the spilled water, then refilled Harry's bowl and the two coffee cups.

"Now, where were we?" she asked, sitting down.

"I asked if you were going to punish Amelia," Jane said.

"No. She didn't do anything wrong," Josie said. "But

I'm glad we're moving away from that old trouble-maker."

"I wish *she'd* move," Jane said. "It will be strange not having you and Amelia living here with me."

"We couldn't have made it without your help, Mom," Josie said. "All your free babysitting. All the times you took Amelia to school or picked her up. You gave me the luxury of a free on-call nanny."

"You gave me a beautiful granddaughter," Jane said. "I'll still be here for you, anytime you need me. She can stay with me if you and Ted need some time together."

Josie squeezed her mother's hand. "Thanks, Mom. But it's time we left your comfortable nest so you can rent this apartment for what it's really worth. More coffee?"

Josie felt uneasy having such an emotional conversation with her mother. She knew Jane loved her, but she'd had high expectations for her only child. When Josie dropped out of school to have Amelia, Jane had been bitterly disappointed—and made sure Josie knew it.

"No, thanks," Jane said. She hesitated, then said, "Josie, I'm sorry."

"For what?" Josie asked.

Jane's voice cracked. "For being so mean when you were carrying Amelia." Tears streamed down Jane's face. "If you weren't such a good daughter, I would have driven you away forever."

"You had good reasons to be angry at me," Josie said.

"I thought I had good reasons," Jane said. "I didn't want you to be dependent on a man for your living, the way I was. I didn't want you to take a job that paid nothing while you raised your daughter. I didn't want you to make my mistakes."

Jane was quietly weeping.

Josie grabbed a handful of tissues and hugged her mother. "Sh. It's okay," she said. "You have nothing to cry about."

"You handled your life better than I did," Jane said, sniffling and mopping her eyes.

"Only because I had your help," Josie said, and kissed her mother on her soft, worn cheek. She caught Jane's familiar scent of Estée Lauder perfume and saw the small bald spot on her crown that her carefully sprayed hair didn't quite cover.

My mother's life was hard and I made it harder, Josie thought. She hugged her again.

Jane blew her nose, straightened up, and said, "Well. I'm sorry for that silly scene. You have enough to worry about."

"I'm glad you said it, Mom," Josie said.

"Don't make me start crying again," Jane said. She sounded annoyed.

Josie was relieved her mother had returned to her prickly self.

"I've saved a little money—about a thousand dollars," Jane said. "I want you and Ted to have it for a down payment on a new home. You don't have any savings and Ted still has his school loans."

"Thanks, Mom," Josie said. "That's way too generous." She wanted to lighten the heavy atmosphere. "Would you like to go along on my last mystery-shopping assignment as a single woman? I have to taste wedding cakes this morning."

"I'd love to," Jane said. "I could use some cake to go with all that coffee. What time is your appointment?"

"I have to make it now."

"Isn't that short notice for a cake tasting?"

"It is," Josie said. "That's part of the customer service test for this assignment."

"I'll take Stuart Little upstairs while you make your call," Jane said, "and meet you at your car."

The shih tzu and Harry were poking paws under the door in an elaborate interspecies game. "I hope Harry gets along with Festus as well as he does with your dog," Josie said.

"It will all work out, Josie," Jane said fiercely. "This time, listen to your mother. Come, Stuart." She climbed the back stairs, Stuart pattering behind her.

Josie smiled through her tears as she called the store for her mystery-shopping assignment.

"Cakes by Cookie, this is Ellen speaking," a woman answered. "How may I help you?"

A pleasant voice, Josie thought. She was glad Ellen gave the proper greeting.

"I'm getting married soon," Josie said. "I need a cake tasting right away."

"Congratulations," Ellen said. "When would you like to come in?"

"Today?" Josie sounded hesitant. "I'm sorry."

"Oh, honey, of course you can come in today," Ellen said. "But we usually make cake-tasting appointments at least two weeks in advance. I can show you photos of our wedding cakes and give samples of similar cakes, but it won't be an actual wedding cake tasting. Will that work for you?"

"Absolutely," Josie said. "My mom will be with me. Could we come this morning?"

"The morning rush is over, so I'll have some time," Ellen said. "Our store is across from the Galleria mall."

"We'll be there in ten minutes," Josie said.

Once again, Josie smelled the sugary aroma of Cakes by Cookie before she saw the store's big polka-dot sign. Ellen was a tall, bosomy woman with straight straw-colored hair.

"I've fixed a little tasting table for you," she said, and ushered Josie and Jane to their seats.

Ellen told them about cake flavors, fillings, icing and decorations, gave Josie and Jane samples of similar cakes, and showed them wedding cake photos in a fat ring binder.

Josie asked the required questions, and Ellen gave detailed answers. "What if I want flowers on my cake?" Josie asked. "Real flowers."

"Those are lovely," Ellen said, "but your florist will have to provide them. Cut flowers are often sprayed with pesticides. Are you sure you want that on your food?"

"What else do you suggest besides sugar roses or ribbons?" Josie asked.

"We have some amusing cake toppers," Ellen said, and turned to the cake toppers section in the binder. "We have a bride and groom with fairy wings and a princess and her knight in armor for fairy-tale weddings."

"Pretty," Josie said. "But ours is more modern."

"Here's a bridal couple both talking on their cell phones," Ellen said.

"A little too modern," Josie said.

"How about this one where the bride wears the groom's pants and he wears boxer shorts with his tux?"

"Interesting, but no," Josie said.

"We have this sexy cake topper." Ellen showed her a bridal couple from the back, grabbing each other's bottoms.

Jane looked shocked.

Ellen quickly turned the page. "For those who take 'till death do us part' seriously," she said, "we have a selection of skeleton brides and grooms. Like this one." The grinning bride had a tattered veil on her skull.

"A little grim," Josie said.

"My daughter is not getting married on Halloween," Jane said.

"You'll love our stylish monogrammed initials," Ellen said. "We have silver, gold, Swarovski crystal, pearls."

"Elegant," Jane said.

They looked at a few more cake toppers, then thanked Ellen and left with brochures, a sample contract, and a promise to call if they decided to go with her store.

Back in Josie's car, Jane said, "I do hope you're going to give that nice Ellen a good report."

"The highest rating. She deserves it," Josie said.

"What now?" Jane said.

"Now I have a wedding errand I need to do alone," Josie said.

I'm having tea with the innocent woman I branded a killer, she thought.

Chapter 26

Tuesday, October 30

It was all over for Rita, except for her arrest.

Josie's lunch with Phoebe Winstid at the Blue Rose Tearoom was a waste of time. But she'd already set up this scheme to politely interrogate George's mother.

I have to go through with this, Josie told herself. I can't waste Phoebe's time, too. At least I'll have a good lunch.

She arrived at the Blue Rose fifteen minutes early and talked to Rachel, the plump, rosy-cheeked hostess. "My friend Phoebe will be asking for me," Josie said. "Lunch is my treat. Please don't bring the check to our table. Here's my credit card. I'll settle the bill after she leaves."

"I'll take care of it for you," Rachel said. She seated Josie at a table by the window and brought tea in a Blue Willow pot. Josie poured herself a cup and studied the antique photo of a young woman stiffly posed in a long dark dress with leg-of-mutton sleeves. She stared solemnly from the wall across from her table.

Phoebe arrived precisely at noon. On the phone, she'd sounded too young to be George's mother. She looked that way, too. Josie guessed her age at about sixty, but she seemed no older than forty-five.

Phoebe was about Josie's height—five feet six—and slender. Rich brown hair framed her heart-shaped face.

She dressed like a woman who'd once had money. Her black pantsuit was well cut but slightly shiny at the cuffs.

Josie introduced herself and a server brought a basket of cranberry scones and a tiered plate of salmon and cucumber sandwiches.

"It's so nice of you to share your lunch with me," Phoebe said.

"I'm happy to do it," Josie said.

"My son says I'm too young for tearooms, but I love them," Phoebe said. "Tea is so gracious, don't you think? This is a return to a gentler time."

Josie glanced at the young woman in the old photo on the wall. Her troubles had been over for more than a century, but Josie doubted that her sorrows, losses, and fears had been any gentler than Josie's.

"Maybe in retrospect," Josie said.

"My late husband, Walter, always said I romanticized the past," Phoebe said.

"When Walt was alive, I'd lunch here once a week with my girlfriends. Now that money's a little tight, I don't come here quite so often. Enough about me. Tell me about yourself. Are you married? Do you work?"

"I'm getting married the day after Thanksgiving," Josie said.

The tea and crustless sandwiches disappeared as Josie told Phoebe about her upcoming wedding at the Jewel Box, the reception, the flowers, and her fiancé the doctor—everything except that the doctor was the notorious Ted Scottsmeyer.

"I've been rattling on too much about my wedding," Josie said.

"I asked you," Phoebe said. "I like hearing happy things. The last time I was here I was with my son, George. My son is a beer drinker, but he made the sacrifice for me."

"He sounds thoughtful," Josie said.

"He's the best," Phoebe said. "I'm so lucky. George is

engaged, but he won't be getting married in St. Louis. He lives in Montana."

"He likes the great outdoors?" Josie said.

"He says Montana is amazing, but that's not why he moved there. He was trying to get away from a woman."

"Unlucky in love?" Josie asked.

"It wasn't love," Phoebe said. "He didn't even like Molly."

"Molly?" Josie said. "Why does that name seem familiar? What's her last name?"

"Molly Deaver," Phoebe said. "You can't turn on the TV without hearing her name lately. She was shot by the mother of a man she was stalking. Molly went to his place of business in a bridal dress and he didn't know anything about the wedding."

"That's right," Josie said. "Now I remember."

"Before she stalked that man, she latched onto my son. All George did was sell Molly some carpet. My son is a top salesman for Brenhoff Carpet and Flooring Corporation. They're a national chain with stores in forty-eight states."

Josie found Phoebe's maternal pride endearing.

"George was working at the Clayton store in St. Louis," Phoebe said, "and sold this Molly Deaver wall-to-wall for her living room. That's all he did. George never showed the slightest interest in her, but she started stalking my son. She turned up at his store, she watched him in the parking lot, even followed him to his apartment. He couldn't turn around without running into Molly Deaver.

"George had no interest in dating her, but I could see why she was attracted to him. My son is handsome, reliable, has a steady job, and he treats me well. You can tell a lot about a man by how he treats his mother. The stalking got so bad, George couldn't even go to the supermarket without running into her."

"Did George get a restraining order?" Josie asked.

"He didn't want one," Phoebe said. "It would have

been bad for his career. Molly told everyone they were engaged and then formally announced it in the paper. When George saw a chance to move to the Billings store in Montana, he jumped at it. I hated to see him go, but I understood.

"I hate to admit it, but he made the right decision. He's just been elected president of the National Carpeting and Floor Covering Association. They have two thousand members."

The Brenhoff Web site said seventeen hundred, Josie thought, but a proud mom was allowed a little exaggeration.

"That's why George was back here this month," Phoebe said. "He was sworn in as president at the big convention in St. Louis. My son is a busy man, but he's not too important to take his mother to her favorite tearoom for lunch.

"When George and I were here, she sat right at that corner table."

"Molly?" Josie asked.

"No, the woman who killed her," Phoebe said. "Lenore something from Florida. Dramatic-looking woman. Liked being the center of attention. She was showing off her pistol in the tearoom. Pretty little thing. She showed off the pearl grips with her initials. She made quite an impression. When I saw her on TV again after she shot that crazy bride, I recognized her right away."

"Do you think Lenore did it?" Josie asked.

"I'm sure, and she did the world a favor," Phoebe said. "Don't believe what you see on TV. Channel Seven made that bride into a victim, but she was insane.

"I told my son I'd testify on Lenore's behalf, but George begged me not to. He wants to forget Molly ever happened.

"But I won't. I lost my son. George had to move to Montana to get away from her. Thanks to one demented woman, I lost my boy. He's living more than thirteen hundred miles away. I don't have the money to fly there, and it's a two- or three-day drive.

"George says the move to Montana turned out better than he hoped. That's where he met Renee, the woman he wants to marry. She'll make a good daughter-in-law."

"Now that Molly's dead, they could move back here," Josie said.

"I'd like that, but I don't think it will happen," Phoebe said. "Renee has her own career. She's the manager of a rental car agency there. Lot of tourists fly into Billings and rent cars to drive to Yellowstone National Park. Renee would have to give up a good job to move back here.

"If it hadn't been for that mental case, my boy would have met a nice St. Louis girl and settled down here to raise a family. And I'd be taking my grandbabies to the zoo, the Arch, and picking apples at Eckert's Orchard in the fall like all the other grandmas.

"Now that won't happen," Phoebe said. "She deprived me of my son and his future life. I'm glad she's dead."

Phoebe slammed down her teacup with such force, there was an audible clink on the saucer. "Sorry," she said. "I didn't mean to get carried away."

"You have good reason to be upset," Josie said. "It's nearly two o'clock. I have to pick up my daughter at school."

"It was a pleasure to meet you," Phoebe said.

Josie walked George's mother to the door of the restaurant. She watched Phoebe unlock her charcoal Chevy Impala, waved good-bye, then returned to pay the bill.

The lunch crowd was clearing out of the tearoom parking lot. Inside her car, Josie opened her cell phone to call Denise's Dreams for the good news. By now Denise would have fired Rita and the cops would have arrested the real killer. Then she could call Ted and tell him Molly's murderer had been arrested.

Time for Josie's dream, she thought as she dialed Denise's Dreams.

A worried, apologetic Denise answered the shop phone. "I'm sorry, Josie," she said. "Rita hasn't reported for work yet. I've called her every half hour since noon. I need a little more time."

"You have until three o'clock," Josie said. "Then I call the police."

"I'll keep trying," Denise said. "She's always so reliable. Maybe she's sick."

Josie was the one who felt sick. Rita knew they were on to her. She'd run.

Chapter 27

Tuesday, October 30

"Josie, I don't know what's wrong," Denise said. "I keep calling and calling, but Rita doesn't answer her phone."

Josie called the shop owner as soon as she got home from school with Amelia. "I can't reach her," Denise said. "I'm worried she's sick."

"And I'm worried Rita skipped town," Josie said. "I gave you till three o'clock. Your time is up. An innocent woman is locked up while Rita goes free."

"There's no way Rita could know what we were planning," Denise said. She had a defensive edge.

"Really? Rita already figured out that Molly knew she was stealing from your shop," Josie said. "I'm calling the police."

"No! Please!" Denise sounded frantic. "Could you go by her apartment first? Just to see if she's okay? I'm really, really worried."

"You want me to go alone to an apartment where there's a killer?" Josie asked. "I saw that movie and didn't like the ending."

"You could take my pepper spray," Denise said.

"I have my own," Josie said. "I'm not going to Rita's apartment alone."

"You don't have to sound so mean," Denise said. "I'd go with you, but I can't leave the shop. I have a customer coming at three thirty. A real bride, not a pretend one who wastes my time and doesn't buy anything."

"I caught your shoplifter," Josie said, trying to tamp down her anger. "I didn't waste your time. I saved your business."

"I know you did, but unless I sell enough to cover Rita's losses, I won't survive," Denise said. Her irritating whine drilled into Josie's ear.

"What if she slipped in the shower and she's lying there hurt?" Denise said. "Anyway, you think she ran away. If you're right, she won't even be home."

I want this over, Josie thought. The longer Denise dithers, the farther Rita can run.

Denise took Josie's hesitation as a sign she was wavering. "Good," she said. "Rita lives in apartment 103. Second building on the right on that little street off Southwest Avenue in Rock Road Village. Her apartment is on the first floor and has big sliding doors. You might be able to see if she's safe without going inside."

I'll take one look and if Rita's at home, I'm calling the police myself, Josie thought. To hell with Denise's precious store. I'll ask Mom to go with me. She can stay in the car and call 911 if I need help.

"Then you'll do it?" Denise asked, her voice shrill with hope.

"Only if my friend is available to go with me. I'll ask her. If she says no, I'm calling the police."

Jane was home. "I'll go with you, Josie," she said. "I need to get out. What's this about?"

"This trip may help us find Molly Deaver's killer," Josie said. "I'll tell you in the car."

Josie stopped by Amelia's room where her daughter was texting with lightning-fast thumbs. "Grandma and I will be gone about an hour," Josie said. "I'm trusting you to stay home alone again."

Amelia jumped up. "I will! I'll be good."

"I hope so," Josie said, running out the door.

On the short drive over, she gave her mother a sanitized version of Rita's role: "She's been stealing from the shop and selling the items on eBay," Josie said. "Molly figured it out. She wanted to tell Denise the next day, but Rita found out and shot her with Lenore's pistol."

"Terrible," Jane said. "But this Rita must be clever. She framed Lenore and got away with murder."

"She's not getting away with anything," Josie said.

"Do you think she has a gun?" Jane asked.

"I think she's skipped town," Josie said. "Molly's murder weapon was left at the scene, remember?"

"I forgot," Jane said. "So much is going on. We won't have to take Rita into custody, will we?"

"No, I just want to make sure she's home and then I'll call the police."

"Is this the place?" Jane asked, wrinkling her nose. "It was so pretty when it was built. But that was in 1968."

"It's not bad," Josie said. But she noticed the mansard roof was missing a few shingles and the doors could use fresh paint. She thought the climber roses on the entrance archway would appeal to Rita's romantic side.

She turned into the parking lot and saw a shiny green Kia in spot 103. Rita was home, Josie decided. At least her car was.

"I'll check the front and back doors, Mom," Josie said. "Wait in the car. If I'm not back in five minutes, call 911."

"You are *not* giving your mother orders," Jane said. "I'm going with you."

"Mom, you can't. What if someone attacks us?"

"I'll stay behind on the sidewalk," Jane said. "I've punched in 911. All I have to do is hit the button if we need help."

Josie didn't argue. She charged up the sidewalk to Rita's porch, prettily framed with golden mums in blue pots. She rang the doorbell, tried the shiny brass handle, and pounded on the door. No answer. She peered in the front window, but the view was blocked by ruffled Cape Cod curtains.

"I'm going around to the back," Josie said.

Josie dodged a toddler's orange plastic tricycle on the sidewalk to the back of the apartment, while Jane trotted behind. Rita lived in a corner unit with sliding doors and a sunny patio with potted mums and lacy wrought-iron furniture.

Josie peered through the back sliders and saw a dark wood dining table with an overturned coffee cup and a dining chair on its side.

"That doesn't look right," Josie said. She knocked on the sliders until they rattled, calling, "Rita!"

No answer. Josie yanked the handle and the glass door slid open.

"Rita?" Josie called. "May I come in?"

Silence.

"Go on in," Jane said, and gave Josie a small impatient push.

Josie's foot crunched on the shattered remains of a china teddy bear cookie jar.

Josie and Jane followed a path of destruction through the kitchen, trying to avoid the broken glass and splintered china.

"Grandma had an old Magic Chef stove like that," Josie said.

"This isn't a house tour," Jane said. "Move!"

They tiptoed around the shards of a glass vase and a smashed plant stand. A trail of teacup fragments spilled down the hall past the living room. Josie stopped suddenly, staring at a fire-engine red vintage Coke machine in the living room. Curly letters declared, "Drink Coca-Cola. 10 Cents."

Jane ran into her daughter's back.

"Rita left the shop so that Coke machine could be delivered," Josie said.

"Wouldn't want it in my living room," Jane said. "It's big as an icebox. Keep moving. We need to get out of here." She nearly dragged Josie down the hall.

Now Josie could see a broken milk-glass lamp in the bedroom doorway.

"Careful, Josie," Jane said. "The burglar could be hiding in the closet."

But Josie had stepped over the lamp and was already inside. The blue satin bedspread was nearly pulled off the mattress.

Josie saw a china foot on the floor by the far side of the bed. A statue? She moved carefully forward. The foot was an odd greenish white and the toenails were painted pale pink. That was no statue. The foot was connected to a slender bare leg in a blue satin robe.

"No, no, no, no," Josie cried.

But no matter how hard she tried to deny it, Josie knew she was looking at a dead woman.

Rita was sprawled next to the bed in a blue satin robe, her golden hair matted with thick black blood.

"Don't come in, Mom," Josie said, her voice shaking. "Rita's dead. Call 911."

"How do you know she's dead?" Jane asked.

"Her head's all crushed in," Josie said. She stumbled out of the bedroom, tripping over the broken lamp.

Jane paled. "I'm going outside," she said. "I think I'm going to be sick."

She must have dragged Josie with her. She and Jane were sitting in matching wrought-iron chairs on Rita's patio.

Jane's queasiness seemed to vanish when she made the call. Now Josie felt dizzy in the hot afternoon sun. The patio tilted and she held on to the chair arm, trying to focus on her mother's conversation with the emergency operator. The chair's wrought-iron curlicue poked Josie in the back.

"Yes, I believe the young woman is dead," Jane was saying. "No, we're not inside the apartment. We're on the back patio. We'll go sit on the front steps and wait for the police. No, I won't hang up."

Jane took Josie's hand and led her to the front steps. Josie sat on a sun-warmed step and mimed to her mother that she was calling Amelia on her cell.

"Amelia," Josie said, her voice thick with phony cheer, "Grandma and I are going to be a little later. I'm trusting you to be on your own. Call my cell phone or Ted's if there's any trouble."

It felt good saying that. She had extra backup now. Josie heard the woeful sound of the sirens and said, "I love you, sweetie. See you soon."

"The police are here," Jane said to the emergency operator, and clicked off her cell phone. "I'm glad you called Amelia," she said. "Now you're going to tell the police exactly what's going on with Rita. It's their job to catch her killer. Her death may have nothing to do with Molly Deaver's murder. She could have been killed by a burglar."

"But, Mom." Josie realized she sounded like Amelia.

"No ifs, ands, or buts," Jane said. "I'm telling the police exactly what happened, and so will you." Her jaw was locked into a stubborn outward thrust. Jane was immovable in that mood. Screeching police car tires ended any more conversation.

Josie had had way too much experience with murder scenes lately. This one was eerily similar to Molly Deaver's death. Jane and Josie were put in separate police cars, questioned, and told to wait for the homicide detective.

Josie knew she'd be dealing with Detective Gray. Rock Road Village was too small to have more than one homicide detective. Her mother was right. She'd have to tell him everything. He'd be furious at her meddling.

The yellow crime scene tape had been strung, and cops and techs were swarming over the apartment complex when Detective Gray's Dodge Charger roared into the parking lot. Gray slammed his door so hard, Josie winced. He was met by a uniform, and the two hiked up the walkway and around the back of the apartment. Gray's coat and tie flapped, he moved so fast.

Josie felt sick. She studied the cage that penned her in the back of the patrol car and wondered if she'd wind up behind bars.

Gray stomped down the sidewalk fifteen minutes later, bristling with rage. Even his iron-colored hair looked angry.

He yanked open Josie's door and said, "You again. Get out and stand over there. I want to hear why you're mixed up in this murder and I want the truth. You get one chance or you go to jail."

Josie climbed shakily out of the car and told Gray everything she could remember: the tiara posted for sale on eBay, why Rita had to be the thief, and Denise's outrage when she discovered her trusted employee was stealing from her.

"So you *gave* this Denise twenty-four hours before you called the police?" the detective asked.

Josie nodded.

"And this Denise was upset?"

"Yes," Josie said in small voice. "She's afraid she's going to lose her store."

"Wonderful, Ms. Marcus," he said. "You probably signed that poor woman's death warrant. You do realize you gave this Denise plenty of time to kill the victim and string you along."

Josie felt the tears coming. She didn't want to appear weak in front of the irate detective. She tried to stop crying but couldn't.

"You'd better cry," he said. "That woman was killed because of your meddling. You know that, don't you?"

Josie nodded. She carried a double burden of guilt: Rita was horribly dead and Josie's investigation had hit another dead end.

She'd have to start again to find Molly's killer.

Chapter 28

"Mom, Ted's car is parked outside our house," Josie said. "Something's wrong. Amelia had to call him for help."

She felt a knot of panic twist her stomach. "I should have insisted that detective let me call my daughter," Josie said. "Instead, we've left her alone for almost five hours. That's the longest she's been on her own. She's only eleven. What if she set a pot holder on fire when she fixed herself dinner? Or cut herself with a butcher knife? What if someone tried to break in?"

"Josie," Jane said. "Amelia knows her way around a kitchen better than you do. You haven't had dinner and you're on edge."

Awful possibilities played in Josie's mind, the trailer for her own personal horror movie. "But—," she said.

"Nothing is wrong, Josie, or Mrs. Mueller would be screaming on the lawn. Remember Amelia's science experiment? That big scare turned out to be nothing, too."

"You're right," Josie said as she backed her car behind Ted's. "If there was trouble, we'd see cop cars, fire trucks, ambulances and Mrs. M doing the happy dance."

Josie glanced at her mother as she straightened out the Honda. "You look tired, Mom," she said. She hurried around the car to help Jane.

Her mother shooed her away. "I can still get out of a car," she said. "I'm not some feeble old woman." Indignation gave Jane a little more color. "Go check on Amelia and Ted."

Josie ran up the walkway. Ted met her halfway, wrapping her in his muscular arms. "What's wrong?" he asked.

"Nothing," she said, inhaling his scent of coffee and wood smoke. She kissed him. The nightmare vision of Rita's corpse faded, along with her fears for Amelia. "Now that you're here, absolutely nothing. How did you know I needed you?"

"Amelia said you were working late," he said.

Josie tensed again. "She called you. Something is wrong."

"I called her," Ted said, "after I went to see Mom in jail."

He stopped, then said, "Never thought I'd say that sentence. Mom has a question for you. You didn't answer your cell phone, so I called your home. Amelia said you and Jane were delayed. I figured you were busy with wedding stuff and you'd be hungry when you got home. Anyway, I wanted to ask you the question in person. Amelia and I made chicken with pine nuts."

"I've died and gone to heaven," Josie said. This time her lips lingered on his. "How did you make dinner? I have chicken in the freezer, but no pine nuts."

"Or parsley, lemon juice, or snow peas," he said. "I picked up the ingredients on my way over. Amelia is making the salad now. Your timing is perfect."

"So is yours," Josie said, leaning against him.

"Seriously, Josie, what's wrong? I can see it in your face. You weren't running wedding errands. Something bad happened."

"I found another dead woman," Josie said. "I thought this poor saleswoman had killed Molly. I went to check on her and found her body. She'd been murdered, Ted."

"Who was she?"

"You didn't know her," Josie said. "Rita. A saleswoman at Denise's Dreams. She was Molly's best friend. She even looked like her. I was sure she'd killed Molly."

"You were going to confront a killer alone?" Ted asked.

"No, I had Mom with me," Josie said.

They could hear Jane's slow tread on the sidewalk, as if she were carrying a burden.

"Your mom," Ted said. "Good choice. The Maplewood cops call her for backup all the time."

"Please," Josie said. "No sarcasm. Jane didn't need muscles to call 911. I saw Rita's body, Ted. Her head was crushed in. It was horrible."

"Tell me," he said, his voice soft with sympathy. Josie wanted to cry on his shoulder. But her weary mother was approaching and dinner was waiting.

"After dinner," she said. "What did your mother want?"

"We'll save that for dessert," he said.

Uh-oh, Josie thought. More bad news.

"Amelia made chocolate mint cookies," Ted said. "Wait till you taste them."

"You've already tried them?" She smiled at him.

"She asked my culinary advice." Ted winked, then reached for Jane. "There's my other girl!" He hugged her.

"It's so good to see you, Ted. I don't want to be rude, but if I don't walk my dog, he'll have an accident," Jane said.

"Already walked him, Jane."

"Mom," Jane corrected. "You can call me Mom. If you want to. I don't want to be disrespectful to your real mother."

"Lenore won't mind. She won't let me call her Mom in public," Ted said. "She says I make her look old. I'd be happy to call you Mom."

Jane stood on her tiptoes to kiss his cheek. "I'm pleased and proud to have such a thoughtful son."

They went up the walk arm in arm to Josie's living room.

Stuart Little greeted them, tail wagging. After his ears were scratched, he pattered into the kitchen and slurped water in his bowl. Harry joined him, crunching his dry food.

Josie's table was set for four with a centerpiece of six peach roses.

"Flowers?" Josie said. "For me?"

"Just grocery store roses," Ted said. "Why are you crying?"

"Because they're so beautiful."

Amelia looked embarrassed. "Mom," she said, "don't be lame. Are we going to eat? I'm starving."

Ted poured the wine, and then they ate their salads. "Delicious," Josie said. "What's in this dressing, Amelia?"

"It's my homemade French," Amelia said, failing to hide her pride. "I make it with garlic, paprika, red wine vinegar, oregano and a little sugar."

"I've had lots of French dressing," Jane said, "but not like this. What's your secret?"

"I use vegetable oil instead of olive oil," Amelia said. "I read online that's how the French make real French dressing. Olive oil is too heavy."

The chicken with pine nuts and snow peas was served over pasta and heaped with more praise.

After dinner, they ate cookies until Josie caught her daughter trying to hide a yawn.

"It's almost ten," Josie told her. "It's time for bed."

"But I have to do the dishes," Amelia said. "That's my chore."

"Your hated chore," Josie said. "You did the cooking. You have the night off."

"Awesome," Amelia said. She slung her cat, Harry, up on her shoulder and said, "Night, Grandma. Night, Ted. Thanks for showing me how to fix the chicken."

Ted gave her a hug. "In less than a month, we can have a cooking lesson every night," he said.

"I'm proud of you, Amelia," Josie said.

"Whatever," Amelia said.

Tonight, Josie thought the ever-flexible word meant her daughter was pleased. But Amelia flinched when her mother hugged her.

Josie heard scraping sounds and saw Jane putting plates in the dishwasher.

"Mom," Josie said, "leave the dishes and take Stuart upstairs."

"We'll finish up," Ted said. "Josie and I need to talk. Go on, Mom. Doctor's orders."

"You're a dog doctor," Jane said, smiling at him.

"And you're dog tired," Ted said.

After Jane and the little shih tzu climbed the back stairs, Josie said, "What did your mom want?"

There was a long pause. This is going to be bad, Josie thought. "Uh, Mom wants to know if you rented chair covers for the reception," Ted said.

"I don't believe this," Josie said. "Your mom is facing death by lethal injection and she wants to know if I have chair covers? No, I don't. We talked about this, Ted. The hall wants eight dollars each for a chair cover—that's more than sixteen hundred dollars. We spent the money on food instead."

Ted looked sheepish. "I couldn't remember," he said. "We talked about so much, it sort of blended together. I'm not even sure what a chair cover is."

"A waste of money," Josie said. She slammed a plate into the dishwasher rack. "The reception hall has perfectly comfortable chairs with blue padded seats. A chair cover is white fabric that covers up the chair."

Clink. Clink. She slammed in more plates.

"Josie, don't get mad at me," he said. "I'm just the messenger. Chair covers are a big deal for Mom."

"Well, I have more important things to think about," Josie said.

Thunk. Thunk. Thunk. Thunk. She added the four china salad bowls and picked up the cookie sheet from the countertop.

"I know," Ted said. He took the cookie sheet away from her and loaded it into the dishwasher. "I know this is incredibly petty. But it's how Lenore survives in jail. She's a strong woman, Josie. Thinking about our wedding is the distraction she needs to keep sane. She wants to pay for the chair cover rental. Please?"

What about my sanity? Josie wanted to say. It's supposed to be my day. I'm losing control of my wedding.

"What harm will it do to let her buy them?" Ted asked.

Josie felt ashamed. If Lenore wanted chair covers, it would only make her wedding look better.

"You can't have naked chairs in Boca," he said, and kissed her forehead. "The sight of exposed legs is shocking." He kissed her nose.

He got down on his knees and said, "Josie Marcus, will you say yes to decently covered chairs?"

Josie laughed and pulled him toward her. "Yes, yes, yes," she said. "Let her have the chair covers for one night. I'm getting you forever."

Ted backed her against the kitchen counter and unbuttoned the first button on her shirt, then the second. She was working on his shirt when a saucer fell off and smashed on the floor, breaking the mood.

"Not with Amelia here," Josie said, and started buttoning up.

"But in a month she'll always be with us," Ted said, kissing her more insistently.

"We'll be married then," Josie said. "We can wait until she's asleep or at school."

"I think I'm going to be coming home for lunch a lot," Ted said.

They heard Amelia giggling and Harry thumping around in her room. Josie reluctantly pulled away.

"Tell me what happened today," Ted said.

Now the romantic mood was deader than Rita. Josie

told him her theory that Rita had killed Molly, the way she'd solved the shoplifting problem, and the horror of seeing Rita's body.

"How did she die?" Ted asked.

"I don't know," Josie said. "But her skull was smashed like that saucer." She shivered, though the night wasn't cold.

"You know the worst part?" Josie asked. "The part I feel so bad about?

"Rita was dead—and I was upset because I'd hit a dead end in the search for Molly's killer."

Chapter 29

"Do you like caviar?" Alyce asked.

"Love it," Josie said. She felt rich and relaxed in the soft leather seats of her friend's Escalade. The luxurious Cadillac SUV seemed the proper place to discuss caviar.

"Good," Alyce said. "I have a terrific caviar recipe for your bridal shower."

"Oh."

Even caviar couldn't make Josie look forward to her shower. "It's really nice of you to give me a shower, but do I have to have one?" she asked.

Josie felt trapped. Alyce was driving her to Brides by Beatrice for the final fitting of her wedding dress. Her wedding heels were in a box on her lap and her bridal lingerie was in a bag at her feet. She wanted to leap out at the next light and run through the traffic to escape the shower.

Josie's blond friend looked soft as whipped cream, but she could be tougher than a two-dollar steak.

"Yes, you do," Alyce said in the same voice she used on two-year-old Justin when she meant business. "I've promised no stupid shower games. Just good food, good drinks, good friends, and good presents."

"But we don't need pots, pans, and sheets. We already have them," Josie said.

"I've seen your cookware, Josie. Goodwill would re-ject it. Ted brings over his own pots when he cooks at your house."

"All cooks have their favorites," Josie said.

"Ted will get more favorites at this shower," Alyce said. "We've made sure his requests are on your wish list."

"Okay," Josie said. "I promise to coo over the Calpha-lon."

"Fortunately, it will be in the boxes when you unwrap it, so you'll know what you're getting," Alyce said. "Oth-erwise, you wouldn't know a panini press from a truffle slicer."

Alyce's voice went slightly sharp with irritation. "This shower isn't about you, Josie Marcus. It's for your mother, who's always wanted a happily married daugh-ter. It's for Amelia, who wants a mom with wedding pic-tures like everyone else at school. And it's for your friends, who want to welcome you to a new stage of your life. We want to celebrate with you, Josie. Are you going to deny us?"

"Well, when you put it that way," Josie said.

"Besides, fancy sheets feel good," Alyce said.

"Ted has these cool pin-striped sheets," Josie said. She thought of their last night together and suppressed a sigh.

"You can have more than one set of good sheets," Alyce said. "Won't it be nice to get rid of your scratchy old towels?"

"Fluffy towels will feel good." Josie was willing to ad-mit that much.

"Your new dinnerware is gorgeous," Alyce said. "I love those square plates in a deep cocoa with the golden brown highlights."

"You make them sound like food," Josie said.

"They're a good showcase for Ted's cooking. I envy you."

"For a set of dishes?" Josie said.

"For marrying at thirty-one," Alyce said. "I got married right after college when my taste wasn't fully developed. I picked boring young-girl china—white plates with timid daisies."

"Is that why you collect china?" Josie asked.

"That's my excuse," Alyce said. "Grown-up weddings are more fun. You know what you want, and I'm not just talking about Ted. You've chosen sophisticated styles. Your shower gifts will be perfect, just like your new life."

"If I get a new life," Josie said. "Yesterday, I thought I had Molly's killer. Instead, I found that poor woman's body."

"That's the third time this morning you've mentioned Rita," Alyce said.

"I keep seeing Rita's foot sticking out from behind the bed. I thought it was a broken statue. Then I saw her head, all crushed in. Rita was a thief, Alyce. She didn't deserve to die for stealing."

"I saw the story on TV," Alyce said. "The police think Rita surprised a burglar and he hit her with a lamp."

"I stepped right over that lamp," Josie said. "I didn't notice any blood."

"You were distracted," Alyce said.

"A botched burglary may be what the police are telling the press, but there's more to her death," Josie said. "Remember Detective Gray, from Rock Road Village?"

"Smart, suspicious, steely-eyed?" Alyce asked. "He investigated Nate's murder."

"I don't know how smart he is," Josie said. "He arrested the wrong killer for Nate. He's the detective in charge of Rita's murder. He all but said I signed Rita's death warrant when I told the shop owner that she'd been stealing expensive items and selling them on eBay. He acted like I murdered Rita."

"He's wrong," Alyce said. "He was wrong about Nate and he's wrong this time, too."

"I hope so," Josie said, "because I keep seeing that

poor silly woman on her bedroom floor. I was so sure she'd killed Molly. It made sense."

"Any other ideas?" Alyce asked.

"Two," Josie said. "The stalker bride's first victim, George Winstid, and his mother, Phoebe."

"You think they killed Molly together?" Alyce asked.

"Maybe. I think the mother did it. I found Molly, remember?"

"Two bodies in one week," Alyce said. "That's too many."

"One is too many," Josie said. "Ever. Molly's car window was rolled down. That was important, and the police overlooked it. That rolled-down window proves Lenore was innocent."

"I'm not following you," Alyce said.

"The night Molly was shot was warm. She'd gone back to stalking Ted. Molly felt safe sitting in the clinic's brightly lit parking lot. She could hear—and see— Lenore's navy rental car and she knew Lenore had a gun. If she'd seen Lenore drive into the lot, Molly would have rolled up her window and roared away. She wouldn't stick around so Lenore could walk over and shoot her in the head."

"Makes sense," Alyce said.

"But she might let her old love, George, get close," Josie said. "Or Phoebe, her future mother-in-law. Both hated Molly, but I think Phoebe wanted her dead."

"Why?" Alyce asked.

"Because George found the woman he wants to marry when he moved to Montana," Josie said. "He's engaged now—for real. Phoebe is a widow and I got the impression she's hard up for money. Thanks to Molly, George, his new wife and their future children will be more than a thousand miles away—and Phoebe can't afford to visit them often. Molly deprived her of the joys of being a St. Louis grandma."

"A good reason," Alyce said. "But how do you prove it?"

"I have to find out where Phoebe was the night Molly was murdered, but I can't figure out how."

"Don't think about it," Alyce said. "Give your brain a rest. We're at the bridal shop. Let's concentrate on your final fitting."

Bridal mannequins stared out of the windows of Brides by Beatrice as if waiting for grooms to rescue them. Beatrice, a grandmotherly woman with her hair tied up in a bun, met Josie at the door. She wore a dress with straight pins stuck in the lapels and a yellow measuring tape around her neck.

"And we're less than three weeks away, my dear," she said with a hint of an Irish lilt. "How are you holding up?"

"Fine," Josie said.

"Come into the fitting room and I'll bring your dress and veil."

Josie changed into her lingerie and white heels for the fitting. Alyce whistled. "A strapless satin corset with garters? That's hot-looking."

"Hope Ted feels the same way," Josie said.

"Any man with a pulse will," Alyce said.

Beatrice carried Josie's wedding gown in her arms and hung it on a hook. "Here," she said, handing Josie a tissue. "Take off your lipstick. I don't want any stains on this dress."

Josie dutifully rubbed the color off her lips. Then Alyce and Beatrice helped her step into the dress. Beatrice zipped it up the back and fastened the hook at the top of the zipper.

"Now, let's take a look at you," she said, and stood back.

"The length is perfect with those heels," Alyce said.

"But the fit is not quite right," Beatrice said. "You've lost weight. We can fix that with a few nips and tucks." She tucked and pinned until she seemed satisfied.

"I'm glad we're taking this dress in instead of letting it out," she said. "That will hide the pin holes. This silk drapes nicely. There. That's perfect. Now let's try the veil. Are you wearing your hair up for your wedding?"

"I'm wearing it like this," Josie said, "except I'll have my hair done at the salon."

"Your swing bob is stylish," Beatrice said. "And you're doing the right thing. Some of my brides pile their hair like Marie Antoinette and spend their wedding day with their hair twisted, pulled, and pinned tight. Gives them headaches, it does, and the last thing you want is a headache on your wedding night. That's no way to start a marriage."

Josie put on the shoulder-length veil of silk illusion trimmed with pearls and crystals.

"So elegant," Beatrice said. "My name means 'bringer of joy.' That's what all my brides bring me. I hope you and Ted have a long, happy life together."

Alyce blinked away tears. "It was just a white dress until you put on the veil," she said. "Now it's a real wedding dress."

If only, Josie thought, I have a real wedding day.

Chapter 30

"Alyce," Josie said, "I've done something wrong and I want to apologize."

Josie was examining a black satin dog bow tie in the bridal shop. She couldn't look her best friend in the eye.

"You're apologizing to me?" Alyce asked. "What did you do?"

"I didn't speak up," Josie said. "You're my best friend, and I sat there and did nothing."

"So what was your terrible crime?" Alyce asked.

"Lenore insisted that Ted's brother, Dick, be in our wedding. Ted didn't even want to invite him. Those two don't get along. Dick plays stupid practical jokes. He can't even hold a job. Last time he was fired for putting his boss's stapler in Jell-O."

"Just like *The Office*," Alyce said. "How original. No wonder he got fired."

"Ted's still furious at him because the idiot super-glued a ball to Festus's paw."

"I don't blame Ted," Alyce said. "How old is his brother?"

"Thirty," Josie said.

"Inexcusable," Alyce said.

"What I did was just as wrong," Josie said. She rubbed the bow's satin, as if she could make a wish and her problem would disappear. "I said Dick could escort you at our wedding."

Alyce laughed. "That's all?"

"That's enough," Josie said. "I should have stood up to Lenore and refused to have that man in my wedding."

"Josie, sweetie, of all the things to worry about," Alyce said. "I can handle him. I'm the mother of a two-year-old. I entertain dozens of ego-flushed lawyers for Jake's career. One idiot brother won't be a problem."

"You're a true friend, Alyce," Josie said.

"Yes, I am. And as your true friend, believe me when I say Ted's brother is one thing you don't have to worry about. Don't fight with your mother-in-law over this. Now, on to important matters." Alyce held up a white satin dog collar with a black bow tie on it. "What do you think of this for Festus?"

"The bow won't show," Josie said. "He's a black Lab."

"Then how about a red bow tie?" Alyce asked.

"Perfect," Josie said. "I'll get a black bow tie for Stuart Little and a cat-sized bow tie for Harry."

"What about Marmalade?"

"Ted's cat should have a girlie white bow," Josie said. "It will look good with her orange fur."

"Will the pets be at the wedding?" Alyce asked.

"No, the clinic interns will bring them to Tower Grove Park. We're having some wedding photos taken there."

"That's where Ted proposed," Alyce said. "That's so romantic. Are you going to Ted Drewes afterward?"

Generations of bridal parties stopped at Ted Drewes Frozen Custard stand to scarf up the city's favorite treats.

"We're going straight to the reception after the photos," Josie said. "But we could go there now. I could use a chocolate chip concrete."

"Deal," Alyce said.

Twenty minutes later, they were parked at the old frozen custard stand. Its peaked gables dripped wooden icicles. Ted Drewes was on Chippewa Street, part of the

legendary Route 66. Ted's concrete shakes were legendary, too.

Alyce ordered a Cardinal Sin with cherries and hot
fudge. Josie wanted a classic chocolate chip concrete.
They sat inside Alyce's SUV with piles of paper napkins
and spooned in their creamy concoctions.

"I still remember the first time Jake took me here,"
Alyce said. "It was an August night and the line wrapped
around the building, but it moved fast. The parking lot
was a party. Jake insisted I get a concrete shake, and
demonstrated how it got its name. He turned the cup
upside-down with the spoon in it and it didn't slide out."

"The concretes are thick as ever," Josie said. She
stopped wolfing hers down. "Brain freeze. Ouch."

Alyce scraped the last of her concrete and licked the
spoon. "Do you have time to swing by Emily's with me?
I want to see how she's doing."

"It must be hard for her," Josie said. "That poor family had to go from planning a wedding to a funeral."

"That's why I want to check on Emily," Alyce said. "I
haven't seen her outside since the funeral—not even to
pick up the mail."

Josie came out of her sugar stupor when Alyce was
waved through the Wood Winds gate. Emily's home jutted out of the ground like a cantilevered crystal. Josie
thought it looked interesting, but cold, like Emily.

"Emily doesn't seem anything like her sister," she
said. "Molly loved antiques, flowers, and ruffles."

"Different hobbies, too," Alyce said. "Molly stalked
men. Emily serves on charity committees. She got all the
practical DNA in that family—and all the good sense.
Good. Looks like she's here. She's working on her roses."

Big-boned Emily wore her overalls like a farmer, over
a worn plaid shirt. A frayed Cardinals ball cap and thick
gardening gloves completed the outfit. She waved, then
hurried to the car with a half-dozen pink roses in a flat
basket.

"Alyce," she said. "Hi. I'm getting the last roses of

summer. I'm sorry, I know we've been introduced, but I can't remember your name."

"This is Joanie," Alyce said, reminding Josie not to say her real name.

"Would you like to come in for coffee and cake?" Emily asked.

"Coffee, yes," Josie said, "but no cake. We stopped at Ted Drewes."

They followed Emily through a two-car garage that dwarfed the bright red Kia Rio. "Is that a new car?" Alyce asked.

"I got rid of that big old Cayenne," Emily said. "It was too hard to handle in traffic. My little Kia is better for the environment. I told Brad it should be green, not red."

Emily slipped off her shoes at the door, and Josie saw her little toe poking through her sock. "The kitchen is a mess," she said.

The kitchen was a shock after Alyce's well-ordered domain. The counter was cluttered with an open loaf of sandwich bread, milk, cereal boxes, ketchup and mustard bottles, and brown-speckled bananas. The sink was piled with dirty dishes.

"Dishwasher broke," Emily said as she plugged in the coffeemaker. "Haven't had time to call the repairman. Come sit in the breakfast room while our coffee perks."

The dining table was a sheet of glass balanced on chrome legs with four stark black chairs. An orange wall added what decorators liked to call a "pop" of color. Josie thought she could trace the faint outlines of a darker rectangle on the wall and wondered if a painting had once hung there.

Josie could see a great room that was bare except for a big-screen television and two plastic lawn chairs on thick gold carpet.

Emily stood at the kitchen island, trimming the roses and dropping them in a vase of water.

"How are you doing?" Alyce asked.

Emily gave a shrug. "Okay," she said.

"Which means not okay," Alyce said.

"Molly was so young," Emily said. "It's hard. We may have to put Aunt Martha in assisted living. She's crushed by Molly's . . . by Molly's . . ." Emily finally said the word, "passing."

"I'm sorry," Alyce said.

"Poor woman," Emily said, wiping her eyes. "She's had enough sorrow for two lifetimes. Molly's killer has been caught and I hope they lock her up forever."

She sliced the rose stem with a sharp *snick!* "Catching the killer is supposed to bring closure, but it doesn't feel like anything at all. Your coffee's ready."

She returned with three mugs and a coffeepot. "There's sugar on the table," she said. "Would you like cream?"

"Black coffee is fine," Josie said. Alyce nodded her agreement.

Emily set the pot on a trivet. "Can I ask for your help?"

"That's why we're here," Alyce said.

"Bring your coffee and follow me," she said.

Emily padded down a hall to an enormous living room with khaki carpeting, orange walls, and a midcentury chandelier. The only furniture was two long gray metal folding tables heaped with boxes. Some were wrapped with white or silver paper. Others were in cardboard shipping boxes.

Molly's wedding presents, Josie thought.

She saw a soup tureen splashed with pink cabbage roses, a cut crystal vase, a scalloped-edged platter and a stack of unopened gift cards.

"I'm trying to deal with Molly's wedding presents," Emily said. "The grief counselor says I should handle them myself to process her death."

"Process?" Alyce asked. Josie heard disapproval in her voice.

"I think she means accept what happened to my sister," Emily said. "But I can't. I try and I try. I open a present, and then I think how much Molly would have

liked it. She really wanted that soup tureen with the cabbage roses. When I unwrapped it, I felt so sad, I put it
right back down. I can't move on—with her things or
with her life. Brad says he's tired of looking at them and
I'm being morbid."

Emily burst into noisy tears. Alyce set her coffee cup
on the edge of the folding table and put her arms around
Emily. "It's okay," she said. "You should cry for your sister."

Josie backed away slightly and noticed a deep dent in
the carpet. She saw five other dents, marking a long rectangle. Did a couch used to be there? In front of the possible couch were four more dents, about the size of a
coffee table.

Alyce was still soothing Emily. "I'm here if you need
me," she said. "You'll get through Molly's loss in your
own way and in your own time."

"Would you and Joanie come tomorrow when Brad's
at work and help me sort her presents?"

"Of course," Alyce said. "What time?"

"He'll be gone by eight thirty. Say, nine thirty?"

"That works for me," Alyce said.

"Me, too," Josie said. She glanced at her watch, and
Alyce caught her signal. "Do you have to pick up your
daughter at school?"

"Yes," Josie said.

"We should go," Alyce said. "We'll see you tomorrow
morning."

Back in Alyce's car, Josie said, "That house looks awfully bare. I wonder if Emily and her husband are short
of money."

"I don't think so," Alyce said. "People in this subdivision keep their display rooms empty until they can afford
the furniture they want."

"I'm pretty sure I saw dents in the carpet where furniture used to be," Josie said. "And who downsizes from
a Porsche to a Kia? If she really cared about the environment, she'd buy a hybrid."

"I'll ask Connie," Alyce said. "She knows all the neighborhood gossip." Her cell phone chimed. "Sorry, Josie, I'd better take this call."

She pulled her Escalade over to the side of the subdivision street. Josie heard her say, "Did my husband and I buy *a what?* A surfboard! Of course not." Alyce ran her fingers through her fine pale hair. "When did this happen? Today! My husband and I are both in St. Louis."

There was a pause, then Alyce said, "I really appreciate your fraud division calling about this out-of-the-ordinary purchase."

She rummaged in her wallet. "My credit card is right here. I can call my husband and check. He usually goes out to lunch. Do you see a lunch charge for today? Sixty-three dollars at a steakhouse in Clayton, Missouri? That sounds legitimate. But not the surfboard. Someone must have gotten our credit card information. Should I cancel our old cards? Yes, please. As soon as I get home, I'll do it. And thank you again."

Alyce turned off her cell. She looked frazzled. "Can you believe it? Someone in Long Beach charged an eight-hundred-dollar surfboard to our credit card. Thank goodness American Express security was alert and called me to check."

"That's it!" Josie said. "Thank you."

"For what?" Alyce looked puzzled.

"You've just told me how I can check Phoebe's alibi," Josie said.

Chapter 31

"Mom, are you pregnant?" Amelia asked.

"Am I what?" Josie was inching behind a line of luxury cars at the four-way stop by the Barrington School. As usual, her daughter waited until Josie was seat-belted in to ask an awkward question.

It was Halloween, and Amelia wore her borrowed witch costume. The pointed hat stuck up in the backseat, but she kept on the black satin cape. Her witchy-dark eye makeup was slightly smeared.

"Zoe told her mom that you were marrying a hot guy," Amelia said. "Her mom said the only reason to get married at your age is if you're pregnant and want to keep the kid."

"I'm not pregnant," Josie said.

"I know. You had me and you didn't get married. But I didn't tell Zoe that."

"Thank the Lord for small favors," Josie said.

"Zoe's mom says it's easier to just live with the guy. Once you get married, you've got to worry about lawyers and sh—"

Josie glared at her.

"Sorry. Stuff when you split."

Josie counted to three before answering. She didn't want to preach, but she didn't like Zoe or her mother.

"Zoe's mom is entitled to her opinion," Josie said. "It's not mine."

"I know. She's a ho."

"Amelia Marcus! You will not use that word."

"But Mom, Zoe came down to breakfast on Saturday and she saw this old dude in his underwear in the kitchen. She didn't even know his name. Her mom didn't, either. She picked him up in some bar."

"That's not how I choose to live," Josie said. "It's risky for a lot of reasons." Time to step off the soapbox, she told herself. "What Zoe's mother did isn't right, but you can't call her a ho."

"A slut?" Amelia said. There was a question in her voice.

"I don't want you using that word, either," Josie said. "Zoe's mom spent the night with a man she didn't know. They're both at fault, but society doesn't have a word for men who bed hop."

"Bed hop," Amelia said. "Good one."

"No, it's not," Josie said. "What I'm trying to say is we have no business judging people when we don't live perfect lives."

Silence. Josie made it through the stop sign and was almost to Lindbergh, a major route toward home, when Amelia bombed her with another question. "Are you sorry you never married Daddy?"

"I'm sorry I couldn't marry your father," Josie said. "I wanted to marry him. I wanted to more than anything in the world. When I found out I was pregnant, I couldn't wait to give him the good news. I knew we'd get married and live happily ever after. Except before I could tell him, your daddy was arrested with a planeload of drugs. He went to prison in Canada."

"But you still could have married him," Amelia said.

"No, I couldn't," Josie said, gently. "I told you why. He was a dealer. He flew in drugs. That attracts big money and bad people. I didn't want you growing up in that environment."

"Were you sad?" Amelia asked.

"I cried for weeks. I thought my life was over. The only thing that kept me going was you. Your grandma was very angry. She said I ruined my life when I dropped out of school. She wanted me to give you up for adoption."

"Grandma wanted to give me away?" Amelia asked.

"That was before she knew you," Josie said. "Now, I think she'd give *me* away first."

Amelia laughed, but Josie could tell she was stunned by this new bit of information.

"Grandma was embarrassed because I wasn't married to your father," Josie said. "We told everyone I was engaged to a pilot who was shot down in the Middle East."

"You lied," Amelia said.

"I did," Josie said. "I was wrong. I convinced myself I did it for Grandma, so she wouldn't have to listen to Mrs. Mueller. But I did it for me, too. Then your father got out of prison when you were nine and everyone knew he was alive."

"He drank," Amelia said.

"Nate had a drinking problem, yes," Josie said. "He developed it in prison. The prisoners made their own illegal alcohol and he was addicted. Nate had problems, Amelia. Lots of problems. Despite them, he was a good man and I loved him so much."

"Did you know he was selling drugs?" Amelia asked.

"No," Josie said. "I knew he had a lot of money—cash money—but I never made the connection between his money and selling drugs. Looking back, I can see the signs were there. But I didn't want to look. That's why I don't think it's fair to judge people like Zoe's mom."

They were nearing Highway 40. They'd be home in less than ten minutes, unless there was a major traffic jam. Amelia slid in another tough question. "Now that you're marrying Ted, are you going to get pregnant?" she asked.

"No," Josie said. "Ted and I talked about it, and we don't want more children." She grinned at her daughter.

"Why have another child when we already have perfection?"

"Whatever," Amelia said.

Josie was relieved when they finally reached Phelan Street. Amelia squeezed in one last question as Josie parallel parked the Honda in front of their flat.

"Why is Mrs. M beastin' Grandma?" she asked.

"Where?" Josie said. She straightened out the car and turned it off.

"On the porch," Amelia said. "Grandma must be decorating it for Halloween tonight. She's got the jack-o'-lanterns on the steps and the plastic skeletons on the railings.

"Mrs. M is arguing away and Grandma is giving it right back."

The two older women looked like gladiators in pant-suits. Mrs. M's helmet of hair didn't move, but her arms windmilled and her face was stroke red. She was pointing her finger at Jane. Josie's mother refused to back down.

"Stay here," Josie said, "while I find out what's going on."

Jane and Mrs. M didn't notice Josie's approach. She listened to them verbally duke it out from the walkway.

"The post office doesn't have to do anything of the kind," Jane said.

"Well, it's ridiculous to deny me service," Mrs. M said. "They could send another mailman."

"We have a woman delivering our mail," Jane said. "Her name is Corrine. For your information, she's a letter carrier. Corrine is allergic to poison ivy."

"I'm not asking her to put my mail in the mums," Mrs. M said. "All she has to do is deliver it to my mailbox, which is four feet nine inches away from the poison ivy. I measured it myself."

"Some people are deathly allergic," Jane said. "They don't even have to touch it. They can catch airborne poison ivy."

"Then the post office can send a mailman who's not allergic," Mrs. M said.

"Or you could get off your bottom and get your mail at the post office yourself," Jane said. "Why waste my tax dollars catering to you? Better yet, why don't you get rid of that stupid poison ivy and then Corrine can deliver your mail?"

"Because I have to catch those thieves," Mrs. M said. "The safety of the neighborhood depends on it."

"My son-in-law installed a system in my plants to catch them," Jane said. "It's safe and good for the environment. It won't hurt the mail carrier or the crooks."

"I don't see any system," Mrs. M said.

"That's the beauty of it," Jane said. "All you see are my mums."

"Hah!" Mrs. M said. "I bet it's not even there."

Josie cleared her throat. "Afternoon, Mom. Is there a problem?"

"Not for me," Jane said. "But our mail carrier is highly allergic to poison ivy. Corrine refuses to come up on Mrs. Mueller's porch until she removes that poison ivy she's growing around her mums. Now, if you'll excuse me, I'm going inside to get ready for the trick-or-treaters."

"You'll be sorry when you wake up and all your mums are gone," Mrs. M said.

"My son-in-law's system will work," Jane said. She slammed her front door. Mrs. M stalked off to her home and firmly shut her own door.

Josie waved Amelia into the house and when she stopped laughing, she called Jane. "Good for you, Mom. You stood up to Mrs. M."

"Was I rude, Josie?" Jane asked. She was having second thoughts now.

"You were perfect, Mom," Josie said. "Want to join us for dinner before the trick-or-treaters arrive?"

"Thanks, dear. I want to rest until the children start ringing my doorbell."

After the revelations on the ride home from school,

Amelia was subdued. She stayed in her room and played with Harry. Josie made her daughter's favorite comfort food, macaroni and cheese. They ate dinner in near silence.

"You're so quiet," Josie said, running her fingers through her daughter's fine red-brown hair.

"Nothing to say," Amelia said. "Did I really ruin your life?"

"No, sweetie. You're my reason for living."

"But you dropped out of school to have me," Amelia said. "You don't want me to do that."

"No, I don't," Josie said. "Life is easier with a college degree. I can go back to school now if I want. Maybe we could go to college together."

Amelia looked stricken.

"I was teasing, honey," she said. "If I go back to school, I'll go to a different college than yours."

"You're not going to be a vet, are you, Mom?" That was Amelia's current career choice. Josie suspected she'd have another one next week.

"Nope, I'm just going to marry one," Josie said.

She stacked five bags of Halloween candy on the kitchen table and poured Hershey's Bars into a big bowl.

"I'm glad you don't give lame healthy treats like raisins," Amelia said. "Can I have a Hershey bar? I'm wearing my witch costume to answer the door."

Josie's neighborhood still had an old-fashioned Halloween. The little kids started coming by with their parents about six o'clock. Their cute costumes would be a good distraction for Amelia, Josie decided.

By eight thirty, she would turn off her porch light. She didn't open her door for the older kids. They were too scary, even if they didn't wear costumes.

"Watch the door, Amelia," Josie said. "I have to make a phone call."

Before she could enjoy Halloween, she had to get Phoebe Winstid's alibi. She checked the date of Molly's murder, got out her cell phone, and draped a handkerchief over the speaker to disguise her voice.

Phoebe answered with a cautious "Yes?"

"Mrs. Winstid, this is the fraud division for your credit card." Josie deliberately did not give a company name.

"Yes," Phoebe said. "Is there something wrong with my MasterCard?"

"I hope not," Josie said. "That's why we're checking. Did you have cocktails and dinner at the Four Seasons restaurant in Manhattan Wednesday, October twenty-fourth?"

"Manhattan?" she said. "I was nowhere near Manhattan. I was here in St. Louis at home. I ate leftovers in front of my television set. Of course, I can't prove that, can I?"

"No, Mrs. Winstid. But we see no other indications that you were traveling then. That's why our computer flagged the charge."

"May I ask how much it's for?" she asked.

"Five hundred sixty-three dollars and thirty-eight cents," Josie said.

"Oh, my word," Phoebe said.

"But you're not responsible for it," Josie said.

"You're sure?" Phoebe's voice was trembling.

"I'm absolutely positive," Josie said. "We'll remove the charge immediately. It won't be on your next bill."

"I'm so glad you called me," Phoebe said.

"Me, too," Josie said.

Now I know for sure you don't have an alibi for the night of Molly Deaver's murder.

Chapter 32

Thursday, November 1

Clunk. Clunk. Clatter.

The sounds rattled through Josie's midnight dreams and she stirred.

Yap! Yap! Yap!

The sharp barks made her sit straight up in bed. That sounded like Stuart Little. Josie slipped on her robe and heard a woman scream, "LET GO OF ME, YOU STUPID MUTT!"

She sounded too young to be Mrs. Mueller.

It was Halloween night. Someone was vandalizing the house.

Josie grabbed her cell phone and the pepper spray off her nightstand, and ran for the porch as the barks, clanks, and shouts increased. Now a police siren howled and tires screeched. Police light bars disco-danced in front of Josie's flat.

She opened the front door and saw her mother doing a triumphant war dance on the front porch.

"I caught the mum thief!" Jane yelled.

"Looks like Stuart caught her," Josie said.

The shih tzu had his teeth firmly in the ankle of a wild-eyed soccer mom. Josie could see blood on her jeans leg, just above her New Balance shoes. Jane's bronze mums were uprooted and potting soil was scattered across the well-swept porch. Ted's tuna-can trap was wrapped around the plants' roots.

The police officer pounded up the porch steps, his smooth face serious. Even his short hair looked earnest.

"Officer, this woman was stealing on my front porch," Jane said.

"This dog attacked me," the soccer mom said. "I was going for a walk. Now my leg is bleeding." The captured thief wore high-rise mom jeans and a dark blue T-shirt.

"Woof!" said Stuart, the tail-wagging attack dog.

"Walking alone at midnight?" Jane said. "I don't think so. She was uprooting my plants, Officer. That's her SUV parked behind my daughter's Honda."

The dark green SUV had the tailgate down. The streetlight showed the back was crammed with flowering plants.

"She was all set to add my mums to her stash," Jane said.

Mrs. M shot out of her front door in a green chenille robe and fuzzy green slippers. Her face was slathered with white cream and her sprayed hair was wrapped in a toilet paper turban to protect it. Officer Earnest's eyes bulged.

"She stole my flowers, too, Officer," Mrs. M said. The TP rustled on her hairdo. "She even stole my poison ivy."

The soccer mom absently scratched her hand at the mention of poison ivy. Josie fought to suppress a giggle.

It took nearly an hour to sort out the crisis. The soccer mom was charged with misdemeanor trespass, with the promise of more charges. "We're restricted from making arrests for most misdemeanor crimes that don't happen in our presence," Officer Earnest said. "But based on the uprooted plant material and the dog bite, I can charge you with trespass and the theft of your neighbor's plants, since she was able to identify her property. Unless you can produce receipts for the other plants in your vehicle, I will also charge you with petty theft and possession of stolen property."

The soccer mom kept . . . well, mum. "I want to call my lawyer," she said, and not another word after that. She even refused to give her name. Her driver's license said she was Trudy Sandusky. Her address was in the well-heeled suburb of Frontenac.

Mrs. M reclaimed her mums from the back of the SUV, but she left the poison ivy. The rest of the stolen plants were taken to the station house. Josie wondered how the homeowners would ID their lost plants. Most were uprooted from their pots and dropped in cardboard boxes. Trudy had lined the cargo bed of her SUV with newspapers to protect it during to her plant-rustling spree.

It was one ten a.m. when the circus folded. Josie helped her mother replant the mums. She could see Mrs. M doing the same thing on her porch. Jane watered her repotted mums. Then, seized with a sudden impulse, she stomped over to Mrs. Mueller's porch.

"I told you my son-in-law's system was a good one," she said. "The thief was too dumb to recognize poison ivy. And you thought gangbangers were stealing your flowers."

Mrs. Mueller gave Jane a glare that should have bored holes in her back, while Josie's sturdy mother marched back home.

Josie checked on Amelia on her way back to bed. Her daughter was sound asleep, her cat, Harry, alert at the foot of Amelia's bed. Josie scratched his oversized ears. "It's okay, old man," she whispered. "You can go back to sleep."

Josie's head barely sank into the pillow when her alarm rang. She opened one sleep-heavy eye. Time to get Amelia off to school. She was grateful her daughter didn't give Josie any trouble this morning. Amelia fed Harry, ate her breakfast, and put on an acceptable school outfit: long white T-shirt, skinny black jeans, and a jade scarf. Josie dressed and pounded down four cups of coffee. All that coffee made Josie jumpy, but she wasn't totally awake—until Amelia asked a question on the way to school: "Are you going to be Mrs. Ted Scottsmeyer, Mom?"

"I'm going to stay Josie Marcus," she said. "That's who I've been for thirty-one years. I've gotten used to my name."

"But how will people know you're married?" Amelia asked.

"I'll have a wedding ring to go with this," Josie said. She wiggled her ring finger and the double-diamond engagement ring sparkled in the sun. "They'll know. And Ted and I will know."

"But you'll still be married even if you don't take his name?" Amelia asked.

Ah, that's what this was about. "Definitely," Josie said. "And we'll have the pictures to prove it. Amelia, many brides don't take their husband's last name—especially older brides. It doesn't mean I don't love Ted, and he doesn't mind. He's not the sort of man who has to own me."

Amelia shrugged.

They were in the Barrington School drive. Amelia ducked her mother's kiss and ran inside. Josie sat for a few seconds, enjoying the crisp fall morning. The campus looked especially pretty. A polite beep from another mom reminded Josie she was taking up valuable space.

Back home, she was sweeping up the potting soil on the front porch when she saw her mother on the walkway, Stuart Little trotting at her side. Jane was glowing after last night's daring capture of the mum thief.

"How's the hero?" Josie asked, scratching the shih tzu's ears. "Did he get another medal for capturing the flower rustler?"

"He was rewarded with a slice of ham," Jane said.

Stuart wagged his tail.

"You may look cute," Josie told him, "but you're one tough dog. You've caught two crooks now. First, you bit a murderer. Now you've nailed a mum stealer."

"He only attacks on command," Jane said. "What are your plans for today?"

I'm bringing Molly's killer to justice, she wanted to say. But Josie knew it was too soon to say that. Rita's murder had been a terrible lesson.

"Alyce and I are going to help Molly's sister deal with the piles of wedding presents in her living room. Emily can't face them."

"That poor girl," Jane said. "What a horrible duty for her."

"It is," Josie said. "But Alyce is good with people. I'm just along as muscle. I want to call Ted, too, before I leave."

Josie's cell rang. She picked it off the porch rail and checked the display. "That's Alyce, Mom. See you later," she said, and went inside.

"Josie, I hope I caught you at home," Alyce said. She could hear Justin fussing in the background.

"What's wrong with your little guy?" Josie asked.

"I think he's coming down with a cold," Alyce said. "He has a low-grade fever—ninety-nine point two—and he's miserable. I don't want to leave him alone with his nanny. He needs his mommy and I want to monitor his temperature. I can't go to Emily's today. Can you go without me?"

"Sure," Josie said. "Do you want to postpone until to-morrow?"

"Connie told me Emily's husband is being difficult," Josie said. "He wants her to clear all Molly's stuff out of the house."

"Brad sounds like a jerk," Josie said. "Does he really believe if Emily removes her sister's wedding gifts, her grief will go away?"

"I don't know how someone like that thinks," Alyce said. "I'm just glad I didn't marry him. Will you help her?"

"Of course," Josie said.

"You were right about Emily being hard up for

money," Alyce said. "I talked with Connie yesterday. She said Emily was asked to resign from her committee because she embezzled eight thousand dollars."

"You're joking," Josie said.

"Happens more than you'd think," Alyce said. "It's not the first time I've seen it. The embezzler quietly resigns and the group pretends it never happened. But this money was for the food bank. The committee is threatening to go to the police and press charges unless Emily gives them back their money."

"Would they really do that?" Josie asked.

"I think they're bluffing," Alyce said. "Emily's embezzling will be difficult to prove and embarrassing for Wood Winds to admit. The rest of St. Louis already thinks this subdivision is in the crooked one percent."

Josie kept silent. That was her opinion, too, with the exception of Alyce and a handful of other residents.

"If Emily doesn't cave," Alyce said, "Wood Winds will probably suck it up and make up her loss. We won't like to, but we can afford it."

"So she'll get away scot-free?" Josie asked.

"Oh, she'll be punished," Alyce said. "She'll be tossed off a major committee, and that will hurt Brad's business. He needs his neighbors. Enough petty subdivision politics. What's going on with you and your investigation? Any progress?"

"Yes," Josie said. "I found out that Phoebe Winstid and her son don't have alibis for the night of Molly's murder."

"How did you manage that?" Alyce asked.

"You inspired me," Josie said, "with that call from your credit card company." She told Alyce how she disguised her voice with a handkerchief over her cell phone and the make-believe call from the credit card company.

"Except I said her card had been used for dinner at the Four Seasons on the day of Molly's murder."

"Brilliant," Alyce said.

"Either the mother or the son killed Molly—and I

think it's probably Phoebe. She even drives the same kind of car that was in the security video: a charcoal Impala."

"Please tell me you're not going to confront Phoebe on your own," Alyce said. "At least wait until Justin feels better, so I can go with you."

"Are you nuts?" Josie said. "Neither of us will do that. I'm giving this information to Lenore's high-priced Boca lawyer. He can earn his keep and use a real detective to investigate the murderous Winstids."

"What did Ted say when you told him?" Alyce asked.

"I couldn't reach him last night," Josie said. "I left a message and he hasn't called back yet. He must have worked late. Speaking of late, I'd better leave if I'm going to make it to Emily's by nine thirty."

Josie heard Justin wailing in the background.

"That's my poor boy," Alyce said. "Thanks for helping Emily with those presents. I'm glad you're not doing anything dangerous."

Chapter 33

"Ted!" Josie was almost to her car when her fiancé called. She sat on the bumper to talk.

"Sorry I didn't call sooner, Josie," Ted said. "I had to euthanize a patient last night and didn't finish until nearly midnight."

Josie thought he sounded subdued. "Who was it?" she asked.

"A thirteen-year-old beagle with cancer," Ted said. "The owner called as I was leaving. Danielle said Buddy was suffering so much, she didn't want to wait until morning. By the time she got here, said good-bye, and I did the procedure, it was too late to call."

"How are you?" Josie said. "I know it's hard for you to put down a pet."

"It was time," Ted said. "Buddy couldn't eat or drink and he'd lost control of his functions. He was a dignified old guy."

"I have news that will cheer you up," Josie said. "I know who killed Molly."

"Really?" No trace of tiredness now. Ted's words tumbled out. "Who? What? Why?"

Josie told him how she'd tracked down Molly's first stalker victim, George, and his mother, Phoebe, then figured out that neither one had an alibi for the time of Molly's murder.

"Both are possibilities," Josie said. "But I think Phoebe killed her. She has a good motive: Bridezilla drove her only son out of St. Louis. Phoebe won't get to see her future grandchildren grow up. She can't afford trips to Montana."

"Money and mother love," Ted said. "Powerful reasons."

"Here's something else: Phoebe drives a dark gray Impala."

"The car in the surveillance video. You got her!" Ted said.

"Not yet," Josie said. "I'm not tackling a killer on my own. It's time for Lenore's lawyer and his investigator to prove it."

"Mom will be out in time for our wedding," Ted said.

"I hope," Josie said. "Will you call Shel Clark?"

"Right now," Ted said. "But Shel may want to talk to you. You're brilliant. And beautiful. Did I tell you I love you?"

"Not since yesterday," Josie said.

Ted kept saying, "I love you," until Josie hung up laughing.

Ted made her feel better. She could face the trip to Emily's house alone.

She sang all the way to the Estates at Wood Winds. As she parked in Emily's driveway, Josie was struck by the stark lines of Emily's house in the midst of the subdivision's fanciful mansions and mock castles.

This morning, Emily's eyes were ringed by bruised circles and her short brown hair needed washing. Egg yolk was dripped down her dark turtleneck.

"Come in," she said. "It's nice of you to help when Alyce can't make it."

Josie followed her to the vast living room with the tangerine walls and the fashionable khaki carpet. Two sculpted dining chairs sat by the metal folding tables heaped with boxes.

"We can open and sort the gifts," Emily said. "I set up a system."

Sheets of paper were on the carpet, with the name of a store's bridal registry: Macy's, Tiffany, Crate & Barrel and Williams-Sonoma.

"Should I keep track of who sent each gift?" Josie asked.

"No reason," Emily said. "People know Molly can't write thank-you notes. You take that table, and I'll do this one. Here's a pair of scissors to open boxes. If you find a gift receipt, tape it to the box." She handed Josie Scotch tape. "Before you add a gift to the store pile, show it to me."

Emily never addressed Josie by her name or offered her anything to eat or drink.

Josie opened a box with a De'Longhi toaster that looked like it could launch a satellite. "Do you want this to go back to Macy's?" she asked.

Emily studied the gleaming metal. "It has the extra-wide slots for bagels," she said. "Ours is an old two-slicer. Put it in the keeper pile."

Josie sought to hide her shock. Emily didn't hesitate to keep Molly's gift for herself.

"What about these?" Josie held up a six-pack of Lenox wineglasses etched with tiny flowers.

"I like my glassware better," Emily said. "Those can go back. Along with this soup tureen." Josie recognized it as the cabbage rose dish she'd wept over yesterday.

"My sister liked all that flowery crap," she said.

This was the woman who couldn't move on with her grief? Josie wanted out of Emily's ice palace. The fastest way was to tear through the mountain of unopened boxes and wrapped presents.

Josie dutifully held up each opened gift for inspection.

Emily wanted the Breville blender and the bright red KitchenAid stand mixer. "I like to bake," she said. Antique silver candlesticks etched with garlands and grapes were rejected as "fussy." So was a dainty porcelain vase.

"I never iron," Emily said, and banished that appliance. "Molly needed one for her ruffles."

Josie had the eerie feeling that Emily was settling an old score with her sister with each acceptance or rejection.

She waved away Molly's blue-flowered everyday dishes, nixed ten place settings of bone china, but said yes to the big Turkish bath towels. "Brad and I have been married ten years," she said. "Our linens are getting worn."

Josie nodded. Emily didn't seem to notice that she was the only one talking. She disemboweled cartons and ripped apart festive paper like a hungry lioness attacking her prey.

"Look at this ten-cup coffeemaker," Emily said. "With a built-in bean grinder." Her excited squeal sickened Josie. "Want to try it?"

I want out of here, Josie thought. "I'm almost done," she said. "Let's finish. That will make your husband happy."

"So will all this loot," Emily said, her eyes glittering with greed.

Josie pulled a round flat tray out of a colorful box.

"Oh. My. God," Emily said softly. "A pizza stone. I've always wanted one."

She grabbed it from Josie and carried the trophy to the keeper pile.

"That was my last box," Josie said.

"I still have more," Emily said. She handed Josie a stack of greeting card envelopes, a notebook, and a pen. "Open these, and write down the amounts."

"After I call my mom," Josie said. "I'll have to ask her to pick up my daughter at school."

She hoped Emily would tell Josie to leave, but she was staring raptly at a vegetable chopper. "I saw these Alligator choppers on TV," she said. "I'm keeping this."

Josie fished her cell phone out of her purse. "Of course I'll pick up Amelia," Jane said. "She wants to learn more about cooking fish. I got some nice tilapia."

"Thanks, Mom," Josie said.

She checked her messages to see if Lenore's lawyer had called, then slipped the cell phone into her pocket. Josie didn't want to miss Shel Clark's call. Maybe the lawyer could spring her, too.

Josie tackled the tower of greeting cards. Most contained checks. A check for fifty thousand dollars was in a card frosted with lace and signed, "Love to my Darling Niece, Aunt Martha." Molly would have loved that card, Josie thought, maybe even more than the check.

Lingering made her feel sadder. Josie opened the last two cards, swiftly added up the checks, and circled the total.

"Done!" she said.

Emily was unwrapping three bamboo storage baskets from Crate & Barrel. Josie was glad she'd included them in her own bridal registry.

"How much?" Emily asked.

"Fifty-eight thousand and twenty-five dollars," Josie said.

"Including Aunt Martha's money?" Emily asked.

Josie nodded.

"I knew my sister would rake in at least fifty thousand for her wedding," Emily said. "Brad and I didn't do nearly as well. Molly always got everything."

Including an early death, Josie thought.

"I appreciate your help," Emily said. "Now all I have to do is take Molly's clothes to a consignment shop, clean out her apartment, and I'm done."

She said this without a trace of sorrow. Emily had processed her grief in record time. She checked her watch. "I should have time to deposit the checks at the bank this afternoon," she said.

"Do you have a special account for Molly's estate?" Josie asked.

"Don't need one," Emily said. "I'm the executor. The money's going to me, anyway. Molly and I already had a joint account, so I could help her with the wedding."

Right. Josie remembered Rita the saleswoman mentioning that. Looks like Molly helped you instead, Josie thought. There's more than enough money here to cover what you embezzled from the Thanksgiving food bank fund. I wonder if a timely check will save your bacon.

"Your friends and family were generous to Molly," she said.

"That was Aunt Martha's doing," Emily said. "Molly was always her favorite. She promised Molly fifty thousand dollars as part of a down payment on a new home."

Just like Mom offered Ted and me money to put toward a down payment, Josie thought. She felt uneasy. Her tidy picture of Molly's killer shifted slightly, but she didn't know why. She was starting to think Aunt Martha's fifty thousand dollars, Molly's wedding gifts, and Molly's death were somehow connected and they had nothing to do with Phoebe Winstid or her son.

"Molly said she'd be a traditional stay-at-home wife," Emily said. "Aunt Martha didn't realize my sister was a master manipulator under all those frills. She fell for Molly's old-fashioned-girl act, wrote her a fat check, and encouraged everyone to help Molly and Ted buy a house."

Josie jumped when Emily said Ted's name.

"Why isn't Ted's name on the checks?" she asked.

"Molly promised Aunt Martha she'd handle the family finances. That was a slap at me. I let Brad handle our money and some of his investments didn't pan out."

"I see," Josie said. She saw the bare walls, the empty living room, and the dents in the carpet where the furniture used to be.

"I never had my sister's advantages," Emily said. "No one helped Brad and me that way. Well, we'll get by. I've put her wedding dress on eBay."

"The one she wore on TV?" Josie asked. "It's been used."

"By a famous person," Emily said. "Denise refused to take back her veil and tiara. The fact that Molly wore those would increase their value. Denise took back Molly's first bridal veil and tiara, like she did for that other ditz who worked there."

"Rita?" Josie asked. "Wasn't she your sister's friend?"

"That's what Rita said," Emily said. "She wanted me to give her Molly's dog. Just hand it to her for nothing. Bella had papers. I sold it for five hundred bucks."

The picture of Phoebe Winstid as Molly's killer was losing focus. "Were you friends with Rita, too?" she asked.

"I met her at the shop," Emily said, "but we didn't socialize. Rita invited me to her apartment to have dinner with Molly, but I said no. I wasn't wasting an evening with those two. Rita was like Molly—obsessed with her looks, her clothes, and her wedding."

"Rita had exquisite taste," Josie said.

"She spent a lot on herself, if that's what you mean," Emily said. "But taste? I don't think so. Rita had an old Coke machine in her living room."

The picture of Molly's killer was coming clearer.

"How did you know about the Coke machine?" Josie asked.

"What?" Emily looked confused.

"How did you know that Rita had a Coke machine in her living room?" Josie asked. "You've never been in her apartment."

"Molly told me about it," she said. "It's all Rita talked about."

Now Josie knew exactly who killed Rita. She pressed 911 on her cell phone and left the line open. She could hear the 911 operator asking, "What is your emergency?" Josie raised her voice to cover the query.

"Molly didn't tell you anything," Josie said. "That vintage Coke machine was delivered after Molly Deaver was murdered." She tried to state as many facts as fast as possible to let the 911 operator know exactly the nature of her emergency.

"You shot your sister in the parking lot at the St. Louis Mobo-Pet Clinic," Josie said. "The one in Rock Road Village. Molly didn't run away when she saw you. She thought she had nothing to fear from you, Emily."

"You're crazy," Emily said. "I didn't kill Molly."

"You did," Josie said, raising her voice even louder. "Then you beat—" What was Rita's last name? She needed it for 911. "Rita Marie Kutchner to death in her apartment. Rita knew you killed your own sister. What happened, Emily? Did Rita find out how badly you needed Molly's money?"

"She was blackmailing me," Emily said. "She got what she deserved. Rita said she'd tell the police unless I gave her eight thousand dollars for that stupid Coke machine. I said we didn't have that kind of money. She said I'd have to find it somewhere."

"And you did," Josie said. "You embezzled it from the food bank committee for the Estates at Wood Winds. Shame on you, Emily Deaver." Good. She'd told 911 her attacker's name and the location.

"I borrowed the money," Emily said. "I'm paying it back."

"Now that you've shot your sister and inherited her money, you can afford to," Josie said.

"Rita lied," Emily said. "She said she'd stop after I gave her the eight thousand, but she didn't. She wanted more antiques."

"Why did you kill your sister?" Josie asked. "Molly wasn't blackmailing you."

"She was ruining my life," Emily said. She was sobbing now. "I needed money, and she spent everything on clothes and those weddings and she got richer. I asked her for a loan and she said no."

"But she was your sister," Josie said.

"Half sister," Emily said. "She was a lunatic, stalking

strangers and saying she was engaged to them. She was hurting Brad's business. Nobody wants an accountant with a crazy relative. We were going broke because of her. Because she wanted this junk."

Emily yanked the massive soup tureen out of the box. Insane rage lit her eyes and reason fled her face.

"Don't!" Josie screamed. "Put that down. You could kill me."

"Exactly," Emily said, and hurled it at Josie.

The tureen shattered against the orange wall like a bomb. Josie hoped the 911 operator heard the noise. She shrieked as loud as she could, picked up the closest cardboard box, and held it in front of her like a shield.

A Waterford vase crashed into the makeshift shield, and Josie's defense crumpled. She dropped to the carpet and crawled to the pile of Macy's presents. Josie hurled the six-pack of Lenox wineglasses. They hit the folding table and shattered.

Wedding presents were flying everywhere. She ducked as the toaster sailed past, and reached for the blender.

It missed Emily and bounced on the thick carpet.

There was nowhere for Josie to hide. She crawled backward, hoping to break for the back door.

More crystal shattered against the wall near Josie. She made it to the bone china place settings and tossed dish after dish, like a drunk at a Greek restaurant. One plate glanced off Emily's shoulder, but it barely stopped her.

Josie ducked behind another pile of boxes, searching for more weapons. She threw the coffeepot at Emily. Emily charged, swung a silver candlestick at Josie's head, and gouged the wall.

Josie felt for something else to throw and connected with the pizza stone. She held the heavy piece by the handles like a shield, turned, and whapped Emily on the head with it.

There was a sound like a gong.

Emily dropped senseless to the carpet.

Chapter 34

Josie stood over the killer's body, still holding the pizza stone. She was prepared to clobber Emily again if she moved.

She pulled her cell phone out of her pocket with one hand and said, "Operator, it's me, Josie Marcus. I called you. I was being attacked by a killer. It's Emily Deaver Destin. She killed two people: her sister, Molly Ann Deaver, and Molly's coworker, Rita Kutchner. I need the police and an ambulance. I'm at Emily's home in the Estates at Wood Winds. It's a big glass house. I'm not sure of the address."

"The police are on the way, ma'am," the operator said. "So you need medical assistance?"

"No, but I think the woman who attacked me does. She's out cold on the floor."

"You should leave the house immediately, ma'am. Go outside and stay on the line until the police arrive."

Josie heard sirens slicing through the subdivision's sleepy silence and saw Alyce sprinting across the lawn, screaming, "Josie! What's happened?" She ran into Emily's living room shouting, "Are you hurt?" Alyce had gone even whiter with worry, and her pale blond hair was flying straight out. Her chest was heaving after the short run from her house.

"I'm okay, Alyce," Josie said. "Go home to Justin."

"Ma'am?" the 911 operator said. "Are you still on the line? Are you in danger?"

"I'm here," Josie said. "I'm fine."

"I've asked you to leave the house immediately. Go outside and stay on the line until the police arrive."

Three patrol cars slammed up the double driveway.

"They're here," Josie said, and hung up. She and Alyce watched the officer emerging from the car. He was about thirty, with a strong jaw and a shaved head. His name tag said RICE.

Officer Rice and another uniformed officer with a soft face entered the front door, hands poised over unsnapped holsters. They walked like prowling cats—poised and alert.

"It's okay, Officers," Josie said. "The killer is passed out on the floor there."

After a quick sweep of the house, they returned. Josie and Alyce followed behind them. "Stay back, ma'am." It was the soft-faced officer. His name tag said DAVIS. Officer Davis had a slight paunch and a five o'clock shadow at three in the afternoon.

"I'm representing Ms. Marcus," Alyce said. "My client has that right."

She was careful not to identify herself as an attorney. Alyce probably knew as much about criminal law as her lawyer husband. Jake's specialty was contracts. While he was in law school, Alyce had audited his early-morning criminal law classes. Her course notes got him an A.

Now she'd successfully bluffed her way into staying inside Emily's house with Josie.

Emily, flat on the floor amid glass shards and shattered china, moaned softly. Josie could see a plum-colored egg forming on her forehead.

Officer Davis directed Josie and her "attorney" to sit in the breakfast room. Alyce didn't correct the man about her title.

"You'll need to surrender your cell phones," he said.

"I live down the street," Alyce said. "I didn't bring mine."

"Mine's right here in my pocket," Josie said, and handed it over. Davis took it and nodded.

"I'd like to speak to my client," Alyce said. "Alone."

A uniformed woman officer stayed in the kitchen, watching them. Officer Davis joined the other policemen in the living room.

From the breakfast room, the two women couldn't see Emily, but they heard her. Sound echoed in the empty, curtainless living room. "Let's listen now and talk later," Alyce whispered.

Josie and Alyce watched three paramedics open a portable stretcher in the entrance hall, then heard it crunch across the ruined wedding presents on the carpet.

"She seems okay, but she should be checked for a concussion at the hospital," one paramedic said.

"Not before I tell these officers how that woman attacked and robbed me," Emily said.

"You're refusing treatment?" the paramedic asked.

"No, but I insist on talking first," Emily said. "Then you can take me to the ER. Give me that paper and I'll sign it."

There was a pause. Josie guessed she was signing the EMS medical release.

"Will you also sign a search waiver?" Officer Rice asked.

"Of course," Emily said. "I have nothing to hide."

Next, Officer Rice cautioned Emily. Both policemen stayed silent as Emily wept and spun her story about "that woman's vicious attack."

"She tried to steal my poor dead sister's money," Emily said through her tears.

Josie's eyes opened wide at the lie. Alyce squeezed her arm. "Don't say a word," she whispered. "Let the police handle this."

"Molly Deaver is my sister," Emily said. "She was shot to death by some woman from Boca, Lenore Something Hall, in the parking lot at a veterinary clinic. She's in jail. Somehow that woman in my breakfast room found out my sister had had her wedding presents delivered here and tried to rob me. I came into this room around three o'clock and caught her red-handed. She'd opened all the wedding cards. I think there was more than fifty thousand dollars in checks in them—gifts for my poor sister. You'll find that woman's fingerprints all over the checks."

Josie started to protest, but Alyce shook her head, warning her to stay silent.

"I don't even know her name," Emily said. That was the only truth in her fantastic tale. "She attacked me with my sister's china and crystal. See that box of broken wineglasses? She threw them at me. I was forced to defend myself with that soup tureen. That's what's left. It was painted with big roses."

Oh, she's good, Josie thought. My prints are on those glasses and the checks. Hers will be on the tureen.

Emily took them on a tour of the war of the wedding presents. "I think I threw that toaster at my attacker," she said. "She tried to hit me with the blender, but she missed. She threw all Molly's china—ten place settings— at me. Her aim wasn't very good. She only hit me once, in the shoulder.

"She also hurled that heavy coffeepot at me. I tried to defend myself with a silver candlestick. I swung at her and missed. You can see where I gouged my wall there.

"I was fighting for my life. I don't think she was injured at all. I tried to run out of the room to call for help, but she slammed me in the head with that heavy pizza stone. It's there on the floor. That's all I remember until I woke up and saw you."

Josie wished she could see the officers' faces.

"What made you decide to come into the living room?" Officer Rice asked. "Did you hear a sound?"

"I'm not sure," Emily said. "This is a big house. More

than five thousand square feet. I think I had a bad feeling."

"Was your front door locked?" Rice asked.

"We don't lock our doors in this neighborhood," Emily said. "It's a gated community."

"How did the attacker get past the gate guard?" Rice asked.

"I don't know," Emily said. "You'll have to ask him."

The officers gave no hint they knew about Josie's 911 call for help.

Emily signed a statement swearing her fairy tale was true. Only then did she let the paramedics wheel her away. A uniformed officer was sent along with the paramedics.

"She's getting her head examined," Alyce said.

"Should have done that years ago," Josie said.

"Want to tell me what really happened?" Alyce asked.

Josie did, then said, "Shouldn't you be home with Justin?"

"He's asleep," Alyce said. "His nanny is watching him. Justin's fever broke about noon."

"I'm so glad," Josie said.

"Me, too. He's as cranky as his daddy when he has a cold," Alyce said. "Must be a guy thing."

Josie thought it was sweet that Alyce seemed proud of her son's so-called manly behavior.

"I can't believe I let you go alone to a killer's house," Alyce said. "I thought she was the sane sister."

"She probably is," Josie said. "That's the sad part."

The two police officers were back in the breakfast room.

"Ms. Marcus will be happy to talk to you," Alyce said. "I'd like to use a phone first to call my nanny. I need to ask her to stay late with my two-year-old son."

Officer Davis checked the recent calls on Josie's cell phone while Alyce used Rice's phone. The nanny reported that Justin was still napping and agreed to stay later.

Josie told a very different—and easily verifiable—

story. Her nine-thirty arrival would be confirmed later by the guard's records. At least two neighbors and a mail carrier had seen Josie's gray Honda in Emily's driveway until the police arrived at three oh four.

It was nearly seven o'clock when Josie signed her statement and Officer Rice said she could go home. Josie retrieved her phone. She was relieved to walk out of Emily's house more than nine hours after she'd entered it.

Alyce left with her. Her shoulders sagged and her pale skin looked dusted with flour. Once outside, Josie still couldn't leave. Haphazardly parked police cars and other official vehicles blocked the street. While Josie waited for them to be moved, she said, "Can I give you a ride home, Alyce?"

"Absolutely," she said. "I can see my house, but I'm too lazy to walk there."

"You're tired," Josie said. "Not lazy."

"At least I caught one break," Alyce said. "Jake's not home yet. He won't know I was mixed up in this mess. I can finish his dinner."

Jake insisted on dinner every evening, come hell, high water, or homicide. Josie thought he was inconsiderate, but Alyce seemed happy with her man and her marriage.

At last, a path was cleared for Josie's car. She backed her Honda out of Emily's drive, then turned toward Alyce's home. She stopped as a dark car tore through the cluster of official vehicles. The driver roared up the Destin driveway, slammed on the brakes, and sprinted toward the front door.

"That's Emily's husband, Brad," Alyce said. "When did he trade in his Beemer for a dark green Chevy Impala?"

"That's it," Josie said. "That wraps up the case."

"It does?"

"A security tape caught a dark Impala on the street by the clinic the night Molly was murdered," Josie said. "Phoebe had one. That's one reason I thought she was the killer. But it was Emily. She drove her husband's car when she shot her sister."

Chapter 35

Thursday, November 1

"Were you hurt when you fought with Emily?" Alyce asked.

"Broke a nail," Josie said. She was parked in Alyce's driveway. Josie held out her right hand and her friend examined the break.

"Just a tiny chip," she said. "You can file it down when you get home. Once your manicurist fixes it, it won't show."

"Where?" Josie looked at her blankly.

"In your wedding photos. You'll want a close-up photo of your hands with your new wedding ring or your hands and Ted's," Alyce said. "It's a tradition. Like a bridal shower."

Josie looked at her frazzled friend. "Are you in any shape to give a shower?" she asked.

"All I need is a night's sleep," Alyce said. "You are not getting out of that shower. You will show up at two o'clock, and if you care about our friendship, you'll have a good time."

"Amelia's looking forward to it," Josie said. "She wants to ask how you make phyllo purses. I don't remember accessories on my wish list."

Alyce laughed. "You eat phyllo purses," she said. "They're made of dough, silly; they don't hold it. See you Saturday."

Josie waved good-bye to the guard at the Wood Winds gate and parked at the first store lot after she left the subdivision to check her phone messages. Both Lenore's lawyer and Jane had called.

She longed to call Ted first with her news, but she knew she had to call Shel Clark. She didn't want the lawyer's investigator bothering innocent Phoebe.

"Ms. Marcus," Clark said. "So nice of you to return my call."

Josie wondered if he was being sarcastic, then realized she was getting high-priced soft soap.

"Dr. Scottsmeyer told me what you learned about Phoebe Winstid," Clark said. "My investigator will be following up. What else do you know?"

"She didn't do it," Josie said. "I was wrong."

"Good of you to admit it," he said. "That will save Mrs. Scottsmeyer Hall time and money."

"The killer has been caught," Josie said. "It's a matter of time before she's arrested." Josie told him about Emily and the 911 tape.

"And you're certain you weren't harmed?" he said.

"Just a chipped fingernail," she said.

"Some of my clients would consider that a major injury," he said. "I'd better move. Once the police make that arrest, I could have my client released within twenty-four hours."

"I'm so glad," Josie said.

"Oh, Ms. Marcus, one more thing. Mrs. Scottsmeyer Hall asked me to convey a concern about your impending wedding."

"What is it?" Josie asked. She was in no mood for Lenore's meddling.

"She wishes to buy the table centerpieces for your reception."

"But we already ordered poinsettias," Josie said.

"She is aware of that," Clark said. "She'll reimburse you for their cost. She'd like you to order something a little more, uh—" Words failed him.

Josie let Clark struggle to find the right one. She suspected the lawyer cost Lenore about six hundred dollars an hour. His three-second pause added about fifty cents to the bill.

"Formal," he said. "Lenore says you can choose roses, orchids, hydrangeas, anything else you like."

For a mean moment, Josie thought about spray-painting plastic flowers gold for the wedding reception tables, but she knew better. She'd only punish herself and embarrass Ted, Amelia, and Jane.

Besides, she'd loved Gretchen's clever centerpieces with the white zinnias, red dahlias, and white tea lights. Josie had wanted those, but they were out of her price range. Why not let Lenore give them?

Because she'll be running our lives, Josie told herself.

But she'll be living more than twelve hundred miles away in Boca. Let Lenore treat you to the flowers you want. You can handle her when she's out of jail. Woman up.

"I have just the flowers in mind," Josie said.

"Super," he said. "Order them and send the bill to my office."

As soon as the lawyer hung up, Josie called Ted.

"I got the real killer," she said, and told him the story. "Come to my house now. We'll celebrate with Mom and Amelia."

"Should I make dinner?" Ted asked.

"I think they've made tilapia," Josie said. "I'd better call and make sure they save us some food."

Josie didn't have to see her mother to know Jane was upset. "It's after seven o'clock," her mother said. "You could have called and said you were going to be so late."

"No, I couldn't, Mom," Josie said. "The police took my phone. I caught Molly's killer—the real killer. I'm okay, Mom. I'll come right home and tell you all about it. Oh, and Ted's coming for dinner. Is there enough for him?"

"Of course," Jane said. "Get home here and tell me everything."

Ted arrived at the flat just before Josie. "I brought wine for the celebration," he said. Their lingering kiss on the lawn made Josie forget how tired she was. Then she heard Amelia call from the porch, "Hi, Ted! Hi, Mom. Hurry up. Dinner's ready."

"To be continued," Josie whispered in Ted's ear.

The food quickly disappeared. Amelia was flattered when Ted asked for the recipe for the Parmesan tilapia. Josie regaled them with how she'd captured the killer. Ted and Jane toasted her success.

Even Amelia dropped her preteen ennui. "Awesome, Mom," she said. "Everyone else's mom is a boring doctor or lawyer, but you catch killers."

"Mostly by accident," Josie said.

"To my beautiful detective," Ted said, and raised his glass again.

"And while we're catching crooks," Jane said, "I want to salute my son for trapping that flower thief." Over their chocolate mousse, Jane told Ted the story of the mum thief.

After dessert, Jane and Amelia started clearing the table.

"No, you don't," Josie said. "Remember the rules: If you make dinner, you don't do the dishes."

Jane kissed everyone good night and climbed the stairs with Stuart Little. "It's nearly ten o'clock," Josie told Amelia. "Past your bedtime."

Amelia hoisted Harry onto her shoulder, said good night, and headed to her room.

"She didn't even protest," Ted said. "She must be tired."

"Or she wants to text her friends about her mom the killer catcher," Josie said.

Five minutes later, Amelia shot out of her room. "Quick! Turn on the TV. There's a special report about Lenore's arrest."

Josie switched on the living room TV in time to hear the announcer say, "Lenore Scottsmeyer Hall has been released from the St. Louis County Jail. As we reported earlier, Emily Deaver Destin was arrested and charged with the first-degree murders of her sister, Molly Ann Deaver, and another woman, Rita Marie Kutchner.

"Lenore Scottsmeyer Hall was wrongly arrested for the murder of Molly Deaver. The newly freed Mrs. Scottsmeyer Hall has agreed to talk to our reporter outside the jail. We're waiting for her to come out now. Here she is with her attorney, Shelford Clark."

The camera panned to Lenore, once again in glamorous black and full makeup. Josie wondered if Clark had brought his client a clean suit and cosmetics.

"How does it feel to be free, Mrs. Scottsmeyer Hall?" the reporter asked.

"Wonderful," Lenore said. "I want to thank my attorney, Shelford Clark of Boca Raton, for expediting the process. I understand it can take more than twenty-four hours to be freed, but Shel had me out within hours after the real killer was arrested."

She hugged Clark and he beamed at her.

"I wonder how much Clark threatened to sue Rock Road Village for unless they hustled Lenore out of jail," Ted said.

"You're so cynical," Josie said, and laughed. But all the while, she was thinking, What about me? Lenore wouldn't be out of prison without my work.

"She didn't even mention me," she said. She couldn't hide her hurt feelings.

Ted hugged her. "She doesn't know the whole story yet," he said.

The reporter said, "What are your plans now, Mrs. Scottsmeyer Hall? Are you taking the first plane back to Boca?"

"Oh no," Lenore said. "My son, Dr. Ted Scottsmeyer, is getting married the day after Thanksgiving. I'm staying in St. Louis to help his bride with their wedding plans."

"There," Ted said. "Mom's going to help. She didn't forget you after all."

Ted's cell phone barked during the commercial break. "I hope that's not a clinic emergency," he said.

He clicked on his phone and smiled. "Mom! You're free. We saw you on TV. You looked wonderful. Thanks for wanting to help Josie with the wedding after all you've been through."

Josie pasted a smile on her face.

"Of course you can talk to her," Ted said. "She's right here."

He handed Josie his cell.

"Josie?" Lenore said. "My attorney says I owe you a debt of gratitude. That's why I agreed to stay and help with your wedding."

"Thank you, but—," Josie said.

"No need to thank me," Lenore said. "My attorney said you got my message about the centerpieces and have something in mind."

"I already sent Mr. Clark the contract," Josie said.

"Excellent," Lenore said. "We're having breakfast at the Ritz tomorrow. I need pampering. Don't forget your wedding plan notebook. We'll go over everything at eight sharp. Don't be late."

Before Josie could say anything, Lenore clicked off her phone.

"I told you Mom didn't forget you," Ted said. He was still grinning when Josie walked him to his car and kissed him good night.

I've got to get Lenore back to Boca, Josie thought, before I go out of my mind.

Chapter 36

How do I get Lenore to go home? Josie wondered.

The time loomed on her bedside clock: 12:08 in the morning.

She had to report to Lenore at the Ritz-Carlton in less than eight hours. Their battle would be fought over eggs and muffins. Lenore would delicately carve away the unique sentiment until Ted and Josie's wedding was one more so-what ceremony.

The process has already started, Josie thought. Lenore insisted that I ditch my plebeian poinsettias and I caved. I gave in on the string quartet and the chair covers. By the time she signs the breakfast check, I'll have as much say-so in our wedding as the bride on my cake.

Unless I can persuade Lenore to go back to Florida.

She has a husband, a successful plastic surgeon, stuck at home with a broken ankle. Boca babes must be prowling the property, eager to pamper a rich, lonely man. I could remind Lenore how easy it is for a woman of a certain age to lose her meal ticket.

Except Ted says his stepfather is a decent guy. It's not fair to suggest Whit is unfaithful. Ted's mother, for all her faults, seems to care about her husband. She just loves herself more.

If only I could get her out of my hair.

Hair! There's my answer. An inspired one, Josie decided, as she drifted off to sleep.

Her alarm rang all too soon. A cold rain lashed the windows, and Amelia fought to stay cocooned in her comfortable bed. Josie prodded her daughter through her morning routine, insisting she wear her yellow rain hoodie. Jane had cheerfully volunteered to chauffeur Amelia to school on this miserable morning.

Josie steeled herself for the fight with another cup of hot coffee. She donned her Ritz-worthy pantsuit like battle armor, adding a bright red scarf to give herself courage. She was ready.

The morning looked the way Josie felt: cold and gloomy. She expertly maneuvered the rain-slick streets in the rush hour. By 8:05, she and Lenore were seated in the cushiony comfort of the restaurant and the server had taken their orders.

"So nice of you to come out on this dreadful day," Lenore said. "Thank you again. My attorney says you helped a little to get me released."

More than a little, Josie thought. You wouldn't be sipping that orange juice without me. She wasn't surprised Shel Clark had skimped on her share of the credit. He couldn't command that fat fee if he admitted a local nobody saved Lenore.

Josie smiled at Lenore. Ted would tell his mother what really happened.

"I'm glad you brought your notebook," Lenore said.

Josie's coffee churned into an acid brew. Brace yourself, she thought.

"Oh, here comes our breakfast," Lenore said. "We'll eat first, then work on your wedding."

Josie blessed the server for her timely reprieve and dawdled over her eggs.

"Something wrong with your breakfast?" Lenore asked.

"Savoring it," Josie said. She finished the last bite of muffin, then launched her plan.

"You look well after your ordeal, Lenore," she said. "Liz, the woman you met in . . ." Could she say *jail* at the Ritz? Josie wondered. Better not. "At the other place you stayed did a lovely job on your hair."

"Thank you," Lenore said. "She is good, isn't she?"

"Too bad she couldn't work on your color," Josie said.

Lenore's face went white as the table linen. "What do you mean?"

"I can see a teeny bit of your roots. I doubt if an untrained eye would notice, but mystery shoppers have to be alert to details."

"I was due for a touch-up last Monday," Lenore said, as if she'd missed an appointment with a parole officer.

"Would you like to see my stylist?" Josie said. "I don't have my hair colored, but I hear Donna is good."

"Here? In St. Louis?" Lenore looked horrified. "I can't go to someone in the middle of nowhere."

"Donna works at the Cheap Chic salon, but she was in New York."

"So was my cook," Lenore said. "Do you have a Frederic Fekkai salon here?"

"No," Josie said.

"What about Dino Laudati? Oribe?"

Josie shook her head. "What's Oribe?" she asked.

"This city is hopeless." Lenore fished a mirror out of her Chanel bag and studied her hair. "But you're correct. My roots are almost an eighth of an inch long. Wait here, Josie. I need to make some calls."

She hurried into the hall like her skirt was on fire. Lenore returned five minutes later, a changed woman. Now she was smiling, calm, and in control. "Josie, dear," she said, "would you mind terribly if I abandoned you? I must leave for home immediately."

"Can I drive you to the airport?" Josie asked.

"No, my attorney's limo will collect me in half an hour. He flies out at noon and there's room on our plane. He'll drop me at my salon."

It worked! Josie thought, and sipped more coffee to hide her relief. This time she really did savor the chocolatey taste.

"There is one problem," Lenore said.

Uh-oh, Josie thought. I'm celebrating too soon.

"If I leave today, I can't return until the morning of the rehearsal dinner," Lenore said. "I lost weight when I stayed at"—there was a delicate pause—"the other place. They served bologna sandwiches."

"Oh dear," Josie said, trying to sound sympathetic.

"I couldn't eat that rubbish," Lenore said. "I'll need to have my dress fitted. I may even need new foundation garments. And of course I'll have to look after my husband. Do you think you can finish planning your wedding on your own?"

"I'll try," Josie said, fighting to keep the glee out of her voice.

Lenore signaled for the check, signed it, then said, "Please finish your coffee. I have to pack and settle my bill."

"I'd love to," Josie said, "but I have things to do. I should go."

"I feel guilty leaving you with so much work," Lenore said.

"Don't worry. I'll manage," Josie said.

The sun was smiling when the valet brought Josie's car. She took that as a good omen.

By the time she reached home, it was raining again. A drenched UPS driver delivered the first wedding presents from Tiffany. Josie didn't recognize the names on the gift cards. Dr. George and Aunt Bitsy sent the stunning Limoges platter. Two other couples, Bunny and Bea and Van and Blair, both gave sterling silver picture frames.

The three gifts totaled more than thirty-five hundred dollars. Their generosity deserved warm, personal thank-you notes, but Josie needed more information about them. Ted would know. She left a message at the clinic.

Ted called back ten minutes later, his voice warming

her on the chilly morning. "Josie, how did the breakfast with Mom go?" he asked.

"We had a nice chat. Lenore is flying back home with her lawyer this morning."

"She's worried about my stepdad," Ted said.

Josie decided it would be petty to tell him Lenore's real reason was all in her head. "We got our first wedding presents," she said. "Three gorgeous gifts from Tiffany. Do you know a Dr. George and Aunt Bitsy?"

"They're my godparents," Ted said.

Josie could hear his smile. They were obvious favorites.

"They sent a fabulous Limoges platter worth more than my car."

"What do we serve on that?" Ted asked.

"Nothing, I hope," Josie said. "I registered at Tiffany because your mother asked me to. I'm grateful for your godparents' generosity, but I have another use for their gift."

"Name it," Ted said.

"We won't be displaying china in a house full of rambunctious pets," she said. "Wedding registry gifts can only be returned for store credit. But we could stash the platter in a safe-deposit box as part of Amelia's college fund. When she needs money, I'll sell it on eBay. If Dr. George and Aunt Bitsy visit us before that, you can whip up a dinner and serve it on their platter."

"I doubt they will," Ted said. "They're eighty-something and rarely leave Palm Beach County."

"There's more. Are Bunny and Bea a gay couple?" Josie asked.

Ted laughed. "They'd be shocked speechless. Bunny is a man's nickname in Mom's circle. Beatrice is his wife. B and B, she calls them. They play bridge with Mom and my stepdad, my godparents, and Van and Blair. Blair is Van's wife."

"B and B and Van and Blair both gave us Tiffany picture frames."

Arf!

"Keep those, will you?" Ted said.

Yap! Yap! Merrrrorow!

"Things going okay at the clinic today?" she asked.

"Better than okay," Ted said. "I found a home for Sammy, the old dachshund whose owner went into assisted living."

"Did you offer any incentives?" Josie asked.

"Just free lifetime vet care," Ted said. "Sammy's fourteen. It wasn't much of an offer."

Woof!

"Gotta go," Ted said. "My patients are getting impatient."

"I love you," Josie said over the clinic's chorus of arfs, yaps, and meows.

She wrote thank-you notes while the rain came down in sheets. It was still pouring when she picked up Amelia at school. Josie's daughter dumped her backpack in the backseat and jumped in the car, water dripping off her yellow hoodie.

Amelia was silent after she said hello. Josie tried to read her silence. It didn't seem brooding or angry. Josie hoped Amelia wouldn't spring one of her awkward questions.

They were almost to the highway when Amelia asked, "Mom, can we have pizza for dinner tonight? I can call Big Dave the pizza dude now."

"Wait till we're home in case we get hung up in traffic," Josie said, "or Big Dave will get there before we do. Why don't you make your own pizza? Yours would probably taste better."

"I like talking to Big Dave," she said. "And pizza that comes in a box tastes better."

"Must be the cardboard," Josie said.

Josie and Amelia spent a quiet evening. "Grandma and I are going to Alyce's early tomorrow," Amelia said. "She's going to show me how she makes the phyllo purses with real caviar. I've never had caviar. Or champagne. Can I have some for the toast?"

"Just a thimbleful," Josie said, and kissed her daughter good night.

Josie woke up to more rain. She was still dreading the bridal shower, and didn't want to go out into the slashing storm.

Once she was inside Alyce's house, Josie's mood lightened. Alyce's white living room managed to look inviting. Bowls and vases of pink, white, and red roses warmed the pale room. A fire crackled and candles glowed.

Josie was engulfed with hugs and congratulations, and given a flute of champagne. Josie was touched by how many people showed up, including many of her mother's church friends. Laura Lavinia Hayes, Josie's former teacher who managed a lingerie shop, was there, too. "I couldn't be happier for you," Laura said. "I'm so grateful you helped me with that problem at my store. I haven't seen you in ages."

Alyce's Wood Winds neighbors clustered in one corner. Connie, the food bank committeewoman, told Josie, "We can't thank you enough for getting that horrible Emily arrested. She nearly destroyed our committee and our hands were tied."

Amelia took her on a tour of the buffet table. "You have to eat a phyllo purse," she said, using the silver tongs to place one on Josie's plate.

"Alyce used American farm-raised caviar," Amelia said. "It's not cool to eat Russian caviar."

"How do you know this?" Josie asked.

"All the good chefs know it," Amelia said.

Josie wasn't sure if she meant herself or Alyce. She took a small forkful of the purse, then a larger one.

"What do you think?" Amelia asked.

"Perfect," Josie said. "The salty caviar accents the creamy mushroom filling."

"You sound like a foodie," Amelia said.

"I like to eat good food," Josie said, "but I can't cook it."

Amelia looked worried. "Um, Mom, I tried one. I didn't like the caviar."

"You will," Josie said. "It takes time for a great chef to develop her palate."

"But what if I don't?" Amelia was still anxious.

"Then you'll discover your own tastes," Josie said.

Josie barely had time to admire the other hors d'oeuvres before she was pulled back into the party. When the guests had settled onto the sofas and the conversation was a chatty buzz, Alyce clinked her glass.

"Let's toast the bride," she said, pouring another round of champagne. "Then, Josie, it's time to open your presents. Amelia, I have hostess duties, so I'll ask you to assist your mother as a bridesmaid."

Josie sat in a thronelike chair next to the pile of presents. The Wood Winds group had demonstrated its gratitude with generous gifts of kitchenware. Amelia helped when Josie was puzzled by a gift.

"A Yukihira pot," Josie read on the box, and held the eight-inch pot awkwardly by the wooden handle.

"Awesome!" Amelia said. "Wait till we make miso soup. See the pouring spouts on the side?"

Laura's ruffle-trimmed coral bikini and cover-up were greeted with wolf whistles. "It's the same style Katy Perry wore," Josie's former teacher said.

"It's a little skimpy," Josie said.

"Not in the islands," Laura said. "You don't want to look dowdy on your honeymoon."

The church ladies had clubbed together for linens. Josie was touched that her mother gave the stand mixer Ted wanted. "I know the whole family will enjoy it," Jane said. "Now open your last present. It's from Alyce."

Josie stripped the silver paper off a flat box. Inside was a photo of a green yard with a family enjoying their deck. Josie saw a table with four chairs and a striped sun umbrella. A Photoshopped Amelia and Josie lounged on two chaises. Ted was grilling at the gas barbecue. Ted's dog, Festus, and his cat, Marmalade, waited by the grill for a burger. Harry was perched on Amelia's shoulder.

"It's my dream," Josie said, and her eyes filled with tears.

"Lift up the photo," Alyce said.

Under it was a gift certificate for a St. Louis outdoor furniture store. The amount would cover all the furniture and the grill.

"You made my dream come true," Josie said.

"No, you did that," Alyce said as the shower guests toasted her with champagne.

Chapter 37

"Ready?" Jane asked.

"Yes," Josie said.

"I've never done this before," Jane said.

"Me, either," Josie said.

She took her mother's arm. She'd leaned on Jane for more than thirty years. Now Josie needed her again to walk down the aisle. Butterflies flapped in her stomach.

"Nervous?" Jane asked.

"No," Josie said. "I mean yes. It's after two o'clock. Let's go."

The Jewel Box was a crystal cathedral bathed in buttery autumn light. Josie glided along the white runner, escorted by her mother.

The string quartet played a fanfare, the notes shimmering in the clear air.

"I'm glad you let Lenore give you that quartet," Jane said to her daughter. "Live music sounds so much better than tapes."

Josie nodded. The aisle seemed a thousand yards long.

"And we couldn't have had better weather if we'd ordered it," Jane said. "We've been through terrible storms."

"So we have," Josie said. "The weather's been scary, too." She grinned at her mother.

The Jewel Box's cantilevered walls were a towering

fifty feet tall, but today the art deco landmark was Josie's sunlit secret garden. Poinsettias bloomed in impossible colors: cool whites, tender pinks, blazing reds. The showy tropical flowers were massed against pygmy date palms and feathery tree ferns. Flower baskets trailed from the ceiling.

Josie and Jane glided down the Fountain Court to an elegant oasis of palms and flowers near the entrance, accompanied by the music and a soft chorus of whispers: "She's beautiful." . . . "Where did she get that jewelry?" . . . "Who would have guessed Josie could look so extraordinary?"

"They're right," Jane said. "You look beautiful. Your grandmother's brooch was meant for your wedding dress."

Josie's gown was deceptively simple: long and white with a V neck. On her left shoulder, Jane had pinned her mother's dramatic art deco pearl-and-diamond brooch.

"You could have sold that pin after my father left and made your life a lot easier," Josie said.

"I was saving it for this day," Jane said. "It was worth the struggle. And so were you." She gave a small, contented sigh.

"You look pretty good yourself, Mom," Josie said. Jane's pale pink dress and matching coat suited her complexion.

"I'm not sophisticated like Lenore," Jane began.

"Lenore is supposed to be admired," Josie said. "You're meant to be loved. I love you, Mom."

"You like the pink?" Jane asked. "I wanted to look special for you. Not many mothers get to escort their daughter down the aisle."

"Not many mothers worked so hard for that privilege," Josie said.

Now Josie saw the wedding party waiting at the palm oasis. Her two bridesmaids—Alyce in rich red velvet and Amelia in soft rose—seemed part of the floral show. On the groom's side, Ted's best friend and clinic partner, Christine, wore a stunning Stella McCartney tuxedo.

Ted's groomsmen — Richard, his brother, and Christine's son, Todd, were blurs.

Josie was dazzled by her groom. Ted was a striking six feet tall, with wide shoulders and a narrow waist. The fine tailoring made his shoulders seem broader. His brown hair was impossibly thick. Josie wanted to grab his hand and run away with him.

But she'd learned something planning this wedding. It wasn't her day, or Ted's. It belonged to their families.

A few more steps and Josie would be with Ted forever.

"Still nervous?" Jane asked, and squeezed Josie's hand.

"Not anymore," Josie said. "Not now when I see Ted ahead of me."

"That's your whole life ahead of you," Jane said.

Jane arranged Josie's sheer veil, gave her daughter a kiss, then took Ted's and Josie's hands. "Take care of each other," she said.

I will, Mom, Josie promised herself. I do.

Christine escorted Jane to her seat.

"You're beautiful," Ted whispered to Josie.

"So are you," Josie said. "I've never seen you in a tux."

"I added a few dog hairs so you'd recognize me," Ted said.

Josie giggled.

The minister, Ted's uncle, Bob Scottsmeyer, cleared his throat. Josie thought Reverend Uncle Bob could be a happy vision of her future. He had Ted's kind brown eyes, a sun-reddened outdoorsy face, and thick white hair.

"Reverend Uncle Bob could be my father's twin," Ted had told her. "He's the next best thing to having Dad here."

The minister was blessed with a resonant voice. "Today, it is my happy privilege to marry my nephew, Ted, and his bride, Josie," he said. "We're here to celebrate their new life together.

"Ted Scottsmeyer, do you take Josie Marcus for your

lawful wedded wife? Will you love, honor, comfort, and cherish her from this day forward, for as long as you both live?"

"I do." Ted's voice rang out in the vast glass building. For generations, couples had made that promise here, and would for years to come. Josie wanted to be part of this past and future love.

Reverend Uncle Bob said, "Josie Marcus, do you take Ted Scottsmeyer for your lawful wedded husband? Will you love, honor, comfort, and cherish him from this day forward, for as long as you both live?"

"Oh, yes," Josie said. "I mean, I do."

The congregation laughed.

Alyce stepped forward to read Shakespeare's eighteenth sonnet in a clear voice.

"'Shall I compare thee to a summer's day?'" she began. "'Thou art more lovely and more temperate . . .'"

For almost four hundred years those words had enchanted lovers. Ted and Josie fell under their spell.

Only when Josie heard Alyce say, "'So long as men can breathe, or eyes can see, / So long lives this, and this gives life to thee,'" did Josie return to her wedding at the Jewel Box.

"It is time for the marriage vows," Reverend Uncle Bob said. "Ted, repeat after me. I, Ted Scottsmeyer, take you, Josie Marcus, to be my wedded wife, to have and to hold from this day forward, for better, for worse, for richer, for poorer, in sickness and in health, to love, honor, and cherish, till death parts us."

Josie and Ted had traded the old-school "obey" for "cherish." "I want an equal partner," he'd said.

He was uneasy about saying "till death parts us," but Josie insisted. "We're together until the very end," she'd said.

She repeated her vows, then Reverend Uncle Bob said, "May I have the bride's ring?"

Christine smoothly produced Josie's wedding ring. The minister blessed it and Ted slipped it on Josie's finger with the twin-diamond engagement ring. Now her wedding set was complete.

Alyce handed Reverend Uncle Bob Ted's gold band. He blessed it. Josie took it with trembling fingers, but she didn't drop the ring. She slid it on Ted's finger.

When the double-ring ceremony was completed, the string quartet burst into triumphant music. Josie had obsessed on choosing the right piece. Now they might as well have played "Pop Goes the Weasel" for all she noticed. The hundred or so guests vanished and it was only her and Ted.

She could hear Reverend Uncle Bob say, "May Ted and Josie continue to give, forgive, and receive more joy with each passing day. May they have the love of their family, the support of their friends, long life, good health, and everlasting love.

"By the power vested in me, I now pronounce Ted Scottsmeyer and Josie Marcus husband and wife. Ted and Josie, you may seal your promises with a kiss."

Their kiss was electric.

Reverend Uncle Bob raised his arms and said, "Ladies and gentlemen, I present this loving couple, Ted Scottsmeyer and Josie Marcus."

The rest of the day seemed to pass by in snapshots. Ted and Josie didn't walk down the aisle together. Their guests engulfed them in a flurry of kisses and congratulations.

For the first time, Josie noticed that Jack Weekler, Amelia's Canadian grandfather, was at the ceremony. "I'm happy for you, Josie," he whispered, but she heard the sadness in his voice. He'd wished Josie had married his son. But Nate was there, too. Josie could see him in Amelia's face. She looked blissfully happy with her grandfather. Josie made sure the photographer took their picture.

Josie had finally met Ted's stepfather at the rehearsal dinner the previous night. Whit Hall had flown up on his plane. He used a silver-headed cane at the wedding, but he would abandon it to dance with Lenore at the reception.

"You're even prettier than Ted said," Whit had told Josie. "Welcome to our family."

Lenore looked like a visitor from a distant, fashionable planet in her black designer dress. "You make a picture-perfect bride, my dear," she said.

And their pictures would be perfect. Josie knew it. She and Ted had hired the legendary Tom Hedtke, a former wire service photographer who was now the city's premier wedding specialist. The old cigar chomper told Josie, "I started shooting during Vietnam, then covered everything from wars to riots for the wires. I took a buyout at fifty-five and sat around getting fat. So I started doing weddings as a favor, and then I was back in the game again—fights, riots, action, and emotion. I'll have a team of photographers capture every moment of your day."

He did, too. The surprisingly agile Tom and his assistants climbed balconies, scaled staircases, and shot photos and video from impossible angles throughout the day. They took scads of photos in the flattering light of the Jewel Box. Tom nearly hung upside down taking video.

Richard, Ted's foolish brother, gave Josie a shy kiss. "May I call you Sis?" he asked.

"Of course," Josie said.

Josie's brother-in-law was not going to be a worry today. Last night, Richard had put plastic ice cubes with fake flies in them in the guests' water glasses at the Ritz.

Lenore had dragged her son out into the hall by his ear, as if he were seven years old. Alyce, coming out of the restroom, heard Lenore hiss, "I am mortified, Richard. You promised." Alyce slipped back behind the door to listen.

"Awww, Mom," he whined. "It didn't hurt anyone."

"It embarrassed me!" Lenore thundered. "Your allowance is cut for one year. You will get a job. And if you ever pull another so-called joke again, you will be disinherited. Do you understand?"

"But, Mom."

"DO YOU UNDERSTAND ME!"

"Yes, Mother."

"Go sit down. I've already apologized to my guests. Now you will."

"I don't know what to say," Richard said.

"Think of something," Lenore said. "Or you'll fly home commercial."

That horror forced Richard to make a rambling apology. He left before dessert.

With the threat of Richard's shenanigans gone, Josie felt free to enjoy her wedding day. She and Ted ran out of the building in a playful shower of wedding bubbles, then posed in front of the statue of St. Francis of Assisi, the patron saint of animals, near the Jewel Box. Ted wanted that photo for the clinic.

Then he helped Josie into his newly waxed vintage Mustang, decorated with white bows and JUST MARRIED signs. Once they were both settled in the car, they kissed. This time, they could let the kiss last.

"Um," Josie said. "I may like legal love even better."

"We'll test that theory on our honeymoon," Ted said as he started the car.

The other wedding guests formed a waving, honking parade through Forest Park and along the streets to Tower Grove Park in the south part of the city. The wedding procession rolled through Tower Grove's Grand Avenue entrance, guarded by lions and griffins.

They waved to another wedding party, a couple on bicycles, and a mom with a baby stroller, all enjoying the pleasures of the park's main drive.

At last, they came to the most romantic spot in the park, the place where Ted had proposed: A three-tiered fountain splashing in a glass-smooth reflecting pool, surrounded by stone ruins.

Even Lenore was impressed. "It looks like a Valenciennes landscape," she said.

Josie guessed he was a painter.

"Was there a mansion on this site?" Lenore asked.

"No, Mom," Ted said. "These are real ruins from an old hotel that burned down almost a hundred and fifty years ago. Henry Shaw, the man who created this park, made the ruins into this folly. They're an artistic recycling."

"Very successful," Lenore said. That was high praise indeed.

Two clinic aides were waiting with the pets. The dogs, Festus and Stuart Little, were freshly washed and wearing their bow ties. Marmalade had bathed herself and wore her white ribbon. Harry tried to claw off his bow tie.

Lenore eyed the pets and the pond warily, as if she expected the orange carp to leap out and attack.

Tom and his assistants posed the wedding party, with Ted and Josie in the center. Alyce, Amelia, and Jane were on Josie's side. Amelia held her rose bouquet and perched Harry on her shoulder. Stuart Little sat obediently at Jane's feet. Ted sat Marmalade on his shoulder and Festus at his feet, where the friendly Lab's tail whipped at Lenore's long skirt. She tried to be a good sport, but she didn't like Festus near her dress. Whit traded places and stood next to Ted, with Lenore at his side.

"Big smiles," Tom said. He had the video camera trained on the group. His assistants were taking the still shots.

"Cheese," said Josie, Jane, Ted and Amelia.

"Money," said Dr. Hall and Lenore.

"Beautiful," Tom said. "One more."

It was one too many for Harry. The striped cat tore off his bow tie and jumped on his friend Stuart's back. The surprised shih tzu leaped up and darted toward Festus. Marmalade jumped off Ted's shoulder and ran under Lenore's dress. "I've got it all," Tom the videographer yelled.

"So do I," Ted said, and gave Josie a joyous kiss.

Epilogue

"How was your honeymoon?" Jane asked. "Never mind. I can see. You're both glowing." She opened her front door and smiled at Ted and Josie.

Josie felt odd being invited into her mother's home like a guest. Her downstairs flat was empty and the blinds were shut. She no longer lived on Phelan Street. After tonight, neither would Amelia.

"Thank you for letting me know you arrived home safely last night," Jane said.

"Good to see you, Mom," Ted said, and kissed Jane on her cheek.

Josie hugged her mother. "How are you? How's my girl?"

"Amelia's fine. She's upstairs making meat loaf, Ted's favorite dinner."

"And what about Mom's favorite dinner?" Josie asked, with mock severity.

"I've never seen you turn down meat loaf," Jane said.

"And you never will," Josie said.

"We've moved Amelia's things into her new room at your place," Jane said. "She's ready to go home with you tonight—after you open your wedding presents. Your nose is peeling, Josie."

"Even a thirty-SPF sunblock couldn't protect it in the tropics," Josie said.

Josie noticed how slowly her mother climbed the

stairs to her flat. Jane seemed frailer than she had before the wedding. Or maybe I've been too wrapped up in myself to notice, Josie thought.

Amelia was waiting at the top of the stairs. "Mom! Ted!"

She launched herself at her mother.

"Oh, I've missed you so much," Josie said, wrapping her arms around her daughter. She was pleased that Amelia didn't pull away, and touched that she wore the pink necklace Josie had given her as a bridesmaid's gift.

Ted gave her a grave kiss on the cheek.

"Woof!" Stuart Little said, dancing at their feet. Harry was curled up on the pile of wedding presents in Jane's living room, pretending to be aloof. Ted and Josie scratched both pets and Ted dropped a shopping bag beside Jane's couch.

He sniffed the air. "I smell something wonderful."

"Meat loaf stuffed with prosciutto and spinach," Amelia said. "I made it with ground pork and beef. Come on. I'll show you."

Josie watched her new husband and daughter retreat to Jane's kitchen.

"She's gotten taller in the week we've been gone," Josie said.

"Amelia is a young woman now," Jane said. "And a born chef."

"Like you," Josie said.

"She's long since surpassed me," Jane said.

Dinner was a noisy celebration. The food disappeared quickly while Amelia peppered them with questions: "Awesome photos of your honeymoon villa. Could you really see the ocean from your porch? Did you go snorkeling? Sailboating? Sit on the beach? Hike?"

"Yes, yes, and yes," Josie said, laughing. "We got all those activities for wedding presents. Some guests gave us scuba diving and sailing. I spent a day at a spa while Ted went deep-sea fishing."

"What did you catch?" Amelia asked.

"Mahi mahi," Ted said.

"Best steaks ever," Josie said.

"I wish they had a gift service like that when I got married," Jane said. "It would be nice to give good memories."

"You don't have to dust them, either," Josie said.

She didn't need photos to remember their tropical nights, the walks on the secluded beaches, or the lazy afternoons at the villa. She'd always have those memories.

"I baked a Bundt cake for dessert," Amelia said. "It's my first."

The four of them ate nearly the entire cake. "That was a spectacular dinner," Ted said.

"What else can we do?" Josie said.

"Please open your wedding gifts," Jane said. "I really do want them out of my living room."

Josie had kept pace with the presents that arrived before their wedding, writing thank-you notes and putting their gifts away at Ted's home. She and Ted still had to formally thank Lenore and Whit for their present. At the rehearsal dinner, Whit had given them a sterling silver box. Inside was a balance transfer for one hundred thousand dollars to Ted and Josie's joint account.

"That's very generous," Josie said after she caught her breath.

"I don't know how to thank you," Ted said.

"That's only part of what Lenore's case would have cost if she'd gone to trial," Whit said. "We hope you'll use it for the down payment on your new home, but the money is yours to do with as you please."

"Thank you," Josie said.

"We owe you much more, Josie," Whit said. "I wouldn't be here tonight with my beautiful bride without you."

He kissed Lenore.

"Ted told us what you did, my dear," Lenore said. "I'm grateful to our attorney for getting me out of jail quickly, but the real credit goes to you."

"And the cash," Whit said, and winked. The silver box was on the dresser in Ted and Josie's room. Josie kept her jewelry in it.

Jane handed Josie the first present, a flat box wrapped in white paper.

"I found this on my porch when Amelia and I came home from the wedding," Jane said. "It's from Mrs. Mueller."

Josie held the box up to her ear. "Does it tick?" she asked.

She read the card out loud. "'Dear Josie,'" it said. "'I'm sorry I am unable to attend your wedding. I hope this gift will help you remember me.'"

"How can I ever forget Mrs. M?" Josie ripped open the paper and burst into laughter when she lifted the box lid. Inside was a gold spray-painted ashtray with a chipped corner.

"Gross," Amelia said.

"Did she get it at Goodwill?" Ted asked.

"More like a garage sale," Josie said. "She caught me smoking behind her garage when I was fifteen and ratted me out to Mom. I got even with Mrs. M by leaving burning dog doo on her porch, and she stamped out the fire."

Ted snorted. Amelia said, "That's way worse than exploding Mentos."

"Give me that," Jane said. "I'm putting it in the trash."

"No, you're not," Josie said. "I'm keeping it. And I'll write her a thank-you note."

"I'm glad she wasn't at your wedding," Jane said. "Everyone at church talked about your beautiful wedding and the wonderful reception and she had nothing to say."

An hour later, Josie and Ted sat with their unwrapped loot.

"Primo swag," Amelia said. "You got all your china and crystal, Mom. Awesome truffle slicer—and we got the truffles, too. Are we going to try those organic aji powders, Ted?"

"It would be wrong to waste hot peppers," Ted said. "We can experiment with spicy recipes. And we have a lot of new cookware to break in. But we still haven't opened all the gifts."

He reached into the bag next to the couch and handed one box to Jane and another to Amelia.

Jane opened hers first. "A green silk pantsuit," she said. "It's so beautiful, I'm afraid to wear it."

"It's not silk," Josie said. "It's bamboo, but it looks like silk. Eco friendly. You can throw it in the washing machine."

"Pictures!" Amelia said. "I got pictures."

She was hugging two of the silver Elsa Peretti frames. The double frame showed Josie in her wedding dress and Amelia dancing at the reception with her grandfather, Jack. The other framed the photo of the wedding party at Tower Grove Park, captured just as Harry had turned the posed photo into chaos.

"What do you think of your photos?" Ted asked.

"Flawless," Amelia said.

Josie and Ted had time to study their wedding photos now that they were back from their honeymoon. One of their favorites showed Lenore and Whit winning the twist contest at the reception. Lenore gave the hundred-dollar prize to Amelia, but she insisted on keeping the plastic trophy. She displays it in her living room, on the same shelf with a Song Dynasty bowl.

Emily Deaver Destin pleaded guilty to two counts of first-degree murder in the deaths of Molly Ann Deaver and Rita Marie Kutchner and avoided the death penalty. She confessed that she'd stolen Lenore's purse at the Blue Rose Tearoom when she took her break, and lifted the pearl-handled pistol. Emily dropped the purse back on a chair at Lenore's table during the confused search. "I had to get rid of Molly," she said. "She refused to go into treatment for stalking. She was ruining my husband's business and my life. She made us laughing-stocks." Emily was sentenced to life without possibility of parole. Emily's husband, Brad, sold the house at the Estates in Wood Winds, to the considerable relief of their neighbors.

Molly had left everything to her sister in her will. But after Emily pleaded guilty, she could not profit from her sister's murder and inherit Molly's estate. Aunt Martha inherited Molly's money, which kept her in comfort in an assisted living facility.

Trudy Sandusky's attorney said the stress of planning her daughter Amy's wedding had triggered her irrational mum thefts. "My client's own plants died when she accidentally sprayed them with weed killer," the lawyer said. "Rather than buy more, she stole mums from Maplewood."

Trudy apologized for stealing and promised to make restitution to everyone in Josie's neighborhood who had lost their flowers. Charges were dropped against the plant rustler—but not before the story made the *St. Louis City Gazette*. Trudy also needed treatment for severe poison ivy. Amy, mortified that her mother was known as the "mum-stealing Mum," eloped with her fiancé. They married on a beach in the Bahamas.

Denise's Dreams closed following Emily's arrest for the double murders. Denise was right—no bride wanted to shop at a store that had two murder victims. Denise sold the shop, and the little house became a successful coffeehouse and Internet café. Denise now sells discount wedding dresses at the Bridal Barn.

George Winstid was promoted to manager of the Brenhoff Carpet and Flooring store in Billings shortly before his marriage to Renee. His mother, Phoebe, traveled to Montana for their wedding and fell in love with the state.

She sold her home in St. Louis, and George and Renee helped pay for her move to Billings. Phoebe enjoys volunteer work and taking her two grandchildren canoeing, hiking, and horseback riding.

Ted, Josie, and Amelia faced more changes as they settled in to their temporary home. Festus abandoned his bed in Ted's office and Marmalade would only sleep by Ted's computer when he was working. Now both animals moved into Amelia's room.

A month after their honeymoon, Josie and Ted stood in the doorway of Amelia's room. Her old night-light glowed softly on the framed wedding photos. Amelia kept them next to the picture of her father, Nate, as a boy, with a cat who looked like Harry's twin.

The real Harry was curled up next to the sleeping Amelia. Festus and Marmalade were sprawled at the foot of her bed.

"Does Amelia have enough room to sleep?" Ted whispered. "The livestock's taken over her bed. What do you think?"

"I think it's flawless," Josie said.

Shopping Tips

Your wedding may be the biggest party you'll ever throw—and your most expensive. The average American wedding costs twenty-nine thousand dollars, according to the *Wedding Report*. That's the down payment on a decent home.

Weddings can be hazardous to your marriage. Couples become so caught up in planning their wedding that they forget why they fell in love. These shopping tips for wedding cakes and flowers will help you survive—and even enjoy—what's supposed to be the happiest day of your life.

Hearts and flowers

Bigger may not be better—not when it comes to bridal bouquets. Petite brides may look lost behind a huge, heavy cascade of flowers. Smaller posy bouquets are lighter and easier to carry. At least that's what some wedding experts claim.

But if your heart is set on a cascade, who cares? Your florist can lighten the heavy look with feathers, beads, or fancy wire.

You may want to tie a photo pendant of an absent parent or friend to a bouquet so you'll have your loved one with you all day. Use a blue ribbon and you've added "something blue" to the ensemble.

You can also give a posy bouquet a "collar" of feathers, foliage, or ornamental grass. A posy bouquet's stems can be wrapped in silk or ribbon to match your wedding colors. Or skip the heavy stem ribbons and set your bouquet in a vase of water at the head table as part of the decorations. It's economical and eco-friendly. Just remember to dry off your bouquet if you carry it again. The water may spot your dress.

Here comes the bling

You may want to add diamante or crystal beads to your flowers or put them on the ribbon handle. These ornaments can accent the crystals on your veil.

Are corsages for the prom?

If you want your bridesmaids, mother, and future mother-in-law to wear corsages, consider their dress fabric first. Heavy shoulder corsages may tear delicate fabrics. Some florists use "corsage magnets" to avoid pins. A small magnet is set in the back of the corsage and a thin metal disk is placed under the material of the jacket or dress to hold the corsage in place.

A corsage will leave your bridesmaids' hands free — but do they really want that? Nervous bridesmaids may feel better holding a bouquet when they make the long walk down the aisle.

It's all in the wrist

Wrist corsages work especially well with short-sleeved or sleeveless dresses. You can also pin flowers to a handbag or a hat. Be courteous, even if it is your wedding. Ask the mothers if they'd rather carry a small bouquet or a single flower. Some women consider corsages too old-fashioned. You may want to give your mother and mother-in-law stylish brooches they can keep as mementos.

Fit for a queen

Queen Elizabeth I was often painted with her favorite pomander. Pomanders—flower balls with pretty ribbon handles—can be carried like purses. Young flower girls or junior bridesmaids love them.

For budget-minded brides, pomanders can be made from inexpensive flowers such as daisies, carnations, or chrysanthemums. Crafty brides may want to make their own with silk or paper flowers.

Bored with flower bouquets?

What about bouquets made from antique buttons, origami flowers, feathers, candy, or seashells? Some winter wedding parties carry fake fur muffs—just brace yourself for the inevitable jokes.

Some of these OffbeatBride.com bouquets are works of art (http://offbeatbride.com/2009/03/wedding-bouquets).

Wedding Thingz offers alternatives from dramatic parasols to playful pinwheels (http://www.weddingth ingz.com/1/post/2012/05/alternatives-to-bridesmaids-carrying-floral-bouquets.html).

DIY brides can make bouquets and boutonnieres from paper. Paper-Source.com has clever kits.

Boutonnieres

If your dude won't wear the traditional flower, give him foliage. Try rosemary (for remembrance, as Shakespeare said), thistle, or heather. A sprig of holly or mistletoe makes a simple holiday boutonniere.

Martha Stewart has this eco-friendly suggestion: "If you and your fiancé have a book or passage that's especially meaningful to you—your vows, perhaps?—turn it into a boutonniere by photocopying or printing out the text and punching it into floral shapes. It won't merely survive your wedding day. It'll last through your golden anniversary." (http://www.marthastewartweddings.com/226648/punched-out-boutonniere-how).

I loved the steampunk boutonniere at OffbeatBride .com (http://offbeatbride.com/2010/09/bad-ass-bouton nieres). Yes, they're really called bad-ass boutonnieres. You must be sick of syrupy bridal-guidese by now.

Reception flowers

Flower arrangements can set the mood for your reception, from small, informal bouquets to impressive arrangements that soar toward the ceiling. Whichever type of centerpiece you choose, make sure your guests aren't hidden behind hedges. They need to see and talk to one another at the tables.

The head table often has long, low arrangements. You can also use a flower runner, garland, or swag. A long head table means the members of your wedding party will be able to talk only to the person on either side. Some couples seat their wedding party members across from one another or at tables for four, with a small arrangement on each table.

Florist-free flowers

Check out wholesale flower markets, usually found near big cities, or scout your local farmers market.

Don't forget your supermarket flower section. These flowers may not be as well-cared for as florists' blooms, but you can find flowers for bouquets, table centerpieces, boutonnieres, floral arches, or pew holders. You may want to buy mixed bouquets and take them apart.

Using a professional florist costs more, but it can save you time. Make sure you or the person arranging your flowers will have enough time for your DIY projects. Allow time for last-minute problems, when Great Aunt Susan's plane is delayed and she needs a ride to her hotel, or the sky looks cloudy and your outdoor wedding may have to be moved indoors.

Flowers on the Web

Bridesign.com has a "wedding in a box." You choose your bouquets, boutonnieres, corsages, centerpieces, and pew holders online, and they're shipped to arrive three days before the wedding. Bridesign.com says couples save "an average of thirty to forty percent." This wedding in a box is only available in the forty-eight contiguous states.

Other florists offer similar flower packages, including Growers Box (http://www.growersbox.com/catalog/wedding-flowers-3/).

Some online flowers look amazingly cheap, but factor in the cost of shipping and time. You'll need someone to care for the flowers once they arrive, arrange them, deliver them to the ceremony and the reception—and a backup plan in case your flowers don't get to you on time. Even the most reliable companies can't prevent delays from snow, tornadoes, or thunderstorms.

If you're using an online florist for the first time, you may want to order a small test bouquet to check for quality and reliability.

Smooth as silk

Some brides choose silk wedding flowers because they're a green alternative. Others are concerned about allergies, or they don't like to kill flowers for their special day. Silk flowers definitely last longer. You'll have your silk wedding bouquet for many years.

Good silk flowers can even fool the experts, but they're almost as expensive as real ones. You may want to mix silk and real flowers for your wedding. You could order silk flower bouquets for the head table or for your wedding ceremony, then use the flowers in your new home or donate them to a nursing home or charity. Silk flower headbands can be worn by your bridesmaids and flower girls after the wedding—or added to a pretty hat.

Tips to trim your flower costs

- A nosegay can do double duty as a bouquet at the head table. Make sure you have a water-filled vase for it.
- Ask your florist if you can rent vases rather than buy them. You may also be able to rent tropical plants and topiaries.
- Nip expensive bridesmaids' bouquets in the bud. Consider a single perfect lily, rose, or gerbera daisy.
- Use flowers in season. Check out the Wedding Flowers Guide (http://www.wedding-flowers-guide.com/seasonal-wedding-flowers.html). The Bliss Wedding Floral Chart (http://www.bliss weddings.com/weddingfloral/) can help you choose flowers by color, season, and region. Stylish hydrangeas are in season in the spring in the East. In the Midwest, you may have to wait until summer. Roses, anthurium, orchids, lilies, and gerbera daisies are usually available year-round.
- Love a romantic Valentine's Day wedding? The cost of your flowers may double, some florists say. You may even have trouble finding a good florist, since this holiday is one of the industry's busiest times. Book your Valentine's wedding early and get your flower prices in writing.
- Float candles and a single large blossom in a glass bowl for table decorations at your reception.
- Use a single live orchid plant on each table. After the wedding, you can keep the plants or give them to friends or members of the wedding party.

- Votive candles and seashells on mirrors make decorative summer centerpieces.
- Candles and framed fun photos of the bride and groom make memorable centerpieces and good conversation starters at your reception tables.
- Use small trees strung with fairy lights in pots for decoration at the ceremony or the reception. You can plant them in your yard afterward or give them to members of the wedding party.
- Concerned about filling a big room with flowers? Martha Stewart recommends these "ginormous paper flowers" (http://thebridesguide. marthastewartweddings.com/2012/03/scene-stealer-oversize-paper-flowers.html).

Grow your own

Brides and grooms with a flair for gardening may grow their own wedding flowers. Experts say you'll need one to three years of advance preparation. Growing your own flowers can give your wedding extra meaning—or give you extra headaches. *Better Homes and Gardens* has this guide: (http://www.bhg.com/gardening/flowers/grow-your-own-wedding-flowers/).

DIY flower arrangements

These can save you money, but make extra work. You'll need to buy vases and get the centerpieces to the reception and the ceremony. Choose flowers that hold up. You don't want to start your new life with vases of wilted flowers. Experts recommend a practice run so you'll know how long it will take to make the arrangements and deliver them.

Green brides

Some brides don't want to leave a big carbon footprint when they walk down the aisle. They're concerned that

.house flowers may be loaded with pesticides and
.own in from overseas. Talk to your florist about using
locally grown organic flowers. Organic Bouquet has
pesticide-free flowers for weddings and other occasions
(http://www.organicbouquet.com/).

Another green choice is using potted flowering plants
or herbs. Rosemary, lavender and sage look and smell
good. Extra green points if you support your local nursery.

Couples can also use centerpieces of colorful citrus—
lemons, limes, oranges—in glass bowls or vases. Baskets
of seasonal fruit—grapes, strawberries, peaches, apples—
make handsome centerpieces and treats for your guests.

Thorns among the roses

Shortchanging brides on the flowers in their bouquets
and centerpieces was part of Josie's mystery shopping
experience. But that's not fiction. Bridaltips.com says it's
one of the top ten bridal scams.

Here's how it works: A florist shows you a stunning
sample bouquet, a knockout centerpiece, or a gorgeous
photo. You love the flowers and the price is perfect. You
sign the contract. At your reception, those stunning centerpieces seem smaller—because they are. The shop
didn't deliver what you fell in love with.

Also, watch out when the florist faxes you a price
quote and "you try to haggle the price down. If they fax
a new quote, check every single item to make sure they
did not remove any items," Bridaltips.com says. "Some
florists get sneaky and say, 'Sure, we can come down on
the price a bit.' When you scrutinize their new quote,
you'll see your 'champagne lace' tablecloth was changed
to a plain tan tablecloth."

Check your contract before you sign. Make sure it
states the number and type of flowers in your bouquets,
centerpieces, and decorations, and exactly how many
centerpieces you'll have at the reception and arrangements at the ceremony.

To prevent disappointments, get florist recommendations from your friends. Check with the Better Business Bureau and the court judgments on your county records Web site.

Don't have time to search the Internet? Enlist your groom or a Web-savvy bridesmaid to help.

Beware of phantom florists

One bride was thrilled when she found an inexpensive florist at an "awesome" price on a wedding board. She lived on the other side of the country. This bride talked with the florist by phone, but felt uneasy. She went back and checked that message board again. The florist had only one review, no address, and no contact name. The photos on the florist's site were stock pictures. The florist explained that her prices were low because she worked out of her home. She wanted to meet at a coffee shop. The florist supplied good reasons, but the bride knew that some so-called florists took the deposit money and disappeared. She chose an established (and more expensive) local florist with a history of happy brides.

Scratch that idea

Some brides get so caught up in the "it's my day" madness, they forget their guests and attendants may have allergies. "The bride chose stargazer lilies for the bridesmaids' bouquets. Two of the girls were highly allergic to these flowers and told the bride ahead of time," a bridesmaid told *St. Louis Bride*. "But the bride insisted on them. The two bridesmaids sneezed throughout the entire ceremony, all the while getting dirty looks from the bride and her mother."

Balloons make colorful, inexpensive decorations, but make sure none of your guests have latex allergies. They may not be able to attend your reception. Latex allergies are so common, some hospitals ban latex balloons.

Your dinner menu, buffet, or desserts should clearly label any food containing nuts. It puts a damper on your wedding when a guest is carried out of your reception gasping for breath.

Cake flower

Fresh flowers or petals can be pretty additions to your wedding cake. Your florist may have a special holder so the flower decorations can be removed when you cut the cake.

If you want real flowers on your wedding cake, make sure they haven't been sprayed with pesticides. Avoid flowers and plants that can be poisonous, including calla lilies, holly, mistletoe, and oleander, or plants that shed pollen or leaves, such as asparagus fern. Amaryllis and poinsettias in pots make pretty winter table decorations, but don't put these poisonous plants near your cake. If you still want these flowers, consider a small bouquet on your cake table.

Silk or artificial flowers are another wedding cake alternative. Some bakers excel at creating lifelike edible flowers (http://www.wedideas.com/).

Tip-top

Many of the wedding cake toppers Josie and Jane saw are available online. Here are some sources: Party City (http://www.partycity.com/category/weddings/cake+toppers.do), Wedding Cake Toppers (http://www.weddingcaketoppers.com/), Wedding Collectibles (http://www.weddingcollectibles.com/WeddingCakeToppers.html), Affectionately Yours & ArtStyle Cake Toppers (http://www.funweddingthings.com/).

Hot weddings

If you have an outdoor wedding, make sure your cake or cupcakes are served safely. Salmonella is not a good wedding souvenir. Display your wedding cake or cupcakes in

a cool, shady place or under a tent. Icing melts in dir
sunlight. Some bakers recommend Italian meringue but
ter cream icing for outdoor events. If you're making the
cake yourself, use pasteurized egg whites to be extra safe.

That takes the cake

Couples are often shocked by the hidden costs of a wedding cake. You may have a delivery fee of fifty dollars or
so, plus a cake-cutting fee ranging from fifty cents to five
dollars a slice. That fee covers the cost of plates and
forks and their cleanup. Some wedding venues waive
these fees if you buy your cake from their baker.

Faking it at your wedding

A traditional wedding cake can cost a week's salary or
more. Some couples order a wedding cake that has one
or two real layers and the other tiers are iced Styrofoam.
The wedding guests are served slices of cheaper sheet
cake stashed in the kitchen. This can save you major
money, especially at a big wedding. Just make sure you
slice into the right layer for the cake cutting photos.

If you consider a traditional wedding cake a big, fat
waste of money, you can rent a fake cake. Rentals start
at about one hundred twenty-five dollars plus shipping,
and you supply your own cake for the hidden compart-
ment. Here's one online cake rental company (http://
www.cakerental.com/index2009.html).

Just make sure your drunken uncle doesn't try to
snitch a piece of your fake cake.

You can serve your guests real sheet cake or some
other sweet alternative.

Is the wedding cake dead?

One Web site is gleefully tolling the bell. "Wedding expert
Cara Davis has included 'Death of the Wedding Cake' in

r top eight wedding trends for 2011," it said. "Citing wedding cupcakes as a major reason for the decline of wedding cakes, Cara also attributes dessert buffets as a contributing factor. Personally, here at wedding-cupcakes. org, we love that Cara has officially announced the Death of the Wedding Cake because it takes a significant chip out of what once was the impenetrable wall of proper wedding etiquette: that wedding cakes were the only suitable dessert for a wedding."

This wedding cupcake site may be a bit biased. But there's no doubt that wedding cupcakes are a significant trend. You can display the cupcakes on tiered stands on a traditional cake table, or organize your reception tables by cupcake flavor—the chocolate cupcake table, the lemon table, the red velvet table.

Green cupcake stands for white weddings

Cupcaketree.com has recyclable cupcake stands in many shapes and sizes, made in the USA. The stands hold from thirty-six to three hundred cupcakes. Clever wedding cupcake displays are at this Web site (http://www.cup caketree.com/).

Experts suggest you order about fifty percent more cupcakes than the number of guests at your wedding feast. If you have a hundred guests, you'll want about one-hundred-fifty cupcakes. Some guests are sure to go back for seconds. Your photographer, DJ, band, and other staff might also like a cupcake. Don't forget to ask your caterer to save two cupcakes for your first anniversary.

Sweet memories

Have your caterer put out small boxes for the cupcakes near the end of the reception, so your guests can take home this memento. If you have only a few cupcakes, give the leftovers to the helpful staff, the catering manager, or a cupcake-loving friend.

How do you handle the cake cutting, Cupcake?

Some couples cut their cupcakes in half. Others have two cupcakes and feed each other. For couples who still want the traditional cake-cutting photo, use a cupcake stand with a top platform large enough to display a small wedding cake. Make sure your cupcake stand is strong enough for a cake cutting, or have the cake on a separate plate and remove it for the cutting photo.

Beyond the butter cream barrier

You're still legally married, even if you don't serve cake at your wedding. Some couples give their guests wedding favors that spotlight their favorite local food—individual gooey butter cakes in St. Louis, apple cider doughnuts in New England, Italian almonds or cannoli . . .

A cookie buffet can be homey and homemade, with lemon bars and chocolate chip, sugar, oatmeal raisin, and peanut butter cookies. It's also a low-cost dessert alternative for a budget wedding.

Or you can serve sophisticated chocolate-dipped biscotti, madeleines, lady fingers, and pinwheels with dessert wine, coffee, or champagne.

Try an upper-crust selection of pies. Peach, cherry, and key lime for summer weddings or hearty apple, chocolate cream, or pecan for winter. Don't forget the whipped cream and ice cream on the side.

Summer wedding guests may appreciate a cool ice cream bar with lots of toppings. You can hire someone to make milk shakes, malteds, and sundaes slathered with whipped cream and chocolate. Or serve chic gelato, sorbets, and ices.

Liquid wedding cake

Pearl Vodka has a Wedding Cake vodka that's supposed to taste just like, well, wedding cake. It's a fun way to ɔast the bride and groom. If you didn't save any wedding cake for your first anniversary, you can toast each other with Wedding Cake vodka (http://pearlvodka .com/).

The groom's cake

This Victorian tradition has been revived and given a new role. Today, the groom's cake is a gift from the bride to her groom. It's supposed to reflect his interests. Many groom's cakes feature his favorite sport or hobby. I've seen groom's cakes shaped like guitars, beer cans, CDs, trophy fish, even a replica of Busch Stadium.

Some groom's cakes are served as the dessert at the rehearsal dinner. You may want your wedding photographer to take pictures of this special cake. Other brides use the groom's cake as a second dessert at the wedding. Or it may be displayed at the reception, then cut and boxed as wedding favors.

Single women are supposed to sleep with a slice of groom's cake under their pillows and dream of their future husband. More likely, they'll wind up with the usual crumbs.

Read on for the next novel in
Elaine Viets's Dead-End Job Mystery series,

Board Stiff

Coming from Obsidian in May 2013

"They're trying to kill me," Sunny Jim Sundusky said. "They nearly succeeded in March, but I'm a tough old buzzard. I survived. They almost got me in April, but I escaped again."

Helen Hawthorne and her husband, Phil Sagemont, sat across from Sunny Jim in their black and chrome chairs at the Coronado Investigations office. Sunny Jim sat in the yellow client chair, looking anything but sunny. Sun-dried was more like it, Helen thought as she studied him.

His face was red leather. His blond hair was dyed and flash-fried in a crinkly permanent. But he did look tough.

"They're gonna keep coming after me until they stop me for good," he said. "That's why I wanna hire you two. I hear you're the best private eyes in South Florida."

"We were lucky to get good publicity," Helen said.

"That wasn't luck," Phil said. "That was good detecting."

"That's what I need," Sunny Jim said. "Detecting. I want you to stop them before they stop me—permanently." He stabbed his chest with a calloused brown hand, right in the smiling sun on his yellow SUNNY JIM'S STAND-UP PADDLEBOARDING T-shirt. His arms and legs were roped with muscle, and his chest was a solid slab of it.

Helen had seen enough steroid hard bodies to know

...t Jim built that beef the old-fashioned way. She thought he was attractive in a dated disco style, except he was too young to have caught the seventies' disco fever. She guessed his age at the shady side of thirty-five.

"So, you gonna save my business or not?" Jim's eyes were hidden behind expensive sunglasses, but his chin jutted in a challenge.

Helen tried to pick up a cue from Phil, but he stayed poker-faced. "Tell us a little about your business," he said.

"Like I said, I own a stand-up paddleboard rental company," Jim said. "I got two locations in Riggs Beach."

"The beach town just south of Fort Lauderdale," Helen said.

"Right," Jim said, and smiled for the first time. "There's Lauderdale, then Riggs Beach, Dania, Holly-wood, and Hallandale Beach. You ever been to Riggs Beach?" He shifted in his chair and Helen tried not to stare at the little golden hairs on his long tanned legs.

"I walk along that beach sometimes," she said. "Nice fishing pier."

"That's where I rent my boards," Sunny Jim said. "Near the base of the pier. Riggs Pier is owned by the city."

"Good fishing off that pier," Phil said.

"Primo," Sunny Jim said. "There's a reef just past the pier. Saw a loggerhead turtle there when I was diving."

"You were telling us about your business," Phil said.

"There's a little restaurant and bait shop on the beach end of the pier, run by Cyrus Reed Horton. The restaurant is called Cy's on the Pier. Locals joke that Cy fries up whatever bait he doesn't sell, but the food's not half bad.

"Cy owns some real estate along Riggs Beach, including a T-shirt shop and a fancy boutique. He's got the parking lot by the pier, too. That place is a gold mine. Tourists are begging to park there.

"I keep a trailer—like a lawn service trailer—at the

foot of the pier and rent my paddleboards, but you go be good to go out on the ocean. I also give lessons a Riggs Lake, about two blocks away: one hour of personal instruction and a half hour of practice for a hundred bucks. The water is quieter and calmer on the lake. It's a good place to learn. You ever do stand-up paddleboard-ing?"

"No," Helen said. "I've seen guys paddling along on those big surfboard-like things on the Intracoastal Waterway. I gather those are paddleboards."

"They are. Stand-up paddleboarding is the hot new sport. Everybody wants a piece of the action, and I've got the best spot in the city. That's why they're after me."

"Who is?" Phil asked.

"My competitors," Jim said, as if it were obvious.

"And they are . . . ?" Phil asked.

"Two main ones—Riggs Beach Water Sports and Bill's Boards. I've caught them both poaching on my territory. Riggs Beach Water Sports was giving lessons right next to my spot on Riggs Lake. Even set up a sign like he belonged there. His lessons are cheaper, but he doesn't have to pay the city to rent the land or buy the license or carry liability insurance like I do. He can afford to under-cut me.

"Bill's Boards parked its trailer next to mine here on the beach and started renting their boards. It was just an employee, not the owner, and I chased him off that time. But Bill himself stands there and defies me.

"Now if I don't open up early and drag my boards out on the beach so Bill's Boards can't park there, he tries to set up his business. I'm out there at six a.m. now, though most of my customers don't show up until after nine in the morning."

"Sounds stressful," Helen said.

"Stress! Hell, it's cutthroat. Those two will do any-thing to put me out of business. Bill's Boards even stole Randy, my best employee."

"How'd he do that?" Phil asked.

"Offered Randy more money," Sunny Jim said. "I can't afford to pay him eleven dollars an hour. Not when I'm stuck with all the costs of being a legitimate businessman."

"Did you complain to Riggs Beach?" Helen asked.

"Hah! Rigged Beach is more like it," Jim said. "I've made more than two hundred complaints to the police, the beach patrol, and Riggs Lake park rangers. The city commission won't do a blessed thing.

"I finally went to a meeting and complained. Put on a suit in Florida. One commissioner said it would cost too much to enforce the rules. Cost too much! What about the fees the city is missing? What about following the rules?

"The commissioners said they wanted proof that my competitors are poaching. I even stood behind a palm tree and took photos, but the commission said that still wasn't proof unless I caught 'em when the money was changing hands. I was never cynical about government, but after that meeting, I saw that same commissioner say hi to his good buddy, the owner of Bill's Boards. Slapped Bill on the back and they left together. In public. That was February.

"Once I turned up the heat, the sabotage started. In March, two of my paddleboards were stolen and twelve paddles were trashed. Someone broke into my trailer at the height of spring break, the busiest time of the year, so I didn't have enough boards or paddles for rentals. By the time my insurance claim was settled, spring break was over and so was the demand.

"That cost me thousands in equipment and even more in lost business. But they weren't counting on my having insurance. See, that's where the extra cost comes in, but it saved my bacon.

"I had video cameras on my beach trailer, and the cameras caught two men on tape. One man is the same size and height as Randy, my old employee, but he and his accomplice are wearing dive suits and masks, so you can't see their faces."

"And even though Randy was a good employe~~e~~" Helen asked, "you think he'd break into your trailer t~~o~~ ruin your business?"

"Yes, I do," Jim said, and stuck out his chin defiantly. "He left me for money. I think he'd break into my trailer for money, too. But I can't prove that. He knew about the cameras, didn't he? So he disguised himself."

"Not sure that means anything," Phil said. "Many businesses use security cameras. What did the police say?"

"They took a report and that's about it." Jim's face showed his disgust. "Riggs Beach police aren't interested in tracking down the thieves. They called it a spring break prank and said the stolen boards were probably strapped to a car roof and heading up north."

"The break-in was in March," Phil said. "What happened next?"

"I started getting tons of calls for reservations and lessons. I was fully booked every day of the week. Thought I was in fat city. Except half of the callers never showed for their lessons or board rentals. After four days of twiddling my thumbs I changed my policy. Now if you want a lesson or you want to rent a board, you gotta give me a credit card. And I run the card while you're on the phone. Nipped that in the bud."

"Who made the false reservations?" Helen asked. "Men? Women?"

"Both," Jim said. "They all sounded young, but then, most of my business is people under thirty."

"Anybody else you can think of who'd want to cause you trouble?" Phil asked.

"Well, there's Cy," Jim said. "He wants my beach spot, too, so he can expand his parking lot. But he told me up front. Those other birds went behind my back. Only my contract with the city is keeping me on Riggs Beach, and the renewal is coming up for a vote in June."

"So what do you want Coronado Investigations to do?" Phil asked.

"Catch 'em!" he said. "Catch them when they're sabo-aging me. I'm still looking for a new employee to replace Randy. I can't find a good one. I'll pay you $7.75 an hour, Phil, to work the pier location. That's in addition to your regular fee. You can keep the money."

"Thanks," Phil said. Jim missed the slight note of sarcasm, but Helen didn't.

"Minimum wage in Florida is $7.65, so I'm overpaying you. And I want your lady to work for me, too."

"You want two people to suddenly start working at your ocean paddleboard rental?" Helen asked. "Won't that look suspicious?"

"You're a smart girl," Sunny Jim said. "But I got a better job for you. I want you to sit on the beach with a video camera. You can document my competitors stealing my business. Make sure you get them exchanging the money. Nobody will think anything of it. Tourists video everything—even palm trees doing nothing but standing there. I want Helen to get to know some of the staff at Cy's restaurant and his two shops. Cy's a tightwad and he has enemies. Some of his employees are angry enough that they'll talk about Cy or whatever else they see here in Riggs Beach."

"My cover can be that I'm a Fort Lauderdale sales-clerk on a 'stay-cation,'" Helen said. "I've got some days off and I'm too broke to go anywhere for a real vacation."

"So are you going to be Phil's wife while he's working for me?" Sunny Jim asked.

"It's better if we don't even know each other for this job," Helen said. "I'll have to take off my wedding ring."

"And put on a bikini," Jim said. "A fine-looking lady like you belongs in a bikini—you know what I mean?"

Helen didn't like his smirk.

"You know that Ms. Hawthorne is my partner—and my wife," Phil said.

"I meant no disrespect," Jim said. "It's hard not to admire a woman like Ms. Hawthorne. Tell you what—I'll

even throw in free paddleboard lessons for you b
ter work. As my personal apology. How about in
start tomorrow at six with me, Phil? Ms. Hawthorne, y
don't have to go to work until nine. What do you say
huh?"

"You can call me Helen," she said. "Apology accepted."

I'm getting paid to sleep late and sit on the beach, she
thought. Finally, a dead-end job I can enjoy. Phil gave her
a slight nod, his signal that he wanted this client.

"It's a deal," she said.

OOK FOR MORE BOOKS BY

ELAINE VIETS

in the Josie Marcus,
Mystery Shopper series

Death on a Platter

Josie Marcus plans to savor sampling the local
St. Louis cuisine for a City Eats food tour. But
her appetite is ruined at Tillie's Off the Hill
Italian Restaurant when another customer is
poisoned. Was the victim the real target—or is
someone trying to ruin Tillie's reputation? It's up
to Josie to find a killer who has no reservations
about preparing a dish to die for...

And don't miss the rest of the series
High Heels Are Murder
Accessory to Murder
Murder with All the Trimmings
The Fashion Hound Murders
An Uplifting Murder

Available wherever books are sold or at
penguin.com

facebook.com/TheCrimeSceneBooks